a dawn like THUNDER

Fiction by Douglas Reeman published by McBooks Press—

A Prayer for the Ship
HMS Saracen
The White Guns
Killing Ground
Battlecruiser
For Valour
Twelve Seconds to Live
The Pride and the Anguish
A Dawn Like Thunder

Badge of Glory
The First to Land
The Horizon
Dust on the Sea
Knife Edge

as Alexander Kent

The Complete Midshipman Bolitho
Stand Into Danger
In Gallant Company
Sloop of War
To Glory We Steer
Command a King's Ship
Passage to Mutiny
With All Despatch
Form Line of Battle!
Enemy in Sight!
The Flag Captain
Signal–Close Action!
The Inshore Squadron
A Tradition of Victory
Success to the Brave
Colours Aloft!
Honour This Day
The Only Victor
Beyond the Reef
The Darkening Sea
For My Country's Freedom
Cross of St George
Sword of Honour
Second to None
Relentless Pursuit
Man of War
Heart of Oak
In the King's Name

DOUGLAS REEMAN

a dawn like THUNDER

Modern Naval Fiction Library

McBooks Press, Inc.
Ithaca, New York

Published by McBooks Press, Inc., 2016. First published by William Heinemann, a division of The Random House Group Ltd.

Cover painting: Geoffrey Huband

Library of Congress Cataloging-in-Publication Data

Names: Reeman, Douglas, author.
Title: A dawn like thunder / Douglas Reeman.
Description: Ithaca, New York : McBooks Press, 2016. | Series: Modern naval fiction library
Identifiers: LCCN 2016018971 (print) | LCCN 2016022578 (ebook) | ISBN 9781590137130 (softcover : acid-free paper) | ISBN 9781590137147 (mobipocket) | ISBN 9781590137154 (ePub) | ISBN 9781590137161 (pdf)
Subjects: LCSH: World War, 1939-1945--Naval operations, British--Fiction. | Great Britain--History, Naval--20th century--Fiction. | Great Britain. Royal Navy--Fiction. | BISAC: FICTION / Sea Stories. | FICTION / Historical. | GSAFD: War stories. | Sea stories. | Historical fiction.
Classification: LCC PR6068.E35 D39 2016 (print) | LCC PR6068.E35 (ebook) DDC 823/.914--dc23
LC record available at https://lccn.loc.gov/2016018971

Visit the McBooks Press website at www.mcbooks.com

Printed in Canada

9 8 7 6 5 4 3 2 1

MIX
Paper from responsible sources
FSC® C004071

For Helen Fraser, my publisher and dear friend

ACKNOWLEDGEMENT—
The author wishes to thank Ulrik Valentiner for providing information, photographs and recognition signals for Operation *Monsun*.

Good-bye, dear.
Protect the spring flowers of
Your beauty. Think of the days
When we were happy together.
If I live I will come back.
If I die, remember me always.

—General Su Wu
second century

(trans. Kenneth Rexroth)

1 | Trust

WAITING WAS the worst part. Everybody said so.

He sat awkwardly in a corner of the submarine's control-room, his thick rubber diving-suit making his whole body pour with sweat. Around him the men on watch stood or sat at their diving stations, barely moving, so tense was their concentration in the oily warmth. In the muted glow of reddish-orange lights, their faces were like parts of an intricate tapestry; only the clicking, purring instruments and dials were alive.

He eased his limbs slightly and saw a young stoker by the lowered periscopes glance at him, but only briefly. Probably wondering why he was risking his life in such dangerous work; more likely seeing the diving-suit as a very real liability, a threat to his own survival and that of his messmates.

The submarine's skipper leaned against the plot-table, his eyes ever watchful. He too would be thinking of the risks to his boat and his men.

The submarine was in shallow water, a good place to conceal the target, not so good for a quick dive. There would be no chance to escape if they were suddenly pinned down by aircraft or a patrol vessel.

He plucked at the tough, narrow rubber cuffs of the suit. In the water it was another thing, supple, protective and familiar after all the hours of training and the wild elation of actual operations against the enemy. Even pushing your head into the tight-fitting hood was painful, and the man who was helping was usually concerned more with haste than comfort.

He glanced at the control-room clock. Dawn was still an hour away. He tried to picture the coastline ahead of the boat's slow-moving bows. *Sicily.* He had studied the plans and the maps, the charts and the Intelligence folios until he felt as if he had already been there.

He turned his head and saw the bridge lookouts lounging by the conning tower ladder. They all wore dark glasses, to prepare their eyes for total darkness if necessary, and in the orange glow they looked like an assembly of blind men.

The boat's first lieutenant was fiddling with his slide rule. One of his duties was to maintain the trim under every condition, pumping water from aft to forward when torpedoes were fired, or in difficult stretches of sea where perhaps the density varied violently when fresh water surged into salt from a nearby estuary. In moments of stress it was not unknown for the trim to be lost, and a submarine's bows to break surface in the middle of an attack.

The boat's commander was probably about his own age, twenty-six, but he looked ten years older. There were dark stains on the long submariner's jersey where he habitually wiped his hands, perhaps to offset his private anxieties. At least in his work he could retain a sense of independence from the greater backdrop of war. Submarines made you like that.

The young commander saw his passenger's brief smile, and walked across the control-room. They had not had much time to chat or become acquainted on this secret mission. He put his hand on the shoulder of the rubber suit and said, "Sorry it's such a drag, Jamie, but I'll have you away before full daylight."

"Thanks. I never doubted it." Something took the commander's attention and he strode back to the compass-repeater. The diving-suit squeaked and another trickle of sweat ran down his spine, like a leak.

One more operation then. Would it really make any difference in the end? Four years of war: retreats and disasters on land, and at sea the mounting losses in an intensified and ruthless U-Boat campaign had almost brought the country down. Almost. Somebody dropped a mug on the deck and several men swung round, their eyes angry, nervous. *Almost.* It made you cynical, frightened to hope too much. He tried to assemble his thoughts in order. One thought predominated. Last month the unbeatable

German Afrika Korps had been driven out of North Africa when, but for the Eighth Army's last stand at a place named El Alamein, they would have smashed on to Cairo, Suez and the final goal, India: Hitler's dream.

Nobody said anything definite, of course, but everyone believed that the next step would be to go on the offensive, to force landings on the Continent and tip the scales as the fighter pilots had done in the Battle of Britain.

He saw the navigating officer tapping the chart with his dividers, his eyes crinkling as he shared a joke with his skipper. Friends . . .

He felt the sweat chill on his spine. Was it possible that this attack on some little-known inlet on the northwest tip of Sicily was a part of that offensive, albeit a small one?

The target at first glance seemed an unlikely one, compared with the great German warships that had sheltered in the icy Norwegian fjords. But this vessel had been reported by Intelligence as being packed from keel to deckhead with new mines, the type created for use on beaches where enemy forces might be expected to land.

The Admiralty and the War Council must have weighed the possibilities carefully: the risk of warning the enemy about a selected invasion area, against the horrendous prospect of an attacking army being decimated by mines even as it pounded up the beaches. As a senior officer had explained, "They need a man who is experienced and determined, not some death-or-glory fanatic."

So it was decided. Lieutenant James Ross was to be that man.

He leaned his head against the steel covered with cork-filled white paint to minimize the discomfort of condensation, and tried to exclude the machinery and the men he would soon be leaving.

So here we are. Late June, 1943, in this tideless, fought-over sea, the bed of which was littered with the wrecks of vessels of every class and size, hunters and hunted alike. *Summer in England.* A beautiful time of year that even air-raids, bomb damage and rationing could not completely destroy, unless you were one of the victims, or a recipient of those feared and hated telegrams: *The Secretary of the Admiralty regrets to inform you that your son,* or husband or lover, *et cetera, et cetera.* It never ended.

He thought of his father, Big Andy as he was called, proud that his son was a naval officer and able to hide his fears and his own memories of that other war. A submariner himself, he had been thrown on the beach with all the thousands who had managed to survive the mines and torpedoes and the mud and wire of Flanders. But he had fought back when so many others had given in to despair, selling bootlaces and matches or playing mouth-organs and tin whistles, their proud medals prominently displayed, to gain sympathy and a few pence when all most people wanted was to forget.

Big Andy had been partly disabled at Zeebrugge in the latter stages of the Great War and had been quickly discharged. But he had been trained as a diver when serving in submarines and that, together with his experience as a stoker in the complex engine- and motor-rooms, had guided him into salvage. From small craft sunk or wrecked along the various coasts to the richer harvest of the scuttled German High Seas Fleet in Scapa Flow, he had worked with a few friends without a break. Brass and bronze propellers were worth a small fortune at a time when industry was still faltering and employers reluctant to invest in new production when salvaged scrap was available from those willing to risk life and limb.

Ross smiled. When he had first learned to wear a diving-suit and, under his father's close supervision, had been allowed down into one of those rusting, unhappy wrecks where German soldiers had once yarned and written home like their British counterparts . . .

He saw some of the watchkeepers stiffen and found himself staring up at the curved deckhead as some alien sound intruded above the gentle whirr of fans and the tremble of electric motors.

Thuds along the hull: a half-submerged boat, or cargo from a wreck. Not a mine's mooring wire dragging deadly horns against this slow-moving intruder.

Out of the corner of his eye he saw the commander's hands rubbing against the stained jersey. This boat had been one of those attacking the retreating Afrika Korps: the cost had been high for both sides. In these waters, a submarine at periscope depth could sometimes easily be spotted by a keen-eyed bomber crew. That was all it took. Despite his outward calm the commander would be remembering, weighing the odds.

The sounds ceased, and he tried to relax. Instead, he found himself picturing the little craft that was attached snugly to the submarine's bulging saddle-tank, like a baby whale on its mother's flank. The two-man torpedo, or chariot, as it was officially known, was the ultimate weapon in a high-risk war, requiring men of courage, or recklessness or whatever you chose to call it. *Volunteers only.* Few even guessed what they were getting into until it was too late to withdraw: in the Navy they always said that a volunteer was a man who had misunderstood the question. But in the bitter Scottish lochs and during those first dangerous exercises at sea they had begun to learn, to accept what this new weapon could do. Curiously enough, the Italian Navy had been the first to use two-man torpedoes against British warships here in the Med. It had prompted Winston Churchill to stir up the War Council and the government to improve on the Italian efforts. The training had not been without incident. Drowning, convulsions and the bends when venturing below thirty feet, even brain damage; the risks were very real.

He found his mind drifting to that last attack in the fjord near Trondheim. Cold to the point of cruel pain, hampered by one obstacle after another, when air reconnaissance and the local Norwegian Resistance had reported the way clear to the target, a brand-new floating dock which had been intended for the German fleet base at Kiel. It had been their last chance. Once into the Baltic with all available air cover and patrol vessels close at hand, that opportunity would have been lost . . .

He jumped as the commander touched his arm. He had not even seen him move.

"All right?"

Ross said, "Of course." It came out too sharply. Then he smiled. "Sorry. What is it?"

The other man looked at the clock. "I'm going up in ten minutes. Need anything else? I'll be a bit busy shortly, but if you want . . ."

Ross shook his head and winced as the rubber tore at his ears. "I just want to get started."

Their eyes met. "I've sent word to your Number Two. He was playing cards with one of my sick ratings. He must be a pretty cool one."

Ross looked away. He had been there on that terrible day in the fjord. Completely dependable: brave was not the description. It went far beyond that.

He said, "Like a rock."

They both looked at the figures in the control-room, the coxswain on the wheel; the men working the hydroplanes, ever watchful, their eyes gleaming in the reflected dials; the stoker by the periscope wells, who looked about twelve years old in the subdued glow; the navigator and the first lieutenant. The team, the heart of any submarine.

The commander murmured, "I wonder if anyone at home really knows what it's like." The mood left him and he said curtly, "Five minutes, Number One. Good listening watch, right?"

Routine maybe, but the essential link between him and the men throughout the boat, who had to trust his every decision, and depend on his skill to keep them alive.

The Intelligence folio had vanished from the chart table; it was already in the skipper's safe. The waiting was over. It was just another target, a small shallow-draught coaster named *Galatea,* commandeered by the Italian Navy for the duration. She had come from the big fleet base at Taranto, moving mostly at night to avoid detection. Her deadly cargo had changed her role and her value. Ross saw one of his helpers moving his breathing apparatus into an open space. Automatically he felt for his diver's knife.

He saw it all in a solitary flash, like a badly taken photograph: water suddenly changing from green to red, the man's eyes like marbles as he had driven the blade through his diving-suit and felt it jar against flesh and bone. Easy. Just as the instructors had described and demonstrated. Not even a whimper.

He had not heard the commander speak again, but he felt the air roaring into the saddle-tanks, the man in question crouching down to his knees even as the thin attack-periscope came hissing out of its well.

"Thirty feet, sir!"

"All quiet, sir."

The skipper was creeping round in his oil-stained boots, his forehead pressed to the periscope pad. He said, "Nothing. Still black as a boot." Then, "Stand by to surface." He slung his binoculars around his neck. "Open the lower lid. Gun's crew and deck handling party in position."

He strode to the men waiting by the conning tower ladder, touching Ross's shoulder briefly as he passed. The wit and the bravado had been lost somewhere in those four years of war, but to Ross, sweating in the uncomfortable rubber suit, that simple gesture meant everything. *The team.*

"Blow all main ballast! *Surface!*"

Further forward from the control-room, and separated from it by sealed watertight doors, was the petty officers' and leading hands' mess. Like the rest of the submarine, it was functional and cramped. Wires, pipes and dials, the arteries of every boat, filled most of the space, but here and there a full-breasted pinup or some newly darned seaboot stockings showed that men lived here, too.

Leading Seaman Mike Tucker was making his own last

preparations before he was finally clamped firmly into his suit. He glanced around at the crowded world he had come to know so well, even before he had volunteered for Special Operations. Large nets containing cans of Spam and bully beef were slung in any small remaining space, and he wondered how men could live in such conditions, just as he knew they would never willingly change them. He smiled slightly as he remembered the youthful and enthusiastic lieutenant at the submarine base before the war: Portsmouth, that sailors' city, flattened now in many parts by persistent bombing. The lieutenant had been warming to his theme that submariners were not unlike the men of Nelson's Navy: men who lived, slept and ate their crude meals between the very guns they would be required to serve, to fight without question until the enemy's flag came down. Tucker had not seen the point at the time, but now he could. The submarine was a weapon first and foremost, but from the cramped discomfort was born a strength, a reliance on your mates that was hard to match elsewhere. Dangerous, demanding, it nevertheless produced a special kind of man for this Navy within a Navy.

He prepared himself unhurriedly: he had even managed to shave, and paused now to regard himself in someone's metal mirror. An open, homely face with eyes the colour of a clear blue sky. Tucker was twenty-five, or would be next month with any luck, and a regular with seven years' service behind him. All that time back, how they had pulled his leg about it at home. He had been born and raised in Winstanley Road in Battersea, South London, and home was a crowded house shared with three brothers and three sisters, not far from Clapham Junction where his father worked as an engine-driver on one of those funny little tank-engines that were used for shunting goods wagons, back and forth, day and night, *clink clink clink,* pushing the trucks into formation, long trains which would eventually head off into the smoke. His father was a firm man, but quiet with it. After a day shunting wagons, he would stroll down to the pub with his fireman on the way home, and once a week he would visit the British Legion. Like so many round there, he was a veteran of that other war, *a survivor* he had called it once when he had had a pint too many. Otherwise he said little about it, hoarded the memories and shared them only with a few, and certainly not with the kids.

Tucker had had a few days' leave before joining the submarine at Portsmouth. Nothing had changed. The house was shabbier, with a few slates missing, like the blind windows in other houses in the street where bomb-blast had damaged them. But the kettle was always on, and there was plenty to eat despite the rationing.

His mother, now seemingly old and tired, had asked him, "Do you still miss her, Mike? Not found another girl yet?"

His father had been sitting at the kitchen table, his driver's cap with the oilskin top and Southern Railway badge still on his head. "Leave it, Mother. So long as *he's* safe, that's the main thing."

They had exchanged glances: understanding, gratitude; many would describe it as love.

The house had seemed empty, somehow. His brothers, willingly or otherwise, were in the Army although Terry, the youngest, was in the Andrew. Two of his sisters had married and were doing war-work and Madge, the baby of the family, was working in a club in the West End which had been opened for the American forces in London. She was breaking her mother's heart with all that make-up and the silk stockings, the late hours and nights when she did not come home at all. He could imagine what she was up to.

His father, of course, had said, "Don't worry so much, Mother. She's young, and there's a war on." They had both laughed at the absurd comment.

Tucker thought of the officer he would be joining shortly: Lieutenant James Ross. At first he had told himself he could never work with an officer, and a regular one at that, but now they were on a first-name basis and had slowly developed a closeness that would have been unthinkable in any other section of the Navy.

Tucker had worked with Ross for almost two years, and trusted him completely. But know him? He knew he never would.

Now, he glanced at the inert shape of the sick rating with whom he had been attempting to play cards. Poor little bugger: his first ever operational cruise in this or any other submarine. Days out from Portsmouth on passage for the Med, they had been on the surface running the diesel engines to charge batteries. It was supposed to be a safe area, and the boat's skipper would have had strict orders not to forget his mission just to give chase to a juicy target. It should have been all right. The skipper and two lookouts had been up on the open bridge, swaying about like drunken seals in their streaming oilskins, when two aircraft had appeared. Out there, it did not matter much if they were "theirs" or "ours." The klaxon had shrilled, *Dive! Dive! Dive!* and the water had thundered into the saddle-tanks to force her down. One of the lookouts had been this young, green seaman, no doubt up until then feeling like part of a war-time film.

Tucker had learned the hard way. When the klaxon sounded, you had fifteen seconds to clear the bridge and get below, pausing only to slam and lock upper and lower "lids" as you went. By then, the hull would be diving fast, the sea already surging into the confined place where you had been standing.

The kid had fallen, breaking his ankle and fracturing a wrist; it had been no help that the others had landed on top of him. A submarine did not carry a doctor, and first aid was simple and basic: the powers that be obviously thought that anything more was needless luxury. In a submarine it was accepted that either everyone lived or everybody died.

Tucker watched the youth's face, drugged, pinched with pain. He would not receive proper attention until the boat returned to base, or to wherever else they might be ordered.

He recalled talking quietly with him before he had slipped

again into a drugged sleep. The boy had asked, "What's he like, Tommy?" Even that had made him smile. So young, and yet already trying to play the Old Jack. If you were a Tucker in this regiment, you were always a Tommy, no matter what your paybook said.

He thought of the lieutenant again. Grey eyes that assessed, calculated, took nothing for granted. He could remember exactly when he had been told he was to be paired off with Ross after his previous partner had been put ashore sick. Bomb-happy, more likely. The captain had said cheerfully, "You'll get along like a house on fire, Tucker. He's bloody good."

Tucker had already known that: Ross would not have lasted otherwise. When the kid had asked him, he had heard himself reply, quite simply, "He's a hero." But he had already dropped off to sleep.

And then there had been that terrible raid in the Norwegian fjord. Two chariots had been involved, the other one commanded by Ross's best friend, some said his only friend.

The floating dock had been the target, but at the last moment the unexpected had changed everything. A German cruiser, damaged by a mine in the North Sea, had entered the fjord and without delay prepared to use the dock, offering them a double target which they could not ignore.

They could not delay either, for as the dock was flooded to receive the damaged cruiser, the narrowing space between the dock's bottom and the bed of the fjord made the attack even more hazardous. Both chariots had been half surfaced between some Norwegian fishing boats. Tucker had seen Ross gripping his friend's wrist, forcing home a point, and the other officer's apparent reluctance. Time was short: as an instructor had once said wryly, "With six hundred pounds of high explosive between your legs, you could do yourself a real injury!"

The attack had gone like a drill. After dodging past a small launch they had dived to some thirty-five feet below the dock and fastened their charges to it without difficulty.

Right on time, while they had hidden amongst the fishing boats, both charges had exploded in one deafening thunderclap. The dock had seemed to fold like cardboard, while the damaged cruiser had rolled over, scattering trestles and wires alike, until both hulls were half submerged. Neither Ross's friend nor his rating were ever seen again. They were probably caught in the mud beneath the dock, and had gone up when the fuse ran out.

For that, Ross had been awarded the Victoria Cross. Tucker was still not sure how he felt about it.

He heard men gathering beneath the forward hatch. This was a submarine's most perilous moment: on the surface with the hatch open. It was time.

He felt very calm, and turned to leave. But before he was sealed completely in his suit he pulled out his wallet in its oil-skin pouch and, after the smallest hesitation, opened it and looked hard at her photograph. *Do you still miss her?* his mother had asked.

He held the picture in the dimmed lights. Eve. *Evie.* So pert and pretty in her bus conductorette's uniform, the huge double-decker towering behind her.

It had begun in the middle of an air-raid, just as the bus returned to the Lambeth garage for the night.

"I'll see you home, love . . ."

And the quick, searching glance he had come to know and love.

She had answered, "All right, sailor, no tricks now!" They had both laughed: her family lived just around the corner in Livingstone Road. He had seen her give as good as she got from boozy passengers when the pubs turned out, or amorous Yanks who thought that every English girl was fair game.

It had ended, too, in an air-raid, although he had been at sea and had not been told about it until much later. They said it had been the worst bombing in London's dockland since the outbreak of war: fifty-seven consecutive nights, until the ware-houses, docks and ships, and eventually the Thames itself, were ablaze. The double-decker bus was completely destroyed. She was never found. Was that why he had volunteered for Special Operations? Because he had nothing to live for?

He did not realize that the injured youth had opened his eyes and was watching him fixedly as he gently kissed the photograph and whispered, "Oh, Evie, where are you?"

He felt the deck tilt and heard the muffled bark of commands. *Going up.*

He began to put his wallet into its pouch, but looked once more at the photograph. He gave a great sigh. "Here we go again, Evie. I'll be back!"

After the stale, oily atmosphere inside the boat, the sea air and stinging droplets of spray were exhilarating, and Ross felt a sense of freedom which never failed to surprise and excite him. It was still very dark, or appeared so, but he could see the cruising white cats'-paws breaking against the rounded hull, and feel the slow roll that was making some of the deck handling party reach for handholds as they stooped over the chariot, fixed to the saddle-tank by special fittings which they had collected at Portsmouth.

He vividly recalled their doubts and uncertainties when, in those early days, they had been introduced to their first human torpedo. About the same size and length as a normal twenty-one-inch torpedo, it carried a ballast tank, pumps and hydroplanes, together with a battery motor that could offer a steady three knots for a limited period. In something rather like a car dashboard, it mounted a compass and an instrument panel fitted with luminous dials. And a joystick. Ross could remember his first trial run, the red-faced instructor's words ringing in his ears. "Like ridin' a bike—just take it nice an' easy." They must have been simple-minded to believe that.

He touched Tucker's arm, glad he had been given him as a partner: a professional seaman, a leading torpedoman, mature and dependable. It made a change from the many volunteers who made up the Special Operations. Telegraphists, cooks, stewards and signalmen: you would never guess their employment from the badges they wore on their uniforms, on the rare occasions when they were wearing them.

Apart from a quiet reserve, the first things you noticed about Tucker were his strength and the light way he moved. His hands were square and powerful, and Ross recalled a time in Scotland when they had been receiving instruction in self-defence and close combat from some battle-tested marine commandos. One, a burly sergeant, had whipped his arm around Tucker's throat from behind and at the same time jabbed an imitation blade up into his ribs. His grin had changed to a cry of agony as Tucker had seized his wrist with one hand and squeezed it. The sergeant's triumph had given way to anger and humiliation. "You nearly broke my arm, you mad bugger!"

Tucker had given his gentle smile. "Only nearly, Sarge? I must be losing my touch!"

A petty officer whispered, "Ready when you are, sir."

Ross lowered himself astride the chariot and felt Tucker watching him now, his outline suddenly sharper against a sky criss-crossed by the submarine's jumping wire. It was so cold. He found he could smile. That was the first thing new recruits noticed about the Med. Too many cruising posters before the war made them imagine the place was full of sunshine, warm seas and smiling Italian girls.

The sky was getting brighter. He could imagine the submarine's skipper up there on his swaying bridge, gripping his night glasses. He smiled again. *Or wiping his hands on his jersey.* He tightened his jaw. He had known men crack even at the simplest reminder, a joke, a face, a memory.

He tested his nose clip; it hurt, but they usually did, especially after so many dives. He adjusted the rubber mouthpiece and fixed the air and oxygen lock until he could breathe easily. He could feel the sailors on the deck-casing staring at him. Willing him to go. The big forehatch was already sealed; if the boat had to dive, these same men would need to race aft to the conning tower, climb it and tumble down to safety with seconds to spare. But this final check could not be rushed. That submerged wreckage, or whatever it had been, might have displaced or damaged something. Pressure-gauge, time-fuse for the massive detachable warhead . . . he looked up and nodded. Tucker climbed on board like a pillion-rider, his position close to the locker where the cutters, wires and magnets were stowed within easy reach.

Ross raised his arm and saw the dark shapes of the seamen on the casing begin to fade, to merge with the conning tower. Only the petty officer remained until the propeller spluttered into life and the sea surged over the legs of the two charioteers. They were free. Then, with a casual wave, he too was gone.

The submarine seemed to move away, the sea trembling as the water roared into her tanks, her hydroplanes already set for diving. Some violent turbulence and more spray like tropical rain on his bare wrists, and then the sea was suddenly theirs.

Ross re-checked his instruments and peered at the small luminous compass. According to all the calculations, it would take two hours to find the inlet and the unsuspecting *Galatea* from Taranto. Unless something had gone wrong, careless talk, like the posters were always warning. Two hours, then; from this to bright sunlight, according to the submarine's navigator. The skipper's friend: you could see it, like something living between them. He tried to shut his mind to it. Like David . . .

He reached back and took Tucker's hand, strong and firm and apparently impervious to the cold water that surged around them, moulding their suits to their limbs and bodies, making them creatures of the sea once again. Tucker knew what to do. All they needed was trust. The grip of his hand gave him that message.

He turned back to his controls, but the thought would not release him.

It was not like David at all. David was dead. *And you killed him.*

• • •

Waiting was the worst part.

The submarine's first lieutenant wiped the lenses of his powerful binoculars and jammed his elbows against the wet plating while he took another slow sweep from bow to bow. It was getting cooler, or perhaps his nerves were playing up. Behind him, the two bridge lookouts were doing much the same, searching for the slightest movement or shadow, while the hull beneath them glided almost imperceptibly across the last great splash of sunset. It was unreal and awesome, one great brushstroke of the deepest red defying even the keenest eyes to discern the darker line separating sea and sky.

Too long. Too bloody long. He bit his lip, imagining for a second that he had spoken aloud. But neither of the lookouts had noticed anything. Noticed what, he thought bitterly. That their first lieutenant had just about taken all he could?

All day, since dropping the chariot at dawn, they had tried to keep out of trouble. These waters were not good for submarines, and he had studied the chart too often to be able to forget it. Twelve fathoms at this point, a mere seventy-two feet. He tried not to think about it. The height of an office building—it was like steering the submarine down a street.

It was too long. Perhaps the chariot had come to grief, or even now was creeping out from the land to look for them. The lieutenant had been on several cloak-and-dagger operations in the Med, dropping agents to work behind enemy lines. It must be a kind of madness which drove them to it, he thought, and they were all the same. Tense, on edge, and yet in some way eager to go, to use and depend on their own resources. One of the agents had been a young French girl; he had tried not to imagine her fate if she were captured and handed over to the Gestapo. One thing was certain: they had never seen the same agents twice.

The skipper would be up in a moment. His decision, then, to remain on the surface or to decide to leave it. *His decision.*

It was strange when you thought about it. He had been

recommended for a command course himself, the perisher, as it was called. But after being first lieutenant to this skipper, and briefly with a previous one, he was far from sure. He had watched what command could do, what it *was* doing to their young skipper.

Almost the worst thing was that shortly after parting with the chariot they had received a brief signal. The mission was aborted. The two charioteers were to be withdrawn. It had already been too late when some bloody stupid staff officer in London had suddenly had a change of heart on the matter. How often did it happen, he wondered. Men thrown away, like the coloured pins on the wall-charts that were dropped so easily into a little box when some ship or other bought it. He stifled a yawn. A sign of nerves. Even fear.

They had run for deep water during the day after seeing a pair of aircraft, like glass chips against the clear sky. It was never good to dwell on the possibility that the enemy had been forewarned about this particular attack, and imagine that these aircraft were just the first of many which were being alerted.

Then, while they had changed course for the rendezvous, the hydrophone operator had picked up the faint effect of a small vessel's engine. Far astern to the southwest, but it was always there. The H.E. was not that of a powerful warship or motor anti-submarine boat, but the Italians, like the Royal Navy, were known to have converted a lot of fishing vessels for the task, and depth-charges were just as deadly no matter who threw them.

He watched the red smear across the sky. A few stars already, but no moon. Soon it would be as black as a pig's belly. *No chance.*

A lookout murmured, "Skipper's on his way, sir."

How did he sound? Nervous, or merely eager that the skipper was coming up to take over? To get them all the hell out of it.

"All quiet, Number One?" He was already raising his glasses, his ear pitched for every sound and movement. He added, "H.E. is still on the same bearing. May be a fisherman, of course."

He gave a dry laugh, and one of the lookouts flinched as if

he had yelled at the top of his voice. "Marsala's over there to the nor'east. Had a lovely lobster there once when I was a young snotty. It was really something, I can tell you."

His mood changed and he said crisply, "You think we should let it go, don't you?"

"It's not for me to say."

"My decision. I know. Look at it this way. There are two chaps out there, maybe hurt for all I know. Depending on us. It matters!"

"I know that, sir." He added savagely, "Makes you sick—the job was aborted anyway."

The skipper was staring at him in the encroaching darkness, his cap-cover touched with red by the strange glow. When that went, they would have to pull out. He said, "We'll hang about a bit longer. Tell the control-room."

The smaller of the two lookouts said, "Aircraft, sir. Starboard bow."

They listened to the uneven drone until it was swallowed up by the sea noises.

The skipper said, "Jerry moving some gear, I expect." He could have been remarking on the weather.

The first lieutenant was still there. He asked, "Anything else, sir?"

"No. Go below and get ready. It won't be long now."

He knew, even as the lieutenant's head disappeared through the hatch that he had not understood.

He levelled his glasses again. How many millions of times, he wondered. Seeking out a kill, trying to avoid the hunters. And they all depended on him, on his eyes, on his conclusions after sighting a target.

This boat had been depth-charged several times, but somehow they had got out of it. He thought he heard the aircraft again, but it was something else.

He felt the small lookout stir and asked, "You all right, Nobby?"

The lookout was actually grinning. "Still thinkin' about your lobster, sir. I'm more used to cod an' chips, or a pint of whelks down th' Old Kent road!"

The skipper looked away, but was greatly moved. *One of his men.* The characters he had come to know and respect; and it went even deeper than just good sense. Like the little seaman from the Old Kent Road. He had seen him at the defaulters' table several times, or had heard him being dragged aboard drunk by a shore patrol. And yet he was able to joke about it. To stand here if ordered until he dropped.

He knew they were staring at him as he leaned over the voicepipe.

"Stand by, control-room. In just a few minutes . . ." He wheeled round as the other lookout gasped, "There they are, sir! Port bow—I wasn't sure for a second, an' then!" He was almost beside himself.

The skipper snapped, "Belay that, Number One. Open the forehatch. Two good hands and a heaving line, *chop chop!*"

The chariot was suddenly right here, swaying alongside, so much smaller without the six-hundred-pound warhead.

"One of them's injured." He gripped the screen with his hand until the rough steel steadied him. He saw Ross's vague outline, could feel his concern as the handling party hauled his Number Two on to the deck-casing.

The chariot was drifting away and already settling down, scuttled to save time. Another minute? How long would he have waited? Then, and only then, did he look up. Tiny bright stars; the red brushstroke had gone.

"Clear the bridge." He jabbed the klaxon and heard it scream through the hull beneath him. The forehatch was shut, the deck empty. He closed the voicepipe cock and bent over the hatch. The small lookout was just about to drop down the ladder when something made them all look up. A great flash lit up the horizon, and the boom of the explosion rolled across the water to sigh against the saddle-tanks like something solid.

Somebody gave a wild cheer in the control-room, but all the

tough little seaman could think of was the emotion in the skipper's eyes.

Through the control-room and forward to the petty officers' mess, the skipper was himself again. He could ignore the grins and the thumbs-up. It was relief, prayers answered, nothing more. *His men.*

He found Ross struggling out of his suit, and two of the deck party cutting away the Number Two's equipment and mask.

The man called Tucker gasped, "Bloody wire, it was. Gashed my suit. Filled with water. Couldn't breathe." His chest was heaving painfully.

Ross said, "Don't talk. Rest now. I'll get some pusser's rum in a minute."

The deck was tilting as the first lieutenant took the boat down, but that was outside. Tucker winced; there was blood on his neck where the net wire had snared him. His voice was suddenly level and clear as he said to Ross, "You came back. How did you know?"

Ross said, "I just knew." He glanced at the submarine's young skipper. "You know these things, don't you, when it matters?"

The skipper nodded and heard the control-room calling him back to his world.

"Yes. When it matters." He walked away. A very near thing. For them all. One more time.

2 | A Different War

THE HOTEL, small by London standards, was well placed on one corner of St James's Square. With even its name hidden by the usual pyramids of piled sandbags to protect the pillared entrance, it had all the appearance of a private club. In happier days it had been the haunt of visiting businessmen from the Far East, and at lunch-times the regular meeting-place of local publishers: a quiet, respectable place which had never accustomed itself to the ways of war.

Lieutenant Charles Villiers paused and glanced across the square. When he had been walking back to the hotel, he had stopped out of curiosity to look up Duke Street towards Piccadilly. In the hot, dusty sunshine he had watched the steady flow of people on either side of the road, and had been astonished that he had seen only one person not in uniform amid the dark and pale blues of the Navy and the Royal Air Force, and the overwhelming tide of men and women in khaki. So many foreigners, too, evidence if any were still needed of the Germans' complete domination of Europe and Scandinavia: Poles and Dutch, Norwegians and Czechs and, of course, the Free French.

Villiers could not remember how long he had been walking, nor could he understand why he was not hungry: he had not eaten since breakfast, and this was early evening. Green Park, then St James's Park, Piccadilly and along Jermyn Street, once the home of many an expensive tailor. Now those same windows displayed officers' uniforms of the three services, rather than the sports jackets and flannel bags of that other world.

He entered the lobby and saw the manager, a feather duster under one arm, speaking busily on the telephone. Exactly as he had known he would be, like a round toby jug, with one lick of hair plastered down on his otherwise bald head. Of necessity he was manager, telephonist and receptionist all in one.

But only for the duration, as he had proclaimed brightly when he had greeted him. A bit of a change from his usual guests, Villiers had thought. Staff officers were the regulars nowadays, not mere lieutenants, especially those wearing the wavy stripes of "temporary gentlemen." The manager managed to bob and smile without missing a word on the telephone.

It was strange and a little unnerving that the manager, as well as the hotel, were so familiar, like old friends. Until he had signed the register two days ago, Villiers had never set foot in the place. Now he could imagine staying nowhere else, and wished he had come earlier. Unable to face it? Afraid of the memories it would release? He was still not sure.

He removed his cap and glanced at himself in an ornate lobby mirror. A young-old face, no longer a youth, not yet a man. Hair so fair that it had no colour in the bright sunlight, and a fine, even tan. Again he felt the uncertainty. The emptiness. His mother would have described it as *the colonial biscuit-coloured tan.*

He frowned slightly, remembering the voice in the park. He had been walking in the Mall when a car had pulled up beside him and a red, angry face had peered out at him. A full R.N. captain, with a small faded woman beside him. Probably his wife, poor thing. The captain had been almost beside himself; it was still hard to believe that he could have worked himself up into such a rage in so short a time.

"What the *hell* do you think you're doing, man? You're improperly dressed, a disgrace to the uniform!"

Villiers glanced at the cap in his hand. He had been carrying it then, enjoying the sun, watching the pigeons and ducks, some Wrens feeding them, probably released from the underground bunkers at the Admiralty nearby. "It's such a nice day, sir."

The captain had exploded, "I am on my way to the Palace, otherwise . . ." Villiers had looked at him steadily and had seen the sudden uncertainty, alarm even. "I don't know what the service is coming to!"

Villiers had heard himself reply, "It's doing very well, sir.

You really should go and see for yourself sometime, instead of behaving like a pompous idiot!"

The captain's wife had pleaded, "Leave it, Henry. The young man is not himself, don't you see?"

The car had driven off at speed. Its driver would have a good yarn to tell when he got back to his mess.

Villiers laid his cap on a table. *Not himself.* Round the bloody bend, more likely.

The bar was not very busy. It was exactly as he had imagined it when his father had described his visits to England. A miniature Raffles. There were two Polish officers at one table, and an Army colonel who kept looking at his watch.

An elderly waiter came over. "Sir?"

"Pink gin, large one, please." He noticed that there was a newspaper on a nearby chair, the headlines almost loud enough to hear.

ALLIES INVADE SICILY. The Eighth Army alongside the Canadians takes all objectives on the southeast coast. The Americans land and swing towards the north.

He picked it up. There was a couple of pictures of Tommies giving the usual thumbs-up, and one of a destroyer at full speed making smoke to conceal an attack. Villiers stared at it. *The way back.* What they had all waited for.

His eyes lingered on the small item at the end of the main article. *The Admiralty released information about operations which were carried out in enemy-held waters by some of their special units before the main assault, as a result of which many lives were saved at a time when the landings were at a crucial stage.* He put the newspaper on the chair. *So easily said.* He wondered who those men had been, whether he had met them. If they had survived.

He looked up, aware that a woman had entered the bar. Both of the Polish officers were watching her like predators. She spoke to the waiter and he waved her to one of the small tables nearby. He obviously did not approve of unescorted women.

Villiers took his glass from the waiter's tray. The latter,

without being asked, said, "Waiting for somebody." He frowned. "She *says*."

Villiers watched her. Young and very pretty, with short, curly hair, she was dressed in a dark two-piece suit, probably grey, although in the filtered sunlight it was hard to tell. The effect was softened by a white, frilly blouse. She had dressed with great care, although she wore no stockings. He had heard the Wrens complaining about the shortage of decent stockings often enough. Above one ankle he saw a tiny scratch of dried blood. He looked away, clenching his fists as he remembered his sister. He had caught her shaving her legs one day and she had wrestled him out of the bathroom . . .

More voices. He looked up again: the scene had changed. The anxious colonel had gone and one of the Poles had moved over to the girl's table, his face set in an amiable grin.

Like a slow film. The officer's hand on her arm, her sudden anger, or was it fear? The rest was obvious. The Pole looked round as Villiers said, "Leave the lady alone."

The man stared at him, the grin fading like the Cheshire Cat's.

Villiers ignored him and said to her, "There's a private lounge where you can wait." He sensed her doubt. Her eyes moved from his face to the wavy stripes on his sleeves. He added, "It's all right, you know. I don't bite." He smiled, and she was to remember long afterwards how difficult it had seemed for him to do so.

The second Pole called out something to his companion, but fell silent as Villiers bent over his table and murmured, "Do you speak English, *good* English, my friend?"

The man snapped, "Of course!"

"Fine. Well, fuck off while you still can, there's a good chap!"

He took her elbow and guided her away from the bar. There was a door, decorated with bamboo inlay and labelled *The Malacca Room. Residents Only.* It was empty—but then, it usually was, unless there was a guest sleeping off a good lunch.

"Are you a resident?"

He looked down at her and smiled. "For the present. Sorry about all that. I expect you're used to it. Pretty girl, the war, and too many servicemen looking for a good time."

She was gazing round the room, so he was able to study her more closely. Brown eyes, nicely shaped hands.

She said, "I *am* waiting for somebody. I hope he's going to give me a job. I don't want people to think . . ." She coloured slightly. "What is your name?"

"Charles Villiers. I'm here for an interview too, of sorts, anyway."

She watched him curiously. "And you really are staying here?"

He held out his sleeve. "Not on a two-ringer's pay. Dinner here would make a real dent in my wallet." Then, "What time is this chap coming for you?"

She glanced at her watch. "Two hours ago. I did telephone, but his secretary told me to wait. I hope it's not much longer. I have to get back."

"Back?"

"Southsea."

There had been a lot of air-raids on the main lines to Portsmouth and attendant areas. It was hardly safe to be out late when that was happening.

She asked, "Are you in a big ship, or shouldn't I ask?" She was very nervous. Making conversation to cover it.

"No, I'm ashore at the moment." He stood up quickly, like a cat. "What's the name of this person? I'll tell the receptionist, and I'll get you a drink at the same time."

She shook her head. "I—I don't really . . ." Then she nodded, her sudden determination making her look more vulnerable. "A sherry, then, thank you."

He found the rotund manager by the entrance, peering out at the square.

"I love these sunny evenings. Not blackout all the time,

people coming and going with money to spend."

Villiers gave him the man's name and the manager said, "Ah, Mr Tweed—he comes in from time to time. I will let the lady know as soon as he calls." He glanced around, his face suddenly grave and troubled.

"I was so *sorry,* Mr Villiers. We all were. I still can't really believe it."

Villiers gripped his arm. "I know. Thank you." He picked up the two glasses and walked back to the Malacca Room.

He almost collided with her and knew instantly that something had happened. "What is it?"

She made to open the door, but he put down the glasses and took her wrist.

"Tell me!"

"You were like the others. Fair game, did you think?" She pointed at the portrait above the empty fireplace: a seafaring man with a telescope, the mast and yards of a tall sailing ship. She exclaimed. *"'Charles Villiers'*—is that where you got the name?" Her eyes were blurred with anger, disappointment.

But she did not resist as he put her down in her chair. Something in his eyes, his voice, his manner compelled her to listen. He said quietly, "That is Captain Charles Villiers—you were right. He was my great grandfather." She was staring at him as he dragged out his wallet and identity card. "See?" Together they looked at the portrait. Villiers had searched it for some likeness to his father, but there was none. As he returned his card, she saw the photograph.

"Who is that, your girlfriend?" She spoke more calmly now and without animosity.

He put the photograph away and said, "My sister."

He knew she was about to ask something and said, almost brusquely, "Take this card. I shall be here for a few days, so please telephone me if you are coming to town. If I am out, leave a message. I want you to promise."

She did not flinch, even when he gripped her wrist again.

"I promise, but I'm not sure . . ."

He smiled at her. "A promise will do."

The door opened an inch and the manager said, "Mr Tweed is here, miss. He has a taxi waiting." She walked out into the lobby and saw a vague figure by the door. But all she could think of was the tall, tanned lieutenant. The door to the Malacca Room was shut. It was as if she had imagined it all.

She hesitated by the desk. "Lieutenant Villiers—do you know him well?"

The manager shrugged and answered warily, "Not that well. A very brave young man, I believe. I knew his family, of course—his mother and father always stayed with us when they came to London. Second home, it was."

The voice intruded, impatient and rather hard. "Sorry I'm a bit late. We'd better get a move on."

But something held her motionless, like his hand on her wrist.

"Where did they live?"

The manager hesitated, afraid he was betraying a secret in some way.

"Singapore."

She could feel her heart beating, beating.

The manager said gently, "They were all killed. Murdered by the Japs."

She thought of the little photograph she had seen in his wallet. Now he was the only one left. She lifted her chin and walked to the door, the manager's words still in her ears: *second home, it was.*

She glanced across the square, golden now in the dying sunshine, then she looked at the man who had arranged to meet her. She was being stupid. She needed that job, more than ever now. A well-cut suit, slicked-back hair like the Brylcreem ads, and a smile that put the Polish officer to shame.

"I've changed my mind." She turned to the taxi. "Will you take me to Waterloo Station, cabby?"

"To the moon if you asks nicely, luv!" He crashed his gears, grinning: the expression on the man's face was a real picture. He had picked him up at a club, kept this nice little piece dangling. Well, *sod him!*

From the back of the taxi she watched the passing scene, so busy, so frantic after the south coast. Uniforms, soldiers with their girls, sandbags and walls cracked wide open by bombing.

She thought of his hand on her wrist, the sudden pain in his eyes, and of the card he had given her. She would never telephone him. How could she? And what might he think?

At Waterloo the concourse was crammed with sailors, returning from leave, a Friday run-up to the Smoke or going to new ships. She saw two lieutenants, made even younger by the massive pipes they were smoking. Wavy stripes like his—going where? Doing what?

She found a compartment that was empty but for a young sailor who was saying goodbye to his mother through the window. She sat in one corner and took out the novel she had brought with her. It would be dark by the time she reached Portsmouth, and with the heavily masked lamps it would be impossible to read.

She heard the woman say, "Don't give all the tarts away, Bobby. I made them myself, so enjoy them." Hands touched and somewhere a whistle shrilled. Most of the sailors would have packed into the other end of the train, ready to leap out at Portsmouth Harbour and charge through the barriers *en masse* to avoid the inspectors and so save their tickets for another journey.

"Write when you can, son." There was a break in the voice. How many people went through this every day of the week, she wondered.

A door slammed and the train began to move slowly along the platform, a few people waving, others sobbing quietly into handkerchiefs. The young sailor sat down and stared out of the window. He said nothing. It was all in his face.

She unclipped her handbag and after a slight hesitation took out the wedding ring and slipped it on to her finger.

She had wanted the job, but she discovered she had no regrets. She had met Mr Tweed once before. She knew he had a riverside flat at Hammersmith; was that where the final interview was to have been, when it was too late for her to get home?

She opened her book, but found herself staring at her wrist where Charles Villiers had gripped it so intensely.

She gazed through the anti-splinter netting at the serried rows of slate-covered roofs, orange now in the sunset that hid the scars and the gaps in every street.

She looked at the ring on her finger and sighed. Just a dream. The lieutenant with the same name as the portrait would already have forgotten her.

Rear-Admiral Oswald Dyer, "Ossie" to all his friends, sat behind the large, empty desk and listened to the muted growl of London's traffic. There was no petrol or diesel fuel available except for essential services, they proclaimed. He frowned. *You could have fooled me.*

He stared around the office, bare and newly decorated—and for what? Dyer was old for his rank and had been retired between the wars as a commander. Being recalled at the outbreak of war had been like a rebirth. Promoted to captain and eventually rear-admiral, he had made his unpromising appointment as head of the Special Operations, underwater weapons section, something of which to be proud. They had started with almost nothing; the Navy had needed every kind of escort vessel, minesweeper and patrol craft just to survive when the daily losses to enemy action had long outstripped their ability to replace them. Nobody had cared much for Ossie Dyer's Special Operations units, his circus—not then. Defence and survival were the priorities: hitting back and hurting the enemy were pipe dreams.

He had helped to change all that. In a small, commandeered Scottish castle overlooking the loch where their training had begun, Dyer had spared nobody, himself least of all. It was crude, dangerous, often fatal, but they never let up. Even the first chariot had been a wooden dummy nicknamed "Cassidy" which, towed by a motor-boat, had put the luckless divers through every possible manoeuvre. A far cry from their recent successes in Norway and Sicily, he thought. He could remember most of their faces, the very young, and the not so young, like Ross, who had won the Victoria Cross.

What now? He would miss the old castle by the loch. Before the war, it had been used as a hotel for keen and wealthy anglers. The huge hall, which even the title of *Wardroom* could not change and which looked like something from an Errol Flynn film, had seen great celebrations and equally intense sadness when a training scheme or an actual operation had gone wrong.

And old Ossie Dyer had nursed them all. With his bald head, the colour of a brown farm egg, and two wings of white hair, he had made himself approachable day or night to his growing teams of divers and, later, the four-man crews of the more sophisticated X-craft or midget submarines. With his old black labrador, Slouch, he had watched them go, and greeted their returns.

He glared at the spartan office. Slouch would miss the heather and the wet grass, chasing the birds back into the water.

Like me, no longer a part of things.

He thought of the man who had been appointed to the new Special Operations Section: Captain Ralph Pryce, D.S.O., Royal Navy, a submariner like his father before him, who had gained a V.C. at Zeebrugge. They needed younger blood, of course. Pryce was probably the right choice. A full captain already, he would soon be offered promotion. The youngest admiral since Nelson, he had heard someone predict.

The war would go on for ages. They would soon forget what it had been like in those first brave desperate years. He would be given some appointment in a vague advisory capacity. He would see it in the eyes of the young officers he visited: the impatient tolerance of men who were forced to put up with one more old duffer who should have been put out to grass long ago.

He banged his fist on the bare desk. But *they would not know,* could not understand what it had been like. A team, a band of brothers which he had helped to mould into a deadly weapon.

The door opened and a severe-looking Wren second officer with a clip of signals in her hand stood watching him.

"Did you call, sir?"

He looked at his clenched fist. "Sorry, Sue, letting off steam."

"Jean," she corrected gently. "It'll be all right, you know, sir. It just takes getting used to, that's all."

He smiled at her. "Not much company today."

She glanced around the office, picturing the new map and where it should hang. The desk, too. Some flowers would not come amiss. She looked at the rows of medal ribbons on the rear-admiral's jacket. She recognized only one: her father had got the same one at Jutland.

He was saying, "My old dog won't like London, not after . . ." He shook himself. "Ah, well—we'll get used to it, like you say." He did not sound very hopeful.

She said, "I've a list of the new units, sir. I knew you'd want to see it."

He glanced at it and noted that Captain Ralph Pryce had already seen and initialled it.

"Let me know when Lieutenant Ross arrives, will you—er, Jean?"

She replied calmly, "He is already here, sir. Lieutenant-Commander Ross, as he is now."

He grimaced. "I didn't know that, either."

She watched his resentment, his hurt. *Stay at a distance. Don't get involved beyond duty and obligation.* But she heard herself say, "I've been out of the service, sir. I was married. He went down in the *Lightning* a few months ago. So I came back. I didn't know how else to get back at them."

She was angry with herself, her eyes too blurred to realize that the old rear-admiral with the two white wings of hair was beside her, holding his handkerchief to her face.

He said quietly, "Right, Jean. New start for both of us. No looking back."

She sat down in a chair and watched while he produced two cups from a filing cabinet.

He smiled down at her. "Sun's *almost* over the yardarm. Brandy, I'm afraid."

She raised the cup, the tears still wet on her cheeks. "Cheers, sir!" Then she smiled back, perhaps for the first time since getting the telegram.

A tired-looking Wren, a petty officer writer, opened the door of the small ante-room and waited for the only occupant to look up at her.

"Captain Pryce will see you now, sir."

James Ross picked up his cap and followed her. He had seen the glances from the other Wrens: curiosity, an eagerness to see one of the men they dealt with every day but rarely met, men represented only by the clattering teleprinters, files of incoming and outgoing signals, and every so often, the casualty lists.

Apart from the new uniform with the two-and-a-half stripes of bright gold lace on the sleeves, he was, he told himself, the same person. And yet everything was different. Being back in England, in the Admiralty itself, and about to be interviewed by a man who, knowingly or otherwise, had always been a part of his life, seemed in some ways more hostile than planning an attack. He recalled again the lull in the busy typewriters when he had arrived, the quick stares and appraisal of the man who had been called a hero more than once in the newspapers. He had seen their eyes move to the crimson ribbon with its miniature cross. *So this is what a hero looks like.* Like the women's faces at one of the funerals after a trial attack had misfired. *Why him, and not my man?*

When he had spoken briefly to his father on the telephone, he had been touched by his excitement and genuine pleasure.

Life was strange, he thought. Captain Ralph Pryce was the son of the man who had been Big Andy's own commanding officer during their attempt to ram the dock with an obsolete submarine filled to the gills with explosives. It had read and sounded like something from *Boys' Own Paper.* Pryce's father had been killed and awarded a posthumous Victoria Cross. Ross himself would never have learned the truth of what really happened on that bloody St George's Day if he had not been entered as a boarder at Highmead School, an old and respected establishment nestling in Dorset where the sons of serving officers and senior civil servants were prepared, usually to follow in their fathers' footsteps. It was an expensive school, and Ross still marvelled at the way his father had used much of his hard-earned salvage money to coax, persuade or threaten the school into accepting a boy from such a lowly family. The reason for his father's choice and determination were immediately apparent. At the top of Highmead's Roll of Honour was the name of Francis Pryce, Victoria Cross, one of the school's heroes.

And on this bright July day their two sons were about to meet for the first time.

The Wren opened the door. "Lieutenant-Commander Ross, sir."

Ross found himself glancing at his sleeve: the new lace made him feel like a stranger.

The captain stood up behind his desk and reached over it to grasp his hand without effort. Ross had the distinct impression that Pryce had been preparing for and even timing the exact moment of this first encounter.

Pryce was tall and lean, his uniform revealing a hardened, athletic physique, as if all surplus and unwanted flesh had been honed or worked away. His hair, dark but slightly grey at the sideburns, was cut very short, so that his face looked narrow, chiselled. A tight mouth with deep lines at the corners and a hooked nose, and the most piercing eyes Ross had ever seen. Very steady, like the man: outwardly controlled, and yet giving all the signs of a consuming, restless energy.

"Sit." He leaned back in his chair. "You don't smoke, do you?"

It was more of a statement than a question.

"A pipe, usually." Ross noticed that apart from a solitary file the desk-top was empty. There was certainly no ashtray.

Pryce said, "You went to Highmead, special entry to Dartmouth. I had to start right at the beginning as a cadet in *Britannia*. But it knocks the rough edges off you. My father went to Highmead too."

Ross saw his fingers move to the unopened file and was reminded of his housemaster at that school. He kept a record of each and every boy: habits, good or bad, qualities and vices. Pryce would have known all about his education and his humble beginnings, and Ross felt a flicker of the same anger he had managed to contain when his father had visited the school for the first Open Day. Recalling the nudges and sniggers at the big, rough character who had called the headmaster "sir." They had not sneered so much the second time, when Big Andy had arrived in his spanking new Bentley.

"Yes, I know, sir. My father served under him at Zeebrugge."

Again the fingers almost touched the file. "Really? But there was only one officer in the passage crew that day when he was killed."

Ross allowed himself to relax, muscle by muscle. "That's right. My father was a stoker."

Pryce regarded him calmly, his eyes strangely opaque. Like a shark's, Ross thought.

"You know, of course, that your recent mission in Sicily should have been aborted. But we lost contact with the submarine, otherwise . . ." The eyes moved quickly as Ross massaged one wrist. Below the cuff of his reefer was a livid red mark on the skin, like a burn. Too many dives, the rawness of working under water against the clock. "Fortunately, the attack was a complete success. I never doubted it would be. But another team could have been sent in your place." It sounded like an accusation.

"Rear-Admiral Dyer was convinced . . ."

Pryce interrupted, "I know. I was not, which is why you are here." He stood up, the movement sparing, like part of an exercise. "Sicily is a beginning. It will be Italy next. Eventually we will be faced with the real task of invading France. A long hard fight, but it can and will be done." He gave a small smile. "*Must* be done. The work of Special Operations must change—the attacks by chariots, even X-craft will become a part of something more fluid, more deadly, and working at close quarters. Several new Special Operations units are being formed, to work in some cases with the Army and other reconnaissance sections. I need a new breed of leadership, officers who put success before all else. I don't care a damn about their motives. I just want results."

Ross waited, wondering if he could ever work with this man.

Pryce said evenly, "The Far East. Where the enemy rules by terror and a brutality unknown in modern warfare. International Law, the rights of sick and wounded, prisoners of war—they regard them as *our* weakness. Perhaps we have been slow to realize it." His eyes flashed in the sunlight. "I want you to take charge of one such unit. A different war, one without rules." He glanced down at the file. "You are not averse to killing the enemy. War cannot always be fought through the impartial distance of a gun or bomb-sight." Again the smile. "As somebody once said, a German I think, 'War demands that sooner or later we must dirty our hands a little.' I believe it."

Ross looked at him, framed against the windows and the clear sky. Two barrage-balloons like tiny silver whales, probably somewhere towards dockland, appeared to be attached to Pryce's left shoulder.

"If you have any doubts, this is the time to say so." Pryce's tone had sharpened. Was that rehearsed, too?

He wondered what Pryce would say if he told him that his father had been killed well before the obsolete submarine, the floating bomb, had reached its objective. That a common, lower-deck stoker had in fact taken the wheel on that unprotected conning tower, and had conned the boat directly to the target. Big Andy would never discuss those last moments. What powerful link had held him to his young skipper both before and after the attack? Ross could not imagine anything like that kind of loyalty, then the idea made him think of Tucker. He smiled faintly. *Tommy* Tucker.

"I would like my leading hand to be advanced to petty officer. It would give him more authority for this sort of job."

Pryce shook his head, momentarily off-balance. "You agree, then? I can put your appointment in orders?" He did not bother to hide his impatience, his eagerness to move on.

"I'll just drop in and see Rear-Admiral Dyer, sir."

Again, the sharp glance. "If you must. I am afraid he doesn't approve of my methods. Where strategy is concerned, we dwell in entirely different worlds."

The telephone rang. Timed to the second.

Pryce snapped, "The Prime Minister. Yes, I'll call back in a few minutes."

He held out his hand. Hard and dry, like the man.

Ross walked from the office and again the typewriters hesitated. By the end of the day every one of those girls would have heard what he had let himself in for. *Never volunteer.* God knew what Tucker would say, or even if he would agree to transfer to yet another section where he was even more likely to be killed.

A fresh start, new faces. He turned towards Dyer's door.

But not David, with all his jokes and youthful optimism.

It was over. Nothing could bring him back.

3 | Men at Arms

THE KHAKI STAFF-CAR slowed at yet another bend and then, all at once, spread out and below them, was the glittering expanse of Portsmouth Harbour. After the green hedgerows of the Surrey countryside with its inviting hotels and pubs, and then the great patchwork of the Hampshire fields, the contrast was almost unexpected: the water, the countless grey shapes of every kind of warship, and the huddle of Portsmouth itself, still too far away to reveal the scars of a city under frequent attack from the air.

Captain Ralph Pryce was sitting in the front seat beside the Royal Marine driver, his cap with the bright gold oak leaves around the peak tilted at an unusually rakish angle. He twisted round to study the other two passengers.

"Good old Pompey—still gives me that feeling, especially from up here on Portsdown Hill. Knocked about, most certainly, but still the same. Where I joined my first ship. Where I took over my first command."

Lieutenant-Commander James Ross glanced at his companion, who had barely said a word since leaving London. He had been told as much about Lieutenant Charles Villiers as Pryce apparently thought prudent, but he hated the way he had thrown them together like this. An hour in one of those quiet little pubs, just the two of them, might have made it easier. He knew about Villiers's parents and his sister who had been killed at Singapore, and the incredible detail Pryce had let slip about Villiers's return there on some secret mission under the noses of the Japanese Occupation Army. Had he been betrayed and captured, his fate would have been horrific. Old Ossie Dyer had also mentioned it when he had called on him at the Admiralty. He had been furious that any senior officer should ever allow such a terrible risk even to be contemplated, let alone taken.

"Pull in here." Pryce never said please. "I have a quick call to make."

They stopped by a telephone booth, and Ross said quietly to Villiers, "Are you settling in all right?" He saw the immediate caution in the young lieutenant's eyes. *Probably thinks Pryce told me to vet him still further.* "You're staying at a pretty posh hotel, I hear."

Villiers smiled. "My uncle's idea. He lives in Sussex, but he has always handled the company's investments over here. Seemed a pity to turn it down."

Ross watched some landgirls passing with rakes over their shoulders. A nation at war. Like the gunsites they had seen, concealed from the air by camouflage netting, and the tall poles in the fields, erected in the first year to prevent troops being landed by gliders. Things were very different now: Sicily had done that, as well as the Eighth Army's victory in North Africa, with the invincible Rommel driven back across the Mediterranean. They were hitting back, instead of lying down and taking it. Yes, it was very different.

Villiers turned suddenly, his elbow on the armrest that lay between them. "Shall we be going to the Far East soon?"

"I expect so. Ceylon as a first step—after that, well, I'm as much in the dark as you." He watched the changing expressions on Villiers's face. "You miss it, don't you?"

"Yes. Despite what's happened. Perhaps because of it. I grew up in Singapore and Malaya and, had I not come to England to finish my education, I'd still have been there when . . ." He did not go on.

Pryce came back and slammed the door. "Some people have got seaweed for brains!"

Ross glanced at his companion and smiled. Pryce had only been gone for a few minutes, and yet in that time he felt he had at least begun to make contact with Villiers. He hoped that he might feel the same.

Villiers turned to watch two low-flying fighters as the car

lurched on to the Portsmouth road again. *Ours.* After all this time, he still found himself clenching his fists when he saw aircraft close by. For some men, it had been the last thing they had ever seen.

He had sensed Ross's scrutiny, his interest, which Villiers had thought genuine from their first meeting. Now he had discovered something else about this rather silent, reserved officer who wore the Victoria Cross: what he had taken to be a purposeful, distant, even aloof attitude he now recognized as a kind of shyness. Ross was an extremely courageous man, even if only half of what they had told him was true; there was no doubt about that. And, personally, he was not like any other regular officer Villiers had ever met. He gave a small, private smile. Especially those like Pryce. A *pretty posh hotel.* It made him seem like somebody else, unable to come to grips with his role and his rank, despite all that had happened.

Pryce said airily, "We shall drop off at the R.N. Hospital at Haslar. I have to see one of the cohort."

The cohort. It was always that: something old-world, and vaguely patronizing.

Pryce was saying, "Captain Trevor Sinclair has performed several missions for Special Operations. First-rate chap." He chuckled. "For a Royal Marine, that is." He nudged the driver. "No offence intended, Brooker."

The marine glared into the driving mirror. "None taken, sir."

"Sinclair's worked in Burma, with Combined Operations and with our people. He was wounded, but I'm told he's raring to get back with us."

Villiers thought of the hotel in St James's. She had left a message for him with the manager, as she had promised, telling him she had got home safely. She had asked the manager over the telephone to thank Lieutenant Villiers for his help. Very correctly, the manager had asked for her name. *Carol.* That was all. And what more was there, or could have been? From a hotel window, he had watched her come to the decision to leave her would-be employer. He did not know her or anything about her, and yet he had been pleased that she had gone away in the taxi alone. But suppose . . . He watched the hedges and trees giving way to houses, barbed-wire checkpoints and the usual drifting throng of sailors.

Could he have told her? Made it somehow different?

He shook his head, unaware that Ross had turned to look at him. No. He would never share it. It would always be there, as if he had actually been at the house where he had grown up when the Japs had burst in. His mind could explore no further than that moment, even though he knew what had happened afterwards.

During his first interview, Pryce had barely touched on that part of his past. Only at the end had he asked, almost casually, "And would you go back to Singapore again, if it was suggested to you?"

It had been like listening to somebody else to hear the voice. So clipped and confident. "If I could do something—anything—yes, I would."

The Royal Naval Hospital at Haslar might have seemed a strange location for a place of healing and peaceful recovery; one side faced the water where, daily and nightly, M.T.B.s and motor gunboats thundered noisily past from their nearby base at H.M.S. *Hornet,* on their way to the Channel and beyond to seek out the enemy in his own coastal waters. It was also only a short walk from *Dolphin,* the submarine base and instruction school where many of the Special Operations people had originally been trained. By comparison with *Hornet, Dolphin* was almost a silent, even sinister part of the harbour complex. Where Pryce had got his first command.

Pryce climbed down from the car and smoothed his jacket into place, not that it ever seemed to need it.

"I have to see the P.M.O. More red tape, I expect." He looked at Ross. "An orderly can take you. Go and see if Captain Sinclair is all packed and ready. I want a word with him, then he can be driven back to his quarters." He shot the driver a searching glance. "Is that all fixed, Brooker?"

"Yes, sir." It sounded like *of course.*

As Pryce strode away, Ross said to Villiers, "You keep with me. O.K. if I call you Charles?" He smiled, and looked about five years younger. "I'm James." He paused, and again Villiers sensed the shyness. "Jamie to my friends." They solemnly shook hands, watched patiently by a white-coated orderly who eventually said, "This way, gentlemen."

Villiers remarked, "Odd place for a hospital." Then he glanced out of a window and saw the water, so near that it appeared to be lapping the terrace.

Ross was watching him at that moment and realized that Villiers was not seeing Portsmouth as it was now, but another harbour which, like the hospital, had flourished in the days of tall masts and pyramids of sails. It moved him, when he had almost believed he was beyond that kind of emotion.

The orderly turned, instantly alert as somebody called urgently, "Nurse, nurse! *Quickly!*"

He said, "Number Ten, sir." Then he was gone.

Ross said harshly, "God, I hate these places."

They looked at one another as, in the sudden silence after the brief commotion, a man's voice shouted, "For God's sake, you should *tell* me; I'm not a bloody mind-reader!" There was silence again as Ross tapped the door. "Come in. Don't be shy!"

The man was in khaki battledress, the rank of Captain, Royal Marines, on each shoulder.

Ross had the instant impression of energy and impatience, and charm. The face smiled warmly enough, his eyes flitting from one to the other with a kind of curious amusement. "Well, this *is* an honour! Two of you!"

Ross half turned to introduce his companion, and felt his mind click into place. Like those other times. When the time-fuse on a mine was disturbed, the sudden tick as loud as Big Ben, when you only had twelve seconds more to live. Or the startled face of an enemy frogman rising beside you in icy water to grapple or to raise the alarm. The briefest second of all, when you know you will kill him. It was all there in Villiers's face. Disbelief, surprise? No, Ross thought, it was shock.

The captain named Sinclair peered towards an open suitcase on the bed and said, "This is my wife, by the way."

Villiers held out his hand and felt her fingers close around his, saw the fear in her eyes change to gratitude as he said casually, "Charles Villiers. Pleased to meet you."

A light flowered dress, but otherwise exactly as he remembered her, had thought of her. Except that she was wearing a wedding ring. She said, "We're almost ready."

Villiers tried not to watch her. Southsea, she had said. Of course. There was a big Royal Marines barracks there, at Eastney.

Ross said, "Captain Pryce wishes to see you before you leave." He looked briefly at Villiers, and knew he had guessed correctly.

Sinclair touched his moustache as if to make certain it was as it should be. "*Captain* Pryce, eh? Well, well. He was a two-and-a-half ringer when we last met." He felt the back of his head and added in a matter-of-fact way, "When I bought *this!*"

Ross opened the door. "I'll send an orderly for the luggage." Then to Villiers: "You wait with Mrs Sinclair. There should be a car shortly."

Then they were alone together. "I'm so *sorry!*" She did not resist as he took her hand again. "So terribly sorry. I didn't know it would happen like this. And—and you were so kind to me at the hotel . . ."

He squeezed her hand. "Don't distress yourself. And thank you for leaving the message." He pulled out his wallet and showed her the page from the pad. "See? *Carol.*" She was close to tears, and there was a strain on her face he had not seen before. He said, "I had no idea, otherwise I'd have made some excuse to get out of this."

"My husband will be serving with you, then?" It was as though she were speaking of a stranger. "If only I'd known . . ."

There were noises outside the door, a wheelchair, or maybe a trolley for the captain's luggage.

He said simply, "I've thought about you a lot. I saw you leave in the taxi."

She stared at him, momentarily pleased, and then openly afraid. "Did you? I'm so glad." She glanced at her watch, but he guessed she did not even see it. "I should go."

He said, "I must see you again."

She shook her head, her dark curls brushing her neck. "Impossible." She was very calm, her eyes quite steady as she looked up at him. "He would kill me." Then she nodded slowly. "I mean it." He watched her hand on his sleeve, her fingers on the wavy stripes. "But thank you. You'll never know."

He said, "Keep my card. If you ever need me . . ."

She shook her head again. "You're a nice person. Find a pretty girl and forget. It was a dream. Just a dream."

A porter banged open the door and peered in at them cheerfully. "Car's alongside, Mrs Sinclair. Your husband is waiting." As she turned towards the door he looked at her bare legs.

Villiers wanted to hit him, and when the door closed behind them, he said aloud, "It's not just a dream to me. Not any more!"

Ross was waiting for him. "Sorry about that, Charles. I didn't know."

Villiers swung on him, his eyes blazing, ready for the innuendo. Then he relented, "No, *I'm* sorry. I didn't know, either."

He felt Ross's hand on his shoulder as they watched Pryce striding briskly out of the building. Then Ross said, "That posh hotel of yours. Do you think we might have an enormous drink there when his lordship gets us back to London?"

Their eyes met. It had been a damned close thing.

Villiers said, too casually, "Best suggestion I've heard all day."

"If you ever want to tell me about it—"

Villiers tried to smile. "Thanks. You can do the same, if you like."

Pryce was back. "Must get cracking. Lot to do." But, for once, there was no bounce in his voice.

As they walked into the sunshine Villiers thought he heard her voice. *He would kill me.* She had meant it.

The severe-looking Wren officer, her chin resting in her hand, raised her eyes from her desk as the door opened slightly. It had been a long day and the air was humid and sticky, as the black-out blinds had already gone up across the windows, and there was no movement or even the hint of a fan.

"Sorry, the office is closed." She shaded her eyes against the desk lamp and recognized the young R.N.V.R. lieutenant watching her. She relaxed slightly. "Lieutenant Villiers. Feeling a bit lonely with all the others gone?"

Villiers glanced at the other door. There was a light on there, too. "I was wondering if I might see the rear-admiral." He felt suddenly lost, out of his depth. It had been stupid to come. But she was right: it *was* different, now that Ross and the others he had met in Pryce's "cohort" had been spirited away. A fast convoy to Colombo, where everything had been set up to receive them.

Pryce had said airily, "You'll be following in a couple of weeks. I want you to take charge of the last party coming down from Scotland. Good experience. Don't worry—the war won't end before you get to Ceylon!"

The Wren was saying, "It's a bit unusual." She saw the strain, the uncertainty on his tanned face. Maybe he had changed his mind about returning to the Far East. She had read his file, and knew as much about Villiers as all the others. Who could blame him?

No, it was not that. As Villiers turned to leave, she said quietly, "I'll see what I can do."

She found the rear-admiral, sleeves rolled up and his jacket hanging over the back of his chair, grasping a clip of signals in both hands with fierce concentration. He looked up, surprised that he had not heard her knock. "Ah, Jean—I was just going to call you. I still don't believe it."

"What is it, sir?"

"They want me back in Scotland! A whole new training schedule for Underwater Weapons is being fixed. The First Sea Lord has asked me himself."

"I'm very glad for you, sir." She was surprised that she felt it so badly. Just a few weeks since he had arrived in the newly decorated office, hurt, baffled and lost. Now he was leaving. She repeated, "I am *so* glad. A lot of others will be, too."

He rubbed his chin. "Fact is, it will mean a lot more work, new weapons, fresh trials to find the people to fit them." He looked at her keenly. "I'll need an assistant, you know, a sort of flag lieutenant." He stood up, as he had that day when she had broken down in this same office. "Will you come to Scotland with me, Jean?"

She said, "I almost forgot, sir. Lieutenant Villiers is here. He wants a few moments of your time." She half opened the door and looked back at him. "Of *course* I'll come. Just say the word."

Villiers walked past her and sat awkwardly in a vacant chair. He had met Ossie Dyer several times since he had arrived and had been amazed by his incredible memory for names and faces, those he had met, trained, or merely fished or played golf with. A good man. A caring one, too, in spite of all the bluster to the contrary.

Ossie came straight to the point, even though he was still bursting both with the unexpected news and his Wren's reaction. Scotland . . . soon it would be cold again, the lochs and the rusting depot-ship as unwelcoming as ever. It would be like heaven.

"You want to ask me something?"

Villiers said, "The others have left, sir." He saw him nod. "I've been trying to keep up to date with the officers who have joined the . . ." he avoided Pryce's *cohort* ". . . new section. Captain Pryce has taken most of the relevant information with him . . ." It was no use at all. He felt like a schoolboy pleading an injured wrist to avoid football.

Ossie Dyer pulled open a drawer. "There is only one recent

entry, and he's not exactly new to Special Operations." He flicked through a small book. "Captain Trevor Sinclair, Royal Marines. But you know him, don't you?"

Villiers said, "I met him at Haslar just before he was returned to duty. I don't really know him."

"Oh, you will. A real goer, that one. His luck almost ran out during a raid behind Jap lines in Burma. Most of his men were killed, but he got back. He was in a bad way. A mine laid near the enemy installations they were going to destroy blew up and killed his sergeant and some of his chaps. Sinclair was wounded by splinters, the last of which were removed only last month. I must say I thought he was going to spend the rest of his life in hospital . . . However, Captain Pryce has assured me that the P.M.O. is quite satisfied. Sinclair is fit and raring to go—if that is so he could be invaluable to your lot. He's worked with the Army in Burma, even with the Chindits. A lot of hard experience for one so young." He sighed. "But everybody's young to me nowadays."

Villiers asked, "Is it possible he might not be completely fit, sir?"

"Well, who can say, when you've gone through something like that. One splinter was about the size of a gramophone needle, can you imagine?"

Villiers remembered how she had told him that she had needed a job. She, too, must have believed her husband was finished, that he would be another wreck left over by the war. And the sharpness in the voice he and Ross had heard through the door at Haslar; the easy, disarming smile Sinclair had used to greet them. His *this is my wife, by the way.* Villiers could recall exactly when he had touched the back of his head and remarked in the same offhand manner, "when I bought *this!*" And she was afraid of him, of what he might do, could do.

Dyer said, "Can't offer you a glass, my boy. I want to get away—bomber's moon tonight."

"I'm sorry, sir. It was good of you to . . ."

Dyer was struggling into his jacket. "Any time. I am very proud to have you in this section. After what you've been through." He looked around, but there was only the Wren in the doorway.

"He's gone, sir."

Dyer dismissed him from his thoughts. "Come and have a drink, and I'll tell you about the castle on the loch." He smiled, happy again. "*Our* castle. Old Slouch will take to you right enough, I can tell you! A bit deaf, like me, but only when he wants to be!"

She took down her tricorn hat, still thinking about Villiers. It had been a long day, and as she switched off the office lights she heard the distant wail of the first air-raid siren. Perhaps Ossie had missed something? Villiers was not the kind to disturb a flag officer without a reason.

It could wait, whatever it was. There was Scotland to think about now.

Charles Villiers turned off the bedside light and opened the heavy black-out curtains for a moment. Bright moonlight, and there were wavering beams from searchlights a long way off, south of the Thames somewhere. He returned to the bed and sat down before switching on the light once more. His unopened newspaper lay beside him; the war in Sicily was all but over, and the friction of retreat was already showing itself between the Germans and their disheartened Italian allies.

He remembered how Ross had come to the hotel on their return from Portsmouth, how they had discussed Pryce's sudden change of demeanour, although he had regained his energy when the orders for Ceylon had been finally approved. Had Pryce's lapse been because of Sinclair's early and obviously unexpected release from medical care?

It was a marvel that old Ossie Dyer hadn't tumbled the reasons for his questions. He was usually sharper than a tack.

The telephone jangled noisily. It would be the manager, as

discreet as ever, announcing the air-raid warning with the courteous suggestion that it might be safer in the hotel cellar-cum-shelter until the all-clear.

An unknown voice said, "Lieutenant Villiers? I have a call for you."

It was a bad line, like a W/T set full of static, but he knew her voice instantly.

She said, "It's me . . ." the slightest hesitation, "Charles?"

He gripped the telephone tightly. "What is it? Where are you?"

She replied, "I just wanted to thank you properly for your kindness when you came to Portsmouth—to Haslar. You were so good, so quick to understand."

Villiers thought of Ross's cool intervention. But for that . . . He said, "I know that your husband has left. Don't say anything about it on the phone. We might get cut off." He tried to smile, to reassure her over the miles. "Careless talk, you know. I know I'm not supposed to say it, but it's wonderful to hear you. You could be right beside me. I wish you were."

For a moment he imagined he had gone too far, that she had hung up.

Then she said, "Good luck, and take care of yourself, won't you?" There was a catch in her voice. It must have cost her a lot to make this call.

He said, "I must see you before I leave." The line crackled but nothing happened. "I promise not to upset you. I want to tell you—no, I *need* to tell you . . ." It was all going wrong.

She said, "I have another interview in two days' time. I—I could meet you afterwards, if you like."

"Like?" He swallowed hard. "Come to the hotel. The Malacca Room, remember?"

She was crying now, but very quietly. "I'll never forget. Your great grandfather. What *did* you say to that Polish officer?"

"You're too young to know." He held the telephone pressed hard to his ear. "We can talk." She could not answer, and he said, "Until Thursday." She had replaced the telephone, but he said, as though she were still listening, "I shall be here."

Then he took a bottle of Plymouth gin marked *Duty Free, H.M. Ships Only* from the cupboard, and groped for a glass.

It was probably madness, but she must not be hurt by it.

When the all-clear wailed across London he was asleep, fully dressed, the gin unopened. He could not remember sleeping without the nightmare for a long, long time.

Lieutenant-Commander James Ross gripped the guardrail and paused to stare up at the ship's superstructure. He had all but forgotten what a big ship was like. Outwardly, this was a powerful cruiser where never a day passed without men mustering for this or that to the lordly summons of a bugle. But H.M.S. *Endeavour* was not what she appeared, and like a few sister ships was in fact a fast minelayer, her belly usually packed with a lethal cargo of some four hundred mines. She was designed to dash in, sow a full field of mines and speed out again before there was time to seek her out from the air. Captain Pryce's cohort had boarded the minelaying cruiser at Liverpool and after the first leg of the passage to Gibraltar they had had cause to be grateful for their choice of transport. *Endeavour* was so fast, in spite of her size, that her escort of four fleet destroyers had been hard put to keep up, even when the minelayer had reduced to her economical cruising speed.

Another world. A full wardroom, meals properly served by white-jacketed stewards: a far cry from the mud and stealth of enemy harbours, where at any minute they might have been sighted and attacked. Out of courtesy, *Endeavour*'s captain had offered Pryce the use of his own quarters. Pryce had accepted with unseemly haste.

The war they had come to know, respect and sometimes fear fell rapidly astern with each turn of the screws. Long-range aircraft, U-Boats and commerce raiders were almost unknown here, and this morning they had sighted the far-off blur of land: Sierra Leone. Africa.

Ross continued with his walk, determined to keep as fit as possible, in spite of the large meals and lack of exercise. He saw Tucker standing by one of the boat davits, shading his eyes to watch some strange birds skimming within inches of the creaming bow-wave.

They met every day, like lost souls in this ship with her complement of over four hundred officers and ratings. Ross had still not become accustomed to the sight of Tucker in his new fore-and-aft rig of petty officer, with its gilt buttons and crossed anchors on the sleeve. But it suited him, just as he had known that Tucker would suit it.

Tucker straightened up when he saw him. "Cheeky little buggers, them birds. It's a wonder they don't drop dead with fatigue!"

Ross nodded. The ship was steering southeast. They would put in to Simonstown, South Africa, in a few days. He had been there before as a young subbie and he knew Tucker had, too. A sailors' town. Hot, not too expensive, and friendly.

Tucker said, "Still find it a bit strange to be messing in the P.O.s' mess. But they're a good bunch—seem to think *we're* the nutcases for doing what we do instead of serving in big ships." He grinned, his eyes crinkling. "Of course, they'd say different if they got tin-fished with a load of mines down below!"

They lapsed into a companionable silence and watched the spray drifting astern from the stem.

Tucker was thinking of his last few days of leave, the consternation when he had appeared in his new uniform. All his father had been able to say was, "Well, blow me. *Blow me!* Just look at our Mike!" Even his old gran had given him a hug and wished him well. Usually she never had a kind word to say for anyone. His mum had questioned him about his next assignment and had warned him to watch out for *them coloured girls.*

It made you laugh, really. His mum had never been further than a trip to Southend for the day.

He said, "Pity Mr Villiers couldn't have come along with us, sir. He'll be feeling a bit out of it, I expect."

Ross smiled. Tucker was a marvel. He spoke to just about everybody and made friends with most of them; he had even dared to caution Captain Pryce when he had been handling a loaded pistol without first checking the safety catch. It was rare to see Pryce at a loss for words.

He thought of that night at the St James's hotel. They had had rather a lot to drink, and in the course of their conversation Villiers had told him about his great grandfather, Captain Charles Villiers, Far East trader and deep-water sailorman; how the business had started at Hong Kong where he had discovered that half of his crew were falling ill, poisoned by the harbour's supply of drinking water for the hundreds of ships that came and left on the tide. He had bought a fresh-water concession with some smart, clean lighters and trustworthy people to handle his business affairs. The name of Villiers had become known world-wide, but few realized that it had all begun with the sale of drinking water.

Villiers had not mentioned his parents and young sister, and Ross had not asked him. It was there in his voice, his eyes, his obvious affection for the life they had all once shared.

He said to Tucker, "A nice chap. Should fit in well. But I agree with you about his being left behind. It's a matter of collecting some last bods for our section—a couple of divers and some mechanics. I don't know the full strength of it yet."

He thought, too, of the girl he had met only briefly at Haslar Hospital, Captain Sinclair's young wife. She was the other reason for wishing Villiers had come with them aboard the minelayer. He tried to dismiss it from his mind. If he had had one reservation about Villiers joining the section it had been because of his past, the obvious hatred he felt for those who had murdered his family, his desire for revenge. Such forces often made a man behave recklessly, and with total disregard for others who relied on him. Ross could well imagine the Royal Marine being like that, the man of action and impulse rather than reason. Now that he knew Villiers a little better, he had no fears in that direction.

But he could see his face, the girl's, too, when they had confronted one another at Haslar. It would be madness for them to become involved. A brief affair? Even that could be destructive.

We are going to a war we know very little about. Ross had always dreaded the possibility of an operation going wrong, and ending as a prisoner of war. But he had never been afraid. He had helped to drag German survivors from the freezing water when minutes earlier they had been doing everything possible to kill one another. A blanket over the shoulders, a cigarette put between shivering lips, a tot of rum if there was one handy. After that, they didn't seem very different from his own men.

But the Japs . . . He had seen it in Villiers's eyes. A young man driven so brutally by grief and horror that he had even agreed to land in Singapore on some crackpot mission or other, no doubt dreamed up by another Pryce, if there could be such a thing.

And what about you? It was like another voice. *What would you do in his place?*

The tannoy squeaked, and then came the trill of a boatswain's call.

"Up spirits! Senior hands of messes muster for rum!"

Ross shook himself mentally and tried to smile. This was reality. All that counted, until the job was over and done with.

When he examined his thoughts again, all he could discover was envy.

4 | The Real Thing

THE ARRIVAL AND DISEMBARKATION of Captain Pryce's Special Operations Reconnaissance Force at Trincomalee, the Fleet's main anchorage on the eastern coast of Ceylon, was something of an anticlimax. Far from feeling like part of a completely new theatre of war, September had brought to them a strange sense of unreality, and isolation from the "real thing."

Some old Army married quarters had been converted into accommodation for the naval party while the chariots, which had travelled from England in the belly of the big minelayer, were transferred to a small depot-ship with all the necessary facilities, and a fine machine shop for the artificers and torpedomen.

Empty blue skies, white uniform shirts and shorts: all the stark changes were matched only by the news from home. As expected, the Allies had invaded southern Italy. Not an island this time, but part of Europe itself. It had not been easy. The Germans had been prepared, and had barely relied on the Italians. They had fought back with artillery and tanks, and an entirely new weapon, a radio-guided rocket which could be homed on to a ship from the air, had made its first appearance. Several major warships had been damaged, including the veteran flagship *Warspite,* the darling of the Mediterranean, and others had been even less fortunate. But despite some misunderstandings between the allied commanders, the attacks had been forced through. Operation *Avalanche* had succeeded.

Pryce's chariot crews, used to the bitter waters of Scottish lochs and the North Sea, were amazed by the beauty and warmth of the coast where they exercised in an underwater world of red and white coral, passages through dark rocks and swaying flowers so exotic and ornate that it was often hard to concentrate on the rules of attack.

There were six chariots altogether, with crews and spare

hands and a considerable back-up of "experts," who ranged from explosives instructors and survival teams to a lecturer on tropical diseases.

On this hot evening, Lieutenant-Commander James Ross walked into a pool of light outside the door marked *Captain-in-Charge* and then hesitated. Pryce had asked him to "pop in," but he obviously had somebody with him: Ross could hear his short, barking laugh. What did he want this time? He thought suddenly of Villiers. His passage to Ceylon had been further delayed, and Ross sometimes wondered if that meant all this had been for nothing; that somebody on high had decided there was no need to proceed with a further expansion of this or any other Special Operations group.

A seaman who was sitting beside a small table with a telephone said formally, "The captain is with a senior Army officer, sir. Shall I call him?"

Ross shook his head. "No, but thanks. Is there anyone in Operations?"

"Only the duty P.O., sir. Ops at Base are still handling the main traffic."

Ross walked away and along one of the newly constructed corridors that had been built to link the various offices and storerooms. The operations room had once been an ordinary bungalow, but had been completely transformed by all the usual hanging maps and signals information. A few Wrens worked here during the day but, unless there was a flap on, it was very much a nine-to-five Navy.

A signal flimsy had been left under a polished piece of stone and he paused to glance at it. It was not vital: it merely warned someone about a forthcoming squash tournament.

"Can I help—" the smallest hesitation. "Sir?"

Ross realized that there was a Wren seated at the biggest desk marked S.O.O. She was hardly a staff officer; Ross was not even certain that the Force rated one at this early stage. On one sleeve she wore a petty officer's rank, like Tucker's but for the colour, and on the other the crossed flags and letter of a coder. She had a pencil in one hand and he saw a half-completed crossword puzzle under her elbow.

"Are you in charge here?"

She regarded him calmly, her eyes almost tawny in the hard glare from the lights. "Yes, sir. Petty Officer Mackenzie."

Her cool manner made him unnecessarily angry. "I'm Lieutenant-Commander . . ."

She stood up in one easy movement. "I know who *you* are, sir. We all do."

It was not exactly insolent. Nor was it respectful.

He said curtly, "The signals file—Immediate." When she showed no response, he added, "Today's. I'd like to see it."

She smiled; it made her look very attractive. "Not possible, sir."

"I'll sign for it, if that's what's bothering you!"

"It's not bothering me, sir. Captain Pryce has ordered that it can only be done with his consent. I would be in trouble if I broke the rules."

Ross said, "I need to see something." It was useless. He had the feeling that she was enjoying it. She had dark glossy hair—it could even be jet black. There was something unusual about her, he thought; foreign, if there was such a thing.

She said, "I can get you anything else, sir—cup of tea if you like?"

"Thank you, no. I'll see Captain Pryce if that is what I must do."

But when he looked back she was bending intently over her crossword.

A strange encounter. Perhaps she disliked officers, or men in general?

I'm losing my sense of humour. Stupid to let it rattle him.

He reached Pryce's door and the rating on duty said, "He's expecting you, sir."

He found Pryce in a jovial mood. "I've been waiting for you. It's restricted; of course, but tomorrow the whole world will know!" He pointed to a chair. "I'll bet they're celebrating up in the lochs tonight, or whatever the damned time is there!"

Ross waited, still puzzled by the girl's hostility.

Pryce said, "All our faith in smaller underwater weapons has been justified, Ross. Some of our X-craft—the signal did not specify how many—penetrated the Norwegian fjord where the *Tirpitz* has been skulking all this time. Nets, booms, patrol boats, the lot! They bloody well did it! Laid their charges and crippled the brute, probably for good!"

Ross stared at him, the picture refusing to form in his mind. He had often thought of transferring to X-craft, the midget submarines that had been one of Ossie Dyer's projects. Small, they carried only a four-man crew, and yet they had done this, the impossible. *Tirpitz* was the most powerful warship in the world, after her sister ship *Bismarck,* which had destroyed the *Hood* in northern waters where a man's survival was limited to minutes. *Bismarck,* too, had been sunk, but it had taken most of the Home Fleet and a lot of luck to do it. And while *Tirpitz* remained, even if she never ventured out from her Norwegian lair, desperately needed ships had had to be tied down just in case she might make a sudden sortie.

He asked quietly, "What happened to our chaps, sir?"

"What?" Pryce was in another world. "Oh, not sure of that either. Some were taken prisoner, but still . . ."

But still. Ross said, "I wish we'd been in on it."

Pryce looked at him curiously. "Which was why I chose you for this job. We will always have casualties. Officers who lead by example are something else." Then he said, "As it's a special occasion . . ." He opened a cupboard and took out a bottle of malt whisky. Then he pressed a bell. "Only one glass, dammit!"

Ross watched him. Pryce was genuinely pleased about the mighty *Tirpitz.* Even Churchill had admitted that it would take at least two British battleships in company to stand a chance against her. But he was on edge. Perhaps in some way he also felt left out.

Ross said, "I was hoping to see the latest signals about our people from England. Lieutenant Villiers . . ."

The door opened, and the petty officer Wren stood there, regarding him with the same cool eyes.

"No tea after all, sir?" To Pryce she said, "I came myself. The messenger has gone to the heads."

Pryce nodded vaguely. "Quite. Quite so. Could you find me another glass?" The door closed.

He opened a drawer. "I've got the signals right here." He gave Ross a searching glance. "I sensed a little tension just now. You've met our formidable Victoria, then?" And he laughed shortly. Then he said briskly, "Say what you like, she did more than anybody to set up these offices and equipment for us. A *very* intelligent girl. Lucky to have her."

Ross considered it. It was rare for Pryce to offer praise so freely. "I'd have thought the Wrens would have provided an officer."

Pryce unscrewed the bottle slowly. "I am sure Miss Mackenzie thinks so, too. She would make a good one."

Ross recalled her eyes, her barely concealed dislike. "Then why not, sir?"

Pryce looked furtively at the door and murmured, "Upbringing—you know how it is. Wrong side of the blanket, does that explain?"

She came back with the glass. "Anything else, sir?"

She was looking at Pryce, but Ross could feel the anger in her voice as if it had been directed at him. *She knows we've been talking about her.*

He felt Pryce put the glass into his hand. It was almost full, and yet he had never seen Pryce take a drink before, not even in the mess.

Pryce was saying, "I imagine many a wardroom Romeo has tried to feel his way into her affections, eh? My guess is she'd have the little buggers for breakfast!"

He held up his glass. "Cheers! To all those chaps we knew who never got back." The mood passed just as quickly, and he turned over the file on his desk.

"You were a great friend of a lieutenant called David Napier." It was not a question. "He died in that last big operation, yes? Not all that far from the bloody *Tirpitz*."

Ross acknowledged it, wondering what was coming, wondering also why he had felt something warning him earlier.

Pryce said, "When our other people arrive there will be one extra chariot team. Sub-Lieutenant Peter Napier is in command."

Ross gripped the arms of his chair, some of the whisky spilling unheeded on to his leg.

"Not Peter." Words eluded him. "He's too young, not experienced. Can't you prevent it, sir?"

"Of course he's young. Most of them were, once." Pryce smiled, but his eyes remained still and cold. "Even you. The training commander had nothing but the highest praise for him—far and away the best applicant he's had for some time. Why should I stop it? He's good and damned keen, just what we need. If it was anyone else you'd accuse me of favouritism, pulling rank, right?"

Ross barely heard. "He was just a kid. Worshipped his brother."

"And you too, by all accounts. We always need somebody to look up to, Ross, even the bloody war doesn't change that!"

He glanced meaningfully at his watch. "I've been having words with our friends in khaki. We shall have to discuss jungle training. Keep them up to the mark, on top line for the real thing."

He turned away. "Something else for you to keep under your hat, and this really is Top Secret. Lord Louis Mountbatten is being given overall command of Southeast Asia: Army, Navy, everything." He smiled at the wall-map with all its bright little flags. "Nobody is going to push *us* into a backwater, not any more."

Ross walked out of a side door and stood in the warm, enveloping darkness. The air was heady with blossom, and yet he could taste the salt on his lips. Here, like the West Country, the sea was never far away.

He thought of the girl with the jet-black hair. *The wrong side of the blanket.* How would someone like Pryce understand?

Somebody to look up to. And would Peter die like his brother for such a stupid reason?

He heard muffled cheering; it seemed to come from the building occupied by the petty officers' mess. He was certain that the name *Tirpitz* was one of the causes of the general celebration.

He found that he could smile, somehow safe in the darkness. So much for Top Secret. "Tommy" Tucker was probably in there with his new mates, with the photo of his London clippie still in his oilskin pouch. He and men like him asked so little, but gave everything in return.

Figures spilled from the petty officers' mess, and he heard somebody thumping on a piano.

The words of the song were so familiar, and yet somehow reassuring because of it. Perhaps David had been right after all. *If it's got your name on it, there's nothing you can do.*

"Roll on the Nelson, the Rodney and Hood,
This long-funnelled bastard is no fucking good!"

Between them, they said it all.

The hotel's Malacca Room was empty. Outside, the evening was growing dark, and there was a hint of autumn in the air. Villiers took the girl's raincoat and said, "Sorry about all this. Not quite what I planned."

It had been an unsatisfactory afternoon, after they had both dared to look forward to it so much. Her interview had been delayed, and by the time she had reached the hotel, the table he had reserved elsewhere for afternoon tea had been given to somebody else. The place they had eventually found off Piccadilly had been crowded, noisy and characterless. The next mistake had been the cinema. To sit in the secret darkness had been nice enough. He had even put his arm around her shoulders while the film, about the Americans in the Pacific, had thundered on. And then the too-familiar slide creaking across the screen, *THE AIR-RAID WARNING HAS JUST BEEN SOUNDED*, had brought even that small privacy to an end, while the audience, mostly servicemen and their girls, had bellowed with indignation and stamped their boots in protest. But the rules were tougher now. Too many crowded cinemas had been hit by bombs, the inmates unaware or indifferent to the danger until it was too late.

She was going to Putney; she had friends there who would put her up for the night. Tomorrow she would hear the result of the interview. It could have been such a perfect day. Now it was spoiled for both of them.

Villiers said, "I'll see if I can get us a drink." He looked at her gravely, remembering her dark curls on his wrist when he had put his arm around her. A lot of other couples had been doing the same, and he gathered from the muffled sounds that some had gone far beyond restraint and caution.

They had walked arm in arm in the fading daylight, had watched the bright pinpricks in the sky, bursting flak, made harmless by distance. The East End again, according to a newspaper seller.

He said abruptly, "I don't like the idea of your going to Putney, wherever that is, tonight. Not alone. It's going to rain—you'd never get a taxi."

The door opened slightly and the manager peered in at them. "It's a bit chilly in here. I could send for an electric fire." He looked at the girl discreetly. "Too early for coal, they say." He held out a buff-coloured letter. "This came this afternoon, Mr Charles. I had to sign for it."

She watched his face and sensed the change in him. Not excited, or even resigned. It was a strangely lost look, she thought, like a little boy.

The manager was saying, "I could arrange for some refreshment. I know it's not officially . . ."

He withdrew.

Villiers folded the letter and said, "Tomorrow then. I have to go north."

She waited, watching his fingers on the paper, the hand she had felt on her collar in the cinema, which had held her arm on the street. She asked, "Overseas?"

He looked at her and through her and then walked to her chair and touched her shoulder. She was not certain he even noticed what he was doing. "I wanted it to be so nice for you. I'm off tomorrow, and you're going to Putney." The smile would not come. "Can't even have a bloody fire in here. Save fuel, save power, save every damned thing except lives. They even have six-inch lines painted on the baths, you know. It's unpatriotic to use more water than you really need!"

She said, "Don't be angry, Charles. I've loved being here . . . with you. It put everything else into proportion. We knew it couldn't last."

He sat down beside her and stared at her. "You could telephone your friends from here. Tell them you've made other arrangements. We could have supper. Just the two of us."

She said, "Do you know what you're asking? What you're doing?" She was surprised at her own calmness. "You know I must go. When we've had our drink. After that . . ."

He took both of her hands. "I want you to stay, Carol. I want it so much it hurts. You can still find out about your interview." He squeezed her hands and looked very young, very vulnerable. "I'm sure you'll get the job you want."

The manager entered with a tray and the drinks. He said, "I had to give old Henry the day off, Mr Charles. His boy, the air-gunner, was reported missing—down in the sea, they say."

Villiers looked at her hands, which she had not attempted to withdraw. "Poor chap. If he needs anything . . . anything I can do. You know."

The manager glanced towards the portrait of the old Captain Villiers. "Yes, I do know. He'd have been very proud of you, if I may say so."

Villiers picked up his glass. "Well, Carol."

She asked, "Have you got your wallet?"

He pulled it out, mystified. "Here."

She opened it and took out the card where he had written her name. She had seen a pencil in the same pocket and reached into his jacket for it. Only for an instant, she felt his body through his shirt. It was hot, as though with fever.

The pencil was gold and had his initials engraved on it. A gift from somebody who loved him, she thought.

He said, "My twenty-first birthday present. From my sister."

She crossed out the name on the card and could feel his sudden emotion, like her own. "You must have it right, Charles. It's *Caryl.*" She reached for the sherry, but turned her face to his and said softly, "If you're *sure.* I don't want you to think . . ." She did not finish, as he kissed her very gently on the cheek. She gripped his hand. So gently, carefully; it seemed likely that he had never been with a girl before.

He said, "I'm sure, Caryl. Never more certain of anything. You see, I've never been in love before, not like this."

She touched his lips with her fingers. "Don't say that. Everything's against us. I'm married to a man I don't love, and we'll probably both regret what we're doing." Then she smiled, as if her true feelings had been lying in wait, even though she had not understood them. "I'll stay. I *want* to stay. I know a lot of girls would jump at the chance and never question the rights and wrongs of it . . . You're very nice-looking—" she touched the medal ribbon on his breast. "What is this?"

He watched her, trying to control the thoughts, the emotions, everything. It was a dream. In a moment he would come out of it. He would wake. "The D.S.C." He tried to make light of it. *"Doing Something Constructive."*

She looked up as the manager came in again. "I have your bag at the desk, Miss. I can try for a taxi, if you wish, but it's raining quite heavily."

Villiers said, "My guest will be staying. Can you arrange it?"

The manager touched the mantelpiece below the portrait as if to seek out some dust. "There is the rule about Identity Cards for overnight guests." He smiled sadly. "The war, you know. But I usually put the register in my safe about now. The formalities can wait until the morning."

Villiers waited until they were alone again. "Are you certain?"

She touched his face, his hair, his mouth. "I never thought it could happen, that I could be like this." She watched his hand on her wrist, like that very first time . . . And it *was* madness. Suppose somebody found out, her father for instance, and all those who would take sides against her on Trevor's behalf. The war hero. She could never begin to imagine him making jokes about his medals and his brave deeds . . . She should have left him that first time. Before she had been made to feel guilty when he had been isolated in one hospital after another. Each visit had been like a penance. He had never spoken, and had barely shown any recognition unless her father or one of his parents had been present. A different man. Or was he? Had she deluded herself over that, too?

She said quickly, "Take me up, Charles. The future can wait. The past is gone."

The room was on the second floor, which was just as well, Villiers thought; the lift was always switched off at night to save something-or-other. Somebody had been in and had turned down the bed. On one side of it his new silk pyjamas, which had so far never been worn, were carefully displayed.

She touched them and exclaimed, "I shall look a proper frump. I brought some warm ones in case I had to go to the shelter."

He watched her, warmed and moved by her excitement, her happiness, which was genuine, if only for the moment.

She held up the pyjama jacket. "I'll wear this. You can have the bottom half."

There was an *en suite* bathroom and she picked up her overnight bag and said, "Luxury! The places I usually stay in have a bathroom down the corridor and on a different floor!"

She paused by the door, suddenly very small and uncertain. "Do you have anything to drink, I—I mean without sending for it?"

He replied, "Only gin, I'm afraid."

She nodded gravely. "Then I shall have some gin."

He smiled. It should have been champagne. He picked up the pyjama trousers defiantly. One day it *would* be champagne.

She came into the room again, her bare feet soundless on the pale carpet. "It's a beautiful bathroom." She took the gin and stared at it dubiously. "Well, here goes!"

He waited for her to finish coughing and said, "You weren't meant to swallow it in one go!"

She rolled on to her back and reached up for his shoulders. "You have a lovely tan. I knew you would."

He said quietly, "Biscuit-coloured."

Then he touched her face and leaned over her for the lamp.

She said, "No. This is our time. We won't hide from it." She watched his fingers on the buttons of her jacket, sensed his shyness, something as strong as guilt.

She said, "Kiss me."

Their mouths came together and she put her hand on his to help him with the buttons.

She felt his hand on her skin, the hesitancy changing to sudden need as he cupped her breasts, lifted them and stroked them until her nipples were hard, painful.

He was kissing her, gently but firmly, her throat, her breasts, the curve of her stomach, until her whole being was roused and slipping out of control. He knelt over her while she reached for him, saw her quick breathing. She found and held him as if they had been lovers for all time.

He was gentle, yet driven by the need to explore her, holding and kissing her like an invader until they could bear separation no longer.

She looked at him with wide, momentarily desperate eyes. She would never think of that other time, when she had been beaten and forced to do things that even now filled her with shame. And then the memory released her and she was surprisingly relaxed as she caressed his tousled hair and said, "Now, Charles . . . take me. Do what you like with me."

Long after they were joined they lay together as if the act had been caught in statuary. On the floor beside the bed the two halves of the pyjamas also lay entwined, symbolic.

Later, she stroked his bare shoulders and his face. She must drive away the past, which had tormented him, and protect him from the future. Her mind hung on the word. *There was no future.* She felt him gently withdraw from her, and prayed he would not wake to see her tears.

And yet I want him so much, in a way I could never have believed. He is rich beyond his own understanding, but he doesn't care, or even accept it.

She let the thought enter her mind as he had entered her.

And he loves me. For what I am. For what he is. It could not be fought because it was real. It could only be surrendered to.

She held him more tightly. But regrets? Never.

5 | Operation *Emma*

JAMES ROSS STOOD beside one of the tables and looked at the ceiling as the thundering roar of rain, which had drowned out every sound, suddenly began to recede.

He said, "I sometimes wish I'd bought shares in corrugated iron. It seems to roof half the world out here!" Several of them laughed, more relaxed perhaps since Pryce had withdrawn after making only a brief appearance.

The operations room was packed, the air so humid that the old-fashioned overhead fans barely disturbed it.

He said, "You may smoke." He watched the pipes being filled, the duty-free cigarettes being handed round. That, too, was something Pryce never encouraged; unless, like his malt whisky, he smoked in secret.

It was remarkable what the weeks of regular training had achieved. They looked tanned and relaxed, their shirts sticking to their bodies in the damp air. A good mixture, Ross thought. Some familiar faces, others becoming more so with each busy day. A Canadian lieutenant and another from New Zealand had joined the others, and they were all watching him now while a seaman trained a light on the big wall-map. Lieutenant Charles Villiers had arrived only two days ago, in company with Sub-Lieutenant Peter Napier, David's younger brother. Villiers had already told him how Napier had spoken of little else but his good fortune at having been posted to this force. Apart from his obvious youth, innocence might be a better description, the likeness was unnerving. The same ready grin, the freckles and the chestnut-coloured hair. Ross tried not to look at him. It was like seeing David alive again.

A paymaster-lieutenant who had been appointed as Pryce's secretary was keeping an eye on everything, a notebook on the arm of his chair. No doubt ready to report every detail of the meeting when Pryce required. There were several Wrens too, pencils and pads at the ready, watched with more than just casual interest by the chief and petty officers who were here to answer any questions about the chariots' readiness for sea.

A bearded lieutenant-commander sat cross-legged, a large briar pipe puffing busily while he waited with the others. Apart from the rest, and yet a vital part of the chain, he commanded the submarine *Turquoise,* with which they had been exercising so regularly that it had become almost routine.

The rain had stopped and they could hear the ripple of countless waterfalls splashing down into the darkness outside.

Ross cleared his throat. This was the first time he had met them all together. It gave him a strange sense of responsibility, even pride. He could still not get used to it. In the past he had sat and listened to the briefing reports and had faced up to the consequences of failure or disaster as an individual.

"We were sent here to seek out targets. We now have one. This operation comes rather earlier than we might have hoped, but speed is of the utmost importance."

He moved to the map and pointed with a long pair of brass dividers. "Here we are, Trincomalee. From this point the attacking force will head due east, then around the northern reaches of Sumatra and into the Malacca Strait." He thought he saw the hint of a smile on Villiers's lips. An old memory perhaps, or something else entirely. "This track has been used for months by our submarines, for landing reconnaissance parties and agents and recovering them when their missions were completed. A hard job at the best of times, and the confines of the Strait have added to the difficulties." He glanced at the bearded submariner and saw several heads turn towards him. "Bob Jessop is no stranger to those waters, and he will be carrying the chariots and their crews to this destination." The dividers made the map shiver. "Salanga. Intelligence have reported that the Japs are building a new r.d.f. installation there, as near to radar as makes no difference. Because of the many islets and other hazards, our submarines always have to surface some six miles away. In the past, for landing special parties, that has been barely sufficient. But we have now learned that the enemy has moved three or four MA/SBs into the nearby harbour."

He saw one of the Wrens bend over to ask Peter Napier something and added, "Sorry. Motor Anti-Submarine Boats. Not exactly a fleet, but with some form of advance warning just one of them would be enough to tear out of harbour and pinpoint our submarine."

Peter was watching him intently and Ross noticed that his hand, which had been resting against the Wren's on the table, did not withdraw.

"We will complete final arrangements tomorrow, but the two chariots for the operation will be Lieutenant Walker's and the new arrival, Sub-Lieutenant Napier's." He saw some surprise, perhaps resentment, on the faces of the others at the latter choice, and said calmly, "Peter Napier's chariot is newer and of slightly different design. It is what he has become used to." They were in fact faster, had a better range and carried almost double the charge of Torpex in their warheads.

He tried not to watch Peter's elation, as if it was one huge game. A privilege and a prank rolled into one. He saw him grip the girl's hand and whisper something, and the way she looked back at him.

It was then that he noticed the Wren petty officer, Victoria Mackenzie. She had been sitting slightly behind the other choice, Lieutenant Walker, the Canadian, her hair very black and shining in the hard lights. She too was taking notes. As he spoke she looked directly at him. "Operation *Emma*—this seems only right as it is timed for Trafalgar Day. I think the little admiral would have approved."

He watched their faces, more composed now. Remembering those other raids, familiar faces which had not returned. He said, "I do not have to remind you of the very real danger in this or any other such plan. If you are captured . . ." He paused. "No, let's think of *Emma*."

He was caught off guard by a sudden outburst of clapping and stamping feet. He saw Walker, the Canadian, applauding and grinning at him and tried not to think that after tomorrow they might never meet again.

The door banged open and they all stood up as Pryce thrust into the room. He looked directly at Ross and then waved one hand in front of his face. "What a bloody stench in here! Thought the whole place was going up in smoke!" Then he smiled. "There will be drinks in the wardroom tonight, gentlemen. In the chief and petty officers' mess too. Compliments of Rear-Admiral Dyer." He coughed and added wryly, "*Ossie.* Though God knows how we'll get the money from him!"

For most of them it was the closest thing to a joke Pryce had ever been heard to make.

The meeting began to break up, the invisible barriers between officers and other ranks asserting themselves once more.

Pryce said, "Went well, I thought. Good show."

"I'd like to go along in *Turquoise,* sir."

He had expected, at best, an argument, but Pryce nodded. "Capital. This time anyway. It might have to be called off at the last minute. Your being there would keep up morale." He nodded again, his hawk nose like a beak. "Good thinking—er, Jamie."

Ross turned to look for the girl named Victoria but she had already gone.

In twos and threes they left the building, trying to avoid the moonlit puddles as they made their way back to the makeshift wardroom.

Pryce sat alone in his office, staring at the door. *One jump ahead.* Instinct or some inner warning, he never questioned it.

"Come!" It was a hesitant tap at the door.

He looked at her impassively. "Ah, Victoria. You've got something?"

She crossed the office to his desk. "I have just decoded it, sir." She looked quite shocked, without her usual self-assurance.

"But you know what it says?" He softened his voice slightly. "Come on, Victoria. I'm not a mind-reader."

For an instant, but no longer, her tawny eyes flashed with anger.

She said, "It's addressed to you, sir. Restricted."

It was brief. He could almost feel her watching him as he read it.

He said, "Lieutenant-Commander Ross's father has been killed in a salvage accident."

There was a long silence. Then she asked, "Will you tell him, sir, or . . . ?"

He toyed with the idea of offering her a drink, and dismissed it just as quickly. *One jump ahead. Never forget.*

It would not do. At any enquiry, let alone a court martial, the gesture might well be seen as something very different.

He said, "Can you keep a secret?" He saw her flinch as if he had sworn at her. "Until Operation *Emma* is over, one way or another? There's nothing he can do, and it might deflect his attention from the job in hand. You do see that."

"I—I suppose so, sir."

Pryce began to relax very slightly. The chink in the armour. "You saw and heard them in Ops this evening. You were there. They're depending on him, surely you must have seen that?"

She stared at the signal on his desk as if it were something obscene. "I shall tell nobody, sir."

He said, "Not even the Colonel."

She looked at him, calm again, defiant, the Victoria he trusted. "No, not even my father, sir."

The door closed and after a momentary hesitation he put a match to the signal and let it burn to ashes.

The girl stood on the wet pathway and looked at the moon. Then she heard footsteps and saw a white figure looming out of the darkness. It was the new sub-lieutenant, Peter Napier. There was some special link between him and Ross, but she could not decide what it was.

He asked brightly, "Have you seen Lieutenant-Commander Ross, my dear?"

So young, she thought, so very young, not like the others, who were young only in years.

She shook her head. "No. He's not with Captain Pryce."

"They're all waiting for him." He sounded lost, suddenly unsure, and she recalled Pryce's incisive voice as if he had just spoken. *They're depending on him, surely you must have seen that?*

"I was wondering. When this stunt is over, perhaps we could have a run ashore together?"

She was glad he could not see her face. He seemed to be doing quite well with the Wren who had sat beside him at the meeting. Perhaps anyone would do.

She said coolly, "We'll have to see." Then she turned impulsively and added, "Good luck with *Emma.* We'll all be thinking of you."

She watched him melt away. Another hero? Or another telegram?

She considered Pryce again. So cold, so certain of everything. He always referred to her father as "The Colonel." So that she should never be allowed to forget.

She heard noisy singing from the wardroom, and wondered if Ross was there with his soft-spoken friend, the other new arrival, Villiers. Somebody else was hurrying in that direction: it was her superior, Second Officer Clarke.

"Glad I caught you, Victoria. Can you hold the fort for me for a couple of hours? I'll fix it with Base Operations." She could barely contain her excitement as she faced towards the singing.

"Of course, ma'am." Who would she be sleeping with next? She never seemed to have any trouble.

She watched the other woman continue towards the wardroom; she was almost running.

Then she stared into the greater darkness where even the lights would not reach. *What is wrong with me?* Some heavy drops of warm rain fell on her shirt. She was alone.

• • •

The *Turquoise's* wardroom, like most of its kind, was small, compact and functional. The bunks that filled much of the compartment mostly had their curtains drawn, their occupants clinging to this small measure of privacy before going on watch again or returning to their other duties.

Ross sat at the table, toying with his mug of sweet tea and listening to the familiar sounds of a submarine running submerged, her electric motors making barely a tremble. A calm sea, the skipper, Bob Jessop, had said, and so it had been for the five leisurely days it had taken them to reach this point on the chart.

He could hear gentle snores from one curtained bunk and some restless thrashing about from another. Should the scream of the alarm klaxon shatter the stillness he knew from experience that these same men, like the others who were resting throughout the boat, would be at their stations in seconds, some of them probably not even realizing how they had got there. They had surfaced during the night to start the noisy diesel engines in order to charge the precious batteries and ventilate the boat. It would be the last time until the operation was finished. Or cancelled. He glanced at his watch: seven in the morning. He tried to remember what the time had been when Nelson had sighted the combined fleets of the enemy on this October day.

He heard sounds from the galley, which was only paces away, its smells of cabbage-water and greasy food constant reminders.

A whole day before they would leave *Turquoise* and head for the land.

And I will not be going with them.

He opened his chart very carefully on the table, but even so the snoring stopped for a few moments. He could almost hear the unspoken complaint: *Don't forget the poor bloody watchkeepers!*

As if on cue, a pair of feet emerged from a bunk and Peter Napier slid down beside him. He looked tousled but fresh, and Ross guessed that he probably did not have to shave yet in any case. He asked, "Want a look?" and studied him as he leaned over the chart. How old was he—nineteen, twenty perhaps? And yet he seemed so much younger.

He said, "We've just passed through the Great Channel, see? The Nicobar Islands to the north of us, and Sabang and the tip of Sumatra about forty miles to the south. Plenty of room, and over a thousand fathoms under the keel." He smiled. "For the moment, anyway."

Napier touched the chart. "And that's our destination?"

"Salanga Island is at the top of the Malacca Strait, which is about one hundred and sixty miles wide around there. It narrows quickly after that—even a submarine would find it tight. So if the Japs are putting some sort of radar on the island, it would make these landing operations even more hairy."

He watched his hand move on the chart as if it were thinking and planning independently. "Just follow the drill. If you think the observations don't match the reports, you pull out." When Napier said nothing, he touched his arm. *"Right?"*

"A piece of cake." He turned and looked at Ross, momentarily uncertain. "You wanted me out of this, didn't you? Because of what happened to David. But, you see, I *needed* to do it. When it was offered, I took it with both hands!"

Ross nodded. So like David for those few seconds: brown eyes, the vivid emotion on the face. Like that day he had wanted to call off the mission—the cruiser and the floating dock. David had not thought it was a "piece of cake."

"I'm sorry. I felt responsible." They both smiled. "I still do."

The messman paused by the curtained entrance. "Breakfast in about fifteen minutes, gents." He smacked his lips. "Tinned bangers and powdered egg! Just the job!"

Ross sighed. They must have stomachs made of iron.

"By the way." Napier sounded casual. "I met that pretty Wren before we shoved off from the base." He hesitated. "You know, the petty officer. A real dish."

Ross replied quietly, "You didn't waste much time."

"Oh, it wasn't that. When I met her I was looking for you." He glanced only briefly at the curved deckhead as the hull gave a sudden shiver. "She was upset. I could tell."

"What about?"

"I don't know. Maybe I imagined it. I don't think so. She's not like the others."

"How so?" It was good to let him talk. Whatever he showed outwardly, he must be nervous about the operation, his first. Or was it something else?

"Well, I heard somebody say at the party that she's—well, half-and-half, if you see what I mean?"

Ross said, "I do believe you're blushing." But all he could think of was her suppressed anger when she had entered Pryce's office, as if she had known they were talking about her. He added lightly, "She's probably cheesed off at being bothered by lovesick subbies!"

"All the same . . ." They both looked up as *Turquoise*'s commander strolled into the wardroom, yawning and scratching his black beard.

"Any char yet?"

A curtain twitched slightly. "Not so much bloody noise!"

Jessop swiped the curtain where he imagined the occupant's backside would be and growled, "Don't be so bloody disrespectful to your captain!" Then he grinned. "All quiet up top. I had a quick peek at first light. Like a mill-pond." He became businesslike again. "We received no signals when we were charging batteries last night. So it's still on." He glanced at the chart. "Our chummy-boat landed a party of squaddies yesterday, so we would have heard something if that had misfired."

Ross, too, was looking at the chart, the neat lines and soundings, depths and compass variations, seeing it as it really would appear. Rocks, small beaches, and the headland where the radar station was said to be. He could guess what the bearded submariner was thinking. How could men volunteer for that kind of work? Put ashore to fend for themselves in an area known to be crawling with Japs. Sheer courage, or was it a kind of madness? An Australian major who had been instructing them in jungle warfare had said, "Keep it in your minds at all times. This enemy is like nothing you've known before. No use bleating about the Geneva Convention and a prisoner's rights if you get captured. All the territory they've taken is held by fear, by sheer bloody savagery. *So keep it in your minds.* Get them first." He had stared around at their intent expressions, face by face. "They kill people like us," he had lingered over the final word, "eventually."

Ross thought suddenly of Villiers. He had actually gone back to Singapore, and he had no doubt that he would go again if it was suggested to him. And what of the girl in England, another man's wife? Perhaps she might change his mind.

Napier stood up and looked for his shoes. "I think I'll go and see how my Number Two is getting on."

He left the wardroom and Jessop said thoughtfully, "When I fix a ship in my crosswires I try not to think of the people who are going to die when I fire a salvo. But this is different. I prefer *my* war." He grimaced suddenly. "God, smell those sausages! Whoever invented them should be marooned on a desert island for a year with nothing else to eat!"

Ross knew his mind was somewhere else, planning, preparing in case the operation had already been discovered by the enemy. But he asked, and he was surprised at how calm he sounded, "By the way, what time *did* Our Nel first sight the combined fleet?"

Jessop paused, a mug of tea half way to his beard. "Six o'clock in the morning. It wasn't until eleven-forty that *Victory* hoisted *England Expects.*" Then he grinned broadly, his teeth very white through his beard. "That would have suited me, Jamie. One hell of a battle, but knowing that the admiral was up there, taking the shit with all the lads!"

Peter Napier paused in the doorway of the heads and dabbed his lips with his handkerchief. He had been sick, without warning. Now, as he splashed his face with brackish water, he looked at himself in a mirror. He had heard Ross and Jessop laughing in the wardroom. The sound had helped to steady him, to restore him.

But the face he saw in the glass was that of fear.

The launching of the two chariots from *Turquoise*'s saddle-tanks had gone like clockwork, or one of those regular drills in Scotland. That was the only similarity: here, the sky was bright with moonlight and stars that appeared to be touching the water, and the sea was almost warm to the touch.

Bill Walker, the Canadian lieutenant, had left first, his being a slower chariot than Napier's newer model.

Walker's Number Two was a taciturn Tynesider named Nash. It was a marvel how they managed to understand one another.

Peter Napier peered at the luminous dials of the compass and depth gauge. He had tested everything within minutes of seeing the submarine swallowed up in the darkness; there had been no faults. He should have felt the usual excitement, that heady exhilaration which had so surprised him after his first dive. Ross had been on the submarine's casing to see them depart, and Napier had sensed his disappointment at being left behind, as well as his concern for his dead friend's brother: he had seen it in his eyes when they had gone through the last briefing before changing into their rubber suits.

The briefing had been yet another grim reminder of danger and the possibility of death when they had packed their additional equipment inside their clothing. Known in the Special Operations Force as the *Just in Case Kit,* it had no longer seemed so funny with the mission and the land a sudden reality. It contained a pistol and ammunition, a small bag of gold sovereigns, compass, knife and compact tool kit, and a square of silk on which was written in several Oriental languages that the British government would reward anybody who helped the bearer in distress. And finally there had been a tablet of poison, as a last defence against capture and what would certainly follow.

Napier waved his arm and felt his Number Two, Nick Rice, pat his shoulder. A slow and careful dive, twenty, thirty feet, the water pressing the suits around their limbs, the control panel gleaming as if it would light up the whole ocean. Then up to surface depth again, the bubbles frothing around their heads and visors while Napier made one more check on the compass. There was a strong undertow, a vague cross-current, which would have to be watched and taken into consideration for the last approach.

Napier pictured the target area as he and the others had seen it through the main periscope at full power when *Turquoise* had risen as close to the surface as her commander had dared. Lush green islands and inviting blue water, the headland little more than a hump with the sheltered water of the natural harbour beyond. Nothing had moved; it had seemed they had the world to themselves, the perfect seascape. And then, brighter even than the reflected glare, they had seen the small but distinct flashes, like some haphazard and meaningless signal. Jessop had said professionally, "The MA/SBs are there all right. Probably moored in two groups—the sun's catching their wheelhouse glass, or something similar. We must have got the right information for once!"

But that was then, just a few hours ago. Now, with every turn of the little propeller, they were drawing closer to something real and hostile, filled with a menace even the bright moonlight could not dispel.

Napier felt his Number Two leaning over to adjust something and wondered what he thought about it. Until he had volunteered for Special Operations, Nick Rice had been a leading telegraphist and had served mostly in destroyers on escort duty. In his late twenties, he was a serious, withdrawn sort of man, but in training and on final exercises they had worked well together, although they had never become quite as close as some of the other teams. Perhaps Rice could not bring himself to trust and have full confidence in an officer he was permitted to call by his first name, like one of his messmates. Or maybe he was waiting to see how they would both react in "the real thing," as Captain Pryce chose to call it.

Napier tried to put everything from his mind, but faces came and went like spirits in the water. His brother; Ross's obvious anxiety over his safety; the awe with which some of the others regarded him because of his prized decoration, although Ross himself never appeared to notice it. No wonder David had said, "The sort of bloke you'd follow anywhere. I know I would!"

Rice was touching his shoulder again, his visor shining in the moon's cool glow.

Napier saw the trailing cloak of green phosphorescence, and when he twisted around in his seat he realized that more of it was writhing away from the chariot's propeller. They had been warned to expect this in tropical waters, but it was still something of a shock. Surely somebody would see it once they had worked closer inshore. The phosphorescence Rice had seen must be from the other chariot, leading the way into the attack. He thought of the Canadian's face during that final briefing. No sign of uncertainty, let alone fear, but then he had taken part in several such attacks, both in Norway and in the Mediterranean. He had even been able to joke about the suicide tablet. In his gentle Ontario drawl he had said, "Well, we'll just have to take their word for it. I don't suppose anybody's been able to report whether it works or not!"

Some drifting seabirds rose, flapping and screaming, only yards away. Napier put his arm across his face without knowing why, and then felt angry and ashamed.

He could just make out the glow from the other chariot's wake. They were about seventy-five yards apart. He eased the throttle to maintain the distance. At any other time they would have been congratulating themselves. It was all going without a hitch—unusual even after so much intense training. It was, many said, still very much a by-guess-and-by-God operation.

Down now. He watched the gauge. Twenty feet, with barely a quiver from the motor. *Slight alteration of course. Check time and compass again.* He could feel his heart pounding like a sledgehammer, his mouth raw from sucking in air from the cylinders.

Now. He eased the joystick and held it steady until they were running with their heads out of the water in a gigantic spearhead of moonlight rippling on the flat water, making it look like beaten silver. He clung to the controls and tried not to yawn. There they were, the two targets, overlapping at this approach angle, hunched and black in the moonlight. He could even make out the stick-like tripod masts on the moored vessels. Small and fast, like the earlier M.T.B.s, about seventy feet long, according to the Intelligence pack, lightly armed but with enough depth-charges to blow a dozen *Turquoises* out of the water.

They were barely moving now and Napier had lost sight of the other chariot completely. Just as well. He was almost thinking aloud. *If I can see them, the enemy can see us.* His skin was hot and clammy and he felt sick again. The moored boats were tied to a large pontoon or lighter. He snapped open his visor and took a deep breath. Whatever the mooring was, it was filled with fuel; so too was the other one. Ready to top up the boats if they were ordered out to investigate a possible intruder. But nothing moved. It might easily have been another exercise, with that red-faced chief petty officer nodding approvingly at the end of it. "Well done, Mr Napier, you could have cracked an egg that time!"

But the voices from the past seemed to mock him. What did they know? Back there, safe and comfortable in their world of tradition and regularity. *What do they know?*

He was just in time to readjust the pump and motor controls before the lighter loomed right over them, solid, like a cliff.

They slithered alongside and came to rest just beneath the surface. The impact was probably little enough, but it felt like a fall of rock. Napier felt the rough metal scrape past and then come to a halt. He peered blindly at the surface, waiting for the lights, the shots. And the agony.

He thought of Lieutenant Walker's chariot. A quick glance

at the clock told him that the other team had probably done its work and was even now preparing to leave, and head back to the submarine.

Rice had already slipped into the water alongside, and was waiting to release the massive eleven-hundred-pound warhead and attach it by its magnets to the moored lighter. His movements showed no sign of anxiety or hesitation, and if he had been alarmed by their clumsy arrival beside and below the target, he did not show it. Teamwork. *Take your time . . . Don't get in a panic.* He was shouting into his mask, *I'm not in a panic! I never panic!* The realization of what he was doing helped to steady his nerves. He leaned over to grip Rice's shoulder, then turned back to the controls and prepared to adjust the water in the trimming tank once the warhead had been released. He pressed his hand to his suit and tried to determine his heartbeat.

It was done. Down there Rice would already be able to hear the relentless tick of the fuse. He felt suddenly wild, lightheaded, as if his oxygen supply had become tainted. When this lot went up, fuel lighter, boats and maybe depth-charges as well, they'd hear it in bloody Whitehall!

He allowed the chariot to rise slowly against the lighter, then opened his visor. In spite of the stench of high-octane fuel, the air tasted like wine.

And here was Rice, slow and careful as he pulled himself level before opening his visor.

Napier exclaimed, "Bloody good show! We did it!" There was a crack in his voice and he did not sense Rice's sudden tension. "Well, chop-chop, old lad—let's get the hell out of it!"

Rice peered up at the nearest boat, the small wheelhouse and a solitary machine-gun very clear in the glacier light. "When we came alongside, we must have got a wire caught." He pointed vaguely to the afterpart of the chariot, his arm half submerged. "It's wrapped around the screw and rudder. We must have been moving too fast."

Napier peered down at him, his mind frozen. "We'll soon

shake it off once we get going. Now climb aboard."

Rice did not budge. "You'll pull the shaft out of the sleeve if you try. We'd not make more than a cable or so." He sounded stubborn, suddenly angry.

"What sort of wire?"

"I expect it was left dangling by some dockyard matey. It doesn't much matter, does it?"

Napier tried to think clearly, the seriousness of the discovery hitting him like a fist. It would be hard enough to rendezvous with *Turquoise* in any case, without faulty steering and the possibility of a complete breakdown.

Rice sensed his despair and said, "Didn't you say there was a beach not far from here?" He added more urgently, "Let's go for it. I can free the prop and rudder as easy as spitting!"

Napier was staring at the land's darkness, where even the moon was held at bay. He said, "They might see us."

"They?" It was almost scornful. Insolent, but for the circumstances. "Jesus, they'd have been here by now with all this row going on!"

Napier peered at him. "Sorry. Not your fault. Didn't mean to snap at you." He made up his mind. "Let's do it."

Rice let out a sigh. He'd seen officers crack before: as a telegraphist, he had been one of the privileged few to be allowed into that separate world of the bridge and those who controlled it. But in the Western Ocean, the killing ground as the men on convoys called it, there were always your mates around you, others to take the strain when things got bloody. He watched the sub-lieutenant as he closed his visor and reached down to his controls. *Here, my son, there's just us.*

The chariot backed slowly away from the moored shapes. Set against the violent beat of his heart, Napier imagined he could hear the fuse ticking.

They stood side by side in the shallows, the heavy chariot swaying and thrusting against them like a dying dolphin.

Rice said between gulps of air, "Nearly got it off!" He peered down and exclaimed, *"Sod it!* I've dropped the cutters!"

Napier wanted to look at his watch, but was afraid of what it might tell him, like the ceiling of stars that seemed to be getting paler by the second.

"Let me!" He snapped down his visor and almost fell, caught in some weed while he groped like a madman until he could feel the cutters' warm metal.

He stood up, confused but vaguely pleased that he had been able to do something. He thrust them out and then realized that Rice was standing as before, gripping the hydroplane but quite motionless.

Napier opened his visor. "Here!" He sensed the change and asked, hoarsely, "What is it, man?"

Then he saw them, pale against the dark undergrowth, three figures, each as motionless as Rice. As in a nightmare, he could neither move nor call out; even his pounding heart seemed to have stopped.

Rice was fumbling with his suit, perhaps trying to get to his pistol. One of the still figures moved, so fast that Napier did not see him leave cover. The next instant he felt a man's arm around his throat, pressing him backwards until he could not swallow. His reeling mind recorded only the dull gleam of steel, the man's steady breathing as he tightened his grip and balanced himself for the kill.

A harsh English voice snapped, *"Easy!"* A small probing light flashed into Napier's eyes, blinding him before it moved on to play across the restless chariot.

The voice sounded angry, or was it strangely disappointed? "Who the bloody hell are you?" As another, taller figure squeaked across the sand he added contemptuously, "Christ, they'll be sending them out in their bloody prams soon!"

Napier swayed and would have fallen but for a steadying grip on his arm. The short, stocky figure who had seized him so expertly and poised a blade across his throat was peering at him, shaking his head and grinning hugely.

Napier managed to say, "I might ask . . ."

The one who had spoken first, crisp and authoritative now, said, "Sinclair, Royal Marines. We've been busy too. Arrived thirty-six hours ago. All done." He and the other man chuckled. "You were lucky just now. The Gurkhas don't usually stop to ask the time of day!"

Rice managed to say, "No Japs, then."

"Not any more. They're all with their ancestors. Except for one."

Two more Gurkhas, dressed in filthy, camouflaged denim battledress, were manhandling a soldier down to the water's edge. He was gagged and had his hands tied behind him.

Napier stepped back, his mouth tasting of vomit. It was a Japanese soldier. Even in the gloom he could recognize the uniform, just like the illustrations in the Intelligence manual.

The one named Sinclair said, "He's the engineer—his men were working on the installation. It's his satchel I want." Then he smiled: afterwards, Napier thought he could have been ten thousand miles from this terrible place. The torch moved to the man's tunic, ripping it open like tearing a piece of newspaper. Sinclair dragged the small satchel from him and said with satisfaction, "The boffins will want to see these. Bloody useful stuff, I shouldn't wonder."

Rice said quietly, "I think we should leave, sir."

But Napier was watching the prisoner's eyes in the small beam of light. Terrified, pleading, resigned—did they, too, know what to expect?

Sinclair came back from his thoughts. "If you see Captain Pryce, give him my best." He laughed. "We'll be making our own way back, eh, Tom?" Then he looked at the pinioned Japanese soldier and said curtly, "Deal with it!"

It was just a blur as the *kukri* flashed across the man's shoulder. He did not even cough, but Napier saw the blood like black tar pouring across his torn tunic as they let the corpse drop into the water.

Napier himself would have fallen if Rice had not helped him to board the chariot. His hands were like claws as he started the motor and Rice pulled the chariot round to face open water.

Rice clambered into his seat and all at once they were *moving, moving.*

When Rice turned to look at the small beach it was empty, as if the whole nightmare had never been.

Turquoise was there, with the other chariot's crew already safely below. Napier, through all of it, the fear and finally the stark horror, had somehow known that Ross would be waiting for him.

The sky was perceptibly lighter when Napier opened the valve to flood the chariot and send it to the bottom. A few pats on the back and some gruff words of greeting as they were both dragged aboard. Hatches slamming, the hull vibrating more noticeably as the submarine began to turn in a tight circle. Faces glanced at them as they were led and half pulled through the boat, and Napier imagined he heard the surge of water under pressure as they began to dive.

And then he was in the wardroom again with all the curtains open, all the bunks empty. He sat down while two of the handling party began to strip off his rubber suit.

Ross handed him a mug of cocoa, well laced with rum. It could have been soda for all he could taste of it.

Ross watched him gravely. The first mission. Would there be another?

He asked quietly, "How was it, Peter?"

Napier looked at the hand on his wet shoulder and almost broke. He replied in a whisper, "Piece of cake." He looked up, his eyes blurred. *"Really!"*

Ross put down the mug by his elbow. "We'll talk later." He smiled and wondered what had happened, afraid that he already knew.

At seven o'clock in the morning, while *Turquoise* was running comfortably at a depth of ninety feet, the two chariot charges exploded, and only minutes later the other laid by Sinclair and his raiding party followed suit.

Operation *Emma* was over.

6 | Thoughts of Home

JAMES Ross picked up the coffee cup but it was empty, although he could not recall drinking it. Pryce's office seemed so still and quiet after the busily contained world of the submarine. This was unreal, with the distant clatter of a single typewriter and the occasional strident call of a telephone.

Captain Ralph Pryce stood with his back to a window, quite motionless and watchful, as he had been while Ross had leafed through the small clip of signals.

Ross felt crumpled and tired and wondered why he could not accept it, come to grips with it. He said, "So you knew, sir? Before we sailed."

Pryce said curtly, "Of course I knew. It was my decision. It was, I hope, the right one. What you yourself would have done under the circumstances."

"Perhaps."

All in white, Pryce seemed to shine against the background of swaying palms and an empty blue sky. Shirt and shorts perfectly pressed, the straps on his shoulders gleaming in the filtered sunshine like gold bars.

"There was nothing you could have done. I made full enquiries while you were away with the team. Everything that could be done *was* done. Your mother has . . ."

Ross said quietly, "Step-mother." Because of the sunlight, he did not see the prickle of annoyance on the captain's face. An oversight, which he should have noticed or known about.

He stared at the signals again. His father had never complained about health problems, and he was careful to keep up with his medical inspections, if only for the Admiralty's sake: most of his salvage contracts were with them. It had been a small wreck near Portland Bill. One of his crew had reported a corroded unexploded bomb jammed in the bridge superstructure just above the surface. Nobody would move it until the sappers of the bomb disposal squad had arrived. Ross could almost have been there, could even hear his father's voice: *Why, you silly wee man, the bomb's a dud! D'you want to lose another day's work?*

The bomb had been a dud, but in wrenching it free Big Andy had suffered a heart attack, and had died soon afterwards at the nearby naval hospital.

Pryce said, "Leave would have been out of the question —agreed?"

Ross nodded. *Too late anyway.* He should have guessed something was wrong. Pryce had sent his own car to pick him up as soon as he had landed from the submarine's depot-ship. Even *Turquoise*'s bluff commander had seemed unusually subdued when he had seen him over the side this morning.

Pryce turned and stared out at the lush green backdrop. "Operation *Emma* was a great success. All objectives destroyed, and no casualties to us. That will make the invincible Japanese feel less secure when they know that determined groups like ours can land and infiltrate their defences. Very pleased, proud too." He bobbed his beaky nose. *"Very."* When Ross remained silent, he asked sharply, "You are too, I trust?"

"Up to a point, sir." It hurt to drag his mind back to it. All he could think of was the bluff, dependable man he had last seen on one of his leaves. The Victoria Cross had been Big Andy's greatest moment. So proud that he had seemed to glow. At the Palace when the King had bestowed the bronze cross on his son he had beamed and exclaimed, "I couldn't be more pleased if it was mine, Your Majesty." Ross looked away. *It should have been.* He said abruptly, "I think Sub-Lieutenant Napier should be withdrawn from active duties for the present. *Emma* was his first-ever operation." *Stunt,* he would have called it. Before.

"I disagree. He did a perfect job, despite a small technical fault. I think he should be encouraged, not made to feel like a bloody amateur."

On their way back to Trincomalee, *Turquoise*'s radio must have been busy at every available and safe moment for Pryce to have been so well informed.

Ross said, "I hadn't realized that our Captain Sinclair was to be in charge of the raiding party."

"Nobody knew outside the operations staff. The fewer the better. As I said to you before, results are all that matter in the end. The motive for such work can be hate or revenge. Equally, it can be dedication—even ambition." He turned swiftly. *"Results,* remember?"

As if from miles away Ross could remember Napier's voice when he had questioned him for the first time. Of Sinclair he had said in a dull, shocked tone, "He was enjoying it. You should have seen him. At one point I thought he was going to have us killed!"

Pryce was saying, "As for Sinclair, his kind of work calls for a special kind of man. Someone who can fight the enemy on his own terms, and without mercy." Almost offhandedly he went on, "His majority is coming through, by the way, another gong too."

"I see."

Pryce said, "If the Japs had caught him . . ." He did not continue. Instead he added, "You can slope off, if you like. A bit tired, I expect?"

"No, sir. I had plenty of time to rest and think on our way back."

"So you see, my decision was the right one. You'd have been in no shape at all if I'd told you this sad news beforehand."

Sad? Did he even know what that meant?

"Actually—ah, Jamie, I have a favour to ask. Things have been moving fast since this last operation. I have to fly up to Bombay to attend a Chiefs-of-Staff conference. I shall most certainly put all of them in the picture!" He did not hide his satisfaction at the thought. "We will be having a visit shortly from Howard Costain, one of the top war-correspondents. Very highly thought of. Could be extremely useful, to us, I mean."

"If you don't mind, sir . . ." He might as well have remained silent.

Pryce was saying, "The admiral has agreed that we should have a party for him." He stared around the office as if it were a cage. "Not in this apology for a naval establishment, and of course not at the base. We thought we should hold it at the Mackenzie estate. More personal, a better impression, we thought."

Ross wondered briefly who *we* were. The admiral, perhaps?

Pryce was watching him again. "I shall leave you in charge during my absence. I can trust you to deal with our people and the day-to-day traffic from Operations." He tapped one immaculate white shoe on the floor. "Of course, if anything urgent comes up you know how to reach me."

Trust, but not that much.

Ross asked, "This Mackenzie—is he the one I've heard referred to as 'The Colonel'?"

"Right. One of the real old sons of Empire. Quit the Army years ago and went into tea—must be rolling in it. Carries a lot of weight, in Ceylon at any rate. Howard Costain will be impressed."

Ross thought of the Wren Peter Napier had been talking about. *Half-and-half.* It made him suddenly quite angry.

Pryce said, "You can go and see him. The Colonel already knows what we have in mind." It seemed to amuse him. "Make sure young Villiers is there too. He knows the territory, even speaks the lingo, I understand." He became serious again, like putting on a mask. "I really am damned sorry about your father. And to think he served with mine. Small world, what?"

The telephone jangled and he snatched it up with a perfect display of annoyance. "I thought I told you . . ." He replaced it and shrugged. "I have to be off." He gave Ross a searching glance. "Go easy on Napier. It will be easier next time." His tone hardened. "Or I shall want to know why!"

Ross walked past the rating at the telephone. Watching him to see if the V.C. made a man different when it came to something as inevitable as grief.

He heard voices outside the door, and saw Peter Napier

smiling broadly while he used his hands to describe something. He was speaking with the same Wren. It was hard to imagine him as the same shocked, gasping figure who had been dragged aboard *Turquoise* after the attack.

He was saying, "You've not forgotten? We've got a date, remember?"

She looked up and saw Ross in the doorway. He was aware of her quick intake of breath, as though the unexpected sight of him left her off balance, even nervous.

Peter exclaimed, "I was just saying . . ."

Ross walked past. "I know. A piece of cake."

Why should it matter? What did anything matter now? But it did.

The reading room, as it was called, was almost next door to the wardroom. There were not many books, and those there were had been well thumbed. There were also magazines and newspapers, some so old that they were hardly relevant any more, but at least it was quiet. From the solitary window you could see the ocean, but little else.

Ross sat in one of the chairs and stared at the pink gin by his elbow. *Not too many of those, my lad, or you'll be the next one.* He did not look round as the door opened and Lieutenant Charles Villiers came into the room.

Villiers said, "If you want me to shove off, please say so. I thought you might want to talk."

Ross smiled. Even after another change of clothing and a tepid bath he still felt jaded, on edge.

"Thanks. I'm getting used to it." He was reminded suddenly, painfully, of Villiers's parents and sister. "I guess I always took the old man for granted. Worked his guts out for us. Then my mother died of the flu. It didn't stop him. He remarried—it was never the same, but he needed somebody to stand by him, to encourage him when things were rough." He grinned in spite of the grief. Maybe his pride in Big Andy was a more fitting memorial. "Not bad for a stoker, eh? The last time I talked to him, he'd just bought another salvage tug. *Never hire anything, Jamie, the cash might run out, then where are you?*" He could almost hear him saying it.

Villiers remarked, "You're a Scot, but you don't sound like one."

Ross said dryly, "What, no curly walking stick and a haggis, like Harry Lauder?" He saw Villiers withdrawing into himself, and added more gently, "We moved south once my dad had got his Scapa contract. Falmouth. I feel at home there, I suppose. What about you?"

Villiers looked at his hands. "Singapore and Malaya, a rare trip or two to England. I called it home, but this last time I felt a stranger there." He seemed to make up his mind. "I must tell you." He shook his head so that the fair hair fell across his forehead. "No, I *want to* tell you. I saw that girl again. Caryl."

Ross noticed the way his tongue seemed to linger over her name. "Thought you might."

Villiers said levelly, "She's Captain Sinclair's wife. She wants to get a divorce." Then he looked him straight in the eye. "You see, Jamie, I love her. I think she loves me."

Ross considered it. A very pleasant, honest young man, who had probably wanted for nothing all his life. Until now. The agony of losing his family in such a horrifying way had made everything else unimportant, incidental. He no longer even considered it a risk. He said, "Sinclair is rejoining the . . ." he smiled ". . . the *cohort* quite soon. He's to be promoted to major and he's getting another gong, or so I am informed. So watch your step."

Villiers stood up and walked to the window. "There's something wrong with the man. She's afraid of him."

Ross watched his anxiety; it was like something physical. Also, he remembered Napier's haphazard account of what had happened after the chariots had laid their charges. He could have been mistaken about several things, but one thought lingered to disturb him. Sinclair had been changed by his experiences. Or had he always been like that?

Villiers touched his breast pocket. "I had a letter from her. The first to get here." He saw the sudden warning in Ross's grey eyes and said almost apologetically, "It's all right. She typed the envelope. Nobody could have recognized where it came from." He stared out at the ocean, the bright horizon between the swaying trees like some huge dam, recalling that last morning when he had awakened in her arms, the sensation of something wonderful, unthinkable: disbelief, too, that it could have happened. They had loved again, had tried to hold the urgency at bay, and make only the moment real.

He smiled to himself. The hotel manager had not asked to see her identity card before she had left. The first Charles Villiers would have approved.

The letter had brought it all back, made the distance less of an obstacle. He said, "I tried to explain to Rear-Admiral Dyer, you see . . ."

"You *what?*"

For a moment Villiers imagined he had gone too far.

Ross said quietly, "Send for more drinks." Then he grinned. "I'll say this for you, Charles, you're determined enough." He held up his hand. "Next time, tell *me,* all right? Ossie Dyer seems very good at his job, but I don't think romance figures much in his strategy!"

They both laughed, the last barriers down. An onlooker, had there been one, would have assumed them to have been friends for a long time.

Ross moved to the window. This peaceful collection of bungalows and storerooms even looked like part of the Navy now, he thought. A White Ensign flapped listlessly from a new mast, which had been encircled by neat, white-painted stones. He felt the warm sill and recalled the age-old joke in the service. *If it moves, salute it; if it doesn't, paint it white!*

He thought of Villiers, his obvious sincerity. If Sinclair ever got wind of it . . . He shook his head. He must not. There would be another meeting with the Intelligence people soon; perhaps after that he might be off somewhere else. He recalled Pryce's summing up, but which one suited Trevor Sinclair? Courage or madness, hatred of the enemy or a genuine desire to kill?

War made some men, but it destroyed many, many more.

Villiers re-entered the room, a steward following him with a tray of glasses. "Feel better already!"

Ross was glad he had come in to join him. He could see it in Villiers's open face: he and the girl had been lovers. Not the usual war-time affair, but lovers in the fullest sense.

When the steward had gone, Ross said quietly, "If ever you want to get out of this and go back to general service or something, just let me know. I'll see what I can do."

Villiers was suddenly very serious. "No, Jamie. I volunteered. It's something I have to do if I'm to live with myself after it's all over. I owe it to them."

Ross did not need to ask who. He raised his glass. "Thanks for telling me."

Villiers said, "I think you knew anyway."

Outside a tannoy squawked loudly, although the whole place was small enough for a man's voice to penetrate.

"D'you hear there? Duty fire party to muster! Libertymen will be piped in one hour!"

Voices filled the wardroom, and there was an immediate clatter of glasses.

Alone with their thoughts, Ross and Villiers finished their drinks.

Somehow, each of them felt he had found a new beginning.

Petty Officer Mike Tucker strode out of the hot sunshine and into the shade of the bungalows. A small board had appeared on the scorched grass in the past few days marked *Quarterdeck,* and he had tossed a solemn salute as he had passed. They could make a naval establishment out of anything these days, he thought. He paused and removed his cap to take advantage of any sea breeze. The strangeness of promotion had completely worn off, much to his surprise. Now he *was* a petty officer.

Three days had passed since the submarine had brought Ross and the others back from Operation *Emma* in the Malacca Strait. Now it was November, although here nothing ever seemed to change. The first excitement and the usual awareness of risk had all but worn off. Apart from checking the chariots on board the depot-ship, and carrying out exercises that seemed so tame after the real thing, nobody appeared to have a clue what to do with them.

He thought of the letter which had arrived from home. His mother never gave away much of her true feelings, her hopes or fears; her letters were very much like her, patient understatements. This last one had been slightly different, though. Young Madge had really done it. Not that it was at all surprising: even that had been evident in his mother's letter. Madge had got herself in the family way. Some Yank, who had immediately been posted elsewhere.

There was other news as well. A pub his father had often used had been bombed flat. She had not written the name; perhaps she had imagined a dedicated censor would have crossed it out, or redirected the letter. A few names were mentioned, and faces sprang to mind, some of which he would never see again. Her main concern, as always, was her son Mike *in foreign parts,* something she had never got used to, let alone accepted, despite his being a regular.

He thought of that first meeting with Ross within hours of his return. It had been easier than either of them had expected to talk of Big Andy's death, perhaps because they knew each other better than they had realized. A firm handshake, and Tucker's honest expression of sympathy, then Ross had said simply, "He's always been there, you see. Even though we didn't meet all that often, he was there, a part of things."

Like his own father, Tucker thought. Quiet, popular with his mates, but firm when need be. God alone knew what he must think about Madge. But surprise would not come into it.

Shunting his little tank engine up at the Junction, working all hours; but luckier than so many during the period of depression and mass unemployment which had been lying in wait for servicemen returning from the Great War. *The survivors.* Yes, their fathers had had more in common than he had realized. That knowledge had come to him gradually as he had slowly become accustomed to working with a straight-laced regular officer on a first-name basis.

Tucker had been used to another kind of officer. Remote, in charge. Decisions made with unquestioned efficiency, almost like a rubber stamp labelled *Duty.* He and Ross had once been in Edinburgh together, to be interviewed by people from the Intelligence Department. They had had half a day to spare, and Ross had told the car's driver to take them on to Leith, to a small, quiet spot along the coast, where they had stopped at a pub for a drink. Ross had pointed to a neat, white-painted house almost opposite and had remarked, "That was my home, Mike. Where I drew my first breath."

Tucker was not sure what he had been expecting. It was a nice enough house, but less than half the size of his own in Battersea.

You never knew, he thought. Tucker had learned the hard way never to take anything for granted. There were officers and officers. He had seen for himself how Ross cared for the people he worked with, and he had felt the bond between Ross and his friend David like a living force. He thought, too, of the new subbie, Peter Napier. Very like his dead brother to look at, but that was as far as it went. The smile, the moments of gravity which were almost as deep as despair had been David's alone. Peter was not the same. He was immature. Tucker grappled with the comparison. *Shallow.*

He rapped on the door, almost expecting to hear Pryce's curt *"Come!"* He and some of the others had had to admit that life at Trincomalee was less boring with Pryce burrowing around.

Ross looked up from the desk and smiled. Tucker had the

impression that he was grateful for the interruption.

Second Officer Jane Clarke, the only Wren officer so far to be directly attached to their Special Operations Force, was leaning over Ross's shoulder while she arranged a clipboard of signals. Blonde, blue-eyed, with a turned-up nose and *such an English face,* as his mother would have put it. She had a candid and very direct way of looking at you. A nice, buxom figure, too: very tasty, as the petty officer cook had described it.

She looked unusually disconcerted as Ross asked, "What can I do for you, Mike?"

Second Officer Clarke stood upright and plucked at her shirt while she looked at the slowly revolving fan. The effect was not lost on Tucker. Very bedworthy. A flirt. It surprised him. He had rarely thought of other women after Eve had been killed.

"There's a car laid on, sir." Tucker contained a smile. It was obvious that Ross had forgotten all about the appointment. "To take you to the Mackenzie estate this evening."

Ross sighed. He had hoped that Pryce would be back before this, but all reports showed that he would be staying in Bombay for at least another four days.

The girl said, "I know the way."

Ross looked at her. The message was clear, if not loud. He had been very aware of the casual touch of her breast against his shoulder, the warm perfume of her body. She sensed his hesitation and added, "I've been there before."

Ross said, "You're on duty this evening. You told me."

She moistened her lower lip. "I can get someone to cover for me. Base Ops know what's happening, anyway."

Tucker said politely, "Mr Villiers will be with you, sir."

Ross smiled at the girl. "Next time, maybe."

She touched his hand. "My friends call me Jane." She walked out of the room without a glance at Tucker.

Ross said, "I didn't know about Charles Villiers."

Tucker shuffled his feet. "Well, I expect he'd *like* to go along."

"Trying to save me, eh, Mike?"

Tucker faced him calmly. "Nice girl. But not your sort."

Ross examined the clip of signals to avoid his eyes. "Four more chariots arriving in the next convoy, two as replacements. I'll leave you to fix things with the chief tiffy." He thought of the girl who had just left. *Not your sort.* But why not? Nothing serious: she was not the kind to expect that. Merely to hold her, let everything go . . . When he looked up, Tucker was still watching him.

He said, "Petty Officer Mackenzie has offered to drive, sir."

Ross stared past him at the blue sky. He had spoken to her a few times but only on the subject of certain signals, because Pryce was away. Then once, when he had been lighting his pipe and she had had her back turned while she locked the filing cabinet, she had said, "I was sorry, sir, so sorry about your father." He had sensed her determination to keep her voice neutral. "I know how I would have felt."

She must have known about the signal before *Turquoise* had sailed. Perhaps she had agreed to suppress it, realizing the effect it would have had on him.

He had asked, "Did you enjoy your date with Sub-Lieutenant Napier?" It had been a stupid remark, merely for something to say.

Her reaction had been swift. "Should I have asked permission, sir? Put in a request through my divisional officer?" It had been like a shield dropping between them.

Tucker said, "There's one thing, sir. I'm a bit bothered about it." He was being serious now, even formal.

"Spit it out."

"Mr Napier's Number Two, Nick Rice. Telegraphist, that was."

"Yes, what about him?" He could sense the sudden concern, the tension in the other man. Tucker had very strong views on loyalty and how far you could take advantage of it. It *was* serious.

"He come to me this morning. I told him straight, 'Don't beat around the bloody bush with me, Nick. Speak up or drink up.'"

"And?"

"He wants a transfer, sir. Change crews when there's an

opportunity. You've just told me about the replacements—well, that might be the time. There's bound to be some new faces as well."

Ross wished there was something to drink in the office. But if Pryce still had anything decent left, it would be under lock and key. He said, "I don't understand it. They seemed to get on so well. First-class reports, nothing that might have prevented me from sending him on such an early mission." *That, and Pryce's pig-headedness.*

Tucker considered it. Nick Rice had blurted out, "Look, Tommy, I'm as game as the next bloke, but the subbie nearly did for both of us. He lost his bottle completely!" He said to Ross, "There's a lack of confidence, sir. Might blow over. I've known it happen."

Ross smiled. *Even with me, I expect.* "Looking round here, you'd never believe it, but this is a front-line operational force. We can't afford any foul-ups, right?"

Tucker grinned, glad he had mentioned it. "Right, sir."

As he turned to go, Ross asked, "Did she really offer to drive us to the estate? I wonder why."

Tucker pressed his famous luck. "Probably wants to defend you against her officer. 'Jane,' isn't it?"

When Ross had taken a shower and changed into a clean shirt and slacks, Tucker was ready and waiting for him, a cardboard box held carefully under one arm.

Ross said, "I don't know how you do it—the Colonel might not even touch the stuff. But thanks, all the same."

Tucker grinned. "His name's Mackenzie. Of course he'll like it. The chief steward arranged it. The same as Captain Pryce favours."

They walked into the evening sunshine and there was another surprise waiting for Ross. He had expected one of the usual overworked staff cars, worn-out springs and completely airless. It was anything but that. Sleek and rounded like a sports car, he recognized it as a Sunbeam Talbot. It had been an expensive rarity in England before the war and now, of course, it was unobtainable. It was cream-coloured, the bonnet covered with the inevitable layer of dust from the roads. Like part of the past, for the lucky ones anyway. It made Ross think of his father's Bentley, which had been laid up for the duration. What would become of that, Big Andy's pride and joy, he wondered? She might marry again and give it to her new husband. He was surprised at how bitter it made him feel.

"Ready when you are, sir." She had been standing beside the car, chatting quite freely with Villiers. She took the box from Tucker, and Ross noted their quick exchange of glances. Then she opened the doors and indicated that he should get into the back. Villiers held the door for her, and then sat beside her while she took the wheel.

Over her shoulder she explained, "It will take about an hour, all being well, sir. The roads are good." In the driving mirror, Ross saw her smile at Villiers. "But the northeast monsoon will soon change all that!"

Past the sentry and out on to the open road, the colours and smells of this exotic country even more striking in the evening light.

Villiers said, "We'll follow the road south along the sea and then head inland and get a bit of height—right, Victoria?"

She nodded, her black hair whipping out from beneath her hat. "Like England—you are never more than eighty miles from the sea in Ceylon!"

Ross stared at some gaunt cattle which were being driven into a field: this was an island of great beauty, and of desperate poverty, too. The others were chatting together, while she occasionally took her hand from the wheel to point out something of interest: a ruined temple, a Catholic church. A place she had come to know, but Ross, who had been told she was born in Singapore, sensed she did not think of it as home.

They were heading away from the sea now, the trees overhanging the car like a green tunnel. He watched her hand as she tightened her grip to take the next slow bend in the road. Small, and strong. Her conversation with Villiers made him feel isolated. He tried to smile. *Jealous, perhaps?*

She said suddenly over her shoulder, "My father is looking forward to your visit, sir. Whatever he says, I think he still misses being a part of things." She glanced at Villiers. "Not far now."

"I could sit and be driven all day!" He ran his fingers through his fair hair. "It's been a long time."

The gates were painted white and were propped open to reveal a long, well tended driveway with flower-beds, and colourful shrubs Ross could not even begin to recognize. There was a fountain, too, where bronze cranes lifted their wings to the cascading water.

The house was impressive. Built on brick stilts to keep termites at bay, it was broad and spacious, with a veranda running from end to end. Ross saw Villiers lean forward for a better look. It was a typical colonial bungalow, and Ross suspected suddenly that it reminded him of his home.

She slowed the car, and must have recognized the expression in Villiers's eyes. She touched his arm and said softly, "You must enjoy today. Do not be sad." Ross felt the simple words turn in his stomach like a knife.

Villiers murmured, "I knew you'd understand. Thank you."

The car pulled up in front of the entrance and a servant in a white coat hurried to greet them.

She opened the door for Ross and handed him Tucker's box. "There will be drinks presently. Please go inside."

Villiers replaced his cap, shaking off the mood. "What a place!"

She studied him gravely. "Like Hollywood? That is what visitors say."

Villiers grinned. "You know exactly what I mean!"

Ross said awkwardly to her, "Will you wait, or are you coming in, too?"

She looked through him, and then at him as if seeing him for the first time. "I live here, sir."

They went up the steps and Ross, trying to recover from his embarrassment, said, "I don't mean to annoy her."

Villiers said casually, "I think you may remind her of someone, Jamie. Somebody who once brought her unhappiness."

Irritated, Ross said, "Old head on young shoulders! You'll have to teach some of it to me."

Villiers paused to admire the broad entrance. There were many Chinese statues and carvings, some Indian ones as well, but mostly souvenirs of the Colonel's Far East travels. He said quietly, "Caryl would love to see all this."

Just like that. She was never far from his thoughts. Such things could, then, happen so quickly; in their case, *had* happened.

Their caps were whisked away and Ross found himself strangely glad that he had come. There was another fountain here, but as he turned to watch it the water fizzled away; at the same time, all the lights dimmed for a few seconds before picking up again. The fountain returned to life.

"Can't rely on anything! My generator was one of the best investments I ever made!"

Colonel Basil Mackenzie strode to greet them. Tall, craggy-faced, with a bushy white moustache and eyebrows to match, he would have been recognizable as a soldier in this or any other century. Very upright, with square shoulders in a well-fitting jacket, he was still that same man, like the pictures at Highmead School and in the various service clubs Ross had visited. Omdurman, Sebastopol, the shoulder-to-shoulder British squares at Waterloo: he would have fitted into any of them.

"Lieutenant-Commander Ross—I shall call you Jamie, if I may. And Lieutenant Villiers. Will 'Charles' suit?"

They shook hands warmly, and he took their arms. *"Officers' Call,* or in your case, the sun is over the yardarm, correct?"

Ross handed him the box. "I hope you like it, sir."

He held it up to the rejuvenated lights. "Islay malt, by God!" He beamed. "You must be not only a man of courage and perception, but a very influential one to boot!" He turned and called to the servant, but not before Ross had seen his eyes. Tawny, like the girl's.

She came in now, her shoes clicking on the tiled floor of the entrance hall. She looked tired, perhaps sorry they were here. The Colonel kissed her on the forehead, and it made Ross realize how tall he was. "I dunno, Jamie, women in uniform!" He smiled, the years leaving his face. "Still, they were well up in the line with us in Flanders."

She said, "I'd like a swim, Daddy. I feel sticky."

He nodded. "Show Charles the garden—and the swimming pool, of course!"

She put her hand gracefully through Villiers's arm. "Come with me, *sir.* Perhaps it is Hollywood after all!"

The Colonel said, "Make a striking pair, eh?" But his eyes were on Ross and his reaction. Then he chuckled. "Come into the Museum—that's what everyone round here calls it—and tell me what you want to do about this bloody war-correspondent fellow." He went towards a closed door and took out a key. "You can tell me about England, too, while you're at it."

It was a large room with only a single lamp on a broad desk. Ross looked around with interest as the other man switched on more lights. Despite what he had said about its being called "the Museum," Ross guessed it was a very private place, and he was surprised and touched that he had been invited to share it.

One wall was lined with books and there were several military engravings interspersed with old swords and eastern knives. Opposite the door, with its own small spotlight, was a portrait of Mackenzie himself, a likeness so good that it could have been a photograph. He was dressed in a green uniform with a white sun helmet balanced on one knee while he stared into the distance.

He heard Mackenzie filling some glasses. "When was that painted, sir?"

Mackenzie replied, "Before I stepped down. Frontier Force Rifles." His voice was casual, matter-of-fact, but Ross knew it was important to him. "The regiment spent a lot of time in Singapore and Malaya after the war, what was left of the poor little buggers. Fought like tigers in Flanders—even that couldn't break them, but British Army cooking nearly did!" He held out a glass. "Pink gin suit you?"

Ross grinned. There were no cobwebs on this old warrior.

"After that I was supposed to leave the Indian Army and be promoted. Drink all right?"

Ross sat down, avoiding the fixed stare of a tiger-skin rug by the desk. Mackenzie went on as though to himself. "My wife and two sons were with me. It was expected in those days."

He moved to the window and peered out between the blinds at the purple sunset.

"I got to love the place. Unfortunately, my wife hated it. I sometimes think she hated the Army, too." He smiled, but it only made him look sad. "A general's daughter at that. You never know, do you?"

Ross wondered why he was telling him all this, when they had only just met: at the same time he felt certain that it was not something the Colonel usually did. Especially here, in this room, which must be so full of memories. "So they went home in a trooper." He sounded far away. "The two boys have done well. One is in the Hampshires, the other in the Royal Armoured Corps."

He said abruptly, "Smoke your pipe if you want to. No rules here, y'know." He watched as Ross pulled out his briar pipe and pouch and said, "We had an *amah* in Singapore, for the boys' sake. She'd been a nurse, and was very good with them." He looked steadily at Ross. "An affair was something else—lots of chaps had those, a mistress perhaps to make the monotony of garrison duty tolerable. But one was never allowed to carry it any further. The honour of the regiment or something like that!" He looked at Ross again, the same searching gaze. "Come over here." He switched on another light above another portrait. A serene, beautiful oriental face with long plaited black hair.

Mackenzie said quietly, "Victoria's mother." He touched the gilt frame very gently. "Jeslene. I often sit here and look at her. She died just after we came to Ceylon."

"And you quit the Army, sir?"

He stroked his white moustache. "No choice in the matter, really. So I had a go at tea planting. Paid off, as it happens, but nowadays I have people to handle everything for me. I'm just the *old soldier* around here."

"Thank you for telling me, sir."

Mackenzie smiled. "Sign of old age. If I lived in London, I'd be lying in wait in the club, ready to bore the pants off anyone stupid enough to listen to how we held Hill Sixteen!"

He expertly mixed another pink gin. Ross hesitated, then asked, "How did your daughter become a Wren?"

"Hated the Army, probably. They formed a women's volunteer unit here shortly after the outbreak of war. She wanted to do something." He stared into his glass. "For the country, she said. But, like that young man you brought with you, she has no country, not to call her own. It needs more than a passport to find that."

Ross saw two pale shapes passing the window, and wondered if Villiers would tell her about his girl, another man's wife, in England.

"I'm glad she's attached to your lot, Jamie. Some of the people at the Base—well, you know how it is." He did not elaborate.

"Captain Pryce said he couldn't manage without her."

"Pryce—oh, yes, he would. She's still only a petty officer." He grinned broadly. "But then, Hitler and Napoleon started as corporals, right?"

Ross heard the girl laugh at something. Mackenzie said, "Don't tell him, not yet anyway, but I used to play golf with his father in Singapore. Didn't *know* him, but like everyone else there I knew the family." He switched off the light above the picture. "I worry about Victoria. When I'm gone." He added angrily, "Let's go and get something to eat. You young chaps must be starving."

Villiers was standing in the hall, studying the ornaments. Mackenzie put his hand on his shoulder and said quite gently, "You miss the old place, don't you, son?"

Villiers looked at him, his face suddenly bare and defenceless. "On days like this, I do." He turned and stared into the shadows, almost as though his ghosts moved there for him.

The girl came to join them, wearing a loose robe and a towel draped over her hair. "It was lovely!" She glanced at Ross and at her father. "You should try it!"

But Ross was thinking of the portrait in the Colonel's room. What their love had cost them, although it had endured, strengthened by adversity.

The others had gone ahead. She asked softly, "Did you have a good talk with my father?"

"I could have listened to him for hours."

"Did he show you the portrait too?"

So casually said, but it was important. Perhaps there had been someone before him, someone who had answered the same question. Villiers might be right after all.

He said, "I can see where you get your looks from. She was lovely."

She stared at him, her eyes startled, but without anger. She exclaimed, "You must not say that! It is not right!"

His voice was surprisingly level. "Someone *should* say it, and mean it, as I do."

Was he just repeating what another man had told her? *I could reach out and touch her, but she is as far away as Charles's girl on the other side of the world.* He thought of his father; there was never any warning. These memories would always ambush him. *What's she like, Jamie? When are we going to meet this girl of yours?*

She said softly, "It wouldn't work. But . . . thank you." She touched his face with her fingertips. "I wouldn't want either of us to be hurt." She walked slowly away, her bare feet leaving small damp prints on the tiled floor.

Then she said without looking round, "I will be going back to my quarters. I'll tell the duty officer to send transport for you."

"No!" He was shocked by the sharpness of his voice. "I'd prefer it if you waited. I don't like the idea of you going back on your own."

He saw the argument and resentment fade, and she answered indifferently, "If you say so. If it's what you want."

He nodded, feeling stupid. "It is."

The others looked at him as he sat down at the supper table, wondering no doubt what had happened between them.

The Colonel banged his fist on the table as a servant entered and said politely, "Telephone call for Commander Ross, please."

"Confound them! Can't they let you off the hook for a second?"

Villiers made to stand as the girl, dressed now, entered by the other door. She waved him down, and he saw that she was quite pale, almost ashen.

At that moment Ross came back, and stared unseeing at the table. "That was the Provost Marshal. A woman's body was found an hour ago in a ditch on the main Trincomalee road." He raised his head, knowing she was there, that she had heard. It was where she would have been driving.

The Colonel exclaimed, "Why did they call you?"

Ross looked at his hands, but they were quite still, even relaxed. Then he said, "It was Second Officer Clarke. She was murdered."

7 | Monsoon

Captain Ralph Pryce moved restlessly about his office and snapped, "I'm away for just a few days, and then I come back to all this!" He waved vaguely at the window. "And now the bloody rain!"

Ross waited by the desk, half listening to the concentrated roar on the iron roof, the memory of the night before last still stark in his mind. The cars in the road; the field ambulance, its red crosses like blood in the headlights; the various lamps carried by the military policemen. He had heard her sharp breathing as she had braked the car, and a redcap had loomed out of the shadows.

He had said, "Wait here. Charles, look after her." Unemotional, cold, although even that was a lie.

The major in charge of the MPs had said curtly, "Sorry to drag you out. I thought it best to keep it in the family." They had met once before; he had a neat, impassive face with a small moustache. A policeman's face—the uniform was irrelevant.

The major said, "Not a very pretty sight, sir, I'm afraid."

The woman had been lying half on her side, one arm outthrust, frozen in the attitude of death. Her body was all but naked, and the torn articles of clothing scattered around in the darkness were being examined and noted by some of the military policemen.

More lights had been switched on and Ross had stooped to brush two ants from her bare shoulder. Her skin had been like ice; it had not seemed possible on such a humid night. He had heard himself ask, "Can she be moved now?"

"Of course. I'll have her covered up. I suppose I've got hardened to this sort of thing."

"It's not that." Ross knelt and looked at the body. So still, and yet he could see her as she had been that same day, offering to drive them to the Mackenzie estate. There was a bruise and a scratch below her right breast. He put his arm around her and raised her slightly towards him. Around him all movement had stopped, and he could feel the redcaps watching him.

The major said, "There's a lot of blood. Just the one wound, though. We'll know more when we get her to the M.O."

Someone lowered a lamp and Ross had leaned over the dead girl's shoulder, seeing the shadow of her spine, and then the wound: narrow, but the thrust so savage that the skin was torn and bruised around it. Like a kind of madness, in his mind he could hear the instructor's voice, laconic, bored even, as he had repeated the lesson for their benefit. *"Thumb on the blade and stab upwards, gentlemen. Otherwise the blade will glance off the ribs and most likely end up in your own leg."*

The major said, "You've seen this sort of thing before, then?"

Ross lowered her with great care and brushed some hair from her unblinking eyes. "I've *done* it, if that's what you mean." So callous, as if he had wanted to shock them, make them realize what it was all about.

He had heard a car door slam and Villiers shouting, "No! Victoria, come back!" She had burst through the scrub and had almost fallen as she saw the nude body on the ground.

Then she had seized the outflung hand and crouched down beside her, stroking her, speaking to her in a small voice until one of the redcaps had brought a groundsheet to cover the body.

There had been a few heavy drops of rain on the trees, and then in seconds had come the downpour. The monsoon. It had not stopped since.

Pryce had returned, fuming at the plane's delayed flight, and further enraged when he found out what had happened. For a while it had seemed he was more angry at the intrusion of the Provost Marshal's men than the girl's brutal murder.

It appeared that the meetings in Bombay had not been as smooth or as full of praise as Pryce had expected.

"They seem to think that Europe and its eventual invasion

by the Allies is all that counts. I told them, *here,* here is the vital role. If we fail against the Japanese, we can say goodbye to the Far East and India for good!"

Now as he watched the rain with barely concealed hatred, as if it were some sort of personal attack, he snapped, "Send for Petty Officer Mackenzie. I want my special file and intelligence pack." His eyebrows went up. *"Well?"*

Ross said, "I sent her home, sir. I thought she had gone through enough."

"I see. I suppose under the circumstances . . . And I *did* leave you in charge." It sounded like an accusation. "Glad you managed to see the Colonel, though. Useful chap, if he wants to be."

There was a tap at the door.

"Come!"

She entered the room and shut the door. "I thought you might want the intelligence file and signals log, sir."

Ross stared at her, trim and neat in her white uniform, her black hair shining; he remembered the rain smashing down on the M.P.s and bouncing off the groundsheet and the dead girl's bare feet. Victoria could have been naked herself as the drenching rain had battered her shirt around her body. She had seemed heedless, unaware of it; even her tears had been concealed by the downpour.

"Pick her up, *please!* Don't leave her lying there!"

Villiers had appeared with a rug or a blanket from the car and had wrapped it round her shoulders. She had not even noticed.

Ross had told Villiers to take her back to the estate, saying, "I'll deal with things here."

She had stared at him with haunted eyes. "She so wanted to drive with you. If she had, she would still be alive. Poor Jane!"

Ross had said, "Explain to the Colonel, Charles. I'll call on him again when I can." Only then had he held her, her body soaking against his, his words almost lost in the roar of the rain.

"Go with Charles, please, Victoria. I didn't want you to see any of this."

She had not moved. "You *knew.* You were afraid for me, weren't you?"

He still was not sure. Second sight, fate; both or neither. But it was not the first time.

She was looking at him now. It was hard to believe she was the same girl.

"I'm sorry, sir. I came back. I thought I might be needed, now that Second Officer . . ." She did not finish it. Then she said to Pryce, "Major Guest is about to leave, sir. He would like to see you before he goes."

Pryce snorted, "Bloody policemen. Oh well, I suppose so."

Like the girl, the military policeman looked smart and alert, with creases on his khaki drill which seemed impervious to the rain.

Pryce waved him to a chair. The major glanced at the girl and asked, "Feeling better?" He did not wait for or expect an answer. "Good, that's the ticket." To Pryce he said, "My sergeant has some of her effects. I expect your people will require them. Identity card, purse and some loose change, that sort of thing." He placed a gold wrist-watch on the desk. The clasp was broken. "Underneath her body. Not a robbery attempt."

Pryce said to Victoria, "You can go, if you wish."

She did not move. "I'd like to stay, sir."

The major shrugged. "The car she had been driving was untouched. Her body was on a—" he glanced at a notebook, "tartan blanket. It would seem that the murderer was known to her. Perhaps she had stopped to offer him a lift, or maybe they met by arrangement. This rain has destroyed any hopes of getting tyre-prints."

Ross thought of the glaring headlights and military police jeeps, the many stamping boots around the body. There would have been no clues left in any case, after that.

Pryce hesitated; he seemed uncomfortable with the girl present.

The major said, "The M.O. carried out an examination, of

course, and the Army is sending a senior man from Colombo when the weather eases." He closed his notebook with a snap. "It was probably an attempted rape, but she put up a good fight and . . ." He glanced sharply at Ross. "The other night you said something about the wound. You said, *I've done it, if that's what you mean.*" He held up the notebook. "I wrote it down. See it if you like. I thought you were upset, that it might have been a sort of bravado to cover it. Nobody would blame you."

Ross could feel her watching him. "It was the wound. It was something we were taught. I had to use the technique myself. That's what I meant."

Guest said, "Could you show me?" He glanced at the girl. "Would you mind?"

Ross said angrily, "She's been through enough, damn it!"

Pryce remained silent.

She took three paces and faced him; her eyes were very steady, like her mother's in the Colonel's portrait. Almond-shaped, with fine black lashes.

She said, "Please. If it would help. I'm not afraid." It seemed to exclude the others, as if they were completely alone.

Ross said quietly, "Stand with your back to me." He looked at the major and Pryce over the girl's head, could feel her tension, like that night in the rain.

He forced himself to speak slowly. "Left arm over the shoulder and round the front of the body." He held her firmly, turning her slightly, his wrist beneath her right breast. She touched his hand, and for a moment he hoped she had changed her mind. But she held his wrist quite calmly, impersonally, and raised it so that he could feel her breast through her shirt.

She said, "There was a bruise and a scratch. I saw them."

The major did not blink. "That is so."

She was looking down at Ross's hand. She said softly, "Where your watch is, sir."

Ross looked away. "Yes. By turning the person slightly, like this, you can use a knife." *Thumb on the blade, sir.* Like the

German frogman, the same hold even though they had been sinking together in the fjord's icy water, as the knife had driven deep and the bubbles around them had changed from pink to scarlet. He thought of the dead girl as she had been in this same office two days ago. Lying down, it would be the same. Up through the ribs, a thrust so savage that it would pierce the heart with one blow.

He said, "A watch could have made those marks."

The major opened his notebook but shut it again. "Any ideas on the weapon?" His casual manner did not conceal his professional interest.

"Narrow blade."

The major interrupted briefly. "Double-edged, the M.O. suggested."

Ross lowered his hand, but she remained with her back to him as if she were under a spell. "A commando dagger, or something like it."

The major stood up. "I'll go and round up my chaps. It wasn't too difficult to check on your people's whereabouts. All accounted for."

Pryce said indignantly, "I should bloody well hope so! This *is* supposed to be a top-security establishment!"

The major was unmoved. "Second Officer Clarke was out of the place, and on her own. She had obtained permission to stand down from her duties, although no security reason was asked for or given!"

"I'll soon change that, believe me!"

The major said, "Won't help Miss Clarke much, will it?"

The door closed very quietly behind him and Pryce said, "What the hell must she have been thinking of? Now I'll have to try and get a replacement. But, until I do—Victoria, can you cover her duties?"

She said without expression, "Yes, sir."

Pryce tapped a sheaf of paper on the desk and laid it down very carefully.

"Staff Officer Intelligence is coming in this afternoon. Lunch first, of course." He glanced at Ross. "The chance of another operation, all being well. Some people seem to think we're all asleep here most of the time!"

They looked round as the door opened and the major peered in at them again. "Almost forgot, sir. Nothing was stolen as far as we know, but the victim's hat-badge was missing. We've searched everywhere. The hat was near the victim's body. But no badge." He looked at the girl. "Blue, isn't it?"

She nodded, and asked, "Why would anyone take that?"

He shrugged. "Souvenir, trophy, who can tell? We'll do our best, but I think this will be a tough one with the thousands of servicemen we've got on the island or out in the troopers." He withdrew.

Pryce said coldly, "He bloody well enjoyed that, didn't he?"

Ross watched as she picked up the small wrist-watch. On the back was engraved *To dear Jane from Tony, with love.*

She said, "He went down in the *Repulse.* I think he was the only one she ever really cared about." She replaced the watch and said softly, "Poor Jane. I hope they catch him . . ." She visibly controlled herself. "I'll make the arrangements for this afternoon, sir."

When she had gone, Pryce said, "That's more like it! Important things are afoot. I'll make a signal to *Turquoise* through Commodore, Submarines. We'll need that boat again if this one is approved—any overhaul will have to be postponed!"

Ross glanced at his own watch. Had she been thinking about it when he had held her? Been imagining him with the knife as he had described? Picturing what it had been like for Jane Clarke? Now no longer a living person; soon she would not even be remembered as a victim, except by a few friends. She would be just another casualty of war, set against so many. A letter from Pryce, even from the admiral perhaps, and a small parcel of belongings, like the broken watch. It was not much to show for a life.

He had been going to press Pryce about the conference or the proposed operation for his "cohort." Instead, he asked, "What about Captain Sinclair, sir?"

"*Major* now. Just confirmed." His eyes were opaque in the steamy glare. "First one I checked on. I don't have my head in the clouds, as some people seem to believe!" He relented slightly. "In Colombo, as a matter of fact. Reports here tomorrow." He gave a faint smile. "Clean as a whistle—satisfied?"

Ross said nothing. Whether Villiers would agree was another matter.

Pryce was reaching for his telephone. He hesitated. "A very ugly incident indeed. But out of our hands. So the 'incident' is closed. We have a war to win!"

Ross left the office and found the girl waiting for him. He said, "I'm sorry you were put through that. I could feel what it was doing to you."

She said softly, "And I felt what it was doing to you. You relived that moment, didn't you?"

He watched the rain on the windows. "I often do. Perhaps it's best to stay at a distance."

She did not look at him. "My father would like you to come for supper soon, and have something to eat this time. You can bring Charles Villiers with you. I feel I let him down the other night . . ."

He shook his head. "You couldn't let anyone down." He smiled. "I'd love to come. But I'm not too sure I can wangle another bottle of Islay malt!"

When she turned, he saw there were tears in her eyes.

She said, "I treated you so badly . . ."

He touched her wrist. "I expect I deserved it."

She walked away towards the Operations Room where they had first met, and he wondered how often her eyes would stray to the empty chair opposite hers.

As far as she was concerned, the "incident" would never be closed. It could so easily have been her.

• • •

Commander John Crookshank, the admiral's senior staff officer for Operational Intelligence, arrived promptly for his lunch with Pryce. He was a round, amiable man who, like so many others, would have been pruned from the Navy, the world he loved most, had there been no war.

Ross met him in the outer office and was immediately aware of the commander's embarrassment, the fact that he had brought another guest, uninvited. The other man was a complete stranger, small, neat and incisive. A military moustache, a lightweight grey suit and a vague tie which might have been regimental, or that of an exclusive London club.

He was introduced as Brigadier Hubert Davis, obviously a very important Intelligence officer, who had only just arrived from London. Davis showed no signs of fatigue, and his suit looked as if it had just been delivered to him by the cleaners.

"Ross, eh?" His eyes moved swiftly over him, missing nothing. "Know a lot about you. Glad you're here."

He might have meant that either way, Ross thought. Pryce was less conciliatory. He said, "I'm afraid the lunch will be rather less than exciting, Brigadier. Had I been told . . ."

The Brigadier was equally forthright. "Well, you know now, so let's get started, eh?"

There was a tap at the door and Villiers, his cap under one arm and his shirt dark with rain, stepped into the office.

Ross waved him to a chair. "You're too early. Had lunch yet?"

Villiers slumped down and turned his cap round in his fingers. "No. You didn't either, I suppose."

Ross shrugged. "Well, what can I do for you? Captain Pryce wants a talk with you. There's a top man from Whitehall in there as well. I shall be sitting in, if that's all right?"

Villiers did not seem to hear him. "I just ran into our old friend Major Sinclair."

Ross tensed. "You didn't say too much, I hope?"

Villiers tried to smile, but it eluded him. "No. He makes me feel uneasy, especially after what young Napier said about him."

"Well, Sinclair may not be here much longer, Charles. I hear he might be sent back to the U.K. to collect his medal in style."

Villiers stared moodily at the window. The rain had stopped, as if a great door had been slammed shut. There was sunshine now, and steam rising everywhere like a fog.

Ross took out his pipe, unable to forget the dead girl's icy body in his arms, her broken, unmoving stare. *Not your sort.* Tucker was upset about it too, probably because of what he had said about her.

"I don't know, Charles, but I think they want to pick your brains."

Villiers looked back at him warmly. "I'll always trust your judgement. About Singapore, you mean?"

"Just a feeling."

"Are you worried that they might want me to go back?"

"It would be madness. No one can force you. If I have any say in the matter . . ." He shrugged again. "Just be prepared, O.K?"

A Wren brought some coffee, and Ross thought of the girl named Victoria down the passageway in Operations. What was really going on in her mind? She was obviously still shocked by her officer's brutal death, and the little gold watch with its engraving seemed particularly to disturb her.

The lunch ended precisely on time. It was somehow typical of Pryce, Ross thought, that it should have been laid out in his office and not in his quarters. Wary of some outsider who might discover something personal about him, a whim or a weakness?

A steward came out carrying a tray of dishes. There were no wine-glasses on it.

Somewhere a telephone rang briefly, and immediately afterwards Petty Officer Mackenzie came to the outer office, a notebook in one hand.

She said, "You're to go in, sir." To Villiers she added, "You are to wait here for a few moments." For all of them, that moment of peace in the Colonel's lovely garden and her swim under the stars seemed a lifetime away.

Ross held open the door for her, remembering the pressure of her body, her scent, when he had held her against him to demonstrate to Major Guest how simple it was to commit murder.

The three faces in the main office looked up as they walked in. Surprisingly, the only one who seemed confused, even startled, was the wiry little brigadier.

"I thought you had a Wren officer seconded to this unit?"

Commander Crookshank said, "She died. Unfortunately at such short notice . . ."

Pryce cut it short. "Petty Officer Mackenzie is the most experienced and certainly the most reliable member of my staff here."

The brigadier's eyes were still on the girl's bare arm, the blue crossed anchors on the sleeve. "If you say so."

Pryce glared at him. "I do say so."

Ross felt a little glow of admiration for him.

Brigadier Davis took out a notebook and said, "Very well—ah, Mackenzie. Shorthand notes, and two complete copies for my file and Captain Pryce's. *Top Secret.*"

Ross studied him surreptitiously. Brigadier of what, he wondered. Or was it one of those fictional titles he had heard were prevalent among the cloak-and-dagger elite?

Davis said, "Now, about Lieutenant Villiers."

Crookshank said carefully, "A very good officer, sir. Temporary war-time commission, but all the same . . ." Keeping the peace. He was well known for it. He had found his niche and did not want to lose it.

Pryce said, "It was all in his report. An extremely wealthy family, famous too, by all accounts. How much he can help your department is something else." He added harshly, "Up to him, don't you think?"

Ross glanced at the girl's tanned arm on the table beside him. She was gripping her pencil so tightly he was surprised that it did not snap. Her eyes were downcast and he wondered if she were hiding anger, as on the occasion when she had known that he and Pryce were discussing her. Or did she resent Davis's hesitation, reluctance even, as another personal, perhaps racial slight?

Davis said distantly, "As long as he can be relied on. Top Secret means just that, in London in any case."

Pryce did not accept it gracefully. "The last time I was lunching at the Savoy, I was sitting next to three staff officers who blabbed so much about the defences at Dover I could have captured the place single-handed."

Crookshank asked quickly, "How was the old Savoy?"

Pryce regarded him and gave a wintry smile. "Still there. Will that do?"

The door opened and Villiers walked into the room, his shoulders still dark with rain.

Again, Ross saw her fingers tighten on the pencil. Reliving it. The drenching, deafening rain, the naked body being covered by the redcaps. Or was it something she felt for Villiers?

Pryce introduced the others and said, "Sit down, old chap."

Villiers glanced at Ross, as if to reassure himself that he had heard correctly. *Old chap.* This was another Pryce neither of them knew.

Davis said, "I am aware of your connections with Singapore and Malaya, or most of them anyway. My department works like bricklayers, putting facts together, trying to discover a pattern, making things fit. We don't disregard any information that might help us and, of course, the country."

Villiers said, "It was my home, sir. In many ways, it still is."

Davis looked into his little book. Like Major Guest, Ross thought. "Do you recall anyone named Richard Tsao, an acquaintance perhaps?"

Villiers stared past him. If he felt surprise, or any other emotion, he concealed it. "I knew him fairly well. He was a junior manager of the South China Lighterage Company of Singapore and Malaya. Has something happened to him?"

Davis did not reply. "The South China Lighterage Company was one of the businesses owned by your family, I believe?"

Villiers nodded, his mind working, trying to anticipate what was coming, why this casual mention of somebody from his past.

Davis glanced coolly at the girl's hand as she scribbled a few more notes. "Richard Tsao is now running that company." He turned his attention to the lieutenant, his eyes very still, like stones. "He is working for the Japanese Occupation Army."

Villiers did not even raise his voice. "If he wanted to stay alive, it was the sensible thing to do. Two of my father's employees were beheaded, simply because they signed their names in English."

Ross watched him, wanting to help, to stop the relentless interrogation. Had Villiers discovered that grisly little piece of information when he had returned to Singapore covertly, when Ossie Dyer had been so furious?

Davis continued, "We have agents there, of course." He sounded very vague. "Richard Tsao has intimated that he might give us certain information."

The pencil moved again. Villiers said, "He'd be a fool to take that kind of risk. He has his whole family to consider."

Davis turned a few more pages. "So have many of us, Lieutenant."

Ross saw Villiers's hand clench into a fist. How could anyone make such a stupid, cruel remark?

"For months now, our combined intelligence forces have been baffled by some German interest in Singapore. They are to all intents brothers in arms, although this seems to be something other than that. There is repeated mention of an operation named *Monsun*." He paused. "For the record, it means monsoon."

Pryce said irritably, "Bloody topical, anyway!"

Davis ignored him. "An agent verified Tsao's knowledge of it, purely by accident." He spread his hands. "It's not much to go on."

Villiers said without expression, "You'd like me to meet him, sir."

"If it can be arranged. You will be consulted every inch of the way, naturally."

"And in return, sir, what is he asking?"

"I am not yet able to say. But Operation *Monsun* is real, and it is necessary to know what it is, no matter how flimsy it might appear."

Villiers said, "I could do it."

Davis sounded neither relieved nor surprised. "There is another snag, but we may be able to overcome it, bypass it, even."

Ross interrupted, "This Tsao chap wants assurance, right? To meet someone less involved with the personal aspect." He looked at Villiers. "I would go with Lieutenant Villiers, if it would help."

Villiers stared at him and shook his head. But he said nothing. Perhaps there were no words.

"Did you get that, ah, Mackenzie?"

Her eyes came to rest on Ross's face, with a shocked disbelief. But she glanced at her pad and said coolly, "I did, sir."

Davis rubbed his hands. "Well, that's it, gentlemen. A good afternoon's work, I think." To Victoria he said, "You may go and type the report, and bring me the shorthand notes afterwards."

He looked at Villiers. "We shall keep you informed. And, thank you."

Pryce said, "I must protest at your handling of this matter, sir!"

"Out of my hands—*our* hands."

He stood up, his suit creaseless. "I shall see you shortly. Right now I have to arrange some signals." He paused with one neat hand on the door. "Don't forget the shorthand notes, will you?"

Pryce watched the door close and snapped, "Does he think she's a spy, for God's sake?"

Ross said, "I thought we had an operation of our own on the cards, sir."

Pryce muttered angrily, "Not in front of him!" To Commander Crookshank he added, "Top Secret goes for this too!"

He got up slowly from his desk, as if to give himself time to calm down. Then he tapped the big wall-map. "It may be useless—too late, anything—but I've alerted the submarine *Turquoise,* and I'll want one chariot crew ready to take passage the minute I get the affirmative." His fingers rested on the coast of Burma. "Not so far as the last operation," he smiled as if at some secret thought, "*Emma*. But we have received information that a large Japanese freighter went aground here, to the west of the Irrawaddy River delta. As I said, it could be too late. They might have moved her, but I doubt it. She was loaded to the deck beams with steel railway tracks and other gear."

Crookshank leaned forward, his earlier discomfort momentarily forgotten. "I read that signal. The Jap Army is constructing a new railway at Rangoon, to run eventually to Mandalay. That's about four hundred miles through very rough territory. So they'll need this cargo and more supplies if they hope to finish it on time."

Pryce said savagely, "No prizes for guessing who's doing all the work."

Crookshank nodded. "Prisoners of war. Dying like flies, I believe."

Pryce let the map fall into place and turned to Ross. "I want you to send young Napier again. I've heard the gossip, but I don't want any arguments. It will be the making of him. I shall see what I can do about advancing his second stripe afterwards."

Ross said, "Don't I have any say in this, sir?"

"I think you've said quite enough!" Surprisingly, he smiled and touched Ross's arm. "I *am* right about this, you know. He's good, but he was simply not ready for *Emma*. This will be a copybook job, like an exercise."

He was almost jovial as he went on, "The pity of it is, young Napier will miss the party for Howard Costain. It's being fixed for next week."

Ross walked out of the room, seething, and yet knowing in his heart that Pryce was probably right. Napier had to rise above his difficulties, otherwise he was finished.

He saw her coming slowly towards him, the typed report in her hand. She held out her notebook. "Shall I burn this in front of them?"

He took her arm very gently. "I could have hit him," he said.

She did not remove her arm from his grip. When he looked at her he saw the expression in her eyes, the way she was studying his face as if she were searching for something. Or somebody.

"I know I must not talk about it. But when you said what you did, what you believed you must do for Charles Villiers, I wanted to stop you, to tell them you've already seen and done enough." She paused: it was difficult for her. "Suppose they really do send you." Her mouth quivered, but she could not stop. "Suppose they . . ."

He pressed her arm gently. "They won't. Charles may be young and in love, but he knows that island as well as you do!"

She wiped her cheek as if she expected to find that a tear had betrayed her. "In love? I'm so glad for him." She was suddenly very serious. "But he must be careful. The Villiers family was very powerful and much admired, by their own sort." She hesitated, wondering if she had gone too far.

Ross said, "I know. The Sons of Empire are not always as popular as they are led to believe."

She heard a bell ringing somewhere. "I must go." She held up the papers. "*Monsun* is German for *Monsoon,* remember?"

As if to make its point, the rain began again.

8 | Next of Kin

FROM SLEEP to an instant awareness, Mike Tucker was no longer surprised at how quick and complete the transition could be. As his hands moved swiftly to the steel cot above where he was lying, his whole body was coiled like a spring, ready to leap out into the dimmed lights of the P.O.s' mess. Piece by piece, his mind was sifting and disposing of the normal sounds and sensations. The quivering vibration of the submerged hulk, the occasional click of machinery, a sense of movement but without any human voice. It was as if the submarine *Turquoise* was an underwater phantom which needed nobody to sustain her.

The air was heavy, too long confined, and without freshness. There had been no opportunity to vent the boat and run the diesels for charging batteries. Four days since they had left Trincomalee, and the closer they had got to their destination on the Burmese mainland, the more aware everyone had been of enemy activity, which had made even casual sightings with the periscope too dangerous to contemplate.

Four days. A lifetime. The submarine's company had one another with whom to share their thoughts. For the chariot crew, Sub-Lieutenant Peter Napier and his Number Two, Telegraphist Nick Rice, there was no such comfort.

Tucker lay back with his head on his clasped hands and stared at the cot above him. Submarines were a way of life if you allowed them to be. He pictured the solitary chariot snugged down on the saddle-tank, inert but deadly. Waiting. A few more hours and it would be time to go. Or to make a decision that was the choice of the submarine skipper, Bob Jessop, alone. To call off the whole operation. Tucker smiled in the gloom. Rather him than me . . .

He thought too of Ross, his expression when he had gone to him to suggest he should go with Napier for support. As one of the old team. The pro. Now Tucker was not so sure. Nick Rice had seen him privately and had repeated his dissatisfaction with Napier as his officer.

Tucker had tried to explain to him that it was too late for complaints or doubts. They were not, after all, green recruits. They were brave, highly skilled men; there was no time or room for sloppiness. Rice would be sitting with his kit right now. Going over it, remembering all the details of the proposed attack. When *Turquoise* had managed to make wireless contact there had been virtually no news which had warranted a change of plan. The damaged freighter was still there; there might be a tug in company. It was possible that the unwieldy cargo of steel rails would have to be offloaded before the ship could be moved and another sent to replace her. All so vague. As usual, Tucker had concentrated on the job in hand. If you banked on a dicey one being cancelled at the last minute, you were usually wrong.

He thought nostalgically of his home in London, the Battersea skyline all the way to the river before the smoke and fog closed in. It would be Christmas soon. The pubs would do well.

He found himself thinking of the girl who had died in Ceylon. He faced it. *Who had been murdered.* He had heard some of the others discussing it, how Ross and the P.O. Wren, Mackenzie, had been there at the scene. Now the girl was just a memory. He tried not to compare her with Eve again. *She* must still be lying there, buried under fallen buildings; they had insisted that it was not so, that she had been laid to rest in one of the big communal graves where the bombing had been at its worst.

But suppose not? Was she still lying there with nobody to care? Or maybe there hadn't been enough of her to bury anywhere.

"What?" He almost snarled at the seaman who had pulled back the curtain.

The sailor said, "The old man wants you in the control-room." He winked. "Just dreaming of a juicy bit, were you?"

Tucker's feet hit the deck almost soundlessly. He glanced

at the curtained bunks, the men off-watch. So many times. He could still remember his first boat, the warnings about getting a move on when the klaxon tore the place apart. He had regarded his messmates with some scorn, thinking, no bloody fear there. One or two of them had been quite plump, not all that fast on their feet.

When the klaxon had sounded, however, he had found himself alone in his mess. They had been able to move when they needed to.

Into the oily air of the control-room: men welded to their seats, eyes watching their instruments. Tucker took a quick look at the depth gauge. One hundred feet, no swell, no other sounds.

The skipper was by the chart table and the plot with his navigating officer. Peter Napier was peering at the chart, his notes under one hand. There was hair like down on his cheeks; perhaps he intended to grow a beard to impress the ladies. Tucker found he could still grin. Some hopes of that. The first bit of wind would blow it off.

Bob Jessop raised his head. "Good weather. The proverbial mill-pond up top. The last run in should be fair enough."

Tucker noticed that the navigator had suddenly vanished, and the duty stoker by the periscope well had also melted away.

Jessop said, "It seems that the Number Two wants to pull out."

Napier looked directly at Tucker, his eyes defensive, resentful. For just a second in that youthful face, Tucker could see Ross's friend David Napier, who had died in that other attack.

Napier said, "I don't know what to say about it. We're a team. Rice is good. I've never worked with anyone else."

Jessop said flatly, "You should have seen Captain Pryce, or Jamie Ross before we left. This is a bit late!"

Napier stared at him. "Well, it's not my fault! I'm ready and geared up for it. A piece of . . ." He coloured slightly and let it drop.

Jessop said, "As far as I can estimate, I shall have to put you off here." His pencil tapped the chart. "It will take you at least three hours to locate the target, do the job and then get back to the pick-up area."

Napier rubbed his chin. "Another three hours. That's a bit of a risk."

Jessop stared past him at the curved hull, the tired, intent faces. "It's a hell of a risk to *my* men, all fifty-eight of them, every time we attempt one of these crackpot schemes!"

Napier looked surprised at the skipper's hostility. "I only meant . . ."

"We sighted a convoy of ten ships yesterday, with just the one clapped-out escort. A full pattern of torpedoes would have taken care of most of them—I might even have had time to reload for a second go. More use, surely, than a grounded hulk full of railway gear?"

Tucker said, "I've brought my own kit, sir. The chariot will carry three, especially if we go on the surface for most of the time."

Napier said sharply, "Was this Commander Ross's idea?"

Tucker grinned. "Even ratings have good ideas sometimes, sir!"

Napier flushed again. "Sorry. Asked for that." He made no further comment, as if it was already settled. Then, hesitantly, he said, "Together we could . . ."

Tucker said casually, "Of course we can." He added, "I'll tell Nick Rice, if you like."

Napier shook his head. "No. I'll tell him." He walked away, his mind apparently resolved.

The skipper said, "What was the subbie's brother like? Jamie Ross's best friend, they tell me."

"I've never seen two men so close, sir. Like brothers, they were." He dodged the question he knew was coming. "Jamie Ross has never got over it."

Jessop said, "I see." Then, "Thanks for sorting it out. When we get back I'll stand you a drink, anything you like. Then the boat's in for an overhaul. About bloody time too!"

The navigator returned, his face suitably blank. "All fixed, sir?"

"Yes. Thanks to our diplomat here, I think we can say just that."

The last hour aboard the submarine went quickly: usually the waiting-time seemed to drag. Dressed in their rubber suits, the three men sat in the petty officers' mess, half listening to the sound of the trimming tanks being adjusted, feeling the slow swell now that the boat had glided up to periscope depth. Tucker did not know what Napier had said to Rice, but he felt that the Number Two was pleased, if surprised, that Tucker himself was going along. He wondered vaguely what Ross would say when he found out. He had already suggested to him that the chariot's two-man crew would feel more confident with one of their own helping them to "take off." He had not said who it might be.

Why had he decided to be the third man? Two men alone took enough risks in the chariots . . . men had died or just silently vanished. Nothing could change that. Why complicate it?

Napier broke into his thoughts. "There are a couple of small islands where the freighter ran aground." He peered at the borrowed chart. "Just a few miles from the Rangoon River, her destination no doubt. Once inshore of the nearest one, we shall get a better idea."

Rice asked sharply, "No booms?"

Tucker noticed that he avoided looking at the young officer.

Napier folded the chart. "They say not. We'll fix the charge and head straight back. No slip-ups. We should make it before full daylight."

Rice muttered, "Christ, I should hope so. The place will be crawling with Japs!"

Tucker said, "I've checked my gear."

Rice nodded. "Me too." He patted his suit. "Pistol, blood-chit, money, the lot." He forced a grin. "Even the headache pill!" But it made him look even more strained.

Napier stood up and groaned. "I'll just have a last word with the skipper."

Rice breathed out very slowly. "D'you reckon he's going to be O.K?"

"Of course. Right as ninepence. The last one was his real test. This'll be like a training cruise."

Rice did not look convinced. "I'm glad you're coming along, Tommy. In your place I'd have thought twice about it." He touched his arm. "You didn't tell Ross, did you?"

Tucker shrugged. "He had enough on his plate."

Napier reappeared in the entrance. "Ready to go." He looked at each of them in turn. Afterwards Tucker remembered it well. As if he was trying to reassure himself, rather than give assurance.

Out and through the control-room, now fully manned although Tucker had barely heard anything. As if the boat was holding her breath.

Jessop glanced at them briefly, his dark beard almost red in the dimmed lights.

"Remember the current, Sub. And watch out for fishing boats—they'll be sleeping with their nets most likely, but don't take anything for granted." He singled out Tucker and said in an undertone, "Keep your head down."

After that, it was like moving to an unspoken drill pattern. The surprisingly cool air after the hull's stuffy confines, water sloshing over their feet while they prepared to release the chariot from its various clamps. Tucker had already noticed that the casing party was only two or three men and the saddle-tanks were already almost awash. The skipper was keeping his command trimmed down, a minimum target should the enemy have any detection gear which might reach this far. Three hours there, three back, Tucker thought. A long night. He watched as Napier slipped into the forward position; he saw the glowing dials on the control panel suddenly light up, and hoped he would remember to adjust the pump and air pressure to allow for the extra man. He could recall when the old rear-admiral, Ossie Dyer, had insisted on donning a full suit and full gear to be dragged through a Scottish loch to see what it was like. It had nearly killed him, but the lads had loved him for it.

Tucker helped Rice to climb aboard and then turned to look up at the conning tower. Not many stars but a clear sky, so that he could see the skipper and his lookouts watching as the motor kicked into life, and a backlash of bubbles and phosphorescence surged against the two seated figures.

A thumbs-up? Or it could have been a casual salute. The next moment he was aboard, his arms wrapped around Rice's body while the chariot dipped heavily and then backed clear of the dark hull. He felt rather than heard the thunder of inrushing water as *Turquoise* began to flood her tanks and prepared to dive.

Napier twisted round in his seat and waved his arm. He was in control, with nothing but the operation in his thoughts.

Tucker adjusted his breathing apparatus and sucked deeply on the air supply. The chariot was answering well in spite of his additional weight. He felt the water surge around his chest and throat, splattering his mask, and wondered what Rice was thinking about. Probably nothing. Yet. They would be all right once they got started.

Tucker doubled his fist and felt Rice tense under it. *Otherwise I'll have to be a bit regimental with the pair of them!*

Far away on the starboard bow they saw a tiny cluster of lights. Fishing boats, but too far off to be dangerous. The Japs were that confident. Hardly surprising when you considered that their armies occupied the whole of Southeast Asia from Burma down to Java, to say nothing of the hundreds of islands in the Pacific, where long-range sea and air battles had already cost so many ships and lives, Japanese and American alike.

Tucker pictured the great warhead of explosive they were carrying. Set against the immensity of war, it might not seem very significant, as *Turquoise*'s skipper had bitterly remarked. Without noticing it, he patted Rice's gleaming rubber suit. But like Sicily, it was a beginning: the road back.

It was the only way to think of it.

The sea grew more choppy closer in to the land, and Tucker knew Napier had his work cut out keeping the chariot on its proper course. When he looked abeam, he noticed that the faint lights from the fishing boats had vanished, as if they had all been doused in response to a secret signal. Half an hour later they began to reappear, and Tucker gave a quiet sigh of relief. The lights had been momentarily hidden by the first small island. They were on course. Napier was doing his job, and he hoped that Rice would regain some confidence by the time they reached their objective.

Provided that nothing delayed them, they should be making their return journey to the rendezvous with precious little darkness left to conceal them.

Tucker smiled. *If you can't take a joke, you shouldn't have joined.* The sailor's answer to just about everything.

He tensed as something dark and shapeless drifted past; Napier must have seen it just in time to avoid hitting it. A half-submerged boat of some kind, doomed to drift up and down the invisible coast until it finally went to the bottom.

It would be almost funny if the target had been moved, or emptied of her much needed cargo. He wondered what Napier would do then. Drop the charge anyway, if only to prove he could do it?

A bright green flare exploded somewhere over the land and floated gently into the darkness. A long way off. The Japanese Army perhaps, or was it some kind of signal to the dozing fishermen?

In spite of his discomfort Tucker almost fell asleep to the even, sluggish motion. He saw Napier and Rice exchanging hand signals and he wished he could see his own watch to check their progress. Like a leaping fish, a white feather of spray broke across the blackness between sea and land. The second island, the offshore current breaking across some scattered rocks like those he had seen on the chart. Three hours? It hardly seemed any time since they had watched the submarine begin to dive, their only contact broken.

He thought he saw Napier hunching his shoulders, ready to dive and shake off their trailing phosphorescence if a strange vessel loomed over them. But there was nothing.

Napier's arm lifted and stiffened, and as he steered the chariot in a shallow turn, Tucker saw the black, motionless wedge of a ship. *Their* ship. It had to be. Napier made no attempt to dive but continued along the side of the blacked-out vessel until they could identify the solitary funnel and old-fashioned bridge, and the derricks that must have been used to load the cargo of rail tracks. Tucker did not need to be reminded of the grim stories now filtering through of wretched Allied prisoners of war being forced to work on road and railway construction for the Japanese Army. Starved, brutally treated, and without medical care, it was no wonder men were calling them the railways of death. But instead of fear at the possibility of what might happen if they were captured, Tucker was surprised to discover that he felt only anger, even hate.

There was a dangling rope ladder, and Tucker saw that some of the lifeboat davits were empty. The Japs had taken no chances. It was probably a native crew, which they had put ashore rather than risk some further disaster. There had been mention of a salvage tug. If it had indeed arrived, it would make an early appearance to begin or complete the work of moving the vessel, or the cargo, to a more suitable position.

Napier and Rice were holding the rope ladder and peering up at the ship's guardrails. Napier opened his visor and said, "The anchor's down. Let's get on with it." He sounded very calm, matter-of-fact, as if it were indeed just another exercise. Rice slipped into the water, his hands fending off the steel plating.

Napier called down to him, "Right here, I think." He closed his visor and twisted round towards Tucker to indicate that he was going to dive.

Tucker slithered into the water to join the other man. It was all going well. The time-fuse was set, and as he helped Rice fix the magnets to a surprisingly clean bilge, he felt the warhead detach and float down beside them until it was suspended firmly beneath the hull. The explosion plus the weight of the cargo would break the vessel's back and scatter the contents across the seabed.

It was done, and Tucker turned round, clinging to the chariot as Rice slapped his shoulder and gestured with excitement.

Napier brought the chariot carefully to the surface again. Not a jolt or a scrape had marred the manoeuvre and all three of them sat in the water, visors open as they sucked in the air and fought down the urge to laugh or cheer.

Napier was peering at his luminous clock again. He found it an effort to remain calm and unruffled.

"Ahead of time, would you believe?" He stared up at the guardrails, still only just visible in the surrounding darkness. He seemed to grin, like his dead brother for just that moment, Tucker thought. He said, "I'm going up for a souvenir. Be ready to cast off, lads!" Then he was clambering up the rope ladder, apparently heedless and unhindered by his breathing apparatus.

Rice said grudgingly, "Like a bloody kid! What do you think, Tommy?"

Tucker stood up, swaying, and then seized the ladder. "I think he's being stupid!" He knew Rice was gaping at him, but he didn't care. Rule One, never take chances. He thought of Bob Jessop's last words. *Keep your head down.* He snapped, "I'll get him back, and then we're bloody well off!"

He climbed swiftly up the ladder, his whole body suddenly cold, as if he were naked.

The freighter's deck was like any other, with loose gear and uncoiled mooring wires scattered about to show the haste of the crew's departure. Tucker lowered himself to his knees and winced as a rivet ground into his leg. He heard Napier rummaging about among the discarded equipment by an open door at the foot of the bridge. *A souvenir.* For the mess, or to impress some girl or other. It made him unreasonably angry, and he was about to call out to him when he glanced at the open door again. There was a tiny glow, where before there had been only blackness. The man, whoever he was, must have been on deck for a quiet smoke when Napier had blundered jubilantly aboard. Tucker could feel his heart lurch as if it might stop altogether and then, as if another's hand were guiding his, he unfastened his knife and pulled the blade carefully from its sheath. Like those other times; like the moment when the German frogman had found them and had been about to raise the alarm. When Ross had gone for him, taken him with him into the swirling water. Ending it.

Napier stood up, something flapping in his hand. Then he froze, his arms flailing as he saw the other man and realized what was happening. Tucker bounded forward, seizing and flinging the man to the deck. Noise no longer mattered. Nothing mattered but survival. He felt the man's buttoned tunic and realized he was a soldier; at the same time he saw him drop a rifle, which had been hidden in the darkness.

He heard Napier cry, *"Oh, my Christ! Christ, help me!"*

Tucker sat astride the soldier and held him between his legs, one arm pinioned so that he could feel the joint cracking. There was a bayonet on the rifle. Napier's screams of agony told him the rest. He said quietly, "Coming, sir." The formality made him want to scream or laugh. If he did either, he knew he would be unable to stop. He saw the soldier's eyes swivel as he tried to look at him, then he drove the blade into his body, counted the seconds before twisting it and dragging it free. Then he moved carefully to Napier, expecting at any moment to hear shouts and challenges, feel the same thrust of steel, then nothing.

"Where is it, sir?"

Napier was gripping his left shoulder, his blood like black paint between his clawed fingers.

"I'll put a dressing on it." He heard Napier choking on a scream as he lifted him bodily and put him over his shoulder. "But first, we get the hell out of here!"

Rice had at last realized something had happened, and

helped him lower the groaning officer back down to the chariot. Before he followed down the ladder, Tucker found time to notice that the dead soldier's cigarette was still glowing on the deck.

He said, "I'll take over, sir. Nick'll hold you."

He sensed Napier's refusal, clinging to some last fragment of authority which refused to give in. "No! I'm in command here!"

Tucker ignored him. "Take a good grip. There's a gash in his suit. If it fills with water . . ." He did not need to go on.

He slipped into the control seat and tested the joystick. They had all been trained for this in case of just such an eventuality. Go out on the surface, and to hell with caution. Only speed counted now. He cursed himself for not dropping the Jap into the sea. Someone might discover what had happened. Even Bob Jessop wouldn't risk his *Turquoise* if a chase was in progress. He made himself take a few deep breaths. *Especially* Bob Jessop.

"Cast off." He watched the compass and felt the chariot edge away from the target. He tried to think it out, put his thoughts in order. *I just killed a man.* But nothing formed in his mind. "Here we go!" *What wouldn't I give for a tot right now!*

He craned his neck and saw the first of the fishing-boat lights. Paler, perhaps? He tried to control his sense of urgency. As they ploughed into a small wave he heard Napier cry out, and Rice's despairing, "For Christ's sake shut it! Haven't you done enough for one bloody night?"

Not officer and rating any more. Just two frightened people who were depending on him.

They would be well clear of the islands soon. After that . . .

The explosion was as deafening as it was vivid, and for a few seconds more Tucker imagined that the charge had exploded prematurely, even though they never did. The darkness that followed was total and enveloping, but Tucker had seen part of an island illuminated by the blast as if it had been touched by fire.

Napier was calling weakly, "What happened? Did the charge blow?" He sounded irritated, querulous, like a small, disgruntled boy.

Rice took a firmer grip on him and stared into the sea. "Can't you smell it? If you'd been in the Western Ocean you'd recognize it quick enough!"

Tucker said dully, "It was *Turquoise*. She's gone." He too could smell the burned oil, could picture the shattered hull falling like a torn leaf to the bottom. He could even hear Jessop's anger. *My men, all fifty-eight of them*. What had happened was anybody's guess. One fact stood out. They were alone.

Napier asked, "What are you doing?"

Tucker shrugged. "Going back. We don't have much time left. I think I can find a place where we can ditch the chariot and our gear." He was thinking aloud, some of his words muffled as water slopped over his open visor.

Rice said, "Going back?" He sounded dazed. "They'll be looking for us."

Tucker responded savagely, "Well, nobody else will be, so shut up and save your breath!"

Surprisingly Rice said, "Sorry, Tommy. I'll stand by you."

Napier called, "It *hurts*. I can't move it!"

Tucker saw the same small lights and wondered what the fishermen would have thought about the explosion. And what about the Japs? An officer was probably roused right now, telephone ringing, perhaps a patrol boat putting to sea to investigate.

Napier muttered, "They won't hear the last of this . . ."

Tucker sighed and watched the compass. *They?* Who, he wondered?

Rice said, "He won't make it." When there was no response from Napier he added, "Sod him!"

Rice spoke as if he had already given up hope. Tucker tightened his grip on the joystick, as he had done on his knife. Aloud or to himself he did not know, he said, "Well, Evie, I'm really in it this time."

A gull rose mewing from the water, disturbed perhaps, or aware of the nearness of dawn and the prospect of fish from the boats. But to Mike Tucker it sounded like a cat calling to be let in.

In his mind he could clearly see his mother opening the telegram.

The evening of the promised party could not have been a better one, offering a clear, bright sky with a new moon riding above its shimmering reflection in the sea. There was even music, provided by a very solid-looking gramophone watched over by one of the Colonel's servants, who cranked it up between the heavy records. Strangely, most of it was dance music, something from the past.

Ross and Villiers handed their caps to a servant and paused uncertainly in the entrance hall. After their other visit it seemed totally different, with naval officers making up the largest number. They, too, looked unfamiliar in their white uniforms, "ice-cream suits," gently suggested by Captain Pryce, who had obviously intended it as an order. Glancing round at the noisy throng, Ross guessed why Pryce had insisted on this rig for the occasion. Medal ribbons were worn, and at a glance one could see the insignia of gallantry on the uniforms of many of those present.

Villiers remarked, "Just a nice bunch of blokes as far as I'm concerned. I never think of them as heroes." His glance dropped to the solitary crimson ribbon on Ross's tunic. "Present company excepted, of course."

They laughed, but Ross had the distinct feeling that his companion was rather depressed. It was neither the time nor the place to question him about it. Perhaps he had not received another letter from his girl, or maybe he had had bad news. He glanced round, wondering if Victoria would be there, or whether she had made a point of staying away.

Villiers said, "So that's the big man, is it?"

Howard Costain, the famous war-correspondent, was not quite the figure he had appeared in his photographs and newsreels. He was shorter than expected, with thinning fair hair, and was quite noticeably plump. His suit was lightweight, well cut, but suitably crushed to show that its owner was a man of action, with little time for the niceties of apparel.

Pryce and Brigadier Davis were with him and, dwarfing them all, the impressive figure of Colonel Basil Mackenzie, resplendent in white dinner-jacket and black tie. Ross suspected that he always dressed for these occasions, or even when he was alone in this house of memories. Major Guest from the Provost Marshal's office was also here, hovering discreetly but obviously by a tall potted palm. He held a full glass of wine in his hand, and looked as if he might have been happier with a pint of ale.

As if to a cue, Howard Costain pivoted round and looked at them.

Pryce frowned. "And this is Lieutenant-Commander Ross, my senior officer in the section."

Ross held out his hand. He had seen the frown and knew it was because he and Villiers were late, their driver having lost his way twice.

The handshake was soft and plump, as Ross knew it would be. But Costain's tan was impressive, golden and perfectly even, as if it had been laid on with a brush.

Costain said abruptly, "Wrote a piece about *you*—two, in fact. You're quite a man, by all accounts."

Ross smiled. Costain spoke sharply and jerkily and sounded much more like the voice on the radio or in the newsreels. *Today I met one of Britain's heroes, not a bit what I might have been expecting.* He saw Villiers watching him over the man's shoulder. He might even have winked.

Pryce said, "We have a very strong team here. I wish I could show you over our establishment, but . . ."

Costain nodded and dragged out a cigarette-case. "Top Secret, of course. But the admiral said he would arrange it. There might be a useful story for the folks at home." He laughed. That was jerky, too.

Brigadier Davis coughed politely. "There are some other people I'd like you to meet, Howard." He took his arm. "Though I doubt they can surprise you much."

Some people stood aside to allow another tray of glasses to pass through, and it was then that Ross saw her.

She was standing on one of the tiled steps and was looking directly at him. Like that other time, as if there was nobody else here. He had never seen her out of uniform before. She wore a simple green silk dress with a high collar and small slits in the hem which was perfect for her hair and eyes; it was more like a gesture of defiance than a desire to impress.

He walked up to her and took her proffered hand.

She said, "I thought you might not come."

"I was thinking the same about you, Victoria. I have to tell you this, even if you hit me. You look wonderful. Stunning."

She watched him, in that same searching way. She did not drag her hand away.

A tray appeared and she selected a glass before saying, "I'm glad you came. I have been thinking about all sorts of things."

"Are you going to tell me?"

She moved slightly away and Ross knew that several faces were turned towards them, watching them. He saw a fine gold chain around her neck, hidden for the most part by her collar.

"I thought I would dress up. My father wanted it." She smiled at the white-haired man across the room. "'It will keep the war away,' he said."

She looked at the white-uniformed figures and added softly, "They give their lives so easily."

"Is something troubling you? If I can help, please tell me."

She touched his arm. "You barely know me." She averted her eyes, almost shyly, he thought. "But thank you. Today I saw the admiral. He has been 'pulling strings' for me." Then she looked back. "Perhaps a commission."

He said carefully, "I'm so glad for you. You more than deserve it. Even Captain Pryce has said so."

She smiled sadly. "Rain in the desert, yes?" She hurried on. "It would mean going to England. Leaving here." She looked at her father's broad shoulders. "Leaving him. Now I can always see him when I am not required in Operations or watchkeeping. It is a privilege, and I am grateful. In England?" She left the rest unsaid.

"Have you ever been there, Victoria?"

She nodded, her voice far away. "My father sent me there to be finished, a good school—you know the way of things, of course."

He wanted to hold her, and watched her hand on his sleeve intently. "Better than you realize, Victoria. I never knew young boys could be so barbaric!"

She seemed surprised. "Because of my mother and me he lost everything, the Army, all the things he loved. He never hesitated. I did not truly understand until I was older, but now I know why my mother loved him."

"And what about you?"

"Me? I once thought I had found love. But it was just a dream. I was foolish, ignorant, if you like."

"I don't like. The fact that you have been hurt, you, of all people."

She smiled, but her eyes were uneasy. "People are staring. They will think all kinds of things!"

"Let them." He hesitated, unable now to discipline himself not to say it. "If I thought I would never see you again, I would feel that I had lost something precious to me."

She said, "Come and look at the fountain." They walked together into the garden, and stood in silence listening to the ripple of water. He was painfully aware of her, of her perfume and her warmth. Like that day when he had held her for Major Guest's benefit.

She said, "And then you will leave, or I will if they decide I am suitable for a commission. The war is between us, as it is for so many."

Ross thought of Villiers. "It can't last forever."

She said, "I shall never forget your face. That night when you were trying to shield me from poor Jane's body. I knew then what you were thinking. That it might have been me lying there with all of them staring at me."

Car doors slammed and Ross heard someone exclaim, "By God, it's Crookshank! Not like him to be late for a free drink!"

Ross looked down as she gripped his arm. "What is it?"

She said, "I saw the guest list. Commander Crookshank was not invited. He is supposed to be with the admiral."

Ross held her arm; it was supple and strong, like the girl. He said casually, "Probably another flap on."

She was staring at him, her eyes very bright in the reflected lights. "But *you* don't think so."

They re-entered the house and a lieutenant Ross had never seen before said, "Captain Pryce wants you, sir."

She nodded, her eyes misty. "You see? You knew."

He saw Villiers and said, "Entertain Miss Mackenzie, will you?" Villiers saw their quick exchange of glances and was reminded of Caryl. Like lovers, or people in love.

They were in the Colonel's study, the Museum, as he knew they would be. Pryce waited for the lieutenant to close the door.

"Bad news, Jamie. The attack was carried out perfectly—Intelligence received word just now. The target was destroyed."

They were all looking at him: Crookshank, sweating from his journey, afraid to use the telephone because of the secrecy; Brigadier Davis, neat and unruffled, his eyes impassively grave, like a general who had just watched a whole division of troops mown down in the wire of that other war.

Pryce continued, "However, *Turquoise* has failed to make contact and must therefore be presumed lost."

Ross heard the muffled laughter and conversation from the adjoining room. The other world.

Pryce said, "The chariot crew may have been able to board the submarine after they had completed the mission. If not, they will be making their way overland."

Mike Tucker was dead. Ross's mind could barely grapple with it.

He said, "Tucker asked if he could go with the chariot crew, to back them up. He had the same feeling as I did about the crew in question." He looked up, his eyes hard, like the North Sea. "I'll lay odds he went with them."

Pryce said, "Very likely. But either way . . ." There was no need to go on.

The brigadier said quietly, "There is something wrong with the whole pattern. It will be more necessary than ever to regain contact with that Tsao chap in Singapore. Some new weapon, perhaps? A device we know nothing about?"

Ross exclaimed, "They died for damn-all, if you ask me!"

Pryce said coldly, "*Easy,* Jamie. It might have been anybody, even you. The raid was a success. In the end, that's all we must consider."

Memories came, assaulting him, and he had no defence against them. The submarine's bearded commander. How they had discussed the sighting of the combined fleet at Trafalgar. Mike Tucker above all of them. Strong, reliable, loyal and understanding. In that shabby street in Battersea they would hear it eventually on the radio news, read by some polished B.B.C. announcer. *"The Secretary of the Admiralty regrets to announce . . ."*

Pryce said, "We still have a few matters to discuss, Jamie. Perhaps you would tell our people."

Ross reached the door. He could almost feel the dead silence that had fallen like a pall over the room beyond. He said bitterly, "They know."

Brigadier Davis snapped irritably, "How could they possibly know?"

Ross looked at Crookshank who lowered his head rather than meet his eyes, and at Pryce, who said in a strangely controlled voice, "This is the Navy, the family if you like. Of course they bloody well know, *sir.*"

Outside they were all waiting, and he thought of Pryce's show of emotion, or as near as he could get. There was absolute silence as he spoke.

"I have to tell you that the loss of the submarine *Turquoise* has just been reported. Most of you will know her and her company." He saw her pale green dress at the end of the room, Villiers close beside her. "The operation carried out by Sub-Lieutenant Peter Napier and his partner Telegraphist Rice was a complete success." He looked around at their expressions, shock, compassion, the dull acceptance of war: it was all here in this room. "We shall not forget any of them. Thank you."

He walked through them, feeling their warmth, aware that some of them had reached out to touch him as he passed. The hero. He wanted to wipe his eyes with his fingers. The man for whom others died.

She held out a glass to him, her eyes dark with concern. "Some of my father's." She raised it to his lips, although he never knew what it had been. "I saw what it cost you. I spoke to Petty Officer Tucker just days ago. He was a good man."

He put down the glass and put his arms around her. "*Is* a good man, Victoria. I think he's alive." He looked at Villiers. "I *feel* it."

Somebody had put on another record, a rather well-used one. *Roses of Picardy.* His father had always liked that one.

She slipped her hand through his arm. "Walk with me."

Villiers watched them until they were swallowed up in the scented darkness. Everything was against both of them, and yet he knew he had never envied anyone so much.

9 | The Enemy

THE EXPLOSION was surprisingly muffled, partly because of the ship's massive cargo of steel rails and also because of the headland. But the effect was like a small tidal wave, and by rising to his knees Tucker could see the sea writhing in a giant whirlpool, the frightened birds flapping above it like blown leaves in a gale.

Rice muttered, "We did it." No pride or satisfaction, just the realization of what had happened to the three of them.

Tucker crawled to the officer's side and was grateful for his silence. It had been a savage effort to wade ashore after scuttling the chariot amongst heavy weed in about ten feet of water. Then they had got rid of their rubber suits and breathing gear, anything that might alert the enemy to their presence and bring all hell down on their heads. When they had finally been forced to cut Napier from his suit the pain had been too much for him. Tucker had carried him the rest of the way, to a small bowl-shaped depression on the side of a hill, well shielded by bushes and some sort of coarse nettle.

Tucker could feel Rice watching him as he re-opened the slit in the young officer's camouflaged denim blouse and lifted the dressing he had used to stem the blood. It was a deep wound: God knew what this place and the climate might do it. Napier groaned but did not open his eyes.

Rice asked anxiously, "What d'you think, Tommy?"

Tucker replaced the dressing. If only they had more of them. He said quietly, "If we can get help . . ."

Rice sounded scornful, angry. "*Help?* Where could we get that?"

"They told me the Burmese are friendly, and often helpful." Rice was still staring towards the sea. "God knows why. We did little enough for them!"

Rice said, as though he was thinking of something else,

"Remember that officer from the Chindits who came to watch us training?"

The officer's face formed itself in Tucker's mind. Screwed up, but so calm, so dangerously calm, not unlike the marine officer, Sinclair. Rice was going on about it. "His mob never took prisoners, he said. Too much of a handful, slowed them down." He watched Tucker almost fearfully. "Like when one of their own was badly wounded and couldn't keep up. They left him. With his gun, or maybe a pill like we've got."

Tucker opened his silk map and studied it. "We're not leaving him, Nick."

"I only meant . . ."

"I know. Now forget it. We'll move at night until we get the feel of things. There'll be fishermen and villages to the northwest of here. Fresh water and food. It'll suit me." He folded the map with great care, Rice's eyes on every move. "If we get jumped by a patrol or a search party, we'll say we were survivors from *Turquoise*. They might go for it."

Napier coughed slightly and opened his eyes. Tucker was surprised that he had not noticed how long his lashes were, like a girl's. Napier licked his lips. "Where are we?"

"Safe for the moment. The charge blew on time, by the way." He knew Napier had not even heard it. "They'll know about it soon enough back at H.Q."

Napier stared up at him vaguely. "There was a soldier." He attempted to reach for his wounded shoulder but Tucker took his hand away. Like a child, he thought. "What happened to him?"

"He'll not bother you again, sir."

Napier let his head fall back. "Thanks. It was my fault, you know."

Tucker saw Rice's mouth begin to open and said harshly, "You made a *mistake*. My dad always said that there was only ever one man who never made a mistake, and they crucified *him!*"

Rice said, "It's raining."

"See if you can collect some of it." He watched Rice crawl

away and then looked down as Napier's hand touched him.

"In my pocket. A flask."

Tucker unbuttoned his pocket and dragged out the flat silver flask. It must have cost an arm and a leg.

Napier stared at him steadily. "Brandy. Have some." As Tucker took a swallow he said, "Rice wants to ditch me. I heard him just now."

Tucker wiped the mouthpiece with his sleeve. At any moment they might be caught, tortured and God alone knew what. But he had wiped the flask as if they were at the bloody Henley Regatta. He said, "Nobody's getting ditched. I'll carry you until we can get help."

The hand tightened on his leg and Napier asked, "Do you think we shall? *Really,* I mean?"

Rice came back with his small folding cup in his hand. "Muddy."

Tucker tipped a few drops of brandy in it. "This'll do the trick."

Napier was raising himself on one elbow, his sweat showing what the effort cost him. "Let me see the map." He peered down at it as Tucker unfolded it again. "We should follow the bay. Better chance. Keep well clear of Rangoon and the inland roads." He groaned suddenly, "Oh, my God!"

Tucker supported his shoulder. *Come on, my son. Keep the grey matter working, like they taught you as an officer. Hang on, don't give in to it.*

Napier twisted round to look at him. "You knew my brother, didn't you?" He sounded quite calm, normal.

Tucker said casually, "Quite well. Liked him, more than I can say for some."

Napier smiled. "You're quite a card yourself!"

Rice hissed, *"Japs, three of 'em!"* He seemed unable to move. "Coming up the hill!" He stared round, his eyes wild. "What'll we do?"

Tucker drew his revolver and put Napier's in his right hand.

"You know what they told us. *Take one with you!*"

Then the rain started, noisy, violent, enveloping. Rice gasped, "Christ, they've run for cover! Don't like the rain!" He sounded crazy with relief.

Napier had his mouth open for the rain, the downpour soaking his bandage and making the blood look fresh, as if it had just happened.

He said softly, "Don't let them take me alive."

Tucker patted his arm and thrust the pistol into his waistband. "Try and rest. I'll have a quiet poke around when the rain eases off."

Rice heard him and said, "You'll come back, won't you?"

Tucker forced a grin. "While there's still some brandy left!"

Poor bastards, he thought. One scared out of his marbles and the other more afraid of letting the side down than of dying. He thought suddenly of Jamie Ross when he had briefed the chariot crews before that last Norwegian raid. "Go in and do the job. No heroics, understood? You're no use to me with your arse blown off!" He could recall it as if it was yesterday. He reached out to brush some wet hair from Napier's eyes. They had all laughed, except one, David Napier. He had been afraid, but nobody had realized it. Until it had been too late.

As the day wore on, they felt the first pangs of hunger. Tucker found a bar of chocolate wrapped in a waterproof bag, but it had melted so much that he had to scrape off the wrapping paper with his knife. He never even considered that the last time he had used the knife had been to kill the sentry.

They could have been on a desert island, or on top of the world. Nothing moved, and there was no sign of voices or vehicles when the rain eventually stopped in its usual abrupt way.

He examined his watch and his small compass. It would not do to creep off in the wrong direction. He had heard of a squaddie who had done that in the desert when his squadron of tanks had laagered up for the night. With the usual sense of cleanliness peculiar to the desert army, the man had walked away from the tanks to ease the demands of nature. He was never seen again, and had probably walked in circles until his strength had given out, and the desert had claimed another victim.

He checked his revolver last, and said, "Keep an eye on things, Nick." He glanced at the sub-lieutenant. "He's passed out again. We'll let him be."

Rice said, "I'll come with you, if you like."

Tucker clapped him on the shoulder. He could feel his apprehension, the fear of being left alone. Like the last one to die in a drifting lifeboat. Alone with a quiet crew of corpses.

As he left the hiding place, Tucker saw the sea fully for the first time, framed by two hills where they must have floundered ashore. Once he looked back, but saw nothing to reveal where his companions were hidden.

His feet slithered on wet leaves and running trails of mud. It was slow going. He thought about Napier. Suppose they could not find help for him?

Something crackled and he swung round, the pistol already at waist level. A youth was squatting beneath a tree, his body covered with what looked like an old army raincoat. He was quite young, about fifteen, and obviously unafraid of Tucker's gun and appearance.

Tucker held up one hand. "Friend."

The youth nodded, but regarded him gravely without speaking.

Tucker tried again. "You friend?"

The youth grinned, his teeth very white against his brown features. "*Yes, friend.* You soldier?"

And so it went on. When Tucker told him his name and asked him for his, the youth replied with such a mouthful that Tucker said, "I shall call you Mango. It's as near as I can get!"

The youth quivered with laughter. "*Mango!*"

Tucker made eating motions. "Food? There are three of us." If he was taking a chance, it was too late now.

The youth stood up and bowed. "I see you in water. Not tell Nippon soldier."

Tucker tensed. "Where are they?"

He shrugged. "Gone now. To my village. You wait, please. I fetch you when night come."

Tucker knew better than to try to follow him as he slipped away amongst the dripping leaves. He probably had ears in the back of his head.

The others were waiting for him. Napier seemed excited. "Mango, eh? First names already, or perhaps second!"

Rice was doubtful. "You trusted him? Just like that? He's probably rabbiting to the Nips right now!"

Tucker massaged his eyes. "He saw us come ashore. He could have blown the horn on us then, might even have got a reward." He looked at the officer. "He's taking us to his village. We might get your wound fixed up."

Napier slumped back again. "If not, you must go on without me."

Tucker groaned. "Don't you start. We're here, and we're going to get away, right?" He saw them nod in unison, the only thing they had done together since it had all started.

True to his word, the youth returned as darkness closed in from the sea. As a sign of good faith he brought a bowl of rice and some kind of sliced fish. He seemed surprised that the three of them were baffled by chopsticks.

Tucker said, "Excuse my manners, mate," and picked up the food with his fingers. "A nice bag of rock and chips would go down a treat right now!"

Then, in single file, they went down the hillside, Tucker carrying the officer over his shoulder like a sack. Rice brought up the rear, his eyes everywhere as if he expected a Jap behind each piece of cover. They came to a road, little more than a rain-rutted track, but left it to take another path through the trees. It was rough going, and Tucker was afraid that Napier might cry out with each savage jolt to his shoulder. But he had seen tyre tracks on the road. It was not as safe as all that, and their guide was well aware of it.

On another occasion when they paused to regain their breath, they heard a far-off, chilling howl, followed by several more from different angles. Like hyenas. Their young guide, in whispers and sign language, explained that the cries were Japanese sentries at the various checkpoints on the road, calling to one another without making any attempt to conceal their whereabouts. It sent shivers up Tucker's spine when he considered how close they were. He eased Napier's body on to his shoulder again and waited for Mango to lead on. God knew if they would ever find their hiding place again, but without Mango they would never even have reached this far.

And then suddenly they reached the village, a collection of huts and dangling fishing nets which seemed to run directly down to a river. Tucker sniffed the warm damp air. The river led to the sea. It was all they had to hold on to.

Several members of the village were present and one, obviously the headman, embraced their guide warmly and then said in good but slightly fractured English, "My son tells me of your plight." He studied Napier as they laid him on some rushes. A pot was bubbling in one corner, and the headman said, "We will use a local balm on your friend's arm." He bent over and ripped open the bandage. Then he sniffed the raw wound for several seconds. "Maybe in time. Save arm."

Napier closed his eyes and groaned. "Not that!"

Tucker knelt beside him. "It may do the trick. Give it a go, eh?"

The headman said, "Be strong." Then in a sharper tone to Rice and Tucker, "Hold him."

Napier fainted before they had completed cleaning the wound. Every touch must have been like a hot iron, each movement an agony. Then they brought the sickly smelling pot and ladled the thick mixture on to his arm where the bayonet had driven into the muscle and flesh. Bandages were brought and the wound rebound with a strange-looking leaf between it and the skin.

Tucker glanced around at the lined, impassive faces. All

fishermen, who would be killed without mercy if the Japs discovered what they were doing.

They brought more fish and rice, and a fresh-tasting green tea which was even more welcome. They all ate, even Napier.

Then the others departed, and Tucker guessed they would be going to prepare their boats for an early start.

The headman waited until they had finished, and seemed surprised when Tucker offered him one of the gold sovereigns. But he took it without comment and Tucker wondered if it had happened before. The headman said, "Tomorrow you hide, get back strength. Then we talk about escape."

Napier whispered, "Escape? How?"

Rice snapped, "Don't ask, just let him get us out of here!"

"My boy will look after you." He spoke his name, but it still sounded like "Mango."

He continued in the same mellow voice, "My people tell me about your underwater ship. Big explosion." He made a gesture like a fish darting through water. "Torpedo, yes?"

"We don't know." There was no point in revealing their role with the chariot. The headman probably imagined that a submarine had somehow managed to move so close inshore, and had fired on the grounded freighter.

The headman's eyes glittered in the lamplight. *"Torpedo."* He sounded definite.

Napier's mind was becoming clearer. He said, "How could the Japs have seen *Turquoise?* It's not possible."

The headman shook his head while he waited for his son to serve more tea. "You not understand. It was another submarine. I have seen it."

He unfolded himself and stood up. "I leave you here. You will be hidden if Nippon soldier comes. I must go and pray now with my fishermen."

"What a dignified old bloke." Tucker glanced around the hut. "Makes me feel a right scruff."

Rice asked, "Could there be a sub around here?"

Napier frowned. "No reports of one. Most Jap subs are being sent to the Pacific to fight the Yanks."

Tucker recalled the briefing, and said, "That's what I understood, too."

In the silence that followed, Napier touched his shoulder and winced. "It's funny, but this feels easier. I wonder how they know . . ."

Tucker leaned back against the wall, his hands behind his head. Napier thought the headman was mistaken, not used to such weapons of war. Tucker considered the man's ageless face, his authority and compassion. *Don't you believe it, my son!* He said, "I'll stand the first watch, right?"

Napier sighed. "Don't you trust them?"

Tucker grinned and loosened his revolver. "The Andrew taught me not to trust anyone, *sir!*"

He saw the headman's son curled up by the stove. "'Cept him, of course!" But the others were asleep.

The four days that followed seemed endless and unreal to Tucker and his companions. It was like being forgotten, written off by the outside world while they waited for something to happen. Most of the fishing boats had sailed and the village itself seemed all but deserted. Very rarely did someone pass their new hiding place, and it was obvious that they had been warned to avoid any contact whatever. A few women and some children had passed within yards of it with neither a glance nor any sign of curiosity. As though they were invisible.

The new hiding place was a long, low-roofed shed with barely enough room to move about. It was filled with spars and old rigging, fragments of fishing net and odd items of boat gear: fishermen were great hoarders, and strongly resented the necessity of docking their craft, thereby losing valuable time at sea.

Only Mango was a regular visitor, always with a ready smile and his usual mixture of odd English phrases and sign language. The one good thing had been Napier's improvement. Although he was still very weak from his wound and from loss of blood, the headman's remedy had worked wonders for him.

On this particular afternoon, Tucker was squatting by a boarded-up window, which he had loosened to give him a restricted view of the river. Once, he had made to draw his knife to prise open another plank, and was reminded of Napier's returning interest and authority when he touched his empty belt.

It had been Napier's suggestion that they bury their diver's knives and the other incriminating evidence like blood-chits, hacksaw blades and any other item that might make things worse for them if they were captured. It made good sense, Tucker realized, and he was thankful to see in Napier's clarity of thought a returning will to survive.

The headman visited them only once, and had touched vaguely on the subject of escaping. A boat would be contacted very shortly when the fishermen were in a certain area. The boat in question was not used for fishing, and the owner might be prepared to help them for payment, rather than out of any patriotic sense of duty.

Napier had hit on it when he had suggested that this mysterious owner was probably a smuggler. It was a risky trade at any time, but in the middle of the Japanese occupation it would be doubly so. If it could be arranged, the boat would carry them to a rendezvous where another "trader" would take them to a place of safety. It was little enough to go on, but it was all they had.

Rice was smoking, having persuaded the youth to bring him some cigarettes and matches. Unlike most sailors, Tucker himself did not smoke, but it was worth it to see Rice so unusually relaxed. At least it would keep him quiet.

Napier said, "I think we should hear something soon. Maybe later when they bring us the food." He looked very young and fresh, considering how rough they were living. Mango had brought soap and a cut-throat razor, a relic of the British garrison hereabouts, and after a careful start they had each shaved for the first time.

Tucker thought of his home again, and wondered if the news had reached them. A lot of young faces had vanished from those familiar streets; people had even begun to take it for granted. Until it came to the front door.

He felt his eyes drooping and Napier said, "Get your head down. I've got the weight."

Eating fish and rice without any kind of exercise would make him as fat as a pig, he thought. But he smiled to himself nonetheless. Napier was an officer again.

He could only have been asleep for minutes when he felt Rice jerking at his arm.

Napier was on his knees with his face to a crack, a bar of sunlight across his eyes like a silk cord. He glanced round at them. "A shot, or shots, I'm not sure!"

Tucker dragged out his revolver, his mouth suddenly dry. It was all so quiet and still, and they were talking of escape. Nothing could go wrong now.

He pressed his face to the boards. The river was moving unhurriedly; a few seabirds were crouching on an upturned boat. Nothing.

"Maybe it was on the road. A patrol, maybe."

Napier pressed himself closer to the crack, and winced with the effort. "No. It was closer. From the village."

Rice said, "I can smell smoke!"

They could all smell it now. Napier dragged himself upright by one of the centre supports until his hair was brushing the roof. "We must get out. Something's happened. We'd be trapped in here."

Tucker stared at him for several seconds. Then he pushed the revolver into his waistband and said, "I agree. But you're not fit to walk, not yet anyway."

The sunlight played across Napier's eyes again. Gratitude, or perhaps shame for being so helpless. But all he said was, "Not for much longer!"

Tucker said, "Open the bloody door, Nick." Then he hoisted

Napier over his shoulder and ducked through the low entrance, momentarily blinded by the river's reflected glare.

Rice had his gun in his hand and seemed to be dragging his heels. "Suppose they come to look for us, to bring us food an' that?"

Napier grunted with pain. "Keep going, for God's sake! It might be somebody else!"

Very slowly, they made their way towards the village, using the path of trodden grass their visitors had used to approach the old shed.

The smell of smoke was stronger and more acrid, and for the first time Tucker saw it drifting above the nearest huts like something solid.

He said, "It's the place where they fixed your wound." He felt Napier shifting against him, trying to see what was happening.

Rice was gulping air like a drowning man, his pistol moving from left to right like a talisman. He gasped, "If we find Mango . . ."

He fell silent as Tucker said harshly, "He can't help." It came out like a sob. "Not any more." With great care he lowered Napier to the ground and waited for him to find his balance, then he walked to the sprawled body lying across the track and stood looking down at it, knowing he would never forget or forgive.

Someone must have discovered that the youth was carrying food and cigarettes to unknown British servicemen. The Japs had stripped him naked and beaten him until his body was bleeding and bruised all over. Either he had been unable to answer their questions or, knowing his simple loyalty, it seemed likely that he had refused. They had tortured him with a heated blade, most likely a bayonet, on his face, his shoulders and his genitals. Tired of it, they had shot him through the heart.

Flames and sparks shot from a nearby roof and, as the hut exploded into flames, two Japanese soldiers ran on to the track. Tucker noticed that they were both laughing, their small pot-like helmets bouncing up and down as they scampered away from the flames, more like two schoolboys playing a prank than men who had brutally tortured and then killed a defenceless boy with an unpronounceable name.

Simultaneously, they saw Tucker and his companions and, like puppets, each unslung his rifle.

Tucker felt the revolver kick into his hand as he fired, hearing nothing, and with no emotion but a deep, grieving sense of loss. There was no time to reload. He flung the revolver away and dragged Napier's from his belt. "Hang on to me! We'll get to the river, find a boat!"

He lifted Napier over his shoulder again and stared round, his eyes blurring and stinging with smoke.

"Lend a hand, Nick! Back to the water, chop, chop!"

Then he began to run, shambling awkwardly with Napier's weight dragging on his shoulder. He croaked, "Bastard's run for it! I should have known!"

He felt something sticky on his fingers and knew Napier's wound had opened again.

It was like watching someone else. He could hear his own rasping breath, could see nothing but the narrow track with the gleam of water at the far end. But it was not getting any closer. He stared down at the ground and with his free hand he dashed the sweat from his eyes. When he looked up again he saw them. They had appeared from nowhere, as if they were figures of fear in his imagination. The same helmets, intent faces, levelled rifles.

In a calm voice he barely recognized he said, "I'm putting you down, sir." He felt Napier clinging to him, bleeding unheeded as they swayed together, hemmed by those same silent figures.

Tucker groped for his gun, but it had gone.

There was nothing more that he could do. Stupidly he heard himself mutter, "Sorry about this, sir . . ." He did not even feel the blow. There was only a sense of falling, and then nothing at all.

10 | A Prayer

THE STAFF-CAR swung round yet another bend in the road, the smart Royal Marine driver handling it with ease, although all his attention was focused on the two officers behind him.

James Ross watched the purple shadows on the hillside, and wondered if the girl named Victoria would be at the house this evening.

He had thought about her a great deal, although he had seen little of her since that night in the Mackenzie house when the news of *Turquoise*'s loss had broken. Ross had been kept unnecessarily occupied exercising the chariots against a moored target, all for the benefit of the famous war-correspondent, Howard Costain: it seemed he had only to make a request in high places to be granted just about anything he desired. If the Admiralty wanted this venture to remain Top Secret, he thought bitterly, they were not going the right way about it.

He sensed Villiers beside him; he was apparently content to remain silent within his own thoughts. Only once had he spoken, when they had passed the place where Second Officer Jane Clarke's body had been found. All that had been forgotten, or so it seemed. Villiers had said, "What kind of man could do that?"

A double question, perhaps. Was he thinking of Sinclair again, and the girl in England from whom he received occasional letters? With Sinclair now sharing their small mess, it was a dangerous thing to do.

The place had its own memories for Ross. How she had clung to the dead woman's hand while the rain roared down and the redcaps tried to cover the body. How he had held her then, and again in Pryce's office, impersonally, for Major Guest's benefit.

He guessed that Villiers was thinking now of the meeting to be held at Mackenzie's estate. Brigadier Davis would be there; like Pryce, he seemed to believe there were too many eyes and ears in and around the unit to keep their discussion secret.

It seemed likely that Davis had got the go-ahead for a landing on Singapore Island to meet the one-time Villiers employee, Richard Tsao. Madness perhaps, but Ross knew he would not let Villiers return on his own this time, no matter what happened.

He tried to find comfort in the thought that the cloak-and-dagger boys probably did it as regularly as clockwork. Even Sinclair had said that there were plenty of agents in Singapore, as well as in Malaya and Burma. A different kind of war; a different sort of man to wage it.

Ross touched his shirt pocket, where he was still carrying a letter he had received from his step-mother. *Evelyn.* The name seemed cool and practical, like her. They were separated now by far more than mere distance. It had read more like a letter from a business associate than one from a woman who had just lost her husband, writing to a son who had lost his father. Ross had never discovered what they had seen in one another, although she had been an undoubted asset to Big Andy's prospering salvage business. Evelyn's cousin was an accountant who had performed miracles with the company's books; his father's old partner and companion was no match for the world of commerce in war-time. She had mentioned another person who might make a welcome addition to the management.

Was that all? Or was Husband Number Three already in sight?

He stared moodily out of the window as two small boys waved at the car: his depression had made him strangely glad to get away from the base. A makeshift choir had been practising carols for Christmas, which was not far away. He recalled Tucker's pungent comment on one such occasion in Scotland: "That's it, mates—a bit of God an' good cheer, and then an almighty piss-up!"

It was impossible to think of him as missing, let alone dead. But as day followed day without news, Ross found it was becoming harder to keep even the faintest flicker of hope alive.

When Howard Costain had been with him at the chariot exercise attack, he had remarked casually, "What makes you all do it, I wonder? A death wish, a need to prove more than the other man?" Costain had been perched comfortably on a shooting-stick, smoking a black cheroot, his expensive suit suitably crumpled. Sleek, untouched, unreachable.

Ross had replied sharply, "Somebody has to do it. If we're to win, that is."

Costain had regarded him with a gentle smile. "You really believe that?"

Ross had been surprised at how angry he had sounded. "I do, as it happens. In my father's war there were no victors. This time that is not enough!"

"Your Major Sinclair seems to think that if the enemy is ruthless, we must be more so."

Ross had thought of the dead girl in his arms: the coldness of her skin, her empty stare, with Tucker's words still there like an echo. *Not your sort.* Now she was nobody's sort.

Villiers said abruptly, "Here we are again." Then, in a more relieved tone, "We're first, thank God."

Ross touched his arm. "Sorry, Charles. I'm bad company today."

Villiers ignored it, suddenly serious, even strained "Look, Jamie. I know what you said. But I won't hold you to it. You don't know Singapore like I do."

Ross found himself hearing the soft, sad voice as Victoria had spoken of it as home. He said, "I'm learning. I'd just feel better if we were together. God knows why."

The Royal Marine driver sank down in his seat as they left the car, disappointed that he had no buzzes to carry back to his mates. Bloody officers, he thought.

They were shown through the house by a servant and found Colonel Mackenzie sitting in a cane chair, immaculate in white jacket, a tall glass by his elbow.

Ross was relieved of his cap and said, "Excuse my rig, sir." A shirt and shorts seemed strangely out of place here.

Villiers sensed his discomfort and leaped in with chit-chat. "Is your daughter not here, sir?"

The Colonel's eyes crinkled, so that the massive white brows almost hid them. "She'll be along later." He looked at Ross. "Had a good day?"

Ross took a perfect pink gin and wished he had not had a drink before leaving the mess.

Villiers said succinctly, "Costain, sir."

Mackenzie chuckled. "Oh, *him!*"

To change the subject, Ross said, "Victoria told me the admiral was backing her commission, sir. Did anything come of it?"

"She'll tell you, I expect." He glanced at Villiers, who stood up quickly and said, "I'll take a stroll round the gardens if I may, sir, before the heavy guns get here!"

Mackenzie watched him leave. "Nice lad." He smiled, but there was no humour in it. "Should be a diplomat." He creaked forward in his chair. "The fact is, Victoria has turned it down. She didn't even think she'd get it, she's like that, but I believed she would after all she's done out here with your lot." He fidgeted uneasily in his chair, and Ross guessed that the Colonel and his daughter rarely shared their secrets with anybody.

"She's afraid I'd be lonely, and that if she goes to England on a course she would lose her local volunteer status, which she has here. She could be posted anywhere, although I think that would be good for her." He fell silent as the servant glided up to refill his glass. Then he said, "I'd miss her, of course, but a hell of a lot of people are going through it every day. You, for instance."

"There's nobody waiting for me, sir." He hesitated. "And in this kind of work . . ."

"God, we used to think the same, my boy! Two weeks was the average life expectancy of a subaltern in Flanders!" He looked beyond, into the garden, which was in darkness now. "We managed."

Brakes squeaked in the driveway and doors banged. There was a sudden sense of urgency.

The Colonel was on his feet; he could move quickly for so powerfully built a man. Then he said, "She may have told you.

There was another man in her life. A naval type, like you. She was in love with him, you see, and I must say I could see nothing against the fellow." He gave Ross a piercing stare. "It was real love, or so she thought."

Ross could hear Pryce's voice, and another's, Brigadier Davis. There was no more time. He asked, "What happened, sir? I'd like to know."

The Colonel looked away, past him. "He went back to England, got promoted, and married a *suitable* girl from Cheltenham. I'd have cheerfully killed the bastard!" He picked up his glass, but it was empty. "I still could!"

Pryce and Davis came into the light, the former in a perfect white uniform, the brigadier in a lightweight grey suit. Pryce shook hands with the Colonel and asked sharply, "Where's young Villiers? We have a lot to talk about."

Ross sat down again, noticing that his glass had been mysteriously refilled.

Pryce said, "Before Villiers comes in." He frowned at Davis, giving him his cue. "Tell him what you know."

Davis said, "I've had a report. They tell me that three survived the submarine's loss, presumably the crew of the chariot and one other."

Ross said, "I knew it. Mike Tucker would have stayed with them. I think he was trying to tell me that before he left. In case anything went wrong." He felt neither relief nor despair. It was simply a confirmation of something, an instinct he had trusted.

Davis frowned slightly, perhaps unused to being interrupted. "The area would have been swarming with Japs of course, after the explosion, but if they follow the drill I see no reason why . . ."

Pryce said, "What are their chances?"

Davis shrugged and took a glass. "Hard to tell. We have people working there but if your chaps are captured they'll probably be taken to Rangoon. The Japs have a big prison camp and jail there. If that happens they'll have to face the Kempetai, the Japanese military police."

Ross said harshly, "Tortured, you mean?"

"It is possible." He considered it. "More than possible."

Ross looked at his hands. They should be shaking. With revulsion and anger, with a burning pity for what had happened.

Davis said calmly, "I shall do what I can, but . . ." The final word was still hanging in the air as Villiers joined them. He saw their expressions, and knew Ross well enough by now to sense something had happened. He sat down without a word.

Pryce cleared his throat. "Still *'on'* for Singapore, Villiers?"

Villiers did not even falter. "Say the word, sir."

Davis looked at Ross. "When we first discussed this . . ."

Ross said, "I'm still *on* too, sir."

Davis pressed his fingertips together. "After what happened to your submarine, Mr Tsao's information may be even more important. It is a risk, but one that we must take."

Pryce murmured, "Hardly *we,* Hubert."

Davis turned a deaf ear. "Speed is everything. I'll have the Intelligence pack here by morning. After that . . . well, who knows?"

Ross asked, "Can I be kept informed about our people, sir?"

"Of course. Mustn't give up hope, what?" He had obviously written them off.

It was a long evening, despite the excellence of the meal, the high point of which was lobster-tail Surabaya. It was all Ross could do to maintain a façade of eating. The old Colonel certainly kept a good table, and must have trained his chef with care to prepare what were obviously his favourite dishes.

Villiers, in contrast to his own mood, seemed far more relaxed, as if he had been preparing himself for his inevitable return to Singapore and now the intolerable tension of waiting and the suspense were over.

Once or twice Ross felt the Colonel watching him, but even his colourful stories of the peacetime Indian Army and the outrageous characters in every officers' mess could not lift the shadows from his mind. Tucker, a survivor, and yet already probably a prisoner of the Japs; Peter Napier who, like his dead brother, had trusted him until it was too late to save him. The restless current of his thoughts made the conversation and the endless procession of wines seem merely a continuation of the same nightmare.

Eventually it was over, but it was obvious that Pryce and Davis had no intention of tearing themselves away from the Colonel's hospitality for a while yet.

Ross shook the Colonel's hand, his head throbbing from the pink gins and wine. When would he ever learn?

Outside, the night was cool, almost cold through the thinness of his shirt. He looked around, aware that the staff-car had gone; only Pryce's car and the smart Sunbeam Talbot were in evidence. He could almost feel her watching him in the darkness, her uniform coming palely towards him like a ghost.

"I will drive." She seemed suddenly uncertain. "Sir?"

Ross swallowed hard. "Where's Charles?"

"He went in the staff-car. I said I would take you back."

Ross grappled with it. "I can imagine what he thinks."

She did not move. "Do you care?"

"No. I'm very honoured." He held his cap in one hand. "I'm so sorry. I've had too much to drink."

She said softly, "It is not like you, I think." She waited for him to climb into the seat before slipping behind the wheel.

He said quietly, "Do you ever stop to wonder what it might be like if life could always be so beautiful?" She said nothing, as if she were afraid to interrupt. "Nice car, a lovely girl beside you—it's a dream. What everyone wants, if only they'd admit it."

She said in a small voice, "You've decided, haven't you? Made up your mind about the mission?" She was gripping the wheel with both hands, but did not flinch as he covered one of them with his own.

"There was really no choice. It's what I'm trained for. What I am." He looked past her, seeing her profile, her hair like a black wing on her cheek. "Your father told me . . ."

She turned on him. "Told you *what?*"

He kept his hand on hers. "That you decided against a commission in the Wrens. You could do it standing on your head, you know."

He felt her tension draining away. It had been like the hostility he had encountered at their first meeting.

"I know I could." One hand moved to the ignition but hesitated. "But you'll forget. I shall pray for you. And for Charles." She looked down. "Mostly for you."

He touched her face and felt the wetness there. "I've done worse."

She looked at him again, very aware of his sincerity with no attempt to impress or shock. "I know."

He said, "So, when I come back you will be here, Victoria?"

She nodded. Then she said, "When? How long?" She switched on the ignition as if she did not wish to hear the answer.

"I may not see you before I leave. There's a flap on, it seems."

"Then I will be brave." She tried to laugh. "For both of us."

He watched the trees gliding past in the headlights. Wanting to tell her, not knowing how. To share. He said, "You were in love?"

She gripped the wheel tightly, her hair flying in the breeze from the open window. "I knew he would tell you. I thought I'd be angry. Now I'm not so sure."

He said, "There is something you can do for me." He put his hand on her shoulder, and felt her whole body tense as if he had threatened her. He dragged the little case from his shirt and laid it beside her. "Keep this for me, Victoria. If anything goes wrong . . ."

She concentrated on the narrow road, her shoulder very warm under his hand.

"Who shall I . . . ?"

He said, "Keep it. There is nobody else."

She swung off the road and sat in silence, the car quivering around them while she switched on a light and opened the case on her lap. She whispered, "Oh, Jamie, it's your medal." She shook her head. "I'm not going to cry!" She looked at him and waited while he took her face in his hands.

How long they remained there like that, they had no idea. Suddenly she said, "Please kiss me now. We're almost there."

At the gates, a white-belted sentry clicked his heels and saluted. "Nice old night, sir!"

He heard the girl laugh as she drove into the compound.

Nice for some, anyway.

Mike Tucker opened his eyes very slowly and groaned as his face scraped across a rough concrete floor. Every part of his body throbbed and ached from the beating he had been given. His mind was still too dazed to remember the order of events, or to combat the wave of utter helplessness and despair which threatened to overwhelm him.

Minute by minute he tried to recall what had happened, but he could only feel the blows of bamboo rods on his back, his head and his legs, with at least four soldiers standing over him, breathless in their efforts to break him.

He moved his hands and was surprised that his wrists were not tied. There was light enough in this confined place to see the livid weals where the cords had been knotted tightly round his wrists. The Japs had dragged him to the truck, and the truck had carried them here. *Them . . .*

He peered around, almost afraid to lift himself in case they had broken his limbs. Where was Napier? At the same time he realized that there was frail sunlight coming through a small barred window. But no sound, except for his own painful breathing. Then he saw Napier. He was lying on his back, and for an instant more Tucker thought he was dead. He was quite still and his eyes were wide open, unmoving.

Carefully, waiting for the stab of agony, he took the weight on his knees. Then, inches at a time, he moved crab-like across the bare floor until he was at the young officer's side. He felt

Napier's chest and was almost moved to tears, something unknown to him. The eyes were on his face now, neither concerned nor frightened. Napier's clothing, like his own, was torn from the rough handling when the Japs had searched them. Tucker felt his own head, the dried blood and the swollen lumps.

Napier tried to lick his dry lips. "What time is it?"

Tucker glanced automatically at his wrist, but his watch had been taken, like everything else. "Early morning, I think."

Napier moved his head from side to side. "I'm so thirsty."

Tucker pushed the hair from Napier's eyes before crouching on his haunches while he examined the cell, and cell it was, not some makeshift prison. There was a pail in one corner, and an old wooden stool. Nothing else. They could be anywhere; he had no idea how long he had been unconscious in the vehicle, or over how much ground they might have travelled.

Napier said, "I hope Rice got away."

Tucker looked down at him. "Maybe he did." To himself he thought, sod him, he ran away and left us like rats in a trap. *Sod him.*

Napier whispered, "What will they do? To us, I mean?" He spoke so calmly, without even a trace of the pain he must be feeling from his wounded shoulder.

"Probably ask us about the explosion." Who cares, he thought. The bastards will kill us anyway.

Napier said, "I knew they were beating you. I wanted to help, to stop them."

Tucker grinned. "You weren't in any position to help anybody." He patted his torn sleeve. "But ta, anyway." He stared at the small window. "I'll bet they burned down the whole village because of what they did to help us. That poor kid."

Napier tried to lift himself on his elbows, but fell back again. "I—I think they took that pill away from me."

Tucker reached out and stretched his arm. They had enjoyed beating him. It would have killed a frailer man. He said, "You wouldn't have swallowed it, you know."

Napier said intensely, "Why do you say that? They might use force to get it out of us!"

Tucker thought about it. He found he could accept it, now that he knew there was no way out. "Get what out of us? What do we know? They'd be stupid not to put two and two together. I mean, we didn't land by parachute, did we?"

He put his finger to his lips and jerked his head towards the door. There were shadows along the bottom of it, somebody's feet, standing right against the outside. He whispered, "Company."

Napier said very steadily, "Name, rank and number. That's all I shall tell them."

Tucker wanted to shake him. But where was the use of that?

Footsteps, but not the clipped sounds of soldiers. Slow and dragging, tired. They stopped outside the door.

Here we go. He sat up slowly and clenched his strong hands into fists. *Not without a bloody fight, mate.*

The door banged open, hard back against the wall. A soldier, his cap pulled down over his eyes and a bayoneted rifle levelled waist-high into the cell, planted himself in the entrance. His eyes flicked from Tucker to the sprawled officer in the corner, then he rattled his rifle bolt and screamed, *"Koskei!"*

When they remained motionless, he stabbed the air with his bayonet and repeated, *"Koskei!"*

Tucker did not understand, but he knew how to obey a command. He stumbled to his feet and stood defensively beside the helpless Napier. It seemed to satisfy the soldier, and he stamped quickly outside into an apparently sun-filled corridor so that another figure could get past.

They stared at one another. He was tall and gaunt, his sunburned arms little more than skin-covered bones, and he wore khaki rags. Stitched to his tattered shorts was a faded red cross, probably once part of an armband. He had sparse grey hair and he was very unsteady on his feet, but his eyes, like his voice, were clear enough. "I'm to examine you." He looked at Napier.

"I am Captain Newton, Royal Army Medical Corps." He knelt down and, helped by Tucker, loosened Napier's deeply stained dressing. "There's not much I can do. I have no medicines and no drugs, nothing. I've lost so many here—malaria, dysentery, ulcers." He spoke in short, quick sentences as if every breath were precious. "They've cleared most of the camp. Some have been sent to Rangoon, others to some new working party, I'm not sure where." He was peering closely at the wound and apologized. "They broke my glasses a few weeks ago."

Tucker licked his lips. A few weeks ago. This man and skeletons like him were being allowed, or encouraged, to die. Newton said, "The only people remaining are here because they cannot walk." He looked up as more feet clattered in the building. "Captain Nishida is in charge here, but he will be leaving soon, I understand. He speaks English very well, but sometimes pretends not to. The one to watch is his sergeant, Ochi. His English is quite good, but he is a savage." He stood up very slowly. "This wound is *not* good." He looked at Tucker. "You will have to help him. I told you, there is nothing I can do."

Tucker asked quietly, "Is there no way to escape from here? Surely after all this time . . ."

Newton gave a small, twisted smile. "I've been here for over a year, I think. There is no escape but the final one." He faced the door, suddenly erect but pathetic in his eagerness. A Japanese soldier, taller and more powerful than most, filled the open doorway. Somehow Tucker sensed that it was Ochi. The savage.

He saw Newton bend over in a low bow, almost losing his balance in the process. The soldier's eyes, like bright black olives, swivelled to Tucker, and he jabbed at him with his cane.

Tucker bent in a similar low bow, hating it, sickened by what he had seen and what he was doing.

The soldier nodded importantly. "So! So! You pay respect to Nippon fighting men!" He slashed the air with his cane. "Otherwise . . ."

The doctor's voice dragged on the name. "Sergeant Ochi,

this officer is wounded and cannot walk."

It was Newton's way of warning them of what was about to happen.

The sergeant strode across the floor and looked down at Napier. "Nippon soldier never surrender. Die first." He made up his mind. "You." He jabbed at Tucker again. "Pick him up, carry like mule. Yes?" He laughed, and Tucker saw that the guard at the door was standing like a ramrod, his eyes staring at the opposite wall. He was frightened of the sergeant.

"Up we get." Tucker bent over Napier and grasped his uninjured shoulder. Then he gasped as the cane slashed him across the spine.

Ochi barked, "No talk. No speak. Here you are nothing!"

Napier gritted his teeth against the pain as he was hoisted over Tucker's broad shoulder. "Sorry to be a bother, Mike."

Ochi raised his cane, but Napier said, almost sharply, "Would brave Nippon soldier strike wounded officer?"

Perhaps the affirmation of rank had done the trick. The cane dropped harmlessly.

It was a short walk to the end of the corridor, but by the time they had reached another guarded door they were both sweating. Tucker noticed dark stains along the floor, and guessed they were his own blood when he had been dragged here. But he could recall none of it.

It was, or had been, some sort of office. There were a few chairs and an empty table, and a view through an opened window of what looked like a parade ground, iron-hard earth, stamped or flattened down over the years to defy even monsoon rain. There were logs scattered at one side of it, and a large blackened area as if there had been fires at one time. A few soldiers were standing about, and beyond them more ragged figures like the R.A.M.C. doctor named Newton. *They cannot walk,* he had said.

Sergeant Ochi shouted, "Officer *sit!*" The cane moved again and came to rest on Tucker's arm. "You are non . . . commissioned . . . rank. You stand!"

Tucker bobbed his head after making Napier as comfortable as he could. "Yes, sergeant." As their eyes met, he added to himself, *you fat-gutted pig!*

Another door was opened by an unseen soldier and an officer Tucker assumed to be Captain Nishida entered. After returning Ochi's salute, he seated himself very carefully on the chair opposite Napier. Tucker thought he was the neatest person he had ever laid eyes on. Very slim, probably in his twenties, and dressed in such a perfectly fitted uniform that the open shirt collar looked as if it had been pressed over the tunic with an iron. He ignored Tucker and asked simply, "What were you doing here?"

Napier steadied himself against the chair-back. "I can give you my name, rank and number. According to International Law . . ."

Nishida raised one hand. He seemed neither angry nor particularly hostile. "Do not waste time. The laws are not made by God, and they are broken by men. You have no place of safety hiding behind such . . ." he hesitated and searched for a word. "Futile deceptions."

Napier said, "I do not understand."

Sergeant Ochi unrolled a blanket on the table. Napier's silver flask, some papers, one of the revolvers and, to Tucker's fury and dismay, his own small oilskin pouch with all the rest.

"You are an officer. You must know what you were doing. You are terrorists, saboteurs, cowards, is that not so?" He did not wait for an answer, but pushed something across the table and watched Napier's reaction with mild interest. "What is this?"

Napier said, "A compass."

Tucker swayed forward and saw the guards raise their rifles instantly. It had to be Rice's compass; he and Napier had buried theirs. Rice must have used it to buy cigarettes. He tried not to recall the boy's burned and mutilated body, left like so much rubbish on the track.

Napier said steadily, "I did my duty."

Nishida touched his chin. "Nippon soldier never surrender. Why did you?"

Napier shrugged and winced. "I was injured. There was no choice." He added hoarsely, "Your men murdered that helpless boy."

"I have my duty also. He was known to be helping you. He refused to co-operate."

"So you killed him."

"Tell me again. What were you doing? How did you blow up the ship?"

Napier asked, "Can I have something to drink, please?"

"Certainly. Presently. I know you were brought by submarine. I know also that the submarine was destroyed, yes? But how did you sink the ship? What kind of explosive, that kind of matter?"

Napier shook his head. "It's no use."

Nishida rapped out three words, and two of his men seized Napier's arms and dragged him on to his back on the floor.

Tucker lunged forward to help him, but two bayonets pricked his chest. The soldiers' intent faces showed no reluctance; they wanted to kill him.

Napier cried out to him, "I won't! Tell them I didn't!"

Tucker nodded heavily, and felt the bayonets' unwavering touch. Napier was losing his strength; one of the soldiers was kneeling on his torn shoulder while the others held his arms and legs. Ochi waited while one soldier pinched Napier's nostrils and then, with obvious concentration, he began to pour a can of water into Napier's mouth.

Tucker had seen men drown before, by accident or design. It made little difference if you did not have the strength to fight it.

Napier was choking, his eyes staring wildly while Ochi continued to pour from the can.

Tucker glanced desperately at Captain Nishida. "Stop them!"

But Nishida had opened the oilskin pouch and was studying the little photograph. He looked up. "Wife? Soldier-woman?"

Tucker wanted to scream, to kill him. Evie in her clippie's uniform, a soldier-woman.

A man appeared in the doorway and muttered to his captain. Nishida raised his hand. "Enough! Put him in the chair!"

Napier was somehow still alive, choking and retching, water pouring from his mouth.

Nishida looked at the raised bayonets and they were instantly withdrawn.

As Ochi gripped Napier's hair and dragged his head up to revive him, he said to Tucker, "My men have found one of the diving suits. The rest is for someone else to decide." He turned towards Napier and raised his voice. "You are stupid, not brave. You will be taken to Rangoon where the Kempetai will attend to you."

Tucker said bluntly, "To be killed, is that what you mean?"

"Eventually, yes. I think you will pray for death for a long while!" He handed the oilskin pouch to Tucker. "Brave woman go fight for her men!"

Tucker carried Napier back to their original cell where, surprisingly, a small amount of rice and tea was brought for them.

Napier said between fierce bouts of coughing, "They should have done for me."

Tucker said, "We came together. We'll stick that way." He pushed the rice-bowl on to his lap. "My guess is we'll be moved today." He tried to smile. "The room's been booked by another guest!"

He saw Napier's head nod with exhaustion. Poor little bugger, he thought, you've just about had it, haven't you?

He watched the sunshine and tensed as he heard the sound of marching feet. Very quietly, he climbed on to the only stool and gripped the window-bars to support himself. There was a squad of soldiers in two lines in the compound, a firing party, perhaps. Then he saw Nishida and the squat sergeant, standing in the shade of an overhanging tree.

Tucker touched the oilskin pouch in his pocket. *She was with him.* Now two soldiers were dragging an inert shape across the beaten ground. He knew immediately that it was Nick Rice. Even at this distance he could see the blood on his face, the way he was groping at the soldiers as if he could not see, as if he did not know what was happening.

Napier sensed the silence. "What's going on?"

Tucker made himself watch as they dragged Rice to one of the abandoned logs and threw him across it. The onlookers, in ragged scraps of khaki, did not even appear to notice. They were beyond caring, beyond every human emotion.

Only then did Rice show some sign of agitation, as he was rolled on to his back with his shoulders across the log. Sergeant Ochi strode into the sunshine and stood over him.

Tucker watched, nauseated, but rendered helpless as if he had been drugged.

The big sword rose above the sergeant's head and shoulders, and seemed to remain motionless in the bright sunshine like glass. Then it dropped.

The black stain Tucker had noticed earlier had not been from fires. It was blood.

He made himself kneel by Napier's side, and without speaking he took his hand. After a long time he said, "It was Rice, sir. They just killed him." He sounded very calm. "I don't know any proper prayers . . ."

Napier stared luminously at him; at his pain and his anger. "I'll say one for the two of us."

It was all they had left.

11 | A Bloody Miracle

THE LAUNCH turned in a wide arc and headed directly towards the big submarine depot-ship, which was moored bows-on to the shore. The two passengers, dressed in light khaki drill with only their shoulder-straps giving any display of rank, watched the passing array of troopships, oilers and fleet escorts in silence. Ross was not sure how he felt: there was, he thought, a certain relief that he was doing something again, rather than merely supervising others. He had noticed the marked change in his companion during the last frantic preparations for the mission to Singapore. Villiers seemed strangely relaxed, with none of the expected signs of strain or anxiety. Like somebody anticipating a return home after long absence.

They would be taking passage in the submarine *Tybalt,* the outboard boat of the only pair remaining alongside the depot-ship. She was a sister boat of *Turquoise,* a grim reminder, if one was needed. Her skipper had been a close friend of Bob Jessop, so it was likely that their presence aboard might be regarded as yet another unnecessary risk factor.

The dapper Brigadier Davis, who had attended the last briefing before taking off for Bombay and eventually London, had been definite about it. "Of course there are *risks,* gentlemen. Four years of war have proved that repeatedly. This Richard Tsao is trustworthy, according to our Intelligence sources, but only up to a point. If he has information of true value, the risks will be justified. If not, Mr Tsao can be given to the Japs with my blessing!"

Ross looked at Villiers. This morning, while they had been waiting to meet Captain Pryce and the brigadier, he had said quite suddenly, "I had another letter."

Ross did not need to be told from whom. He had been aware of Villiers's anxiety during that last dinner with Colonel Mackenzie, when the girl had waited to drive him back to the unit H.Q. When he had held her and they had kissed. Now, more like a dream than ever.

But he had sensed that Villiers had been putting up a brave front throughout the meal, and now the reason was very clear.

"She wants to break it off, Jamie. She was hoping for a divorce, but now she thinks it's impossible. Even her father seems to think she should stick with Sinclair." He had hesitated. "She's afraid of him, you see."

"And what about you? Do you still feel the same?"

Villiers nodded, and had looked very young and vulnerable. No wonder she had fallen for him. "I love her. I can't think of anybody else."

Sinclair was not being sent to England after all. Not yet, anyway, and it seemed increasingly possible that Pryce might want to use his particular skills if the Singapore venture proved to be more than a red herring.

Nor did Sinclair improve on acquaintance. He had been in the mess one evening when somebody was reading an item in the newspaper aloud: some old dear being interviewed about war-time marriages. Sinclair had interrupted coldly, "What the hell does a happy marriage have to do with it? These sentimental fools make me want to puke. A marriage is either suitable or it is not. Everything else is a tedious obstacle."

A newcomer to the mess had asked jovially, "Doesn't a woman have any point of view in this, Major?"

Sinclair had stared through him. "If you think like that, any woman would walk right over *you!* You really are pathetic!" Then he had stalked out of the mess. Ross had been glad that Villiers had not been present. It would have confirmed his worst fears.

Villiers said with a quiet intensity, "If he lays a hand on her, I'll kill him."

Ross touched his arm as the towering shadow of the depot-ship shut out the sunlight. "Take it easy. We'll talk about it later, if you like."

Villiers said tightly, "Yes. I *would* like."

The launch's wash surged against the outboard submarine's saddle-tank and Ross found himself thinking of *Turquoise*. What it must have been like for Mike Tucker and the chariot's crew. Perhaps Brigadier Davis was right to dismiss so casually the conventional standards of war. Why should they matter? What was the difference between bombing a town or city from the sky, regardless of the innocent who suffered, and torturing a man to death to obtain vital information for the survival of your country?

But he was not convinced. There were always standards, no matter which side you were on. Man must have the last word. Only the bomb and the torpedo were impartial, indifferent.

It was a different sort of war in the jungles of Burma: no wonder the famous Fourteenth Army was bitterly called "the Forgotten Army" by the troops who fought each day against an enemy so ruthless that they had themselves become equally hard. No prisoners, no quarter, no mercy. Their war was more like a savage struggle to stamp out a terrible disease than an effort to defeat human beings.

Have we come to that?

They crossed the two submarines and ran lightly up the long accommodation ladder where the O.O.D. was waiting to receive them. Ross imagined he could feel their eyes watching them. *Where to this time? What are the odds on getting away with it?*

He thought of the girl's nearness in the car, the break in her voice when she had opened the little case and realized it contained his Victoria Cross.

Of course it mattered. Lives mattered; faith mattered; hope and decency mattered. Davis was wrong if he believed otherwise.

At the top of the ladder they exchanged salutes, and Ross found himself glancing at the nearest troopship, its rigging adorned with khaki clothing hung out to dry.

Was there someone aboard her, or the next one beyond, who had a Wren officer's hat-badge hidden away, a souvenir, or "trophy" as Guest had put it, to remind him of assault and murder?

Could you ever live with it? Perhaps even take pleasure in a girl's dying appeals?

He touched his pocket, wishing he had something Victoria had held or used. Like Mike Tucker with his photograph.

The O.O.D. said, "The Commodore, Submarines will see you now, sir." Ross stared up at the sky. Clouding over. All the better for what they must do.

If Tucker had been here, he would have said, "One more time, eh? The old firm!"

He turned and clapped Villiers on the shoulder, unaware that two seamen with brooms had stopped to watch them. "Here we go, Charles. We'll be back. Remember, we've both got a lot to live for."

At the end of the day, as the sunset ran deep red down the horizon, a submarine, low and dark like a shark, slipped her moorings and headed away from the crowded anchorage with barely a ripple to mark her departure.

On the coast road above the bay a solitary car was parked without lights, the windows open so that the girl had an unhindered view. She stared at the small dark sliver until it became confused with the wakes of fussy launches and the slow, even swell of the ocean beyond.

It was like losing part of herself. Something she had found was already slipping away out there in the shadows. She could almost hear his voice, so close that he could have been beside her. *It's what I'm trained for. What I am.*

She wound up the windows and said aloud, "I will not cry." And in a smaller voice, "I love him. I cannot help myself."

She wiped her face and switched on the ignition. But any passer-by would have noticed that it was quite a long time before the car drove away. Then there was only darkness.

Charles Villiers licked the flap of the envelope and sealed it down on the wardroom table with his fist. It was like some sort of private statement or pledge.

Ross said, "One for the skipper's safe, Charles?"

"Just in case." He looked up at the curved deckhead, his mind only partly adjusted to the sound of the submarine's discreet machinery. "I wish to *God* we could get started!"

Ross glanced again at his folio of secret orders and instructions. During their four days at sea after leaving Trincomalee he must have studied them a hundred times, seeking flaws, or some misinterpretation of local information. It was totally unlike all those other times. Then he had had all possible resources at his disposal. On this mission, mercifully unnamed, they were listed as passengers. In many ways, it was true. Once off the submarine, they would have little more than trust in people they did not know, and only the clothes they stood up in, to sustain them.

It was strange to realize that he was even more of a passenger than Villiers. *He* was the key to the whole operation, the only one who knew their contact, the man who had worked for his father and the once-powerful company.

Often, in the privacy of his bunk with the curtains drawn, he had thought of Victoria. If they ever got back from this harebrained scheme . . . He tightened his jaw. *When* they got back, she would still be there.

The general information from Naval Intelligence was surprisingly good, up to a point. But there were still a lot of *ifs* and *maybes* that might cause the operation to be cancelled. To face up to the worst option, someone down the line might already have betrayed them.

The wardroom curtain was pushed aside and *Tybalt*'s commanding officer, in crumpled shirt and shorts, entered and sat down beside them. Lieutenant John Tarrant was not new to submarines, and he knew the hazards in these restricted waters probably as well as his dead friend Bob Jessop.

Ross had noticed that he was short on humour, both with his officers and his ratings, something fairly unusual in this elite branch of the service. It was Tarrant's first command, so maybe that was the reason for his somewhat rigid approach to almost everything. Perhaps he was also very conscious that he was outranked by at least one of the "passengers." Whatever it was, he seemed unable to unbend.

He said, "It looks like a go, sir. No signals to the contrary." He stared at the quivering curtain and seemed to see the whole chart laid out in his mind. "I shall surface tomorrow night as arranged, twenty miles southwest of Penang Island. If signals are satisfactory, I will transfer you to the other vessel."

Ross nodded. Most submariners would have said *about* twenty miles, to be on the safe side, but not this one.

Villiers looked up, aware of the vague tension between them. "The vessel is the tug *Success,* a big sea-going job. Worth her weight in gold in the lighterage business."

Tarrant eyed him calmly. "Is that a fact?"

Ross ignored it. "What would she be doing in Penang, Charles? D'you have any idea?"

Villiers shrugged. "Georgetown used to be quite a busy port until the Japs invaded Malaya. Our people dismantled some of the docks before the pull-out, but lighters might still be needed there. A well-known tug, presumably in the employ of the Japanese, would be the obvious choice for us."

Tarrant said to Ross, in the same detached tone, "The Malacca Strait is less than a hundred and fifty miles wide at that point, with a maximum of forty fathoms to play with. It *should* be all right, but one sign of a trap and I'll blow the thing out of the water!" He stood up. "Please excuse me, sir. I have to tell my people what we're doing." He hesitated by the entrance. "Once you are aboard that vessel, there's *nothing* I can do."

Ross sighed as the curtain fell back into place. "A real little ray of sunshine!"

Villiers laughed. "I'm glad you decided to come along, Jamie."

Ross smiled. *Jamie.* Tarrant would address him as—*sir* until orders directed otherwise.

It was always a difficult command to hold. Some failed because they needed to be popular, others because they could find no common ground with their officers and men. One thing about Tarrant, like him or otherwise: he would never crack, even at the gates of hell. He could imagine Pryce being much the same when he had commanded a submarine.

Villiers said suddenly, "If Richard Tsao says we can slip into Singapore, then I trust him."

Ross looked at the sealed letter. It was about four hundred miles to Singapore from the pick-up point off Penang. They would need a little more than trust.

True to Tarrant's promise, the submarine flooded tanks and dived well before dawn. The watches settled down, and the boat was soon filled with the smells of greasy tinned sausages and a welcome and unexpected issue of bacon.

The other officers were friendly enough, but Ross could sense their eagerness to get the mission, or their part of it, over and done with. Above on the surface, in that other world where men fought and died, or hunted one another like animals in the jungle, the hourly problems were entirely different.

Here, war showed its face in many devious ways. The first lieutenant raised his mug of tea and exclaimed suddenly, "Happy Christmas, gents!" They stared at one another with surprise and disbelief until the sub-lieutenant, the youngest member of the wardroom, lowered his head and sobbed quietly over his plate.

The first lieutenant watched him push away from the table, but said nothing. Ross remembered that someone had told him the subbie's family had been wiped out in an air-raid on Portsmouth. The mention of Christmas had broken him.

The first lieutenant met his eye and lifted his shoulders with a slight shrug. There was nothing anyone could say. No words. Not any more.

"All set?" Ross gripped Villiers's arm. "I'm depending on you." In the restricted lighting of the control-room he saw the white, reassuring grin.

"I hope you don't regret it, *sir!*"

Tarrant was waiting by the periscope, and said impatiently, "She's there, right enough. Starboard bow." Over his shoulder he snapped, "Stand by to surface."

Everything else was prepared: gun crew at the foot of the ladder with the lookouts, the deck party up forward ready to open the main hatch and launch the small dinghy.

As an afterthought Tarrant asked, "Care for a look, sir?"

Ross crouched over as the smaller attack-periscope hissed out of its well. Then he saw it: the irregular blink of a light, something which could if necessary be explained or excused as an unfastened deadlight swinging open across a scuttle with each roll of the hull.

He said, "Let's go." To Tarrant he added, "Thanks for the ride."

They walked from the control-room, feeling the silent stares from the men they were leaving behind. Tarrant called after them, "Good luck!" The rest was lost in the roar of compressed air, while the deck tilted to the angle of surfacing.

Villiers was tense, but managed to retort, "Actually, sir, we rely on skill!" It was unlikely that anyone heard him.

The damp air rushed to greet them through the open hatch. Men in oilskins were already tilting the dinghy over the edge of the casing. There was low cloud, and one bright star to break the darkness.

Ross heard the sharp click of the deck gun's breech-block and could picture the slender barrel training round towards the tug, as clearly as if he were up there with them. If the tug intended to ram them it would do little good, he thought. Like stopping a charging elephant with a boat-hook.

Then they were in the pitching dinghy, water slopping over them, surprisingly icy after the heat of the day. It seemed no time at all before they were bouncing alongside the tug's overhanging quarter, where a ladder was already in position. Ross seized it, conscious of the pressure of his revolver against his hip.

Somebody in the dinghy reached up to touch his shoulder. The last contact. Like all those times. A voice called, "What a bleedin' way to spend Christmas!"

He reached the deck, with Villiers pitching over the bulwark beside him.

A quick glance at the heaving black water. But they were alone.

Mike Tucker gritted his teeth against the pain and tried to steady himself beside a pile of sacks filled with rice. Apart from the other beatings he had received from his captors, he had been punched in the face by the Japanese sergeant, Ochi, when they had been bundled into the truck for their journey to Rangoon. His face was badly bruised and his eye was still swelling, so that he could barely see out of it.

The road was very narrow and deeply rutted, and branches and fronds occasionally scraped the sides of the truck like claws. It was an old three-ton Bedford, abandoned by or captured from the British Army, its original camouflage paintwork crudely daubed with vivid Japanese characters. From the way it was lurching and rattling, it seemed likely that it had not been serviced since it had changed ownership. There were two armed soldiers with them at the rear of the truck, smoking cigarettes, and making threatening gestures with their rifles whenever a local cart or wagon had appeared to be blocking their progress. A big wagon drawn by two yoked oxen had almost toppled over the edge of the track when they had fired their rifles in the air to frighten them and their owner out of the way. The soldiers had laughed delightedly, like the two Tucker had shot after finding Mango's mutilated corpse. It was hard to think clearly: there was too much pain, and an increasing desperation, which left him unable even to guess how long it had been since they had first stumbled ashore from the scuttled chariot.

His hands were cruelly tied behind his back; his arms throbbed, as if all circulation had stopped. Napier lay with his head against Tucker's outstretched leg, unconscious or uncaring it was hard to tell. They had not bothered to tie his arms, either because they saw that he was helpless or because their code required them to respect his rank as an officer. It was just another part of the madness.

Occasionally Tucker could hear the Japanese sergeant's voice; he was in front with the driver. Making sure, Tucker thought, that he wouldn't miss the opportunity of seeing them handed over to the military police for further questioning.

Tucker clenched his fists and bit back a groan as the pain lanced through his wrists. To get his hands round that pig's neck, for only a few seconds. It would be something. He felt Napier move his head and heard him mutter, "Thirsty. Where are we?" He was trying to roll over in order to see him. "Where's Rice?"

Tucker answered patiently, "He's dead, sir. They done for him, remember?"

"Yes." He gripped his wounded shoulder. "What happened to the Jap officer, Nishida?"

Tucker sighed. Napier's memory was coming back. Perhaps it would be better if it did not. He said, "Gone ahead in style, in a posh car. Enjoying his little self!"

Napier said in a small voice, "He stole my flask. My father gave me that." His words trailed away and for a moment Tucker imagined he had fainted. But he continued eventually, "They were so pleased when I told them I was with James Ross, David's friend." His own words seemed to hit him like a physical blow. "Oh God, what will they think when they hear what's happened? First David, now me!"

Tucker watched the two soldiers; he could just see their caps above the pile of rice sacks. This was madness too, of course. Like a chum of his, who'd caught a dose off some tom in Chatham. He had been married, and so shocked and disgusted by what had happened that he had hanged himself in an air-raid shelter at the barracks. Madness. But maybe it had seemed that there was no other way out.

He was surprised to hear himself sound so calm, but he had to make Napier understand. *Understand.* "My hands are tied." He watched the two heads beyond the sacks. "Are you listening?"

A long pause. "Yes. I—I'm sorry . . ."

Tucker said, "*Listen.* If I roll over, do you think you could untie them?" He closed his eyes, and felt the injured one throb with pain. *What was the use?*

At first he thought Napier was confused. "Get away, you mean? Escape?" Then it sounded more like sudden fear, the thought of being alone.

Tucker said, "Together, remember? Good or bloody useless, we keep together."

"I don't know. My mother once said . . ." He fell silent again, and Tucker gasped as one of the wheels crashed into a deep rut. The whole vehicle felt as if it were falling apart.

One of the soldiers was on his feet, swaying about like a dockside drunk as he tried to keep his balance while he urinated over the tailboard.

If my hands were free . . . He stared at the muzzle of the soldier's rifle where it rested on the sacks. It would not be there for long. The bloody place would be alive with the bastards if they escaped. But to have a go, even kill a couple before they finished them, as they had finished Nick Rice. The soldier said something and his companion chuckled, then he slumped down again and the rifle moved out of reach.

For an instant more Tucker believed he had imagined it. There was so little feeling in his arms. But he leaned over, his eyes still on the two heads while Napier's fingers found and then fumbled with the tightly knotted cords behind him.

"That's it, my son." *Poor little sod.* He could hear Napier's sharp, painful breathing; every movement must be agony for his wounded shoulder, as if the bloody truck wasn't bad enough.

If Sergeant Ochi chose to stop the old Bedford for any reason, or came round to inspect his charges, it might at least spare them the horrors of the military police.

Napier was not going to be able to do it. What little strength he had left would soon fail. His fingers were pulling at the cords as if entirely separate from their owner, who lay much as before with his head against Tucker's leg.

Napier murmured, it sounded more like a sob, *"One!"* Even through and beyond the pain, Tucker could feel his triumph.

"That's more like it, sir. Just a couple more."

Napier's head moved as if he were trying to nod. "Never any good at it, you know. Nor wire-splicing. Didn't see the point of it, really."

Tucker waited, his heart thudding. "Right, sir. Whoever heard of an officer soiling his hands with that kind of lark?"

Napier almost laughed. "You really are a card. I told you before." His fingers lost their grip and he swore quietly. He could not go on.

Tucker sighed. "A real bundle of laughs, that's me."

Napier said softly, "Sorry I let you down. Can't quite manage—"

For a split second, Tucker imagined they had run over a landmine or collided head-on with another truck, even though his mind screamed that it was impossible.

It was an explosion, not close but not far away either. There were other sounds too: something breaking or falling, much closer to the truck, which had lurched to a violent halt. Tucker heard things crashing amongst the trees, birds screaming as they flapped away from the violent disturbance. Napier gasped, "What was it?"

"Never mind that. One more go—*come on,* sir." He felt the sweat pouring down his face and chest. It was too late. Someone had climbed down from the driving cab and the two soldiers were leaning over the tailboard, pointing and shouting, obviously alarmed by the sudden explosion.

Tucker raised his head slightly and saw part of the road behind the truck, dust hovering above it like haze. Maybe it had been a plane crashing. But there was no smoke, nor any smell of fire. Then he saw the ox wagon, the one they had frightened off the road. It was standing quite still, as if the man in charge had not decided what to do.

Ochi's unmistakable voice was shouting angrily, and he saw

the man by the wagon wave a stick, as if to point out that he had no room to turn or move aside to allow the truck to reverse along the track.

Napier whispered, *"Three!"*

Tucker moved his hands very carefully, the sudden pain almost unnoticed as he realized what Napier had managed to do. The sergeant was just below the tailboard, and when he shouted again the truck began to reverse, no doubt intending to force the wagon off the road. What was the point, Tucker wondered. Why not drive on? The man with the wagon was waving his stick again, jabbering, pleading perhaps. He turned in a shaft of dusty sunlight, and Tucker felt a hand tighten on his heart.

He whispered to Napier, "I don't believe it. It's the old bloke, sir—the village headman. Mango's dad." It made no sense. He saw Ochi turn to glare at his men, his face contorted with fury. Tucker remembered the skeletal doctor. A savage, he had called him.

He whispered urgently, "Stay here an' lie doggo! It's now or bloody never!" He gripped the sacks and knew that Napier was reaching out to him with one hand. To wish him luck, to prevent him from leaving? None of it mattered. Just his legs and his hands. If they gave out now . . .

With a great heave he hurled himself over the sacks, and he had a rifle in his hands almost without knowing how it had got there. There was no time to discover how it worked, or even if it had one up the spout. The rifle shone in the sunlight like a club, smashing the face of one of the soldiers to a bloody pulp, knocking him bodily out of the truck. The engine was roaring and grinding, so that nobody even heard his short, frantic scream as the rearmost wheel rolled over him. The other soldier, the one he had disarmed, had vaulted over the tailboard and was shouting for assistance.

Tucker jerked the rifle bolt and heard a bullet click into place. If there was a safety-catch, it made no difference now. He almost fell as he dropped down to the road. Ochi was standing beside the crushed body near the truck's wheels, a pistol in one hand while he drew, so unhurriedly that it seemed like a film in slow motion, the heavy sword that hung from his belt. The last thing Nick Rice had seen on earth.

The old Bedford had stopped, and in the silence it seemed as though he had suddenly gone completely deaf. All Ochi had to do was pull the trigger, and yet he did not move.

Tucker saw a movement from the trees, and then another. There was a glint of weapons, too. It must be more Japs, and he couldn't even get back to Napier, comfort him, prepare him . . .

The men who stepped on to the road were filthy, their camouflaged uniforms stained and torn as if they had been living in ditches and swamps for a long time.

Tucker raised the rifle very slightly to waist level, the muzzle towards the motionless Sergeant Ochi.

One ragged figure, a Sten-gun carried loosely in the crook of his arm, snapped, "*Easy,* now! Just lower the bloody thing, will you?"

Tucker's mind almost cracked. To hear the level, educated voice coming from such a scarecrow: it could have been one of his own officers. The Sten-gun jerked slightly, and more men spread out across the road.

The voice continued calmly, "We're a bit pushed for time, old son. I'm Percy Townsend, Gurkha Rifles." His free hand gestured to the roadside, while the Sten remained quite still. "And this reprobate is Teddy, our illustrious sapper from the Royal Engineers. I expect you heard his handiwork just now, what?"

Tucker said nothing, barely able to grapple with it. *Chindits.*

"We blew the bridge over yonder. Afraid a Jap staff-car went up with it." He and the sapper were grinning like conspirators. "Now, if you'd been any closer behind it . . ." He shrugged. "No need to elaborate."

Somebody called, "There's rice on the truck, sir!"

"Good. Bring as much as we can carry." To Tucker he said, "You must be one of the naval types we heard about."

Teddy, the sapper, held out a tin of cigarettes. "I thought there were three of you?"

Tucker looked at the ground. It had only just stopped moving. "They beheaded one. My officer's in the truck. He's badly hurt."

He saw their quick exchange of glances and exclaimed, *"I'm not leaving him!* Not after what he's been through!"

They studied his bruised face and lacerated wrists, then the Gurkha officer said, "You've not done too badly yourself."

Tucker felt someone beside him and turned as the old headman put his arms around his shoulders.

"They kill my son! He was your friend."

For the first time Tucker was aware that there were other Burmese present. Some with Lee-Enfield rifles, some armed only with knives and crude spears. They were all victims now. He said, "I was so sorry about your boy. I am proud he was my friend."

What would happen now to this man and his companions? How might they be judged? Guerrillas? Terrorists? Patriots?

Townsend watched his Gurkhas while they disarmed Ochi and the other two Japanese. Matted and wild-looking they might be, but Tucker recognized the tough, disciplined little soldiers underneath. To their officer he remarked, "You're lucky, sir, to have men like these."

Townsend smiled. "Time to move, *chop, chop!"*

Orders were being passed and Tucker asked, "Where are we off to, sir?"

"A safe place. It will be hard going, I'm afraid. But after that they'll come and pick us up."

Tucker did not ask who *they* were, and he guessed that this filthy, well-spoken officer would not have told him anyway.

Townsend said, "Don't worry. We'll get you out of here." He must have recognized the desperation in Tucker's face. "And your travelling companion, too."

As Tucker climbed back on to the truck, from which two Gurkhas were already unloading sacks of rice, Townsend turned to the sapper named Teddy and said, "Must seem like a bloody miracle to them. Poor devils, brave as tigers, but they don't have a clue what it's all about, do they?"

They both laughed, their cigarette smoke drifting above them. Like the laughter, it seemed unreal.

Tucker crawled over to Napier, and raised his shoulders very carefully. Napier was staring at the Gurkhas, one of whom grinned at him as if it was all perfectly normal. "Where—where are we going? What's happening, for God's sake?"

Tucker was glad Napier could not see his face, or the emotion that was ripping him apart. "I think they're taking us out of here, sir."

Napier allowed himself to be lifted from the truck, while the soldiers stopped work to watch. He said, "But for them . . ."

Tucker glanced once towards the Japanese, but they had been tied up and were already being dragged through the trees by the old headman's people. He felt no pity, only disgust and hatred.

Let them pray for death before the end. It was all he could think of. He hoisted Napier over his shoulder. There was not a whisper of complaint from him, no murmur of pain. All he said was, "Together."

For Tucker, it was the only reward he needed.

12 | Thumbs-up, and You're Dead

After their stumbling arrival on board the steam tug *Success,* the modest lighting in the master's small cabin seemed blinding. Apart from an occasional guiding hand when they were in danger of falling over some winch or coiled wire cables, they could have been invisible. Nobody spoke, and in the darkness it was impossible to see any expression, or to gauge the extent of their welcome. Villiers sat down gingerly on a battered bench seat, and looked at a litter of plates and cups mingled with various charts, and a long, old-fashioned telescope. He said, "I've known this tug since I was a little boy. Built in England. She was twice as powerful as anything else when she was new."

Ross watched him. *There it was again.* Villiers was searching for something, trying to identify the events which had changed his life. He asked, "What's Richard Tsao like? And where is he, I wonder?"

"I think he was up in the wheelhouse with the master." Villiers frowned. "*Like?* Just an ordinary sort of chap. Hard-working, I believe." He smiled ruefully. "You had to be that, above all else." Ross recalled what the girl had told him of the powerful Villiers family.

Villiers was saying, "Must be in his middle or late thirties now. He's taking a hell of a risk, so he must be pretty eager to help."

Ross nodded. *So are we.* "Our information points to a lack of trust between the Japanese and their German allies. The sooner we get to the bottom of it, the better." He leaned back against a cupboard and listened to the engine's powerful beat, felt the easy roll of the hull, which was built like a battleship. With luck, they would reach Singapore in two days. After that, everything would depend on Richard Tsao.

The cabin door opened, and Ross studied the newcomer with

interest. Late thirties, perhaps, but looked older. His carefully combed black hair was edged with grey, like frost, and although he was casually dressed in a well-worn reefer jacket he had an air of authority, and a confidence which Ross had recognized in other men who risked their lives without question.

Villiers scrambled to his feet and thrust out his hand. "Richard Tsao! I can barely believe it, after all this time!"

Tsao shook hands, his dark eyes examining the youthful lieutenant as if searching for something. He said, "It seemed the right way for us to meet." He gave the merest hint of a smile. "*Success* has a suitable ring to it!" He turned to Ross. Again the scrutiny, calm and unhurried.

"Lieutenant-Commander James Ross. I have read about you." He nodded. "I am pleased you decided to come." He opened a pack of cigarettes and offered them automatically. To give himself time. To decide how much to divulge. Richard Tsao was not what Ross had expected. Even when he had spoken with Villiers, the son of his formidable late employer, there had been no attempt to ingratiate himself, as might be usual in one who was likely to ask for favours or rewards for what he was doing. The exact opposite. With Villiers, he had more the air of a potential employer himself than that of a man who had survived the Japanese invasion by working under their supervision.

Tsao said, "We shall be off Kalang tomorrow. We might be boarded by the inshore patrols. It is not uncommon." He bobbed his head. "This vessel has a secure place where you can be concealed. It was constructed originally for smuggling refugees out of Singapore and Western Malaya, when many believed that the Japanese victory would soon be reversed. But it was not to happen." He said it without bitterness, without emotion of any kind. Something which he had learned to contain under his new masters, Ross thought. "The next day, all being well, we will reach Singapore Strait and enter Keppel Harbour, where we will take on fuel." He stabbed the air with his cigarette and watched the smoke being drawn into a ventilator. "Coal can be a nuisance, but it does have an advantage in that we will be undisturbed."

Villiers was staring into the distance. "Keppel Harbour? That's taking a chance, isn't it?"

"Life is a risk, my friend. Each one of my men on board is putting his life at stake, every hour of the day. Which is why the Japanese are not afraid we might try to escape. Our families are their hostages. They are totally ruthless—cruelty is like a ritual to them. Men, women and children are not spared." He stubbed out the cigarette and selected a fresh one. "But you will be safe. You may become like a passport to the future—it is not a mere dream, it is our fervent belief. It may take years, who can say? But we will win." He looked intently at Villiers. "The British will always be welcome here and on the Peninsula. Planters, merchants, engineers—there will be much to do for our people." He shook his head sharply, as if he had heard a contradiction. "But not as colonial governors and rulers. To exchange one yoke for another would be a form of insanity!"

Ross said evenly, "We are in your hands. Our aim is the same as yours. Just tell me . . ."

Tsao gave a brief smile. "I shall do better. I will *show* you."

Villiers asked, "My home, the house—what's happened to it?"

Tsao regarded him impassively, as if to sound out his strength. "It was burned. Much of it was looted, as you are aware. Had I known about your other visit, I would have prevented it. It was reckless, without thought for those who would suffer if they were caught helping you."

Ross watched and listened. This was no downtrodden junior manager. *I would have prevented it.* It spoke volumes.

Villiers said, "I—I know. But I wanted to see for myself."

Tsao seemed satisfied. "I obtained part of the property. I am little liked because of it, and because of my work with the Japanese."

"I don't blame you for that. I was told what they did to some of my father's employees."

Tsao glanced up at the stained deckhead. "The tug's master

had a sister, too. They took her away, and made her become a comfort-woman for their loathsome army! He does not forget. Neither must you!"

Villiers asked abruptly, "May I go on deck?"

Tsao smiled. "Of course. You are a guest, not a prisoner. But do not try to speak with my people. They will not talk. Safety is like a chain. Each link must be secure."

He watched Villiers pause by the door, waiting for the deck to fall heavily as *Success* ploughed into a deep trough. There was a brief smell of funnel smoke, and then he was gone.

Tsao said, "I would have felt easier if you had come alone, Commander Ross. The lieutenant," again the small, tight smile, "Mr Charles, as we were expected to call him, is still unable to come to terms with what happened. It is like a deep scar. He may never lose it."

"I like him very much." Ross smiled. It had sounded like defiance.

"In war-time it is sometimes safer to hold friendships at a distance." Tsao leaned forward and tapped his knee. "I admire you for that. Such frankness can be rare." He smiled again. "In war-time!" He stood up. "I shall leave you now. Food will be brought soon."

Ross said, "Don't worry about Villiers. He won't let you down."

Tsao paused by the door, his mind already elsewhere. "If we are stopped, you will be taken instantly to the hiding place. But they have searched this vessel many times, before trust was established, so unless we have an informer . . ." He shrugged. "We shall soon know."

Ross said, "What happened to Charles's sister? He's never spoken of her."

For only an instant, Tsao showed genuine surprise. Then he said in the same controlled voice, "She was a very pretty girl. When the soldiers burst into the house, they killed Mr Villiers because he tried to stop them. The soldiers took the girl and raped her." He put down his pack of cigarettes and Ross saw that his fingers were shaking. "They forced her mother to watch." He bunched his fingers into an obedient fist and added coldly, "Then they shot her, too." He looked straight into Ross's grey eyes. "The girl, you were about to ask? I do not know. I never heard of her again."

Ross said, "Thank you."

Tsao was about to close the door behind him. "I have learned something about you, Commander. It is a quality you have, which is rarer even than courage. It is compassion." He paused. "I see now why you lead and others follow."

The door closed silently.

Ross thought about it for a long time, and realized that he was glad he had been allowed to accompany Villiers on what was, at best, a perilous escapade.

He was surprised also to discover that he was not afraid.

Richard Tsao unbolted the steel door and stood aside to allow the two officers to stumble out into the sunshine. Both were covered in coal-dust, their khaki shirts and slacks plastered to their bodies like filthy skins.

He said, "It is safe now."

Ross rubbed his eyes and felt the coal-grit under his fingers. Although they were well hidden below the tug's bridge structure, the sunlight was blinding. He managed to reply, "Thanks. I began to wonder . . ."

He glanced at his companion. Villiers's fair hair was as dirty as his face, but he managed to grin. "In this boat, when you *hide,* you really hide!"

Tsao regarded him with the same opaque stare. "I am sorry for the delay. It was unusual." He looked directly at Ross. "This time there was an officer with them. Young and eager. He wanted to see everything. Usually it is a formality—they know the *Success* like one of their own." He glanced up at the tall funnel and the plume of smoke that drifted past the flapping flag of the Rising Sun at the gaff. "Which she is, of course."

He showed no sign of anxiety, any more than when the patrol boat had been sighted tearing down on them, a great moustache of white foam bursting beneath her stem. He had merely directed them below, to the "safe place," a small, cramped addition welded to one of the coal-bunkers. It was right above the boiler-room and it had been like a sealed oven; at times the concealment had been almost unbearable, especially as they did not know what was happening.

Tsao said, "You will be able to clean yourselves soon. Tomorrow we will reach Keppel Harbour. Then we shall see."

Ross glanced up in time to see the tug's master step back from the glass screen. What must he have felt when the Japanese had come aboard? What must he always think when he saw them on his own streets, free to do whatever they liked while his own sister was forced into prostitution?

And how much would it take to make just one of the crew betray them? He stared at the tug-master's clenched fist on the rail, all that was visible now that he had stepped back from view. The fist opened slightly and after the smallest hesitation gave a brief salute, as if it alone had decided upon the gesture. Ross looked at Tsao, and wondered if he had noticed this first small gesture of welcome, or trust. If he had, it did not show in his dark eyes.

In the cabin, Tsao produced a bottle of sake, a gift, he explained, from a previous encounter with a Japanese patrol vessel. Ross had never tasted it before, and thought it foul, but it helped to ease away the tension of waiting, sweating in the steel box above the boiler-room and straining their ears for every sound.

Tsao said, "You must keep out of sight from now on. There will be much shipping and many curious eyes." As he lit another cigarette, he ticked off the points in the same unemotional manner, as if it were an everyday occurrence.

"We will go alongside and take on coal. It is a long task as the bunkers are almost empty of everything but dust. It will give us time to go ashore." He saw Villiers's surprise, and added, "I have a permit to use a company car." He almost smiled; it seemed to amuse him. "The Nippon soldier is a great respecter of permits if signed by his own masters."

"And then?" Ross hoped he sounded as detached as Tsao.

"I have some papers for you to see, and some pictures for you to take with you when you leave us."

Leave us. An old tug flying the Japanese flag, with patrol boats and the risk of a stop-and-search exercise at any time of the day: it made the prospect of leaving, even surviving, seem like a fool's dream.

That evening, as a deep gold sunset closed down the visibility, they washed in buckets of steaming water from the engine-room, with a coarse slab of soap which was as black as coal, and reminded Ross of the stuff his father had used to clean the grease and rust from his hands after working on some salvage job or other. What would Villiers's girl say if she could see him now, standing naked while his superior officer washed his back for him? He thought of Victoria Mackenzie. What would she think?

They emptied the buckets over the side, and Villiers pointed. "Look. A junk."

Caught in the last of the golden sunset and framed against the water like a huge bat, the strange-looking craft seemed as timeless as the place itself. Like Richard Tsao: no matter how long it took, or what terrible cost it demanded, he and his sort could wait, and triumph.

Later, after yet another meal of rice and fish and a second bottle of sake, Tsao raised the curtain a little more on what lay ahead.

"The Germans have been here for a matter of months. But mostly they are in Penang, where they have better facilities. Co-operation between them and the Japanese is poor—the Japanese perhaps resent their intrusion more than they appreciate what they are doing. For their part, the Germans take exception at being treated as anything but the Master Race. They see their ally as inefficient, wasteful of resources and, for the most part, over-confident." He glanced at his watch. "They are not even allowed to wear their uniforms ashore, something they probably hate more than anything else."

Villiers asked, "And what are they hoping to do there?"

Tsao stood. "I told you. I will show you." He gestured to some neatly folded khaki clothing. "There are several sizes. Some should fit you."

Villiers bent over the pile. "What are these?"

"The same as the Germans wear when they are in town."

Ross said, "If we wore these, and were caught wearing them . . ."

"You would be treated as spies. Either way, you would die. But then, you knew that before you came to me, yes?"

Villiers said flatly, "Yes. We knew."

Tsao said, "I must leave you now. You must try to rest. I do not think you will be disturbed again."

When they were alone Villiers said, "What do you think they're up to?"

"The Master Race?" It had sounded almost comical, coming from Tsao. "The Japs have conquered most of Southeast Asia. And only now are they being held by the Americans in the Pacific. I would have thought the last thing the Japs need is advice or military training. It's a different war, a different set of rules."

Villiers said, half to himself, "I don't think I could take being tortured." He did not look up. "Not a very brave thing to admit."

Ross reached for the sake. Foul though it was, it seemed to help. He could almost hear Mike Tucker saying scornfully, *You shouldn't have joined . . .* He thought, too, of Tsao's summing up. *You lead and others follow.* It was suddenly important that Villiers did not lose the drive that had brought him this far. "Think of that girl of yours. Caryl, isn't it?" He watched Villiers look up, saw the effect of her name. "She'll be waiting. She just wants to protect you, you know. Needs you to think of yourself, and not drop your guard around Sinclair, even for a moment." It was like hearing someone else. What the hell did he know about it? "When I was a boy, I thought only brave men won battles, that even if they were killed in action there was something glorious about it." He looked down at his hands, recalling the feel of her body when he had held her in Pryce's office, and on that last night in the car, when she had kissed him. "We know the truth now. War is ugly and brutal, and for the most part death in battle is anything but glorious. Ask any old sweat!"

Villiers said, "Then why do we do it?"

"Because it matters. To those who depend on us, who have to trust us, whether they like us or hate our guts. And for girls like Caryl . . ."

Villiers reached across the table, sharing it. "And Victoria."

The next morning, after a quick meal, they changed into their borrowed clothing while Tsao collected all their personal belongings, identity cards and discs, anything that might betray them. Even their pistols were taken away and placed in a waterproof bag. Tsao allowed them to retain the suicide pills, without any comment. He knew that they understood the consequences of failure, not only for them but for all those found to be involved.

It was a strange, eerie feeling, watching the occasional masthead or stain of funnel smoke appear briefly above the tug's foredeck as they entered harbour. Maddening not to be able to see what was happening, although they were surrounded by shipping, some moored, others threading their way in or out of the anchorage as if nothing, not even the suffering or devastation of war, would ever change it. Ross was aware of his own excitement, strangely at odds with their circumstances: the sheer sense of anticipation at entering any foreign country, rather than apprehension at this covert penetration into the midst of a ruthless enemy.

The *Success* sounded her whistle and Ross heard another vessel reply.

If only I could see it. When he glanced at Villiers he saw that his head was thrown back, as if he too were listening, forming a picture of everything he had once known and loved, which had gone for ever.

Tsao clattered down a ladder from the bridge. "We are

permitted to go alongside the fuel jetty. My company clerk is waiting, but he will not come aboard." He looked at each of them in turn. "His presence means that we are safe to take up moorings. Tomorrow we shall head north again, for Penang. There I will show you . . ." He broke off as somebody called from the wheelhouse. He ran lightly up the ladder, but was gone for only a minute. He was not even out of breath.

But he was changed. Different, in a way that Ross could not define. Excited? Unlikely, and yet . . .

Tsao took each of them by the arm. "You will not have to wait as long as I thought." His fingers were like steel. "Into the cabin. You will see from there."

Ross almost fell in his eagerness to reach the cabin's only scuttle. With Villiers pressed against him, he peered through the salt-smeared glass, not knowing what he expected to see.

He tried again to define the change in Tsao's demeanour. *Triumph.* It was triumph, which even he could not conceal.

A great rusting barrier of steel almost blocked out the light as the tug pushed abeam of a moored freighter. The waterline was so thick with weed that it seemed likely she had not moved for many months. Then the sunshine came to greet them past the freighter's overhanging bows and anchors, and he heard Villiers's sharp intake of breath as he, too, saw the other vessel, stark and vivid in the glare.

Ross was a submariner, but it did not require his professional eye to identify the shark-like, raked bows with the jagged net-cutter above the stem. Abaft the conning tower, the scarlet flag with its black cross and swastika hung motionless in the warm air. As if it had been waiting, just for them.

Victoria paused by a window, one of the few in the small headquarters building from which you could see the ocean, and watched the motionless trees and the haze of heat and dust which gave the only pretence of movement. It was unusually hot; even she, who was used to it, found it oppressive, like an open furnace. Ninety degrees. It was Saturday, and the place was deserted but for the small operational staff and the duty officers. The rest had probably gone swimming, or hitched into town in the search for pleasure. She plucked the shirt away from her body. A swim. Later perhaps . . . But she knew she would not. It was like being adrift, unable to concentrate.

She watched the hard blue line of the horizon, remembering the night he had sailed in the submarine with the lieutenant who had once lived in Singapore. It was as if they had vanished, as if they had never been. But she never forgot, and as the weeks had dragged by each memory had become clearer, more vivid: they were all that she might ever have. Except for the precious medal he had left in her care. She had looked at it every night before she had turned in, held it against her bare breast as if to bring him back, to hold on to the only link she had.

She turned away from the window and heard hammering somewhere. The fans had broken down again; no wonder it was so hot, so crushing. The rating by the door looked up from his magazine, then covered it with his elbow. But not before she had seen the heavy-breasted nude on the cover.

"The Captain's expecting you." He grinned. "He's got company."

She knocked and pushed open the door, knowing that the seaman was looking at her legs. She felt no anger or resentment. He had probably been out here so long that he had forgotten anyone he might once have cared for.

Captain Pryce stood, arms folded, by his desk. Commander John Crookshank from Operations Intelligence sat comfortably in one of the deep chairs. She glanced at the desk. No signal-pad, no envelope marked Top Secret. Her heart sank. Nothing, then.

Pryce said, "Glad you were aboard. Thought you should meet your new boss, so to speak." He sounded vaguely uneasy, which was unusual for him. She realized for the first time that a Wren officer was sitting near Crookshank, clean and crisp in her white uniform, her eyes hidden in the slatted shadow thrown by the sun through the lowered blinds. Pryce said, "Second Officer Blandford. Celia Blandford."

Victoria waited; it was hard to see her in the shadows. Slim, fresh skin and dark brown hair. At least she wasn't fair, as Jane Clarke had been. Victoria brushed her own hair from her forehead without even realizing she had moved. She had always envied Jane's hair and her English complexion. But she no longer missed her. It was like losing a friend: people came and went; it happened often enough these days. Nevertheless, she felt a strange resentment that a stranger was to take her place, to use the chair in the operations room that had remained empty since that terrible night.

Second Officer Blandford said, "We'll get to know each other pretty well, I expect." She smiled briefly. "I understand that you turned down the opportunity of a commission?"

Victoria answered, "It was my choice."

Pryce said, "I think you were wrong, but I said as much at the time. You have to put the service first. It can't always suit your personal needs, you know."

As usual, Crookshank remained firmly on the fence. "Well, of course, my dear, there are two sides to everything, right?"

"Anyway," Blandford continued as if there had been no interruption. "There won't be too many changes, not as far as I'm concerned. Smartness, punctuality, efficiency—what I've been used to."

Victoria noticed how her lips formed into a smile during each sentence which vanished before the end of it. A nervous habit, or a calculated one to cover her true feelings? Celia Blandford was probably about her own age, a year older at the most, and yet there was something stiff and formal about her that reminded Victoria of a teacher she had known at the exclusive finishing-school in England, which her father had considered "only right and proper" for his daughter. Love, defiance, pride, it was a part of them all. How could she leave him? How could she have gone without waiting to see Jamie again?

Crookshank said heavily, "Some good news you should know about. Sub-Lieutenant Napier and P.O. Tucker are back."

The Wren officer said in a sharp little voice, "I was going to tell her when it had been cleared."

Victoria said, "I'm so glad. What about . . . ?"

Pryce interjected, "Telegraphist Rice didn't make it. They did a fine job before they were captured by the Japs. The Chindits got them out—bloody marvellous, when you think of it. I shall see Napier, and Tucker of course, when they're cleared by the P.M.O. I've already put Napier down for advanced promotion and some suitable decoration."

Crookshank went on gravely, "No news of Commander Ross, though. But early days. We should hear something quite soon." That was as far as he intended to commit himself.

She heard herself say, "P.O. Tucker doesn't know about Commander Ross, sir."

Second Officer Blandford eyed her curiously. "Should he?"

"They are very close." She felt sick, and angry with herself because of it. She saw the impatience and added, "Ma'am."

Crookshank said, "Are you feeling unwell, my dear?" He looked at Pryce. "A chair, I think."

She replied, "The heat. I'm all right, sir."

Blandford said, "It is pretty close, I must say. Bit of a change from England." The smile came and went just as quickly. "I'd have thought you would have been used to it, er, Mackenzie?"

She might have meant it either way. Victoria no longer cared. "I manage."

Pryce looked at them with a mixture of disappointment and satisfaction. It was not going to work. It had been a mistake to send the new second officer without first consulting him. This was not the Royal Naval Barracks, or some operations section in a bomb-proof shelter deep under ground, where the war was fought with little flags and crosses on wall-charts.

The new officer turned to look up at him. "What happened to this man Rice, sir?"

Crookshank spread his plump hands. "It's all in the report. We were fortunate not to lose the whole crew. We still don't know what happened to *Turquoise,* although there have been plenty of ideas bandied about."

Pryce said curtly, "Rice was killed by the Japs. Beheaded."

Victoria saw her new officer's hands clench into fists, the sudden tension. Pryce had caused it deliberately, for her sake, thinking she herself could not be shocked, not after Jane Clarke. He was wrong about that, too.

She asked, "May I go and see Mike Tucker, sir?"

"I don't see why not. The P.M.O. will probably release him soon."

Crookshank leaned forward in his chair. "Commander Ross's mission is *not* for discussion. Please remember that."

Pryce glanced at him briefly, and with dislike. If he had said *Don't be such a bloody fool; everyone knows anyway* out loud, he could not have made it plainer.

"I know that, sir." *I love him, don't you understand?* It was almost as if she had shouted at them. "They'll be feeling it. You know how they are after an operation." The words seemed to mock her. She had had plenty of time to observe their strange behaviour after Jamie had gone away. At Christmas, the place had been a madhouse of wild, drunken celebration, and the juvenile high spirits had been at their worst in the wardroom. The young subbies and lieutenants had gone through their usual destructive form of field-gun drill, using sofas as guns and the wardroom table as the barrier they were expected to surmount. The damage, like the mess bills, had been horrendous.

Then, only the following day or so it had seemed, the news of the sinking of the German battle-cruiser *Scharnhorst* had been announced. She had fallen to the guns of Admiral Fraser's *Duke of York* in the freezing seas off North Cape. The last of Germany's major warships, a ship with a charmed life, which had outlived and outfought all the others.

But a matter of rejoicing? She had watched with astonishment as those same young officers had raised their glasses in salute, not to a vanquished enemy, but to a brave ship and her equally gallant company. She would never understand them.

So she was different after all. She belonged, but she did not fit in. Suppose she had chosen to accept the chance of promotion, had gone to England for it. She would know nobody, least of all her father's relations. They would never accept her, would blame her for ever as a symbol of Colonel Mackenzie's disgrace, and his removal from the Army List. Yes, she might meet someone else, but that was not what she wanted. She *knew* what she wanted. Surely she could not be so wrong again.

Pryce was saying, "I shall speak to them as soon as possible. Throw some more light on things."

She reached the door and heard him add, "You should have a few days' leave before there's another flap."

She looked at him directly. *Don't you understand either?* "We're short-handed, sir."

He watched her leave, her black hair shining as she walked past a window. As if to a signal, all the fans began to revolve. Until the next time.

Pryce closed the door. "Well?"

Second Officer Blandford took a cigarette from Crookshank and tapped it on the desk. "Good record. I can see why you chose her. Perhaps a bit free and easy. But we shall have to see."

"Your predecessor . . ."

"Jane Clarke? A bit slack, was she?"

Crookshank sighed. "A lively girl. Had everything to live for."

Pryce ignored him. "Everybody liked her."

She said coolly, "Popularity isn't everything, sir."

Pryce smiled for the first time. "Very true. I've always found it something of a hindrance!"

But he was still thinking of Victoria Mackenzie. He had noticed the shadows under her eyes, sensed her emotion when she had spoken from time to time about Ross.

He said abruptly, "Now let's get those restricted signals out again. We're in the dark. If we don't hear something soon, we'll have to postpone operations. Can't afford another unexplained sinking."

Crookshank took out his reading glasses, something he tried to avoid doing in the presence of women. "The admiral wouldn't like that."

Pryce gave him a pitying stare. "More to the point, neither would I!"

The hospital was a small one, and had been completely taken over by the Navy. It was mostly used for incoming convoy survivors landed in Ceylon after an encounter with the enemy. If a convoy outward bound from Britain suffered casualties they had to complete the remainder of the passage as well as they could, with men suffering from scalds, oil-fuel poisoning, and every sort of shock. Ceylon would seem like a piece of heaven for the lucky ones.

A medical orderly guided the girl along a well-polished corridor. A few injured men sat or strolled in the surrounding gardens, and several of them whistled at her as she passed.

The orderly said, "Your captain phoned to say you were coming."

To say I was to be trusted, she thought.

He added, "I'll fetch Petty Officer Tucker if you'll sit here. He's in pretty good shape, considering."

She waited by the partly open door. It was a cool, white room, mercifully protected from the sun by long green blinds. There were just four beds, and each was occupied; the inmates were quite still, sleeping or drugged it was impossible to know.

She heard a step and saw Tucker walking towards her. He wore a dressing-gown, and apart from a plaster on his head he looked much the same. He stopped dead and stared at her. "I—I thought—" Then he smiled. "My God, girl, it's good to see you!"

He held her as she put her arms around him, her face against his shoulder.

Close to, the strain was very visible on his homely features, and the gashes and bruises made the enemy suddenly stark and real, not an indefinable menace far beyond that dark horizon.

He said gently, "I heard about Jamie Ross. He'll be all right."

She hugged him. "He knew you were alive, Mike. Don't ask me how. He just knew."

"Well," he said, "we go back a long way."

She looked up at him, trying to understand what he had gone through, afraid to imagine it. "Captain Pryce is getting Sub-Lieutenant Napier a decoration, promotion too."

He turned his head, as if he had heard something. "He's still drugged. Really been through it, poor little sod." She was shocked to see the tears in his eyes. "All that way, hardly a peep out of him, trying to prove he was as good as his brother!" He stepped away and wiped his face with his cuff. "Sorry." He took her hands in his. "When Jamie gets in, you hang on to him. You're so right together."

Then he said quietly, "I'd better get back and sit with him."

She watched his despair, his sense of loss. "What is it? Please tell me."

He looked at her, although she knew he did not see her. He was somewhere else.

He said, "All that way. Then a submarine, a Dutch one, to bring us here."

There was a small sound from the room and he began to move away. "So they took off his bloody arm today. A fat lot of good a medal will do after that."

The orderly returned and passed them, going into the room without a glance at either of them. From miles away she heard a bell ringing, felt Tucker releasing her. She said, "I'll wait for you. As long as you like."

His face was very calm again. "Yes. I'd like that. Just want to be here when . . ." His eyes hardened as a white-coated doctor and another orderly bustled along the corridor. "I owe him that at least."

She found a stone bench beside a fountain and leaned back

against it, feeling the roughness pressing through her shirt and into her skin. She wanted to cry, to grieve for him, but knew she could do neither. She could scarcely remember Peter Napier now; his was just another youthful face among so many, like the ones who had whooped and yelled as they had charged over the wardroom table, or the ones who had raised their glasses to a brave enemy they had known only by reputation. Boys into men; and others like Mike Tucker, who held the whole machine together. Faces of war. Like those in her father's old photographs. *Thumbs-up, and you're dead.*

It was dark and she was still sitting beside the fountain when Tucker came to find her.

He wore a borrowed uniform. He said, "Will you buy me a drink, Petty Officer Mackenzie? I've got no cash till I see the paybob."

Together they walked out to the car, and she said quietly, "Welcome back."

He squeezed her arm. "Jamie's a lucky lad." Perhaps to give himself time, he asked, "Do you have a fag to spare?"

She shook her head. "I didn't think you smoked."

"I don't. Just feel like it." He stared past her and saw the faint shimmering gleam of the ocean. Waiting, he thought.

She said, "I'll get us that drink." But still she hesitated. "How was it with Peter? Did you manage to speak to him?"

Tucker made himself relive it. She was as much a part of it as they all were. He said quietly, "I think he understood. But he just lay there and looked up at me. Then he said, *'Not so much of me for you to carry next time.'* Then he passed out, thank God."

She slid into the car beside him and switched on the engine. There was the ocean; you were never far from it here. Like the night she had watched the submarine slip away and merge with the dark water.

"Come and meet my father. I can phone the section from there."

Tucker watched the gates open to let them through. A nice

car, a lovely girl in a crumpled shirt with the same badges as his own. What would Evie have thought about that?

Then he said, "He'll blame himself for this, you know. Because of his brother who was killed in Norway."

He did not need to say it was Ross he was troubled about.

She replied firmly, "It's up to us then, isn't it?"

Tucker glanced out of the open window and laughed. It was almost unnerving. He had never expected he would ever laugh again.

13 | The Signal

CHARLES VILLIERS stared through the stained scuttle, watching a mixed procession of harbour craft weaving amongst the anchored shipping.

He said, "Do *you* think it can be done?" He turned and saw his companion, like a stranger in his fresh khaki shirt and slacks. "I mean, in broad daylight?"

Ross touched the small black and yellow cockade attached to the left pocket of his shirt. Richard Tsao had already informed them that every German in Singapore was required to wear it as a recognition symbol when he was outside their dockyard facilities, or away from supervision. The idea was still hard to accept. The whole of Europe and Scandinavia, apart from Sweden, were under the German heel, where the sight of a uniform would bring at best, caution, and at worst, terror. It was incredible that that same Germany would permit the Japanese to impose a rule of servility, where any kind of German uniform or decoration was forbidden.

Ross said, "We cross the wharf and get into the van. Did you see it?"

He saw the disbelief in Villiers's face. "Yes. It's one of our old company vans. You can just make out the crest through the paintwork." He clenched his fists. "God, the whole place must be falling to pieces!"

Ross listened to the thumps and scrapes on deck as the tug's crew prepared to take on coal.

He said, "You know Tsao pretty well. What do you think he'll want for all this information he says he's got?"

Villiers said firmly, "He's got it all right. He wouldn't risk his life and everyone else's for a gamble." He seemed to consider it. "I always thought him such a quiet, unobtrusive chap. His job wasn't all that important—there must have been more to him than any of us realized." He recalled the question. "Maybe money. Gold. Maybe a firm commitment to get him and his family out of here, perhaps to Australia. He'd be safe there, for the moment anyway."

The door opened and Richard Tsao stepped over the coaming. He had found time to put on a fresh shirt, and looked remarkably relaxed. He said, "We wait for the signal. Then we go. It is not unusual for the *Success* to carry a passenger or two back and forth to Penang." He handed them two well-worn passes, each with the Nazi eagle embossed on the cover, and added, "There will be guards, but they want little contact with the Germans."

He hesitated, his head cocked to listen to the clatter of derricks and dockside equipment. "Well, gentlemen, you saw the submarine. Were you impressed?" He smiled. "I could tell from your expressions that you were unaware of their presence here."

Ross said, "A well kept secret."

Tsao's smile was gone. "The Japanese went to some pains to ensure such secrecy. Many of our people have been killed, or have disappeared without trace." Somebody stamped on the deck overhead and he said calmly, "So let us go forth and discover, shall we?"

They climbed a ladder and crossed the vessel's deck, their shoes scraping on the first layers of drifting coal-dust. Neither the crew nor the dock-workers gave them so much as a glance. Perhaps they really did not care, Ross thought. They were working and being paid: under a ruthless enemy occupation, that was more than most people could boast.

Tsao had lit a fresh cigarette, and handed a worn briefcase to his clerk, a small, bespectacled man who dropped his eyes if either Villiers or Ross looked in his direction.

It was the strangest sensation Ross had ever experienced, walking through the dockside litter, shoulders growing hotter in the dusty sunshine. Like being naked, or completely invisible. He glanced at Villiers: against the moving mass of Chinese and Malay faces he looked even more vulnerable, lost in a place he no longer recognized. Or was it all too familiar even now?

The van was standing with several other battered vehicles, the rear door hanging open to allow some air to enter. A normal precaution, nothing which might arouse suspicion. Ross glanced around. It did not appear as though anybody was interested.

Tsao said quickly, "We shall leave tomorrow." He added, "Do not look back. There are soldiers by the gates. Get into the van." He watched his clerk, probably guessing that the little man was terrified. "I will drive. You go to the office." He called after him as he hurried away, "*Walk!* I am depending on you!" In a more contained voice he said, "He is useful in many ways, but . . ." He switched on the engine and gripped the wheel. "Remember what I told you. *They* are the enemy."

The van jolted over some old iron tracks and lurched towards the gates.

Ross crouched on a small wooden bench and peered over Tsao's shoulder. He could feel Villiers's tension like something physical, although when he glanced at his profile he looked surprisingly calm. Then he forgot him and everything else and watched the soldiers. There were three of them, one lounging against a notice-board, alien and yet immediately recognizable. He found himself wishing he still had his revolver, or even his diving-knife. It was like going into a trap. He could feel the sweat around his waistband, but it was cold, like the murdered girl had been.

Tsao breathed out sharply as one of the soldiers stepped into the road and raised his hand. He whispered, *"Remember!"*

Ross saw the soldier peering through the open window, his dark eyes flitting from the official passes on the windscreen to the one Tsao was holding out to him.

Then he looked directly at Ross. It seemed to take minutes before he said something.

Tsao turned slightly. "Passes."

Ross took Villiers's pass and held them out together. It was impossible to guess what the soldier was thinking. Then he nodded to his companions and returned the passes without a word.

Ross waited, counting seconds, expecting that at any moment they would be ordered out of the van. What might Tsao do then? Claim ignorance, or drive on without a backward glance? It was not likely that he would get very far.

The van rolled forward, and when he glanced back Ross saw that the three soldiers had stopped a man who was carrying a large sack from the harbour. He turned away, sickened, as one of the soldiers hit the man with the butt of his rifle; he did not even bother to unsling it from his shoulder. The other soldiers were laughing as he kicked the man, while he lay on the road covering his face as though to protect it. Nobody stopped to protest, or to offer a hand to the victim. It was as though he was invisible. As they had been when they had stepped off the tug.

Tsao said, "I told you. There is no love between the Japanese and the Germans. It is your greatest protection."

Villiers asked huskily, "What had that man done, the one they were beating?"

Tsao swerved to avoid a sprawled figure beside the road. Sick, drunk or dead, no one seemed to care. "Probably nothing. It is their way. How it has been since the British surrendered here."

Ross frowned. There it was again: like a barb, and yet without any obvious malice or bitterness. Was he really a friend? They had to trust him, that was obvious.

He saw Villiers's fingers whiten on the bench seat as he leaned forward to watch the passing shops and houses. There seemed to be so much damage left uncleared after the original invasion, buildings no more than heaps of rubble, where mortar and shellfire had speeded the inevitable.

They turned off the main road and Tsao said, "We go inland here." He gestured to the road they had left. "Follow that road and you sometime get to Changi, where thousands of your people are prisoners. It is a place of darkness."

Ross thought unwillingly of Tucker and his companions,

wondering if they were in such a terrible place, or even if they were still alive.

Nor could he help thinking of the Mackenzie estate, and the old Colonel opening his heart to him. What would he think if he could see his beloved island now? Where, despite all the rules and unspoken laws of a closed society, he had fallen in love and had paid for it ever since, no matter how he spoke of the "old country." And Victoria? It would break her heart.

He heard Tsao say, "You know where we are going, Lieutenant?"

Ross saw Villiers nod, his fingers still gripping the bench as if he would never be able to let go.

Tsao said, "You will be strong. Nothing can change what happened. You are not alone."

Villiers leaned back and said quietly to Ross, "My home is a few minutes away. Where my parents died," he did not try to hide his bitterness, "while I was strutting around in my new uniform, looking for somebody to salute me!"

"Don't be so bloody hard on yourself. It's the war. It happens."

It sounded almost brutal, and he knew Villiers resented it. He went on, relentlessly, "My best friend died because of me. Because of an attack, one that was so important I couldn't see anything else. His nerve had gone." He was shocked by his own voice, his words. As if he had just betrayed him. Richard Tsao had summed it up better than anybody. *Others follow.* He touched Villiers's arm and felt it tense. "So try to find comfort in the hope that something we do might help to end all this bloody misery."

Eventually Villiers said, "Sorry, Jamie. I keep expecting . . ." He ran his fingers through his fair hair. "Well, I just do—that's all."

They were stopped at two more checkpoints, and Ross was amazed that he could accept it without flinching. When one of the Japanese soldiers had tossed him a casual salute, he had acknowledged it with a curt nod and *"Heil Hitler!"* Even the inscrutable Tsao had given a nod of approval.

"That is better!"

They entered a weed-choked access road and Tsao stopped the van. "We walk from here." It was then, and only then, that Ross realized it had once been a magnificent driveway, and the pile of blackened ruins, now almost overgrown with creeper, must have been Villiers's home. His mind lingered on Tsao's words. A *place of darkness.* He could smell it, feel the chill and the sickness like the early symptoms of some fever.

They eventually stepped out on to a cleared pathway, where a bungalow stood detached from the rest of the property. Ross wanted to ask Villiers about it, but said nothing when he saw the pain on his face. Where an employee had once lived, perhaps the manager whom Richard Tsao had replaced.

Inside, the bungalow was comfortable and well furnished, with some ornaments and pictures which would not have seemed out of place in the Colonel's house.

Villiers sat down in a leather chair as if his legs had been cut from under him.

Tsao said, "I have sent my family to visit friends." His dark eyes flashed between them. "We will not be disturbed. I will make certain that food is brought."

Ross had seen several motionless figures at the back of the bungalow. Tsao's status seemed to increase by the minute.

Villiers rubbed the arms of his chair. He murmured, "This used to be my father's." He shook his head. "No, don't worry, I'm all right. I knew what I was getting into."

Ross said sharply, "I'm banking on it!"

Tsao returned and threw his jacket across a chair. "I have arranged matters."

Ross wondered if he had left them alone merely to settle their differences, which might have been apparent to him in the van, or even earlier aboard the *Success.*

Tsao said bluntly, "There is not much time. Here, we come and go to Japanese clocks!" He took out his cigarettes. "I would like to speak with *you,* Commander Ross, just the two of us for a few minutes." Without looking at him, he included Villiers. "If you would like to walk in the garden, my man will see that you are safe and left alone."

Villiers stood up, and Ross said, "That O.K. with you?"

Villiers said dully, "Yes, it's O.K." Then, "I was the one who talked you into this, remember?"

Tsao did not even appear to notice that he had left the room. Watching his cigarette-smoke as it hung almost motionless in the humid air, he said, "You were impressed by what you saw in the harbour, Commander?"

Ross nodded. "Are you prepared to tell me more? About Operation *Monsun,* for instance?"

Tsao blew the smoke aside. "The Germans came here a year ago. At first we thought it was a token presence, something to prove to the Emperor that they were on the same side. Herr Hitler even presented the Emperor with a U-Boat, and a team of sailors to instruct a Japanese crew." He smiled. "You do not have the right face for a secret agent, Commander. I can see from your expression that you were told nothing of this, that you *knew* nothing of it."

Ross smiled. "I will not lie to you."

Tsao continued, "The Germans became more ambitious. They sent their own submarines, not to free the Japanese to fight the Americans in the Pacific as we first thought, but to act as blockade runners, to carry vital cargoes of materials which are either in very short supply or totally unobtainable in Germany. It was this German group which was called *Monsun,* not an operation as such. Several submarines are known to have been sunk by British and American aircraft before they could reach Singapore, but nobody, not even your Intelligence, knew what they were attempting to do. Since those early days, the group has expanded, and its facilities have been improved by the Japanese, albeit grudgingly. There are docking arrangements here in Singapore and at Tandjok Priok at Batavia, but German headquarters for *Monsun* is in Georgetown at Penang. There, too, they have improved the dock—it was dismantled by the British during the retreat. It is useful for their mooring and smaller refittings, which are essential in this climate." He kept his bombshell to the last. "The Germans even have two Arado float planes in Penang, just to oversee who comes and goes." He shrugged. "But they feel safe, invulnerable. Out of range of bombing aircraft, and separated from their enemies by islands which they dominate, and by the Indian Ocean for good measure."

Ross waited. "Your English is excellent, if I may say so."

Tsao smiled broadly, perhaps for the first time. "When you worked for Mr Charles's father, it was taken for granted, believe me!" Then he became businesslike again. "I can give you all the information you require for an attack on the German base, or their depot-ship, which is daily expected from Japan. It would be a triumph for you, and create an even deeper rift between the two countries."

"You are certain we could do it?"

"With our help and guidance, I am sure. Without that, you will make no progress, and your future coastal operations against the Japanese will be under constant threat."

"And in return?"

Tsao tossed the empty cigarette pack away. "I have prepared a list. It would mostly consist of weapons and explosives, and of course transmitters if we are to play a part in the last battle."

Oddly, Villiers had expected him to ask for money, gold, he had suggested, and a carefully planned escape from this constant danger.

Tsao eyed him calmly. "I can see you are surprised, Commander. Again? Is that not so?"

Ross stood up. "I'll fetch Lieutenant Villiers now." He looked around the room. "I will await your instructions." He hesitated at the door. "Surprised? Yes." He held out his hand. "But pleasantly so."

He walked into the garden and beyond, where fallen bricks and charred wood were partly hidden by pastel orchids, masses of them, perhaps wild, perhaps once cultivated as houseplants. He found Villiers in the hot sunlight, one of Tsao's servants, perhaps "guard" would be a more fitting description, loitering nearby in the shade.

He said quietly, "I've finished. I think it was worthwhile, if I can make our people understand what's needed."

Villiers stared at him, his eyes very clear. Afterwards, Ross thought it was the best he had looked for some time.

He said, "We're together now, Jamie. My family are here. I know it." He stood up as Ross took his arm. "They're at peace now."

Captain Ralph Pryce pushed open the door of the operations room and very deliberately laid his cap with its peak of gold oak leaves on an empty table. Outside the building it was dark, as black as pitch, the air hot and heavy as though a storm were brewing, although the Met boffins denied it. In here it was peaceful, deserted, the only sounds being the overhead fans and the persistent tap of insects against the sealed windows.

Second Officer Celia Blandford began to rise, but Pryce said curtly, "Nobody stands up for rank in here, except perhaps for the admiral—but I think he's only been here once."

She stifled a yawn and glanced at her watch. "All quiet, sir."

Pryce grunted and glanced at the signals folder. He need not have bothered. A ship wanting this, a commanding officer demanding that, some vague instruction about base security. He said, "No news yet." She did not answer, and he asked, "Settling in all right?"

She shrugged, and he noticed that her shirt was defaced by dark patches of perspiration under her arms. A far cry from England, he thought.

"Petty Officer Mackenzie still on board?"

She looked up at the revolving fan. "I sent her for some tea." She almost smiled. "I think she resented it."

"She has been running things since your predecessor

was . . ." He hesitated, and wondered why she made him so ill at ease when it should be the other way around.

"Murdered? Well, sir, I have to do it my way. I'm not really a first-name type, not this early."

Pryce walked around the room, glancing at graphs and lists, maps and notices so faded that they were barely readable. He said, "I've just been out to the hospital ship. She'll be weighing in about an hour. Not much you can say on such occasions. I've written to his people, of course."

She nodded. "Sub-Lieutenant Napier. How was he taking it?"

Pryce considered. The young face, pinched and lined with pain and drugs. A shadow of the officer Ross had wanted to protect. He should be used to it. He had seen enough men die . . . he glanced at the serious-looking Wren officer. Women too. "It's the end of his career." It was like slamming a watertight door. But what other way was there? He thought of Petty Officer Tucker; he had been aboard the white-painted hospital ship, too. Pryce had not asked how he had wangled that. Another odd bird. Could be on his way home for a long and well-deserved leave. He had survived a brief but brutal captivity, and from what Pryce could gather from the secret reports, he had all but carried young Napier most of the way to safety with the Chindit sabotage party. But no, he had firmly resisted it. *I want to stay, sir. I belong here. My family will know about me now, that was my main worry.*

Pryce considered Tucker's views on the *Turquoise*'s disappearance, and what he had been told by some Burmese headman. Sunk by another submarine. It seemed very unlikely, and he wondered what they would make of it at the Admiralty. He had sent Tucker's statement, as would be expected, though he had been careful not to offer a private opinion either way. But somebody should have discovered something. He glanced at a wall-map, thinking vaguely of Ross and Villiers. *Tybalt*'s commanding officer had signalled that he had completed the first part of the mission. Since then, nothing.

The door opened. Petty Officer Victoria Mackenzie walked

in with a tray of tea and saw Pryce. "I'm sorry, sir, I thought you were out on board the hospital ship."

Pryce watched her. "I'm not in any mood for tea, thank you." He noticed that she had brought only one cup, for her officer. It said quite a lot.

"How was Sub-Lieutenant Napier, sir?"

He replied, "As well as can be expected." Then, for something to say, "No news from Singapore, I'm afraid." He tugged out his personal key. "Fetch my special file, will you?" He watched her leave, and tried not to imagine how it might be.

Second Officer Blandford said, "I can have a word with her, if you like, sir. I could even arrange a transfer."

Pryce faced her, tired of waiting, sick of people who did not or would not understand. "Actually, you can't. I wouldn't like it."

Surprisingly she smiled, as if she had discovered a weakness and not the other way round.

The girl returned and laid the heavy pack on a table before handing him the key. She glanced only briefly at the tea. It was untouched.

"Get me the clip of signals from Flag Officer, Submarines. There might be some glimmer amongst all that bumf." He added casually, "The submarine *Tybalt* will remain in her selected area until it is time to recover the Singapore chaps." He saw the sudden gratitude in her eyes, which he had not suspected.

She said, "Thank you, sir."

He picked up his fine cap and looked at it. *The youngest admiral since Nelson.* He smiled faintly. *Not at this rate, you won't be.* "I'll be in my office for another hour."

Victoria sat and looked at the signals. Pryce knew exactly what was happening. He was always a jump ahead, everyone said so. She thought of Mike Tucker's bruised and beaten face, and found strength in the fact that he had refused to leave, and could still raise a grin when it was most needed.

He had understood when she had tried to explain. He had touched her bare arm and had said, "Then we'll wait together."

The smile had gone just as quickly, and he had murmured, "*Together.* It was what the poor little bugger said to me. And for what?"

A shadow fell across the table, and she looked up at the new officer, feeling the familiar tension between them. Jane Clarke had been difficult at times, always wanting her to stand in for her while she pursued her latest heart-throb. But there had been no side to the girl, no pulling of rank.

Blandford said, "I gather you're pretty fond of the section commander, James Ross? He must be quite a man. A hero."

Victoria waited. Perhaps it had been a bad start. She might be trying to make amends, and it took two to do that. She replied, "I love him. I never thought it could happen like that. I was sitting here when he first walked in. I used him badly . . . even so, something must have told me."

Blandford smiled, but only briefly. "The war has a lot to answer for. It's something you've always got to guard against—it's so easy to let things slide, to throw it all away. Do you really think you know what you're doing where he is concerned?"

Victoria felt herself flushing hotly, and was angry with herself. "I love him. You must know what I mean?" She saw Blandford's sudden impatience and knew the rift was as strong as ever. She looked away. *"Ma'am?"*

Blandford said curtly, "I'm going to the S.D.O. I'll be back in a moment." She glanced at the inner door. "I'll be here if Captain Pryce needs anything."

She went out and slammed the door behind her. Victoria stood up and walked vaguely to the other desk. Suppose she had accepted the offer of a commission? She picked up the second officer's white hat and stared at it. *Do you really think you know what you're doing where he is concerned?* It was as if Jane had come back to taunt her. Maybe someone in Blandford's life had let her down . . . She hung the hat on the chair again and returned to the table. Another night of anxiety lay ahead, and even when she fell into an exhausted sleep the dreams would still be there.

Ross taking the prized medal and saying, "No, I want to give it to somebody else!"

She put her face in her hands. "Oh God, I do love him so! Don't let anything hurt him."

The door banged open and she jerked upright with surprise. But it was Major Trevor Sinclair, his tanned skin very dark against fresh khakis. He seemed to be having difficulty in focusing his eyes. "Oh, it's you! A bit late for such a pretty girl to be on watch?"

She clenched her fists under the table. He was usually so cold and correct. A little like Pryce, or so she had believed. But not this time. His normally neat hair was disordered, and his voice was slightly slurred.

He snapped, "Well?" He seemed to have forgotten what he had been saying, and exclaimed, "Where's the Boss? He wants to see me about something. *Needs* to see me more likely, *what?*"

If only somebody else would come in. Anybody. She said, "Captain Pryce is in his office, sir. Is there anything I can do?" She saw the trap immediately, and added quickly, "Fetch him for you?"

He walked to the table and leaned on it with both hands, his face just six inches from hers. "Oh yes, my little teaser, there's a lot you can do for me." He reached out and touched her shoulder, his hand hot through her shirt. She could smell the gin, just as she could feel the sudden presence of danger. Of fear.

"Not shy, are you?" The fingers gripped her shoulder, harder, until she wanted to tear herself away. And yet somehow she knew it was what he wanted. Expected.

"Please don't, sir."

He smiled, and his hand began to move again. "You know you like it. Whose word would they take? Come on, don't play hard to get with me."

Something rattled against the window and he turned his head, his hand gripping her arm now, so that she could feel her own wild pulse beating against his wrist. She saw his expression change, the wildness replaced by disbelief, shock, so that for a second she believed he was losing his mind.

He was staring at Second Officer Blandford's hat, the badge very bright in the overhead lights.

"*What?—What?*" He seemed to be choking. "Is this some bloody joke? *Is that it?*" But his anger was without menace now, and she made herself sit quite motionless until the fingers released her arm, and he straightened his back as if he had been carrying some invisible burden.

She heard herself say coolly, "Second Officer Blandford, sir. You didn't know? She's the new officer here." It was like listening to somebody else. A small, quiet voice, her only defence against the sudden terror and understanding. She could almost hear the redcap, Guest, describing the scene, talking about the missing badge from Jane Clarke's hat. A *souvenir, a trophy.*

The door opened, and Second Officer Blandford stared in. "I thought I heard voices."

Victoria touched her arm. Surely there would be bruises? Otherwise she could have put it down to imagination and strain. She had not even seen him leave. She said quietly, "Major Sinclair, ma'am. Looking for Captain Pryce." *Was that all?* Could she just leave it and walk away?

The lips flickered again in a smile. "You should have called me. I've yet to meet him. He's another hero, isn't he?"

But the taunt failed to move her, to mean anything.

They had said it was impossible. She recalled his words—how long ago? Minutes, no more than minutes. *Whose word would they take?*

She thought of Ross, trying to shield her from the girl's naked body and the stares of the M.P.s while the rain had battered down.

He touched me. Her hand was on her arm again, loathing it, wanting to scour it away. *The grip of a murderer.*

Blandford said, "Well, if you've nothing to add . . ." She snatched up a telephone before it had rung more than twice.

Then she said, "Captain Pryce wants you." The girl did not move, and she added abruptly, "That means now!"

Victoria did not remember walking the length of the corridor, or even if she passed anyone. She was suddenly in Pryce's office, knuckles pressed hard against her thighs as if she was on parade. Her control was all she had; she knew only that she must not give way.

Sinclair was here, very relaxed in a cane chair, a glass in his hand. He smiled at her, almost indifferently, as he might greet a stranger in his mess. She realized that Commander Crookshank was present also. He too was drinking, and very flushed, as if he had run all the miles from the main base. She shook her head and felt her hair clinging damply to her skin. That was silly. The base was too far away.

Pryce was watching her as though unsure, like that other time in this same office when James Ross had held her and pretended to stab her for Guest's benefit. He frowned as Crookshank gestured with his glass. "You've been overdoing it, my dear. I think we can bend the rules. You should have a drink."

She tried to shake her head, but it was too painful. "What is it, sir?" Perhaps Sinclair had made some allegation against her, then she was certain he had not. He was not even the same man.

Pryce said coolly, "You know Commander Crookshank's mistrust of the teleprinter, or even of science's latest triumph, the telephone?" But even he could not prolong it. He said, "Signal from *Tybalt: Operation terminated. Both passengers recovered safely. Returning to base with all despatch.*"

She knew she was falling, just as she knew Pryce had been expecting it. He half carried her to a chair, and somebody held a glass of water to her lips.

She wanted to say something. To hear the signal again. He was safe. He was coming back. But nothing came.

She vaguely heard Major Sinclair say, "I'll escort her to her quarters, if you like?"

No. No. But again, nothing came.

Then there was another voice. The woman with the quick, nervous smile. "That will not be necessary, Major Sinclair. I'll attend to Petty Officer Mackenzie."

Victoria reached out and grasped her hand. "Thank you." She almost called her Jane. Her hand was cold, as Jane's had been that night. *Or is it mine?*

Then she did faint.

14 | A Good Show

JAMES Ross covered his mouth with his hand to stifle a yawn, and fought back the desire to look at his watch. By his elbow his favourite pipe lay, filled with tobacco but as yet unlit. Each time he had considered lighting it either Captain Pryce or Commander Crookshank had fired another question at him. It was unreal and oppressive, the surrounding darkness and the bright lights of the operations room making him feel as if he was on trial.

When he had come ashore from the submarine depot-ship, he had hoped she might be there on some pretext or another. But it was Pryce's car with its usual Royal Marine driver that had been waiting, and had brought him at a hair-raising speed to this debriefing.

There were two other officers of his own rank present but they had not been introduced or, if they had, it must have slipped his mind.

After the rendezvous with the submarine *Tybalt,* the apparent ease with which the tug *Success* had been able to contact and transfer them to safety had amazed them both. Perhaps neither of them had really expected still to be alive. Even then, things had almost gone against them. The submarine had been about to surface so that her skipper could make a signal reporting that the operation was over when they had been attacked by two Japanese patrol vessels. Luck, some hazy information as to their presence, they would never know; but it had been a close thing. Ross had served in submarines, and the suspense and fear of a determined attack by surface vessels had not changed. One pattern of depth-charges had been so close that they had heard the firing-pins click before the world exploded about them. Lights had shattered and paint chips had fallen like snow on the dazed and deafened watchkeepers. There had been one enormous crack, as if the pressure-hull had been crushed in a giant vice; then they had heard the sounds of engines fading, moving away, then going altogether. The hydrophone operator had reported all clear, and the young commanding officer had called each sealed compartment himself to make certain that all of his men were safe. Apart from a few nose-bleeds and a broken finger, they had got off lightly.

Tarrant was probably an officer one would never really know, but although it was his first command he had handled the submarine like a true veteran. He must have had some good skippers along the way. Ross had shaken hands with him when they had left to board the depot-ship. The conning tower had been savagely buckled like a tin can, and part of the deck-casing had vanished altogether. It had been as close as that.

Perhaps at any other time it might not have happened. It was a well-known fact that many submarines were lost when returning from patrol, and not at the height of some attack. Never relax, never take anything for granted.

Tarrant had smiled. "At least it will mean a proper refit. You'll have to take a different taxi for the next stunt, sir." He had gazed at the damage, probably recalling the typical submariner's comment. *The most expensive coffin in the world.*

A hand reached out for another note-pad, and Ross saw the Wren look at him for several seconds. The new second officer, the replacement. She made him feel awkward, uneasy. It seemed wrong to be discussing so openly what he and Charles Villiers had seen and done together. There was another Wren present, too, a Leading Writer from Crookshank's department, a small, dark girl with freckles, whose pencil was flying now across her pad as she noted every comment, question and answer.

If Victoria was here . . . He rubbed his eyes, angry that he was so tired. When he had stepped ashore, he had felt more alive than he could remember for some while.

Then Pryce had told him about Napier and, of course, about Mike Tucker. Peter Napier had apparently sailed in the hospital ship. *I must write to him.* In the same instant he knew he would not. If or when they met, it might be different. He thought of Tucker, the warmth he had felt when Pryce had told him of his part in the operation. When Rice had been beheaded. It was still hard to stomach.

Crookshank fiddled with his reading-glasses, and Ross had time to notice Pryce's annoyance.

"And you really believe this Richard Tsao chap is straight up?"

Pryce snapped, "For God's sake, John, Commander Ross is not under oath at a bloody court martial!"

The little leading Wren lowered her head to hide a smile. Second Officer Blandford glared at her.

"I *do* believe that, sir. He is taking a lot of chances, but he knows that, and so are his people. The U-Boats are there, and have been on and off for months." He saw Pryce staring at the little cockade on his shirt: he had not even found time to change into clean clothing. "The group called *Monsun* intends to take vital materials through our blockade. Not in any vast quantity, of course, but it will mount up."

Crookshank rubbed his chin. "In the Great War the Jerries had a big cargo submarine named the *Deutschesland*. She ran the Atlantic blockade to the U.S.A., but of course she was built for the job, not for fighting."

Ross said, "I take your point, sir. These U-Boats are long-range IX D-class. They carry all that they can, raw rubber, wolfram, zinc, ballbearings, but they're still able to hunt well enough. As I've put in my report, with Lieutenant Villiers's help, the Germans also have two Arado seaplanes at their disposal. Their headquarters is at Penang and under the command of *Fregattenkapitän* Dommes." He recalled Richard Tsao's rare display of amusement when he had explained that the overall Japanese commander was a Vice-Admiral Uozumi, the vast difference in rank being another chasm between the unlikely allies.

Pryce said, "This list Tsao made out. Weapons, transmitters?"

Ross attempted to focus his thoughts, already drifting towards images of a bath and a long drink. Villiers was probably in bed by now, dreaming of his unreachable girl in England, or recalling that small moment of peace in the ruined garden where he had once played as a boy.

"He wants to fight, sir."

Pryce grunted. "Don't know what Whitehall will have to say about that." Then he was his old brisk self again, all doubts dispelled. "That's their problem. As soon as I get clearance from D.N.I., the admiral can make the right noises to Southeast Asia Command itself. Go right to the top."

Crookshank looked worried. "Lord Mountbatten?"

Pryce gave a thin smile. "Of course. He usually gets what he wants."

Ross said, "The new depot-ship will arrive any day, sir. A Japanese merchantman, but now properly converted with the right machine-shops for servicing U-Boats. That was another stumbling-block between them, apparently."

Pryce said sharply, "Would be. I wouldn't want to entrust my old sub to a bunch of bloody coolies."

He walked to a shuttered window and back again. "I think this is exactly what we want." He almost reached out to touch Ross's shoulder, but changed his mind. Perhaps the gesture seemed too intimate to him. "You did damn well, Jamie. I'll see that it all goes in my report."

Ross looked away. Like poor Peter Napier and his promotion; a medal too, Pryce had said. Mike Tucker would pull no punches. He would tell him what really happened.

As if reading his mind, Crookshank said helpfully, "Your Petty Officer Tucker insists it was a submarine that put paid to *Turquoise*."

Pryce stared at the wall-maps. "I shall enjoy having a word with Brigadier Davis. So much for his chain of secret agents!"

Crookshank said, "But some of his information . . ." He got no further. Pryce was leafing angrily through his private file, to prove or disprove something.

Ross turned as the second officer spoke to him for the first time. "It must have been a fearful risk."

Ross smiled. "Not so bad once we got started." He saw the doubt in her eyes. "The only time I was really worried was when the *Tybalt* was attacked. I suppose I've grown used to being on my own, being free to act in my own way."

She smiled briefly. "If you say so."

Pryce glanced at them, frowning. "By the way, Jamie, I'll want you to keep your head down for a while. The admiral's got that damned war-correspondent Howard Costain back again." The same irritation, as if he did not approve of someone else holding the apron-strings, not even the admiral.

Ross picked up his pipe, but found that he no longer wanted a smoke. "Whatever you say, sir."

Pryce glanced through his papers again. "And this Tsao has promised recognition signals, boat-markings, everything?"

Ross saw Tsao's composed features, the inner steel of the man and the knowledge he carried with him. While they had been lying at Penang, surrounded by the enemy, and had watched the submarines at their moorings, Tsao had come and gone with the cool confidence of a professional agent, not the junior clerk Villiers had once known. And yet at any hour, day or night, the door could burst open and he would be dragged away to endure the Kempetai's hideous tortures, or forced to watch his family and friends die at their hands.

Ross said, "I would trust him with my life again if need be. He is a man who believes in victory, not just against the Japanese, but against anyone who tries to dominate his country, his people."

Blandford asked gently, "Even against us, Commander Ross? Or the Dutch in Java and Sumatra and their dependencies? Will they not be allowed to recover what was rightly theirs?"

Was she laughing at him? Perhaps his simple explanation seemed shallow here, where there was no danger.

Pryce interrupted rudely, "Not our concern. Our job is to hit them where it hurts, not to worry too much about the price!"

Just for an instant, it seemed as if he and Pryce were quite alone. Ross heard the unspoken words in his mind, like all those other times. *Did we ever, sir?*

And somewhere back there in the shadows, the young Peter Napier, so eager to please. *A piece of cake.*

It was dark when Ross finally escaped from the operations building, and it seemed even darker because of his immense fatigue after the endless questions, the explanations required for the benefit of the Wren who had been taking shorthand.

Two sailors strolled past, only their white caps giving a hint of identity. Ross could smell the heady aroma of rum, and guessed they had been celebrating with an illegal bottle of hoarded tots. It seemed so long since he had been here, months rather than weeks. It was like being a stranger. Charles Villiers had thought the same.

And then he saw her. She was standing quite still beside one of the khaki vehicles parked in the compound. It could have been one of the other Wrens, but he knew instantly that it was Victoria.

She came to meet him, shaking her head as if with disbelief before she threw her arms around him.

He held her tightly and whispered, "I'm a mess. I haven't been able to change for days!"

She did not appear to hear. "I knew you were coming. I was sent to fetch some documents from Colombo." She was trying to smile, to hide the strain and the past anxiety. "I—I think Captain Pryce did it on purpose. To have you all to himself!"

Then she seemed to realize what he had said, and rubbed her hands across his shoulders. "I don't care. You're back, you're safe." She leaned against his arms. "You *are* safe?"

He pulled her closer, remembering all the times when he had thought of her like this. Now that it was happening it was different, unbelievable. "Yes. Good as new." He touched her hair and, very gently, her face, aware of her warmth, her eyes which, even though in shadow, were exactly as he had seen them in his thoughts.

"Was it bad?"

He glanced up at the clouds behind her, and the solitary star which was drifting among them. "I believe it was worthwhile." He thought of all their intent faces, Pryce's rare satisfaction at Tsao's information and lists. "But I kept thinking of you, what it must have been like when you left there as a child."

She lowered her face against his chest, and ignored his protests. "I have waited for this. You are a man. You smell of ships, that other world you described to me."

She allowed him to lead her away from the compound, to the path that led to the sea. She said quietly, so quietly that her words were almost lost in the regular swish of fronds overhead, "I prayed for you. I was so afraid you would be hurt, that you might not come back." A small hesitation, *"To me."*

Somewhere else doors banged and there was a burst of noisy laughter. Perhaps Mike Tucker was one of them. Getting over it.

He stopped and faced her. "Colombo? You drove there and back?"

She stared up at him, her black hair lifting in the warm breeze from the sea. He could feel her studying him, and remembering too. She shook her head. "It was *all right.* I had a marine driver. It was quite safe." She waited for him to hold her again. "You never forget, do you, Jamie?"

It was the first time she had used his name since they had met in the compound.

He said, "I never forget. You are so very precious to me."

She started, and for a moment he thought she was unwilling for him to speak his thoughts.

But she answered softly, "Each night I prayed for you." Her teeth showed in a quick smile. "Several gods, but the same prayer!" She touched his hip and he felt her shiver. "You carry a gun?"

He did not want to release her. "Orders." He did not elaborate. It all seemed so far away, hard to accept that right at this moment men were risking everything, and many were paying for it. In the past, it had been easier to disguise. *A bad show,* or somebody-or-other had *bought it.* Not just the hardness of young men at war, but a necessary shield, a forced callousness to allow the survivors to carry on. From what his father had told him, it had always been like that. Instead, he said, "I've been told to lie low for a bit. Three days, Pryce said. The famous war-correspondent is back, apparently."

She held his arm with both hands. They felt hot, almost feverish through the borrowed shirt with its black and yellow cockade. "I know. He has been asking questions. The security people don't like it."

He smiled. "Careless talk. But in his case it will more likely be another of his *'At last the story of this secret and dangerous war can be told. A spokesman said . . .'* et cetera."

She looked away. "My father wants you to use the house. You can call the base every day, even the section operations."

He sensed the doubt in her voice. "I met your Second Officer Blandford, by the way . . ."

She shrugged. Even that small movement made him want to share all of it with her, his doubts, his fears . . . His mind lingered over it. Fears came in all guises. He knew he would never share it with anybody else.

She said, "She will learn. Perhaps."

A car started up very noisily and some birds clicked nervously in the undergrowth. She paused and looked at him. "You could bring Lieutenant Villiers. My father would like that."

"I'm not sure." He hesitated, hating his own shyness. "People might take it the wrong way, although I can tell you now that I'd deal with anybody who tried to make trouble for you!"

She seemed to relax. As if she had been unsure of his reaction. "Three days? Captain Pryce wanted me to take some leave. But I needed to be here, in case you wanted me." She touched her eyes with her fingers. "All those miles of ocean, but you were never far away, not from me, Jamie."

So Pryce accepted it, even if he did not agree. He tried to

picture Pryce as the young submarine commander, loving someone, being loved. But the picture refused to form.

"I'll speak with Charles Villiers. I'm sure he'd jump at it."

She said gravely, "It was hard for him, I expect. His Singapore is gone." She looked down. "Perhaps mine, too."

He held her against him again. Supple, warm and so trusting. "I'd never hurt you, Victoria."

"I knew that was what you were thinking. My name, my honour, my father's feelings—you worry about everyone but yourself!"

Some headlights flicked on and off, and she said, "I must go now. Commander Crookshank is leaving. I am working for him also now."

He protested, "I'll wait! Please let me do that!"

She released herself and said, "Tomorrow. Now you sleep, have a drink maybe." She tried to laugh. "But not with Second Officer Blandford, she might steal you away!"

More doors slammed and she put her hands on his shoulders again and kissed him on the mouth. "There now, *I must go.*"

"Victoria!" He saw her hesitate as she walked along the same path. She said nothing. "I love you, Victoria. I've never said that to anyone before." He repeated it: it was like hearing someone else. "I love you!"

Then she called, "I know!"

He waited, his heart pounding while he listened to the voices in the compound, Crookshank's thick whisky laugh, Pryce's cool brevity. He ran his fingers through his hair. *I love you.*

He thought suddenly of all those young faces which had been lost, had *bought it.* For this one precious moment in his life perhaps they were able to share it.

Ross stepped down from the big staff-car and looked around in the bright sunshine. From the imposing frontage of the Mackenzie house, to the scarlet flowers and the clattering palms, still fresh from an overnight rainfall, it was a perfect welcome.

He signed a chit for Pryce's marine driver, all very official, to show that he and Villiers had been delivered safely and without incident. It seemed almost absurd after what they had done together. Even the driver had been too attentive to his duties to speak, and had not appeared to be listening to his passengers behind him.

It was always the same in this outfit, Ross thought. Openly all very relaxed and informal, until there was just one hint of another flap forthcoming. Then, as always, the whole section would close up like a giant clam.

The car moved away and Villiers said, "There were times . . ."

Ross smiled. "I know. Me too." He turned his head. "What's that smell? Incense?"

Villiers stared at him as if he had misheard. Then he snapped his fingers, his face suddenly excited and very young.

"Of course, it's Chinese New Year! How could I have forgotten?"

Ross picked up his small grip and looked at the sunshine through the trees. "New Year? I'll bet they had snow in England for ours!"

Strange that it was so hard to accept that he was here, when he had taken his arrival at their small headquarters almost for granted. It had come to him during the night. Tossing and turning, perhaps calling out as his troubled sleep changed into nightmare. He had met Mike Tucker for a few moments just before the car had come for him. They had studied one another, each unsure, looking for something. There were few words: those might come later. It would not have done for Dartmouth, or Flag Officer Submarines, but they had embraced, each feeling the other's pain and bruised relief.

Ross had said, "You could have gone home—you know that, you rascal!"

Tucker had given his lazy grin. "You'd never make it without me. The old firm, remember?" The rest would come out later. When it was possible to talk about it.

Villiers said, "There was a letter waiting for me. Caryl's taken legal advice about a divorce." He grimaced. "Her father's no bloody help, though. Saw her marriage as a bit of a flag-day, apparently. He's a local bank manager—thinks the sun shines out of Major Sinclair's . . ." He broke off and flushed.

Ross turned and saw her on the steps, framed against the house's shadowed interior. She was wearing a white dress, with her arms bare, one of the scarlet flowers pinned in her hair.

Villiers took her hand. *"Kung Hai Fat Choy!"* He lowered his head to kiss it.

She smiled. "And a Happy New Year to you too, Lieutenant Villiers!" But she was looking directly at Ross, her eyes concerned, perhaps sad, as if Villiers's greeting had brought back another memory.

Then she walked slowly down the steps and said, "You are so welcome here." She tilted her face for him to kiss her cheek. "You look so much better now."

He grinned. "Do I? I must have been a real sight!"

She linked their arms with hers and together they walked into the house. More incense, and some red and golden orchids beside one of the Colonel's figurines.

Ross glanced at Villiers, and the shadow was there, too, in his face. Another reminder of what he had seen in Singapore? Of what he had lost?

A small servant appeared, bowing. Victoria said to Villiers, "He will take you to your room. We will meet you when you are ready."

Alone with Ross by the two pillars, she said, "My father is playing chess with his old friend, the doctor here. I will show you round the gardens, in daylight this time."

He felt her arm in his fingers, smooth and so tanned. It was strange that he felt so awkward with her. Had she been in uniform, perhaps it would have been different. Part of their world.

She said, "You are staring."

"Are you surprised?"

"I'm glad." She squeezed his arm. "I still cannot believe you are here, you are like this, with me."

He stopped and held her gently. "I will not have you hurt again." He watched her mouth, the small pulse beating in her throat. "But I have to be sure that you understand."

She watched him searchingly. "Understand? What is there to understand?"

He gripped her arms and said, "I love you, girl. I have since I first laid eyes on you. But it doesn't give me the right, the freedom . . ."

She pulled him firmly around and fell in step beside him.

"You think I may do something I will regret? Like that other time my father told you of?" She shook her head, the black wings of hair hiding her eyes. "I was to blame, too. I wanted love. I thought I had found it."

"I needed you to know."

She gazed up at him, her eyes bright in the reflected sunlight. "Yes, Jamie. Now I know." She watched him for several seconds. "We are not supposed to speak of such things." She shook his arm. "No, don't look at me. But we both know there is a big operation coming, something very dangerous, something which will take you away from me."

"Yes. It seems very likely." There was no room for denials or lies, no time now to make things appear what they were not. What they might never be, for either of them. "I don't believe the top brass will be able to resist it."

She smiled. "*Top brass.* You are so disrespectful, Jamie! What would our Captain Pryce think of that?" But her eyes were troubled again.

He kissed her very carefully. "Or *this,* Victoria?" He could feel her holding back, frightened perhaps; for her, for him, it was impossible to tell.

She said quietly, "Three days. What would you like to do with them?"

He thought of the telephone. Surely Pryce could leave them alone for three days?

She said, "We can walk and talk, swim or just sit in the sun." She watched his hand on her arm, surprised.

He said, "You have a beautiful tan. Second Officer Blandford will envy that."

She corrected him just as seriously. "She will envy me that *also.*" Then she pointed to the rear of the property, a plain white-painted building like a blockhouse. "The water storage is inside. It has a flat roof. Very private. Nobody can see me up there!" She smiled, but could not look at him. "I used to wonder why I bothered." She pressed his arm again very tightly. "Now I know why."

They paused beside the swimming-pool and she said, "Are you tired of water, Jamie?"

She seemed to pause each time she used his name. Unable or unwilling to drop her defences.

She watched him as he knelt beside the pool and put his hand in the clear water. Cool, and after the heat and the dust, so inviting. And it was because of her. Their being together. Something which people had almost given up taking for granted.

She touched her arm, as she had when Major Sinclair had released her. If there was a bruise, it did not show. She saw the pleasure on Ross's face when he turned to look up at her, the tension smoothed away as if it had never existed.

How could I tell him ? It would prove nothing and might put his life in even greater danger when Pryce's "flap" became a reality. She could hear Sinclair's slurred voice. *Whose word would they take?* Captain Pryce had asked Sinclair to postpone his return to England for his new decoration, his gong, as Mike Tucker had called it. If he even suspected that she had informed her superiors, he would blame Jamie: indirectly or otherwise, it would amount to the same. Sinclair's enmity would impose a terrible risk in addition to those other dangers he was already expected to accept without protest.

She could feel her eyes stinging, her body trembling with sudden anger, remembering how she had fainted after the news of Jamie's safe rendezvous. Who could she tell, anyway? What proof did she have? *Whose word would they take?*

He was beside her and she had not heard or seen him move. "What is it? Is it me?"

She shook her head and wanted to cry. "No, Jamie. It's neither of us . . . It's not a dream, either." She lifted her chin and looked at him quite calmly. "I love you, Jamie. I don't want to lose you. Not now."

Colonel Mackenzie got up from the chess table and walked to a window. "Care for a gin, George?"

His friend, the doctor, another old warrior, nodded while he studied the ranks of chessmen. He asked, "What are they doing now?"

Mackenzie pushed his fingers between the slats of the blind and peeped out at the unmoving couple beside the pool. No use getting sentimental and protective about it: if it wasn't for the bloody war, he'd have been more than satisfied. Jamie Ross was a fine officer, a brave young man who had proved his courage over and over again. Sometimes luck stayed with you. People often said that if it had your number on it there was nothing you could do anyway. *But what would become of her if that happened, and I was gone?* Without turning his head, he knew that the portrait of her mother, Jeslene, was watching him. Just as he knew what she would have said about it. He dropped the blind again and reached for a bottle of gin. It was stamped *Duty Free, H.M. Ships Only.* Charles Villiers was a thoughtful lad.

He replied, "*Doing*, George?" He touched his white moustache with his knuckle. "They're living. That's good enough for me." Then he did look at the portrait, suddenly aware that he meant it.

It was on the second of their promised three days that the call came. Surprisingly, it was Pryce himself, undaunted by the security of the telephone.

She had watched Ross's face when he had come back into the room. He had said, "I have to go tomorrow. They're sending a car. There's no need for you to leave here."

The old Colonel had looked at each of them, feeling it, sharing it, as if the life he had been forced to abandon was still a part of him.

Ross had added quietly, "I shall come back—if I may, sir?" But his eyes were on her, her mouth, her breathing, the way she was clenching her hands with desperation, and with courage, too.

He did not even hear the Colonel's gruff assent. It was like being broken, forced down into the abyss where all hope is finally extinguished, like the lightless depths of the sea.

To Villiers, he had said, "You too, I'm afraid." But still his eyes did not leave hers. Pryce had sounded firm and convinced, without emotion, as might have been expected.

Ross had been suddenly reminded of Highmead School, the place to which his father had been desperate to send him, even though he had been so short of money. Just so that his son could go to the same school as the man who had once been his young commanding officer: Pryce's father, who had been awarded the V.C. after Zeebrugge. The decoration which should by rights have been his own. Ross sometimes wondered if Pryce knew or had ever guessed the truth of that affair. But more than that, in a school so full of tradition, and with such strong ties to the armed services, he had found himself thinking of morning assembly in the Hall, and the school's roll of honour. His own name was on it now, although he knew he would never go back to see it. There had been some verse beneath the long list of names from the Great War: lines from Kipling.

What stands if Freedom fall?
Who dies if England live?

The car had come for them in the early morning, and he had seen her watching him from a window, her face in shadow. She had reached out as if to grip his hand, and then placed hers against her breast. As though she had been able to take and lay his own hand there.

The car had swung out of the driveway and headed back towards the coast. Once, Ross looked back, but the estate, like a dream, was lost from view.

Captain Ralph Pryce was showing unusual signs of strain, as if he had been working sleeplessly throughout much of the night. He waved Ross to a seat and said simply, "Sorry to drag you back so soon, but this matter can't wait."

Ross prepared himself, surprised that he felt nothing. No nerves, no fear, only a kind of emptiness. Awaiting the inevitable, not for the first time.

There were a lot of cars in the compound, and even from Pryce's office he could hear the murmur of voices from the operations room along the corridor. He tried not to think of her at the window, her courage.

He had thought it strange that Pryce should hold the briefing here: the Base Operations section had far more room and better facilities, and was used to dealing with the needs of a fleet, not merely a tiny part of it. He had even seen the Chief-of-Staff's car. As *he* was second only to the admiral, it must be important. Then Ross had understood why Pryce had persuaded the brass to meet here. He was in control. It was, after all, his show.

Pryce said, "Before we go into the wolves' lair, I just want to make matters clear to you. If you agree, *you* will be the main player." He turned over some papers without looking at them. "At first I thought it was some extraordinary coincidence—and but for your meeting with that Tsao chap and getting that priceless information from him, the whole thing might have gone down the drain." He leaned forward, and in the light from the lamp on the desk Ross could see his fatigue, the redness in the eyes, so unlike the man. Pryce said, "Last week, apparently off Lisbon, an R.A.F. Sunderland spotted a U-Boat on the surface. It attacked with depth-charges and destroyed it. Nothing unusual, just a 'good show' as the high-fly boys would put it, but they did manage to photograph the end of the attack. Then some bright lad in air-reconnaissance spotted something interesting about it. The Intelligence department had circulated all branches, but it took one man to notice it. This is it." He dragged out a glossy enlargement of the original photograph and laid it carefully beneath the light.

It was familiar enough: a submarine caught at the moment of diving, the great whirlpools of torn water where the depth-charges had burst around the shark-like hull in a lethal straddle. Some unknown character had written in one corner, *The Perfect Kill!* To others, it would be. Ross glanced at Pryce's cold eyes and knew how he was seeing it. A submarine in her death agony, men like themselves being taken to the bottom, crushed and mangled—no one ever could know the true horror of such a death. *The Perfect Kill.* As submariners, they both saw the scene in a different light.

Pryce said, "Take a closer look."

Ross studied the dying U-Boat, the moment frozen in time. He could almost hear Tsao's calm voice describing the boats in Group *Monsun.* As part of the German and Japanese recognition system, the U-Boats were to have two broad white stripes fore and aft athwart their decks, and the German flag painted on the conning tower. Unnerving to think that he had seen it for himself in the harbour at Penang, peering through a tiny shutter in the tug-master's cabin like an amateur spy. In the photograph it was not possible to see the painted flag, but the white stripes had stood out stark and bright even as the sea had boiled over the casing. There were some metal containers, too, immediately abaft the conning tower: extra stowage for non-perishable cargo on the return passage. Ross looked up and saw the feverish brightness in Pryce's eyes.

Pryce said, "We shall have the correct recognition signals if Tsao keeps his promise. The rest is up to us."

Ross looked at the photograph again. "We'd use a submarine, sir?"

"We *have* a submarine, Jamie. I've got the go-ahead, and the

Fleet Engineering Officer has the matter in hand." He added with his usual impatience, "*Tybalt* is pretty well knocked about. The enemy will have no idea that another of their boats was sunk. There were no signals. It was over in seconds." His mouth lost its customary hardness. "Poor bastards."

He might have taken Ross's silence for doubt, and went on sharply, "It's a chance in a lifetime. We have no time to lose. All we need is the location of the new submarine depot-ship—Intelligence are voting for Penang. I don't think so. Too many eggs in one basket. The Germans may be difficult to understand sometimes, but their submariners are still the best. Admit that, and you're half way there."

From far away they heard a bell ring, and somebody's deep voice calling for order. The stage was set.

Ross said quietly, "You want me to command the attack, sir?"

Pryce swung round and seized the telephone before it buzzed twice. "Yes? I told you I was not to be disturbed!" A pause, and Ross saw his eyes return to the photograph. "He'll just have to wait." He slammed it down. "Bloody woman, I'll explain to her what *I* think is important." He took several seconds to calm himself. "It will probably never come again, and in any case we should probably be elsewhere if it did." He walked to a window and stared emptily at the palms. "Fate, some would call it. My father and yours in the Great War, with a clapped-out submarine full of explosives. Who said history can't be repeated?" He patted his pockets. "Well? I can't order you to do it."

Ross picked up his cap and turned it over in his hands. "You don't have to. I'll ask for volunteers when we're closer to the time." He realized that Pryce had not followed him to the door. "What is it, sir?"

Pryce shrugged. "I just wish one thing." He looked at him, searching for something, perhaps. "I wish to God I was coming with you."

They walked out into the corridor and Ross noticed the messenger and some seamen watching as they passed. They knew.

Soon everyone would know about the proposed attack, and the secret would be safe. He thought of Mike Tucker. *The old firm.*

He realized that a solitary officer was waiting as if to intercept them. In his smart white drill, he was barely recognizable as the distant Tarrant, who had conned his submarine with such admirable skill through that last attack.

Pryce stopped and said curtly, "There is nothing to add, Lieutenant Tarrant. You will get another command in due course, and I would be obliged if you would keep the whole matter to yourself."

Tarrant turned to Ross. "They're taking my command, sir! To be thrown away on another crazy operation!"

There was nothing to say. He knew and understood what Tarrant was going through. He would have felt the same way himself.

Pryce had no such doubts. With one eye on the widening slit in the operations room door, he said coolly, "A submarine is a weapon, Lieutenant Tarrant, to be used to its best advantage, and under any given circumstance. That is all."

Ross hesitated, but the other man looked through him, his eyes empty. There *was* nothing to be said.

The long room seemed to close around him, shining red or tanned faces, smart drill uniforms or crumpled shirts of khaki and white. Officers who had come from all branches and every kind of duty to be a part of Special Operations, their reasons as varied as themselves.

The Chief-of-Staff sat with his black walking stick beside him. Before this important staff appointment, he had commanded a light cruiser in the Mediterranean, which had eventually been sunk by dive-bombers on a Malta convoy. He had made no secret of the fact that he would have preferred another sea command to a position with the top brass. The thought touched Ross like a spoken word. *You are so disrespectful, Jamie.*

Pryce was on his feet, describing the situation with his usual precise efficiency, and without giving too much away. He did not even mention Richard Tsao by name, and Ross wondered what the others might think if they had heard his rare disclosure, which on recollection Pryce himself would regard as a weakness. *I wish to God I was coming with you.* Ross had come across plenty of people who had said as much, knowing that in fact they were quite safe from any such risk.

He saw Second Officer Blandford watching him thoughtfully, tapping a pencil against her teeth. Victoria should have been here, and yet in his heart he was grateful that she was not.

Pryce was saying, "This is probably the most intrepid and daring operation we have undertaken. Some might even suggest it is impossible. But they said the *Bismarck* was unsinkable, and others claimed that nobody would ever be able to penetrate the fjords of Norway and blow the bottom out of the *Tirpitz,* the world's mightiest battleship. But it was done, gentlemen, and there will always be men to attempt such impossible missions."

Ross saw Commander Crookshank, sweating in the crowded room, his face composed and empty of doubt. Others far more senior would bear the true responsibility.

Pryce said, "It will be weeks rather than months, so let us waste no time." He was looking directly at Ross.

Waste no time. It was like an epitaph.

15 | No More Time

His Majesty's Submarine *Tybalt* lay close alongside her depot-ship, her casing and conning tower busy with boiler-suited artificers and mechanics. Large tarpaulins were spread over much of the work, a normal precaution in Trincomalee where blistering sunshine and soaking rain could come in liberal proportions. To the casual onlooker and passing boat, she looked what she was: a submarine undergoing another overhaul and refit.

Only down below, away from the snaking power-lines and diamond-bright welding torches, was it possible to appreciate the change.

Lieutenant Charles Villiers entered the control-room and glanced at the base engineers, the "plumbers" as they were nicknamed, studying a rough pencilled plan and making notes to be passed on to their team of experts.

Villiers had felt the difference. It was if the submarine had been suddenly abandoned without warning, the officers and ratings swept away like some modern *Marie Celeste.* Lockers left open, but with a few scraps, remnants left behind to remind anyone who cared of the men who had lived, worked and survived as one company. A few garish pin-ups, a newly darned sock, forgotten in the haste to leave the boat as ordered. Only in the control-room was there a sense of purpose, something preserved. The chart table and plot, the tightly packed and well-thumbed publications close to hand. Time and tide tables, recognition manuals, some of the regularly used charts, and of course the navigator's bible, *The Nautical Almanac.* But how quiet and still. The only power, which came from the depot-ship, was muffled; even the plumbers spoke quietly, like people in church. Villiers grimaced. Or at a funeral.

Less than a week, and they had barely paused for breath. Two containers had been fixed just aft of the conning tower. Each one would carry and conceal a chariot, a two-man torpedo, as some still called them. They had even erected something like a bandstand at the rear of the bridge, where a U-Boat would normally carry her antiaircraft weapons. The structure had then been buckled to match the damaged conning tower. It was often said that a lookout only saw what he expected to see. How many bobbing pieces of wood, like broom-handles, had been mistaken for enemy periscopes? And vice versa, when it had already been too late.

When he had walked from forward to the control-room, Villiers had realized, perhaps for the first time, what it all meant. The many cases of high explosives, the treble system of fuses in case one failed. *Tybalt,* within one week, had become a floating bomb.

He heard Ross's level voice, and turned to see him clap the two engineer officers on the shoulders. Did he ever doubt? Did he see even the remotest chance of survival, let alone the success of this attack?

Villiers had worked in and from submarines often enough, and in his papers at Special Operations he was described as an explosives and demolition officer, but the classrooms and the experiments at H.M.S. *Vernon,* the Navy's mine and torpedo school, had been nothing like this.

Ross walked over to him. He wore overalls which had once been white, but were now streaked with grease and blotchy with oil. He must have been right over the boat, Villiers thought, and he wondered if Ross had felt the ghosts watching as he passed.

Ross said, "They've done well, Charles. Just got to top up the bunkers and fix the guns . . ." He hesitated and glanced along the narrow passageway, the line of oval-shaped watertight doors, now open from torpedo tubes to engine- and motor-rooms. He was speaking his thoughts, his mind checking and re-checking. Villiers could almost feel it. But then, Ross was a true submariner, and he had once heard him say that he had even served in one of the original *Thunderbolt* Class boats. Like this one, *Tybalt.* Good, dependable craft. A maximum of twenty-two knots surfaced, and eleven submerged. She was armed with ten twenty-one-inch torpedo tubes. Villiers had quickly noticed that they carried no extra torpedoes. It was obviously considered unlikely that there would be time or room for a reload. It was a chilling thought.

Ross had seen his emotions: Villiers had too open a face to hide anything. He felt the hull quiver as something heavy was moved overhead. It was as if the boat was resisting, trying to assert herself. He thought of Pryce's words to her stricken skipper: *A submarine is a weapon, to be used to its best advantage.* Some might agree. Ross glanced again at the deserted spaces where men had been packed together under every kind of condition. As he had been. Hoping and dreaming. Holding back the fear which was a constant crewman on every patrol.

Even now many of *Tybalt*'s company would be on their way, perhaps to a different theatre of war. Some to be drafted to other submarines, others glad to be leaving, grateful to be going home. *Home . . .*

He touched the lowered attack-periscope and felt the grease on his fingers. Not just a weapon. As Mike Tucker would say, it was a way of life.

Feet scraped on a ladder, and tall khaki figures ducked beneath unfamiliar obstructions. Major Trevor Sinclair grinned broadly at them. "Thought you might be here. This is my second-in-command, Captain Pleydell, Royal Marines."

Ross shook hands with the newcomer and wondered what it must be like to work with Sinclair. Pleydell looked very young, and the large moustache he sported made him appear even younger. Like some of the R.A.F. pilots Ross had seen, the *high-fly boys* as Pryce had termed them. There would be a landing party of marines with them, and a few Gurkhas who were well trained, and unmoved by the prospect of working behind enemy lines. It reminded him again of Peter Napier and what he had said about Sinclair.

"We'll go over it again with the N.C.O.s, Bobby."

Pleydell, "Bobby," nodded, frowning at the same time. "A bit dicey, I'd have thought, Major?"

"If you can't do it, say so, and I'll get some bugger who can!"

Villiers said, "I know what he means, sir . . ."

Sinclair eyed him. "Bully for you, Lieutenant Villiers. But when I need advice I shall ask for it." He gave the huge grin again. "Or more likely yawn, eh?"

Ross said, "We'll *all* discuss it when we get the word." He looked from one to the other, feeling the tension, especially where Villiers was concerned. The cracks were beginning to show. He would have to watch it. Step on it, if need be.

Sinclair was looking at a list. "Come along, we'll see where they're putting our chaps. Must have room to strip their weapons and lay out the gear." He was quite calm again, as if nothing had been said.

Ross glanced at Villiers. Could Sinclair know about him and his wife? It was unlikely, but not impossible. He half smiled. *God, I'm getting as bad as him.*

They stood beneath the conning tower and looked up at the two open hatches, the upper and lower lids. It seemed wrong not to see an oval of blue sky. Just canvas, and a dangling drill on a cable.

They climbed the ladder to the bridge. How many times had the klaxon screamed out from here, to the tilt of the deck and the fierce inrush of water?

They stepped out into the sunshine, and Villiers said quietly, "Will you come back to submarines afterwards, sir?"

So simply said. *Afterwards.* The operation, the whole bloody war—what was afterwards?

He saw a boatswain's mate in smart belt and gaiters peering at him anxiously from the catamaran. The Commodore, Submarines did not go in for oily sweaters and scruffy grey flannel bags in his depot-ship.

"What is it?"

The sailor saluted. "Captain Pryce has come aboard, sir. He's with the Commodore." He made a clumsy point of not including Villiers. "When you're ready, sir."

Ross jammed his cap on to his tousled hair. The Commodore would just have to put up with the overalls for once. He said, "I have the strangest feeling that the balloon is about to go up to an enormous height, Charles." He tried to lighten his tone. "Do you want a run ashore with me?"

Villiers hesitated. "If you don't mind, sir. I've a letter to write." He looked lost, rather helpless. "I want her to know . . ."

Ross said, "I understand."

Villiers watched him, seeing someone very different from the man he had come to hold on to as a friend. Then he said, "She means so much, you see."

Ross looked at the glittering water alongside. Villiers was speaking for both of them.

Colonel Basil Mackenzie leaned back in his cane chair and watched with some amusement while Ross topped up his pink gin with water. "You Navy chaps. I don't know how you can drink that stuff. It rots your guts!"

Ross looked across the veranda at the lush gardens, with their heavy flowers and winding paths, carefully swept. So peaceful.

Mackenzie said, "She won't be long. She was having a swim. I don't think she was expecting you quite so soon." He smiled. "Glad you could get away."

The information had been verified. The converted depot-ship had arrived. She would soon be moving to her new anchorage, not far from the place where the chariots had blown up the motor anti-submarine boats. Peter Napier's first-ever operational job, and almost his last.

Pryce had been definite. "We're putting real pressure on the Japs now—they're even falling back in some places. We've got a new army in the field: tough, hard and determined. So if we can pull this one off, it will be a real stab in the back for the Japanese as well as the Germans." He had glanced at his ever-present folder. "Operation *Trident*. It will make a few people sit up and take notice!"

Surely, Ross thought, it must mean more than that?

Mackenzie had been watching him steadily. "Having a rough time, are you?"

Ross smiled. "Sorry, sir. Does it show?"

Mackenzie brushed something invisible from his immaculate white jacket. "It's something you never forget. I never have." He looked at him very directly. "There's something in the air, right?" He held up one hand. "I don't expect you to tell me." He sighed. "You don't need to."

"I want to tell you something, if I may, sir."

The bushy eyebrows rose and fell. "How you feel? That you're afraid for Victoria, the one living creature I care about?"

"Something like that." He had always thought it wrong to become too deeply involved because of the war: he had seen too many heartbreaks to allow it to happen to himself. Until now.

He said quietly, "I love her. I want to ask her to marry me." The Colonel said nothing but stared into his gardens, his eyes distant. "It's just that . . . if anything goes wrong . . ."

Mackenzie said, "If you think like that, then it will. I've seen it happen." He glared round for his servant and gestured at their empty glasses. "For one so young you're a funny sort of chap, a bit old fashioned. I'm told you don't think so much of yourself as you do of others." He paused. "I like that. Pretty rare these days. All mouth and trousers now, as my old batman would put it!" He was suddenly very serious. "I know you love her. Saw it the first time you were here together. I have to admit I was bloody jealous at the idea of losing her. Eventually." He leaned over and gripped his wrist. "You're right for each other. Don't fight it. Take it while you can!" He released him and added, "She's coming."

She wore a white bath-robe and was rubbing her hair with a towel when she saw them together. She looked from Ross to her father, her eyes steady and questioning, one bare foot on the lower step like that other time.

Then she said, "I knew." She nodded as if to confirm or accept it. "I have to go back tomorrow. I'll be on stand by, they said."

Then she walked towards him, the towel falling unnoticed to the floor. "I prayed. But deep down, I knew it was going to happen." She moved against him as he put his arms around her, her hair damp against his face. It seemed so natural, as if it had never been any other way. Then she did look up. "When?"

He watched her eyes, and the way she was holding her head. For his benefit and for hers. She tried to smile. "You may as well tell me. I will know tomorrow anyway."

He turned her towards the garden. "Twenty-four hours. After that . . ."

She tried to give herself time. "What have you two been talking about?" But when they looked round, the Colonel had discreetly disappeared.

Ross held her for several seconds, so aware of her, her breathing, her private anguish.

"I told your father I want to marry you, if you'll have me." She watched him, her eyes never leaving his face as he said, "When this is over, we can talk." He shook her gently. "Talk and talk. I can tell you what you might be letting yourself in for . . ."

She answered in a whisper, "When this is over, Jamie? That is beyond time. How can we wait?"

He brushed the hair from her forehead. "Will you?"

She looked away. "Do you have a handkerchief?"

He gave her his and watched her dab her eyes with it.

She said lightly, "I'm all right, Jamie. I'm not going to spoil it. Twenty-four hours? They might cancel it, whatever it is—I've known it happen before. So must you?" She looked at him, her eyes pleading. "It happens, doesn't it?" Then she threw her arms around his neck and exclaimed, "But you don't think so. You *know,* don't you?"

He touched her hair, and her neck where he could feel the thin gold chain she always wore. "Too much at stake, Victoria." So many lives, reputations too; no, they would not cancel it unless the enemy were one jump ahead. He held her even closer. *Am I afraid? Like poor David. Would I know if I was afraid?*

He thought of Villiers and Sinclair, and the young Royal Marine captain with the absurd moustache. And all the others. Mike Tucker would be there as well. He would know, too. Mike had changed in some way: there were fewer jokes now, and he had acquired a calm maturity which had taken Ross by surprise. After being a prisoner he must have seen how narrow was the margin between hope and despair. He had come through it, but what had really changed him?

He said quietly, "I love you so much, Victoria." It felt as if he had shouted it aloud. "I don't want to hurt you any more. You deserve so much more than I can offer." He touched her mouth and throat. "But nobody could love you more."

She thrust her hand through his arm. "That's settled then. It's up to us." They paused by one of the pillars. "Now kiss me, as if you mean it." She smiled up at him, some small tears on her dark lashes unheeded. "Just keep on loving me!"

He kissed her. The smile was still on her lips, and he could taste the salt of her tears.

Second Officer Celia Blandford looked around the operations room and plucked the shirt away from her damp shoulder. There were two sailors on duty beside the array of telephones and one glanced up to watch, but averted his eyes when he saw her irritation.

She compared this to the operations room where she had served before: the bustle, the orderly comings and goings of messengers, senior officers and other Wrens like herself. She glanced at the damp, curling notices and faded maps on the walls. This place was a shambles, more like a seedy club than the springboard of Special Operations.

She recalled Pryce's precise instructions about signals and Intelligence reports. He at least was a true professional, whereas some of the others . . .

Then there was Lieutenant-Commander Ross. What was he really like? The Victoria Cross should have said it all, but it only scratched the surface. Also there was that half-Chinese Wren petty officer. She had confessed out loud that she was in love with James Ross, had even seemed rather shy about it: perhaps she would have been more open with Jane Clarke. Love—what could she know about it? Although she had an influential father; she would be very wealthy one day . . .

It was so unfair. But get a commission? She smiled quickly. They needed good officers in the Wrens, but there were standards, limits. Perhaps she ought to take her aside and have a talk with her.

She looked up, frowning, as the door opened very slightly and a khaki arm came around it. For a moment she thought it was that dashing Major Sinclair, who had made such a name for himself in Burma and Malaya, and whose fierce manner intrigued her. But it was not. Anyway, Sinclair was married, or so she had heard.

"Yes? Do you wish to see somebody here?" It came out more sharply than she had intended, and she tried to soften it. "I'm Second Officer Blandford . . ."

The officer entered the room. He was wearing smart khaki drill, well pressed, somehow at odds with the tanned, lean features and steely eyes above it.

He said calmly, "I know who you are. I want to see Captain Pryce."

She smiled, on firm ground again. *I want.* "Captain Pryce is not here at present." She made a careful note of the crown on his shoulder and the Military Police flash on his sleeve. "I'm sorry, er, Major . . . ?"

"Guest. George Guest. I need to see him."

He sauntered across the room, the eyes of the two sailors following him like lamps.

"I can call the Base, Major Guest, if it really is so urgent. We've been rather busy . . ."

The steely eyes settled on her. "A flap on, right?" He saw her flush and smiled. "I've seen a few come and go here. I felt it as I drove in." He recalled what she had said. "Yes, give him a buzz. I should have come earlier, but this sort of thing takes time, and tenacity."

"May I tell him what it's about?"

He watched her hands, their quick, nervous movements. "It's about your predecessor. Jane Clarke."

"I—I see." The cool way he had spoken her name, and without her rank: it made her sound like a suspect. But she was dead.

Guest walked to the door. "Where's Petty Officer Mackenzie?"

She said, "Ashore, sir. On local leave. I have a number where she can be reached."

Guest nodded. *I'll bet you have.* "I'll not disturb her." He closed the door behind him without a sound.

His sergeant was waiting for him, his red cap shining like blood in the police-light by the compound.

"All right, sir?"

Guest smiled. "We'll have to get a move on." He compared the dead girl with the one he had just met. How could they send her to a place like this, he wondered. Surrounded by all those young tearaways, most of whom had probably never been with a woman in their lives. But this one, Blandford, would run a mile if a man so much as smiled at her. *If I'm any judge.*

Like his sergeant, he had been a copper on the beat long before he had joined the Military Police for the duration. He listened to the piano and the lusty singing coming from the petty officers' mess, and then headed towards the wardroom. A far cry from the East End of London, with its jellied eels and Saturday night punch-ups at the old *Salmon and Ball* pub. To go back to it after this was unthinkable.

He was himself again. "We may not have enough to make it stick, but a court of enquiry—well, that would be something else."

They both grinned. *Once a cop . . .*

• • •

The hospital seemed very quiet, even deserted, not at all the way that he remembered it. Petty Officer Mike Tucker held up his arm and looked at the small red mark where the needle had gone in. It was almost funny when you thought about it. While he had been here in this same hospital with the delirious Sub-Lieutenant Napier, some busybody had noticed in his paybook that one of his inoculations was out of date. He clenched his fist. It should cause no pain; with him it almost never did. Must keep the naval records up to date, even when you stood a fair chance of having your arse blown off. He picked up his cap, his best one, and wondered why he had bothered. Then he glanced at a closed door, where he had waited by Napier's bedside, when the girl had come to him. He smiled again. *Jamie's girl.* He hoped so, anyway.

He glanced at his reflection in a window and tilted his cap to a rakish angle. His family would know he was safe. They would never know he was already off again. He had even had some letters, some so old that they were still talking about the nearness of Christmas. Young Madge had had the kid, his mother had written. He had been able to feel her indignation through her sloping handwriting. It was more black than white, apparently. He could smile about it now, but it must have lit a fuse under his mum and dad. Madge and her bloody Yanks, another benefit of the Lease-Lend agreement.

"Why, hello! Didn't expect to see *you* back here!"

He swung round, shading his eyes from the sunlight that filled the corridor. The nurse was small and neat in her tropical uniform: pretty, too, with a nice smile.

He said, "Oh, just for a jab from the doc."

She shook her head. "You don't remember me at all, do you?"

It was like turning back a page. He said quietly, "Nurse Julyan. I'm hardly likely to forget you." He saw her surprise and uncertainty. "You were such a help to young Mr Napier, before they took off his arm. You must be used to it, I suppose."

She seemed to consider it. "Not really." She hesitated. "He

was such a nice young chap. One night when he was able to speak properly, he told me all about you, how you saved him and carried him for miles." She saw his face cloud over. "Sometimes he was too drugged to know what he was saying. He kept talking about somebody called Mango." She smiled. "You'd fallen asleep in the chair by his bed."

"Mango was just a kid caught up in somebody else's war. He was killed."

She said, "I see *you* don't get used to it, either."

He said, "You told me about your brother."

"Did I?" She glanced at her wrist; it was bandaged, but Tucker had not noticed it before. She said, "One poor chap tried to kill himself. Some clot had left the scissors where he could get at them. I stopped him, but he had a go at me instead." She tried to smile. "He didn't know about my famous right hook!"

All at once they were walking together towards the entrance. She said, "Did I really tell you about Jack?"

"Yeah. He was a rear-gunner on a Lanc. Bought it over Germany." She nodded. "And you come from Hendon. North London. Very posh."

She smiled again, her teeth white in her tanned face. "Not our part of it!"

There was a naval van in front of the drive, with the Special Operations flash painted on the wing.

He said, "I'll cadge a lift. Got some gear to pack." She said nothing, but stood quite still watching him as if she were waiting for something. "I was wondering." He looked down at her: she was short, and had a pretty, turned-up nose. "Bit of a cheek—I'm not even sure if I'll be back in these parts. But would you care to come out for a drink, a meal or something? Maybe we could see a flick down at the army cinema?"

"Thought you'd never ask." She studied his face, where the cruel bruises had been. Like the scars on his back. It must have been agony, but he had not complained like some men did when they were on the mend. Before that they were like small, lost boys, ashamed of their wounds or injuries, embarrassed at being washed, swabbed and handled, and suffering every indignity thrown their way. Mike Tucker had not been like that. She had been easily able to picture him carrying poor Napier mile after mile. Once, Napier had gripped her hand and said in a level, conversational voice, "He could have left me, you know. Or killed me. It's what they do over there."

What they do. She looked at the line of closed doors behind him. *We don't even know the half of it. We only pick up the pieces.*

Tucker was looking at her, as if they had met somewhere before.

"I really ought to know your name, Nurse Julyan. You know mine!"

She wished they were somewhere else. There were so many things. She replied, "Actually, it's Eve. No cracks now, if you don't mind!"

He took her hands in his, very careful not to touch the bandage.

"Eve." He looked at her for several seconds. "*Eve.* It would be. Eve." He stooped and kissed her on the cheek, then turned away before she could speak.

A sick-berth attendant passed with a large jug of lemon juice. "There now, Nurse Julyan! What did I just see?"

She smiled. After all, he couldn't help being the way he was. He was called Flossie by his workmates, and he seemed to enjoy it.

He said suddenly, "That was Mike Tucker, just had a jab. Can't see the sense in it, if the buzz I've heard is true. I should forget about him if I were you."

But she was staring after the van as it moved towards the gates. It had blurred over like a painting left out in the rain. A light began to flash above one of the doors and she automatically straightened her cap before hurrying towards it.

She touched her cheek where he had kissed her, remembering his face when she had told him her name. *It would be.* What had he meant? She gripped the door-handle so hard that it hurt her fingers. She might never know.

James Ross lay on top of the bed and watched the moonlight through the mosquito netting spreading patterns across the opposite wall. The house was full of creaks and small sounds, although he guessed that everyone else was asleep. He could see the close, brilliant stars through the window and imagined a warm breeze playing through the palm fronds. There had been no rain after all, although he had heard the Colonel predicting it to his old friend, the doctor, over dinner. An awkward meal despite everyone's kindness, and the unmasked interest of the doctor. Had it been planned, or had it just happened that way?

She had been seated opposite him and each time their eyes had met over another course, he had felt their emotion like physical pain. She had worn a plain silk dress with her throat bare; he had seen the gold chain moving even when she had kept her features composed.

Tomorrow. Or was it today? She would be in uniform. That would be the hardest time . . . He had thought he might lose himself in the preparations, the "ifs" and "maybes" of Pryce's Operation *Trident,* but there was nothing more to do. He had forgotten nothing, had even seen all their faces in his mind when he had gone over it yet again. *The volunteers.* If they had accepted all the volunteers, they would have needed four submarines and more chariots as well. He had been deeply touched that men he had come to know as friends could offer their lives so freely. The target and the location were set. Even if something changed at the last minute, or the vital recognition signals were never discovered, he knew, just as he had known other significant things in his life, that the operation would not be cancelled. When he tried to think ahead, beyond the nerve-stretching strategy which had seemed so clear in the operations room, the shock really hit him. Beyond the deed there had been nothing. Like a last chapter being torn out of a book.

He thought of the faces again. The Canadian lieutenant Bill Walker would be in charge of the chariots; Major Trevor Sinclair was to supervise the landing party once the target had been reached. Surprise was everything. Without it, they were dead and buried.

He looked over at the drink on the bedside table, some of the Colonel's special malt. "Make you sleep, my boy!" But even that had been said with a certain sadness. Ross had known plenty of men who had drunk themselves stupid before an operation. A good defence, but not for long.

He had kissed Victoria goodnight on the veranda. Like parting at a railway station; it was nothing new. No words when they were needed so badly, then so many when it was too late and the train was moving from the station.

Charles Villiers would be thinking of it, too. Remembering . . . The hotel off St James's owned by the Villiers family. Yes, he would be thinking of his girl right now; and every time he bumped into Sinclair it would remind him of what could never be.

If only. He stared at the ceiling. If only what? The war would step between them; yet but for the war they would never have met. Never seen her? Never heard her laugh? He rolled over and reached for the glass.

For an instant he believed that he was dreaming, had imagined it. Round the bend.

She stood in the doorway beyond the filmy curtain, framed against the darkened corridor, all in white, her feet bare on the carpet.

Then she closed the door and deliberately locked it. "I came."

He swung himself out of the bed and through the netting like a dream, and held her against him. He could feel her heart beating against him, the thrust of her breasts as if she could barely breathe.

She said, "I had to. I feel no doubt, no shame. I could not bear to lie there, aching for you, knowing what we must go through together."

He kissed her hair, saw her eyes shine in the moonlight as she raised her mouth to his. She was trembling but her body was warm, even hot, and he knew what it had cost her, *was* costing her while they kissed with an intimacy unfamiliar to them both.

She looked down as he pulled at the ribbons of her gown and allowed it to fall to the floor. For a while longer he held her at arms' length, knowing that this was meant to happen, that even if she had protested it might have been too late.

He laid her carefully on the bed and watched the moon drench her tanned body, so that the skin shone in the cold light like bronze. He sat beside her, kissing her, exploring her neck, her uplifted breasts, feeling her excitement rising to match his own as he stroked her nipples and the smooth curve of stomach. He did not even recall throwing off his underpants to lie naked beside her; he knew only that she wanted him as much as he needed her. Not merely an act, not some passing encounter, but passion, real and overwhelming.

She was kissing him again, her mouth seeking his, their tongues meeting like temptation itself.

She arched her back and gasped as he slipped his hand deeper. There was no more time. Perhaps there never was.

She looked at him as he lifted over her, her eyes like flames in the moonlight.

She gasped, "I can't wait! Not any more! Take me, Jamie! Take me!"

It was like nothing else, and he heard her cry out just once as he found and entered her.

Then and only then she murmured, "I couldn't wait. It had to be."

Her head lolled against his shoulder but when he made to move away she held him tightly. "No. Stay, Jamie. I want to feel you inside me."

Eventually they slept, and the moon moved, and left them in peace.

16 | The Sailor's Way

CAPTAIN RALPH PRYCE rested his elbows on the depot-ship's guardrail, but withdrew them instantly as the heat penetrated his drill sleeves. The sun was high overhead and even the ship's tightly spread awnings afforded very little relief.

He said, "It's all in the Intelligence pack. I've checked it myself." He glanced at Ross's profile. "I don't have to tell you about ditching them."

"No, sir." Ross watched the outboard submarine with professional interest as white-clad seamen bustled across the brows with sacks, boxes and every kind of supply for the next patrol. More heavily built than the other submarines, she bore the old pre-war K lettering to mark her as one of the Royal Netherlands Navy's East Indies Fleet. Ross had often wondered what it must be like for such men. Free Dutch, Free Norwegians and all the others. Still fighting the common enemy, with the terrible knowledge that their own countries were overrun and occupied. How would we feel, he thought. Would we still be able to fight with such determination and at such risk if London and Edinburgh were thronged with German uniforms? If every ration-card, postage stamp and newspaper came only with the enemy's consent?

K-21 was the Dutch submarine which had lifted Mike Tucker and Peter Napier to safety. Once *Tybalt* left Trincomalee, the Dutchman would follow. Her commander was well used to these waters; in peacetime he had probably been based out here, at one of the ports mentioned by Richard Tsao which were now in Japanese hands.

Pryce was saying, "Our people in Singapore got the recognition signals from Richard Tsao. They might be changed—we can't be sure . . ."

"Of anything, sir." He turned and looked at Pryce, surprised by this unusual display of uncertainty. They both straightened up and walked across the depot-ship's broad deck; it seemed like a parade-ground. A few seamen paused in their work and looked up as they passed. Like those who had also been watching in Trincomalee's Royal Navy Yard, where they had been driven, to be collected by the depot-ship's smart launch.

Faces that watched them, but what did they see? Brave men or fools, heroes or lunatics? Ross had even hoped that she would somehow have been able to drive them, although he knew it was impossible. It had been bad enough when he had left the estate: Victoria once more in uniform, smiling at him and holding up her cheek to be kissed. Did her father sense the difference in their manner? If he did, he was good at concealing it. Would she tell him that they had been lovers, giving and taking without hesitation and without regrets? If he did not already know, he had probably guessed.

All he had said was, "Come back, Jamie." He had put his arm around the girl's shoulder and for the first time Ross had seen her resolve falter.

Just a few hours ago. It was already a lifetime.

With Pryce, he reached the opposite rail and looked down at the partly concealed *Tybalt. A* few figures were moving on her casing, and the chariots had been carefully stowed in their special containers, which, if seen from the air, should be taken for deck cargo. The chariot crews had had no time to practise launching their craft from the containers, but as they had always said in those long-ago days of training in Scotland, *it will be all right on the night.*

But *Tybalt* was different in another way. The air above her after-casing was blue with drifting diesel exhaust, and the throaty growl of her engines was returning her to life.

Two of *Tybalt*'s original company had volunteered for Operation *Trident*. "Insisted" would be a better description, and Pryce had accepted both of them without hesitation. One was the boat's first lieutenant, and the other, equally valuable, was the Chief, a senior commissioned engineer. The latter had passed it off scornfully by saying, "I'd hardly leave the old girl in the hands of a bunch of amateurs!" Pryce had thanked him, and had said nothing of the fact that the Chief's wife and son had been reported killed in an air-raid.

Pryce said, "We've just got to get the marines and the Gurkhas packed aboard and that will be it. You can leave on schedule."

Ross stared at the glittering water, the sedate line of anchored troopships. Like that other time: slip out under cover of darkness. Like the assassin. He looked at his watch. What would she be doing now? Back at operations with all her signals and codes. Essential to Pryce and to the men of Operation *Trident.* But unknown at the Admiralty, like so many others. He smiled. *Like me.*

Pryce saw the smile and was partly satisfied. *Trident,* a three-pronged attack, was entirely his creation. There would be no mercy if things went wrong. Others would make certain of that.

"By the way, Jamie." He hesitated; he still found it hard to share such confidences. "That war-correspondent will be going out in the Dutch boat. He's been a bit of a menace, a security risk in my view. But the admiral likes him, so that's the end of that."

Ross thought he had misheard. "But the Dutch boat may become completely involved, sir."

Pryce said coldly, staring into the light, "Good experience for him. Unique, if what I've heard is true."

Then he turned towards him. "I'll be off then, Jamie. I'm more use to you back in my H.Q. than out here being nostalgic." He glanced once more at the boat alongside. "Strange, don't you think? Like our fathers . . . the same challenge."

Ross ignored it, suddenly impatient to go. "If anything happens, sir . . ."

Pryce said, "I know. All taken care of. What we used to say in those first impossible days. 'You can have my egg if I don't make it.'" His tone hardened. "But you will." He looked briefly into Ross's level grey eyes, unable to confirm his suspicions. He had never understood why they allowed women to serve alongside officers and ratings, and still expected everything to remain normal. Bad enough for the civilians. He shut it from his mind. "Good luck." Then, surprisingly, he saluted.

Ross watched him leave, lightly down the varnished accommodation ladder to a swaying launch. It could have been a scene from peacetime, he thought, wondering what on earth Pryce would do when it all ended.

Tybalt's first lieutenant, a regular officer named Tom Murray, was waiting in the control-room, his eyes everywhere as he observed the comings and goings of seamen and marines, most of whom were total strangers to him.

"All set, Number One?"

Murray smiled. The easy use of his title had done much to break down any last barriers.

"Everything's stowed, sir. The marines have got their boats folded and handy near the forrard hatch. Rather them than me."

Ross looked around at the gleaming dials and gauges, the periscopes shining greasily in their wells. Above the navigator's table someone had even found time to polish the builder's plate, *Camell-Laird, 1939*. The boat was the same age as the war. They built fine submarines, but not to be used like this, on a one-way ticket.

Murray said quietly, "She'll not let you down. She's a good lass."

"Is that why you volunteered?" Then he shrugged. "I have no right to ask. I'm sorry."

Murray shook his head. "You have every right, sir. You more than anyone. I just thought you should have somebody who knows her funny ways."

They both laughed, breaking the tension. Mike Tucker, who had been appointed acting-coxswain for the mission, paused by a watertight door and saw the difference in Ross immediately. *She was his girl*. Whatever happened now, nothing could change that.

Ross turned, his eyes questioning. "You look pretty pleased with yourself, Mike."

Tucker thought of the girl in nurse's uniform. It wouldn't be wrong or disloyal. Not now. Her name was Eve. *I must have looked a right twit.* "I'll tell you some time, sir." The grin came back. "You won't believe it!"

The first lieutenant watched and listened. He had never really got to know Tarrant, the previous C.O. This one he felt he had known all his life.

Ross said, "I'll speak to everybody an hour before we cast off."

"The officers, sir?"

He smiled. "Everybody. Provided there are no foul-ups we've got just four days to iron out the creases. That means everybody, right?"

Murray grinned. "Understood, loud and clear, sir!"

At sunset, without ceremony or fuss, *Tybalt* cast off her wires and lowered her flag.

Ross stood on the narrow bridge with the lookouts and listened to Tucker repeating his orders through the voicepipe. He felt the easy lift and thrust of the raked stem and turned to watch as a car headlight probed briefly from the dark mass of land.

He bunched his hands into fists inside his coat and tried not to think that it might be the only time. The last farewell.

He heard the main periscope move in its sheath, easing away the stiffness of time in harbour.

He thought of her in his arms, the frenzy and the gentleness of their embraces.

Ross knew he was not alone. Not any more. No matter how far or to what end, she was with him.

"First Lieutenant requests permission to relieve you, sir."

"Very well." He heard the man's feet on the ladder, felt the air being sucked past him to feed the growling diesels.

He glanced once more towards the land. But there was nothing.

He adjusted his thoughts as the lieutenant's head and shoulders came through the hatch.

I couldn't wait! It had to be! It was as if she had spoken aloud.

He dropped quickly on to the ladder and left Murray to make his own private farewell.

Captain Ralph Pryce stood, arms folded, and watched the guards on the main gate checking a civilian van before allowing it to enter. Behind him, his makeshift headquarters building sounded busy, alive: he heard the clatter of a typewriter and at least two telephones in use at the same time. *The first day.* He glanced at the big wall-map and pictured the submarine, probably submerging for the first time after using full speed to find open water and seclusion. Heading due east, into the sun.

He turned and looked at the Wren officer who was sitting, legs crossed, while she checked through the list of instructions he had just given her.

"I want our Operations on full stand by from now on. I've arranged with the Base to monitor all incoming signals which may have even the smallest connection with what we're doing. Can't be too careful." He frowned as one of the overhead fans gave a warning squeak. It was going to be another scorching day. If the fans broke down . . .

Second Officer Blandford said without looking up, "I've had a word with the O.O.D., sir. Someone will be sent to check the fans as soon as possible."

"Hmmm." He looked at her. So neat, so self-assured. And yet . . . He walked to his desk and picked up a cup of fresh coffee. After Operation *Trident,* what then? Maybe they would close this place down, and move the section elsewhere. Australia, perhaps. It would be like the backwoods after here, and London.

She asked, "Anything else, sir?"

"No. Commander Crookshank will be dropping in during the forenoon." Worried and anxious, no doubt, in case he was left holding the baby. He snapped, "Enter!"

The door opened and he saw Victoria Mackenzie in petty officer's uniform; composed, as if nothing had changed.

She said, "Major Guest to see you, sir."

Pryce said, "Not a chance! God, does that man think we've nothing else to do around here?"

Second Officer Blandford uncrossed her legs. "He was trying to get hold of you before." She added softly, "I did tell you, sir."

"Did you? Oh yes—I was pretty busy." He squared his shoulders. "I still am!"

Victoria Mackenzie looked past him at the big map. It had always been part of the job, but not close and personal, as it was now. *He* was out there somewhere. How did he feel? What must it be like?

She heard herself say, "Major Guest has seen the Chief-of-Staff, sir."

Pryce sat down. "Crafty bugger!" He looked at the office clock. One signal, then nothing more. The Dutch submarine would slip her moorings and leave at sunset. It was not just a plan any more. It had started.

He said, "All right, ask him to come in. I'll make some excuse and get rid of him."

As the door closed he said, "Mackenzie's a fine girl. She should go for that commission."

"Really, sir?"

Pryce did not smile. A raw point. A weakness. Always useful to know.

Major Guest came into the office, followed by a tall sergeant.

Guest said, "Sorry to barge in like this. I've been trying to see you." He glanced through the window as another incoming vehicle was stopped for inspection. "But I can see you're somewhat pushed for time today."

Pryce was looking questioningly at the sergeant. Guest said, "In this job I need Sergeant Penrose in case I forget something." He smiled, but it was completely without warmth. "In the early days out here things were so simple. The Captain-in-Charge was in Colombo, and he was always available when the Provost Marshal needed help or information." He waved his hand. "Now there's an admiral, more ships than you can count, and right in the middle there's your Special Operations Section."

Pryce said sharply, "Yes, it's the war. Bloody nuisance really. So what do you want of me?"

Guest sat down uninvited opposite the Wren officer. "My chaps have been investigating the unlawful issue of petrol, among other things, as well as the improper use of vehicles. Mostly an Army matter, but all sorts become involved."

"I hardly think it's of any interest to me."

A telephone rang noisily and Second Officer Blandford covered the mouthpiece with her hand.

"Commander Crookshank has come aboard, sir." She saw the major's mouth twitch in another cold smile, obviously amused at the use of naval expressions even this far from the sea. But she was used to it, and at the same time irritated by the man's arrogance. Misuse of petrol indeed!

Pryce said, "Go and take care of him, will you, Victoria? Give him some tea or something." He added meaningfully, "I shouldn't be very long now."

Guest cleared his throat. "We detained two men, and charges will follow in due course. However, during the investigations evidence was found that one of the men had been using service vehicles on a regular basis. Doubtless other arrests will be made shortly."

Pryce said unhelpfully, "So what does this have to do with me? I would have thought that the whole thing shows a lack of proper discipline and control. Any soldier, or rating for that matter, is only as good as his officers dictate, right?"

"Up to a point, sir." Guest glanced at the Wren officer's legs as she crossed them again. "One of the arrested men has claimed in his defence that he was ordered to use the car without proper authority. To take an officer on some private journey, which in itself is an offence."

"I am aware of that, Major." Pryce looked pointedly at his watch. "Does it concern this section?"

Guest took his time. "On the night that Second Officer Jane Clarke was murdered, the arrested man dropped the officer on that same road, and was told to call back for him after visiting a shop on someone's behalf. We are pretty certain that the officer was Major Trevor Sinclair, Royal Marines, who is attached to this section."

Pryce stared at him. "But I thought *you* had checked every detail. I thought you knew where everybody was. I seem to recall that you were quick enough to criticize the security *here,* when all the time . . ."

Guest shrugged. "We were wrong. But that was then. We had thousands of enquiries to carry out, passes to check, everything."

"Are you suggesting that Major Sinclair is a suspect?"

"We have to follow up enquiries, sir. I have seen the Chief-of-Staff." He hesitated. "You understand that I had no alternative when I was unable to make contact with you."

"And he passed the buck, did he?"

Guest met his angry stare and said, "I am empowered to interview Major Sinclair, sir. There are questions which have to be answered. We might then avoid the involvement of the S.I.B., or even worse, detectives from London. It would all take time. This way . . ."

Pryce stood up lightly. "Major Sinclair is not available. I am not permitted to discuss it further, but the nature of our work here should be self-explanatory."

Guest also rose. "It is. Thank you for your co-operation, sir." He nodded to his sergeant. "Some other time, then. I should like to be informed of his return as soon as possible."

Pryce rubbed his chin. "Major Sinclair is a very courageous officer, one who has more than earned the decorations he has received. But for his present, ah, commitment, he would have been on his way to England to receive an even higher decoration from the King in person."

Guest watched him curiously. "In your kind of work, sir, where men risk their lives again and again without question, the distinction must be a fine one."

"Distinction?"

"Between hero and trained killer, sir."

The door closed, and in the silence their boots could be heard thumping down the passageway to the entrance.

Pryce said at length, "Do you have a cigarette, er, Celia?"

She took a packet from her shoulder-bag, her eyes never leaving his face. "I thought you didn't smoke, sir."

He took a cigarette and waited for her to light it. Then he coughed and said, "I gave it up. Now I'm starting again."

"Is it true, sir? I mean, could they be wrong?"

"*'In our kind of work'*—what the hell does he know about it?" He watched the smoke rising into the fan. "Nothing changes the fact that Operation *Trident* is under way, and Major Sinclair is an essential part of it. His experience and his courage are rare, even in Special Operations. He is dedicated. Totally."

She nodded, thinking busily. So Captain Pryce had deliberately avoided meeting with Guest until he knew the operation had started. Had he suspected Sinclair all along, or did he simply not care, provided the attack was a success?

She said, "I thought Petty Officer Mackenzie was quite troubled on one occasion when Major Sinclair came to Operations. I was out of the room. She was alone with him. She seemed very nervous, frightened."

"That's the first I've heard of it."

She smiled. Passing the buck. "Would you like me to tell her, sir? Put her in the picture?"

"No." It came out too sharply. "What good would it do? I need everyone here on top line." He swung round as Commander Crookshank ambled into the office, his face set in an anxious smile. Victoria was with him.

But the Wren officer was thinking about her subordinate, the way she held her head. Pride, defiance: whatever it was, you could never forget her. There was no need to tell her. You could see it in her fine, tawny eyes.

And at that moment she knew that the girl named Victoria was stronger than all of them.

"All present, sir."

Ross looked around the control-room. All the officers, including the two chariot crews and those who had been standing watch-and-watch throughout the passage, and also the chief and petty officers not on duty, were crammed into the *Tybalt*'s nerve-centre. Others overflowed into the passageway; one was even standing on the bottom rung of the conning tower ladder for a better view. Ross could feel their eyes, the power of them, searching his face for some sign of confidence or of doubt. The measure of life and death.

Three-and-a-half days since they had slipped away from the depot-ship, crowded days during which every sort of preparation was made, and instructions were rammed home so that nobody would forget when it was too late to ask questions. Major Trevor Sinclair had been a tower of strength. Ross did not know why it should have surprised him, when the man had such a reputation. It was as if he needed a challenge, like oxygen, like blood. He never seemed to lose his temper, and he had been seen sharing a joke with his handful of Gurkhas on several occasions. Any rift between him and his youthful captain, Pleydell, had been forgotten, or so it appeared. Ross had seen Sinclair sitting in on Pleydell's briefing of the N.C.O.s, who would be responsible for launching the collapsible boats and getting them away from the submarine within minutes of reaching a suitable position. Watchful, listening to every point and question, he was a different man entirely.

Ross said, "We shall surface in about twenty minutes." Somebody dropped a pan in the galley and he added, "Which is why I got you up so bloody early for breakfast!"

Several of them laughed or nudged a companion. Ordinary, commonplace things. He glanced at the curved steel, listening to the muted hum of electric motors. A weapon, Pryce had called

Tybalt. But to these men she was home, even though all but two of them were complete strangers to the boat and, in many cases, to one another. The sailor's way. The Navy's way. Ross had seen men walk along the upended keel of their sinking ship, rather than leave her and swim to safety before she sucked them down with her. Few outside the service really understood; fewer still could explain it.

He saw Mike Tucker watching him, his jaw still moving on the remains of his breakfast. It made him think of Peter Napier. He should have been here . . . How many times had that been said? And how many more?

"At present, we are passing between the Andaman and Nicobar Islands. When we surface we shall be able to see if the navigation has been accurate or not!" More grins, but each one would be hiding a mounting tension, a fervent wish to get on and get it over with.

"According to my instructions, we should be prepared to be challenged, most likely by aircraft." He did not need to tell them that any first encounter would reveal the value of Tsao's information, or the lack of it. Each man would know and be prepared for the worst. "The enemy will assume we are heading for Penang. It would have been our destination if we were in fact the missing U-Boat. But we shall alter course and head straight for the Peninsula. To the target." He looked around at their faces; even the planesman seemed to be listening, although his back was turned while he watched his instruments. "It is a prime one: the depot-ship and, we hope, some U-Boats alongside. As for our chariot crews from the Colonies . . ." He waited for the laughter and cheers to die away and saw the Canadian, Bill Walker, wink at him. The other chariot skipper was Lieutenant Dick Challice, a New Zealander from Wellington. "They will make for the other vessel, a supply tanker." He paused. There was no humour now. "It will not be easy. If it was, we wouldn't be here. I can't even warn you about heroics. In my book you have proved your courage more than enough—anything else would be an insult."

He thought suddenly of her lovely face against his in the night, in the moonlight. Her mother must have been very like her. No wonder the old Colonel had lost his heart, and had turned his back on those who had condemned him.

He saw the first lieutenant bending over the chart, his fingers busy with parallel rulers and dividers. A submarine could almost think for herself, but a human brain was still needed to make a decision.

He said, "Go to your stations now. Gun crews stand by." He turned away and heard the gathering break up. They knew what to do. To wish them good luck was pointless; even to consider the margin of safety was a waste of breath.

He looked at the first lieutenant. "All set?"

Murray nodded. "Pity that bloody war-correspondent didn't come with us. He would have seen a few sights he'd remember for a long time!"

Mike Tucker, waiting to take over the helm, said, "He'll probably shit himself anyway when he finds out the Dutchman isn't just along for the laughs!"

Ross watched the clock's second hand: it seemed to drag across each mark. What if Richard Tsao had been betrayed, and was even at this moment gasping out his life under torture? The target was anchored in comparatively shallow water, ensuring that any submarine would have to surface when making a final approach. The Germans were too professional to miss something like that. Perhaps Tsao was right, and the Japanese *were* too confident about their overall domination, and the power of the fear they used like an additional weapon.

Odd that it had taken somebody like Richard Tsao at last to recognize their weakness.

He leaned over the chart and moved the light to obtain a better look. One to two thousand fathoms under the keel in this span of open water. Straight down. Total darkness. Creatures still unknown to man, unreachable even with the most modern detection gear.

It was getting to him. He straightened his back and moved to the periscope wells.

"No point in hanging about, Number One. Take her up to periscope depth and mark it in the log." He gave a wry smile. Who would ever read it?

He listened to the first lieutenant's voice, quiet and confident, as it had been during the depth-charge attack, the straddles, the savage jerks and lurches, the groan and crack of metal under pressure. He was probably remembering it right now.

Ross saw the dials and their quivering needles, felt the gradual tilt of the deck under his shoes. Ninety feet, eighty, seventy . . . He wiped his eyes with his wrist. It was wet. Forty feet, thirty . . . Steady, the hull without motion, hanging in space above the chasm.

Ross lowered himself almost to his knees and snapped down the periscope handles as it hissed smoothly out of the well.

The darkness changing to misty grey; the flurry of foam you always thought you would feel; then the periscope stopped. Ross moved carefully around the well, snapping the lenses to full power, probing through one hundred and eighty degrees and then reversing along the other beam. Dark water, only the hint of a grey light beyond. It was a contrast, nothing more: there was no true vision as yet. Somebody handed him a pair of binoculars, which he slung around his neck and covered with his open shirt. It might seem cold up top; better that than feeling half asleep.

Their eyes met. "Open the lower lid. Surface, Number One. Fast as you like."

He pushed through the waiting gun crews, the trailing snakes of bright ammunition for the two Brownings, the lookouts with their dark glasses. Somebody touched his arm and a voice, barely audible, murmured, "I'll be thoroughly browned off if the war's over an' we've not been told, sir!"

Ross was thankful for the shadows and their protection. They could not see his face. *Help me.*

"Surface!" Then it was happening, like a released spring. Hands clawing at the ladder, shoulders, arms and legs all crammed into the small pressurized tube; and then with a crash the upper hatch was open, water spitting down on their bodies as *Tybalt* lurched violently to the surface. Then the scamper of feet was stilled, the clang of the four-inch gun's breech-block went unnoticed. It was cold, compared with the oily warmth they had just abandoned. The bridge was still running with trapped water, the voicepipe cover blurred with salt.

"Dawn coming up, sir!"

Ross held his breath and watched it. A sliver of red, like blood on the horizon, the living division of sea and sky. It would be full daylight in no time. What then?

He heard Murray's voice through the voicepipe. "Course to steer is one-one-zero." Somebody spoke in the background, probably Mike Tucker. Down there instead of here with me, Ross thought.

"No H.E., sir."

"Very good, Number One."

Murray sounded as if he was pressed against the voicepipe, so close. He replied, "We're on our own. Sea's pretty calm." He heard the periscope move, and knew Murray was seeing for himself.

Ross raised his glasses. "No ships anyway." He was thinking aloud. "Aircraft then. From the land. Out of the sun." He saw one of them acknowledge him. "So be ready." Any U-Boat commander who had survived the incredible passage from France, around the Cape of Good Hope and across the Indian Ocean, would be on his toes. Every ship or aircraft would be regarded as an enemy until proved otherwise. It was exactly the same for British submarines in the North Sea or Mediterranean. Many a boat had been depth-charged or bombed by an over-eager pilot who had seen only an enemy.

"Bend on the flag." He glanced around to see the German ensign flap weakly from the small staff on the buckled "bandstand."

The seaman who had hoisted it said, "Don't forget yer titfer, sir!"

It was Ross's own cap, with its white cover and a crudely fashioned German badge. All U-Boat commanders were distinguished by their white caps: if anyone got close enough to see that the badge was a mock-up, it would be too late in any case.

When it came there was neither shock nor surprise, merely the sense of something inevitable.

"Aircraft, sir! Bearing Red four-five!" Excited, but without fear. "Low down, sir. Angle of sight about two-zero!"

Ross leaned over the voicepipe and saw his own breath like mist on the brass mouth.

"Sound action stations, Number One. We've got company!"

He turned away from the insane sound of the alarm and watched the small, slow-moving aircraft. Like a flaw against the fierce dawn sky.

Then he saw the slender grey muzzle of the four-inch gun training round, seeking out the intruder, the next shell already waiting to be rammed home.

He tried to remember the poem beneath the school's Roll of Honour, but like everything else, it was gone. There was only now.

17 | Begin the Attack

LIEUTENANT CHARLES VILLIERS clambered through the hatch and wedged himself between Ross and one of the lookouts. The red dawn made him appear flushed, and deepened the lines of tension around his mouth.

Ross did not lower his glasses. "You once told me you were on top line as far as aircraft recognition went." Then he did glance at him. "I think that little bugger is having a good look at us. Can't be sure."

Villiers lifted his binoculars from inside his shirt and trained them carefully over the wet metal. Ross could well imagine him under training, keen and very serious. Life had been hard on him since then.

Villiers said, "It's a Jap all right. A seaplane. At this range . . ." He hesitated as if studying some remembered wall-chart. "It would be an Aichi reconnaissance plane. Some carry a couple of bombs, but out here I think it's unlikely. Mounts a pair of twenty-millimetre cannon, among other guns." Surprisingly, he grinned. "But not very fast—about two hundred and a bit, flat out."

Ross touched his arm. "Spot on. Pass the word to the gun crews." He dragged his eyes from the slow-moving aircraft and tried to picture the submarine as the Jap airman would see her. The damage, real and faked, would be visible, and without looking he knew that a long silver snake of leaking diesel fuel, one of the Base engineers' tricks, should carry some additional weight. It would look more convincing if most of the hands were on deck: in safe waters it was customary to give crewmen as much freedom of movement as possible, especially if they really had just completed a long and dangerous passage. But suppose the enemy were not deceived? Or worse, if they already knew about Operation *Trident?* They might die anyway, but to dive the boat under attack and leave so many men to drown or be machine-gunned in the water was not even a consideration.

He heard Villiers switching on the bridge signalling-lamp.

The starboard lookout muttered, "The bastard's getting brave, sir!"

The aircraft was much lower. If the sky were brighter, they would see its reflection as it flew above the undulating water like a giant hornet. Lower and lower, turning now as if to cross astern of them. The pilot must surely see the oily stains on the water?

The machine-gunners were ready, sights set, the ammunition trailing over the side of the bandstand, with fresh belts close to hand.

The pilot had obviously made his decision. The seaplane changed course again and flew towards the sun, the harsh glare shining on the markings and the perspex of the cockpit cover. Villiers exclaimed, "The signal!" They stared at the winking light from the cockpit. Villiers said, "H . . . R." He triggered off an acknowledgement and added, "Here we go." The lamp clicked in his hand. *R . . . K.*

There were shouts of alarm from the four-inch gun as a sudden burst of fire spat from the slow-moving seaplane.

Ross cupped his hands. "Stand fast, lads!" He knew that two of the gun crew had turned to stare up at him, caught as they were on the open deck-casing.

The shells exploded with vivid flashes, which even the sun could not quench. Ten small starshells. Ross rubbed his mouth. Exactly as Tsao had predicted. The seaplane was already heading away, its part played: it was up to others more senior to decide matters from now on. Much the same as in any service, in any country.

Ross spoke deliberately into the voicepipe. "Signals exchanged, Number One. The natives are friendly." He thought he heard somebody give an ironic cheer. "We shall continue surfaced until it's time to alter course."

He gripped the pipe's bell mouth, the decision still to be made holding him like a wire spring. There was no cancellation, no change of plans. He knew Villiers was watching him, wanting to help in some way. He could see them all in that shabby building they used as their headquarters, the palm trees, the ocean like a dark barrier beyond. When the signal was received there . . . still he hesitated. It might very likely be Victoria who would decode it. He doubted if Pryce trusted anybody else.

He looked at Villiers and smiled. "As you said, Charles. Here we go!" He lowered his mouth to the voicepipe again. He was speaking to the first lieutenant, but also to Mike Tucker, to all the others who had to depend on him. And, not least, to her.

"Make the signal, Number One." Then he gripped the warm steel and leaned back to ease the stiffness in his body. When he looked again for the aircraft, it had vanished. The German flag and the white stripes across the hull had probably convinced the pilot as much as any simple recognition code.

If a German aircraft came out to investigate it might not be so easy. But Richard Tsao had said there were only two German seaplanes, and they were at Penang, a further two hundred miles beyond the intended target.

They would have to submerge and risk the reduced speed for their final approach. To meet with an inquisitive warship or casual patrol boat would ruin everything. He glanced at his watch and saw how hard he was gripping the bridge rail, and released his hold one whitened finger at a time. Something he had taught himself to do all those years ago, whenever the true realization had reached him. Twenty-four hours and it would be over. Twenty-four hours to live, or to die.

He thought of Bob Jessop, the submarine *Turquoise*'s commander, his bitterness at what he considered a waste of lives when compared with a normal patrol. Jessop had to be wrong. It had to matter what they were doing.

Surely a dying man had a right to know that it must have been for *something*?

He said, "Go below, Charles. Have another run through it.

Number One can relieve me when he's ready."

Villiers paused on the ladder and looked back at him, his eyes troubled. Up there with the ocean and the clearing sky it was remote: even the circling Jap plane had not seemed real. He lowered himself the rest of the way and saw a seaman handing out mugs of tea.

Ross had wanted to be left alone. Alone, and yet strangely at peace.

Petty Officer Mike Tucker strolled from the submarine's wardroom, where he had been helping to dress the two chariot crews, and found himself wishing that things would get a move on. It seemed wrong not to be sitting with the others while the diving-suits and equipment were dragged and belted into place. Like being an outsider.

In the forward part of the hull it was just the same, as the marines and the small detachment of Gurkhas struggled in the limited space to prepare their boats for hoisting through the forward torpedo hatch. He did not envy them: with all their weapons and gear, they would be out of breath by the time they had paddled their way ashore. They were well trained and experienced, but get used to it? He shook his head. They must be nuts!

He glanced through the control-room, deserted now but for the first lieutenant and a small group of watchkeepers. *Tybalt* had already taken on a stark, abandoned look; the rest had been a pretence to guard them against what lay ahead. Tucker had seen Lieutenant Villiers creeping on his hands and knees while he checked the various coloured wires, the timers, or, as a last desperate resort, the detonator which could blow the whole boat to hell with one press . . .

Here on the chart table lay the last of the notes and plans. There was even a print of their main target, the depot-ship. Once named the *Java Maru,* she had been a passenger and cargo vessel of the Osaka Mercantile Steamship Company. Eight thousand tons, and built only a few years before Pearl Harbor, she was a good choice. Tucker had seen the two chariot officers going over the final details with Ross. The fuel tanker was their target, and although there were no proper details available about it the attack would be straightforward, just like the drill. They always said that.

Tybalt had been forced to dive earlier than planned because of several aircraft sightings. Now that their presence was known and had obviously been reported, there was no point in inviting a closer inspection.

"Are you all right, Mike?"

Tucker turned and saw Ross watching him, an unlit pipe jammed in his mouth. "So-so, sir. Getting a bit twitchy, I suppose." During the afternoon he had mentioned the nurse named Eve to him, although he had not intended to let it come out until he felt more certain. But Jamie Ross was like that, easy to talk to, rarely too busy to listen.

Ross had seemed genuinely pleased, relieved even. "I'd like to meet her."

He had meant it, something which had always made him seem very special to Mike Tucker. Not like some regular officers: said one thing, but that was as far as it went. No wonder that sort stayed in General Service. They wouldn't last five minutes in this mob.

Tucker glanced around. "D'you think we'll catch them with their pants down?"

Ross smiled, his eyes distant. He had been reminded of Peter Napier. *A piece of cake.* And before that, of David.

"It's all *ifs,* Mike. You know how it is. *If* Major Sinclair manages to set his raiding party down without being jumped, *if* Lieutenants Walker and Challice can place their warheads under the tanker and do it without setting off an alarm, and *if* all the other diversions work out . . ." He shrugged. "Then I think we have a fair chance." He saw Sinclair by the lowered periscopes. The complete fighting man, Ross thought, something that even the stained denims could not disguise. Ammunition, grenade pack, pistol and binoculars. When he turned slightly to look at the clock, Ross saw the commando dagger and water-flask.

Sinclair said, "Still calm up top?" He hurried on without waiting for an answer. "I'd like to get my boats on deck and assembled as soon as we surface. No sense in hanging about. If we get separated, my chaps know where to meet up. Not that far from our little trip before, eh?" He smiled. "Makes it simpler."

Ross asked, "You know this whole area well, Major?"

"Pretty well." He grinned. "You know the Corps motto, *By sea and by land.* That's all right in this cohort, as that silly ass Pryce would call it!" It seemed to amuse him greatly. Then he raised his wrist and Ross saw the black compass strapped to it like a watch. But larger, and probably sharper, than any watch. It was like a cold hand upon his spine. He was back there beside the road, turning the dead girl's body in his arms. Seeing the deep scratch beneath her breast . . .

Sinclair raised his eyebrows. "Never seen one of these before? Better than a white stick in the bloody jungle, I can tell you!"

He saw one of his men waiting for him and snapped, "Don't give it a thought. If the plan misfires I'll get you out of it. It's surprising what a few gold sovereigns or the nasty end of a revolver can do for you when you need it most!"

As he strode off Tucker remarked, "With all respect, sir, I really don't like that officer."

Ross said curtly, "I didn't hear that." *What is the matter with me?* Sinclair had been nowhere near that road on the night of the murder. Pryce had made sure of that; so had the Provost Marshal's men. If there had been even a shadow of doubt Sinclair would not have been sent on this mission. But all he could hear was Tucker's comment.

Tucker said, "He's married, isn't he, sir?" He saw him nod. "Then I pity her, whoever she is."

Ross thought of what Charles Villiers had told him, and of that which he kept bottled up inside. But he could not, must not discuss it. It was too late, even if somebody had slipped up where

Sinclair was concerned. He stared at the shining deckhead, the tell-tale wires which had been taped to the various fittings so that nobody would fall over them. *A floating bomb.*

Tucker saw his eyes and said, "Did I tell you about my kid sister, sir? Got herself knocked up by some Yank."

Ross smiled. The olive branch. None could do it better.

He pictured the old Colonel, alone, or with his friend the doctor. It must seem strange without Victoria coming to see him whenever she was off duty. After tomorrow, nothing would ever be the same for any of them.

Tybalt surfaced slowly, the water still streaming and gurgling from the bridge and conning tower as the first figures appeared from below. The sea was very calm, with a slow, undulating swell like breathing.

Ross wedged himself in the forepart of the bridge and snapped open the main voicepipe. The moon was very bright, touching the wet hull and the sea itself with trailing patterns of silver. It made him feel naked, although the hydrophone operator had reported that the area was empty of ship movements. He stared at the great expanse of stars. The sense of nakedness was merely an uncomfortable delusion; he knew that from experience. If any aircraft chose this moment to fly over, it would see nothing. *Tybalt,* like any surfaced submarine, would be like a small black stick, lost amidst the moonlight on the sea's face.

He pictured the chart in his mind. The nearest land was less than six miles beyond the dark wedge of the bows. With some twenty-seven fathoms under the keel, there was still enough room to manoeuvre. He peered at his watch, the luminous dial very clear in the glacier light. Like that night when she had come to him, her body held in the moon's glow like a living statue.

He said, "Open the forrard hatch." At least they would not have to keep it open and vulnerable when the chariots were eventually launched from their protective cases aft. Dark figures moved around the four-inch gun and he heard some tackle being dragged along the casing. A less war-like use for it this time: the gun, with block and lowering gear lashed to its muzzle, would be used like a derrick to launch Sinclair's collapsible boats, with the men already packed inside them. The sea was calm, and this should avoid any risk of capsizing them on the submarine's bulging saddle-tanks. Marines and Gurkhas loaded with weapons and grenades would sink like stones.

He spoke directly into the voicepipe. "The first boats are on deck, Number One. Shut the hatch when I say the word."

He watched the dark shapes move from the hatch, and first one then another of the boats was opened out near the gun. One figure stood motionless in the centre of all the preparations. Ross knew it was Sinclair.

Unreachable and unafraid. No wonder his men respected him. Or was it not respect, but fear?

There were a few splashes and then the paddles took charge, taking the boats clear of the swaying hull. The next pair were already in place. What would the people at home think if they could see their sons and brothers preparing here to risk everything without argument or protest?

A lookout said, "All away, sir." He was whispering.

"Close the hatch." Again Ross stared at the sky. It was as if they were the only creatures alive.

"Chariot party in position!"

The first lieutenant was proving his worth. He would trim the boat down just enough to allow the handling party to release the chariots, but not enough to sweep them over the side.

Ross looked around for the boats, but they had been swallowed up completely despite the moonlight. He thought of Sinclair's heavy wrist-compass . . . the cold, nude body in the rain . . . Villiers's gratitude when he had been confronted unexpectedly with Sinclair's pretty wife . . . Did he know? Did he suspect?

He thrust the thoughts away angrily. "Ready to launch!"

He saw the froth of the first propeller, somebody waving at the conning tower as he himself had often done. He raised his arm in a private salute while the two-man submarine backed away to avoid damage or collision.

Down below at the helm, Mike Tucker would be sharing it. Reliving the numbing excitement and the fear.

"Second one's away, sir." The seaman sighed. "Never volunteer!"

Ross scanned the night for movement. The flares of fishing boats perhaps, but otherwise there was nothing.

He rubbed his eyes to hold any weariness at bay. A lot might depend on the alertness of the enemy depot-ship's men. But provided they had discovered nothing about this operation from some unknown source, the first moves should be a complete surprise.

He thought of the main target, the *Java Maru.* In happier times she had been on regular runs from Japan to Hong Kong and Singapore, as well as other Far Eastern ports. In those casual days when strict security was a joke, it would have been simple for such a well-known visitor to record all the warships and defences, the regiments and the preparations, if any, for possible hostilities. No wonder men like Richard Tsao were determined that it would never happen again, and were prepared to fight for what they believed in: their own independence.

Men clambered up and past him before vanishing below to prepare for the next hours of waiting.

No turning back. The chariots were on their way, miniature submarines in a vast ocean. Elsewhere, Sinclair's men were paddling towards the land, probably too busy to consider the risks awaiting them.

"Clear the bridge." The lookouts were gone in seconds, glad to be joining the rest of the skeleton crew.

He could picture the faces in the control-room, waiting to sever the last link. A quick look at the stars and the endless pattern of silver beyond the bows.

"Take her down, Number One. Periscope depth."

Then he closed the voicepipe. *Begin the attack.*

18 | Together

James Ross looked at the control-room clock and then at the few men who would remain here until the last possible moment. How empty the boat had seemed when he had walked through it, from the fore ends and the empty torpedo tubes, then right aft to where Arthur Pound, *Tybalt*'s original Chief, had been watching over his engines and electric motors as if this were a normal patrol. One with a return trip.

There had been a few grins, but mostly there was only a set determination now, something almost physical.

Ross said, "As soon as it's full daylight they'll be looking for us when we don't appear anywhere near Penang. It should be too late by then. We'll go straight in. I'll want a handling party on deck, and the forward hatch open to make it appear genuine. I can't dive the boat anyway, it's too shallow there for comfort. We could get stranded before we were anywhere near the target." He looked around at their intent faces. "*Straight in.* We'll open the bow doors and scuttle her slowly—the main hatch will do the rest. We shall clear the boat and fire the fuses." He saw Villiers nod, living his part of it. A three-pronged attack, what Pryce had wanted. The two chariots at the far end of the anchorage, Sinclair's landing party, and the final hammer blow, *Tybalt* herself. They all knew what to do: only the survivors would know if it had worked. In war that was always the worst part, as he had heard his father say so many times. Young men dying, bravely and without hesitation. But they would never know if their sacrifice had been worthwhile.

He looked towards the conning tower. "I'm going up." He saw the gratitude on Mike Tucker's face as he added, "You come with me. I think we can safely leave Number One and his team to make the last run-in."

He pulled himself up the ladder, the rungs very cold under

his fingers. *Or is it me?* He heard Tucker humming to himself as he followed close behind him, as if he had been done some immense favour. The old firm.

They had surfaced for the last time around midnight, the stars partly dimmed by layers of drifting cloud, like smoke. It would be a hot day again. Shortly after surfacing they had passed the two tiny islands of Goh Raja Yai and Goh Raja Noi and had fixed their position exactly before steering almost due north. Ross had watched the gyro repeater ticking round, the chart a ruthless reminder that they were on course, with the Malay Peninsula reaching out across the bows to embrace or crush them.

The two tiny islands, like tips of sea-bed mountains, had been a great help. But they must have torn the keels out of many lesser vessels over the centuries.

"The information is that the Germans have two Arado seaplanes at Penang. One will be sent to look for us, I expect." He was amazed that he could joke about it. "Provided their Nippon friends have bothered to tell them!"

Tucker said, "And if we can't get out of it . . ."

"We'll go overland. Anything. I'm not throwing in the towel for anybody."

Tucker sounded satisfied. "That goes for me, too. I don't fancy a second helping of their hospitality!"

They felt the bridge shudder as the Chief cut the motors and brought the powerful diesels into play. Right on time. What was he thinking about? His dead family, how it might have been? Ross pushed it from his mind. There was no room for pity now. There never was.

"One thing, Mike." He looked up at the German ensign as it flapped weakly in the damp air. "If we get a chance . . ."

Tucker's grin was very white against the sea's backdrop. "I guessed you'd think of that. I've got *Tybalt*'s White Ensign right here."

Ross tensed as a lookout said, "I think it's getting a bit lighter to starboard, sir."

"Yes. It is. Call the gun crews." The handling party. They would be cut down in seconds if the surprise did not work. It took real guts to stand on an exposed deck while they approached the target. Ross clenched his pipe in his pocket so hard that he was surprised it did not snap. They *had* real guts. Otherwise they would not be here.

Some birds rose flapping and screeching as the submarine's bow-wave sluiced over their resting place. Ross watched them until they had vanished into the darkness. Tonight the birds would be back again. *By then . . . ?* Men clambered past them, and practised fingers soon had the heavy machine-guns mounted and ready.

Ross found himself thinking of his father. Was this how it had been for him? Two men alone on a tiny conning tower in that obsolete submarine, with all hell breaking loose around them? Big Andy and Ralph Pryce's father, side by side. He glanced quickly at his companion. *Like us.*

He leaned forward to watch as other figures appeared near the four-inch gun. He hoped they had remembered to lay out some mooring wires to make the boat appear normal to anybody who was on watch when they burst in. He had the chart fixed in his mind as if it were printed there: the scattered islets and the larger island of Salang with its harbour at Phuket. To the east of it was the anchorage. A good choice. Ross smiled faintly. Unless you were the idiot who was trying to crack it.

It was so sudden, like the glow of an unexpected flare. It was the sun, barely making an appearance, but in no time at all . . . Ross swallowed hard; his mouth felt like leather. He ducked over the voicepipe.

"First light, Number One."

Murray replied, "Course is three-five-zero. Ready and waiting."

"Very good." It was something which had been set in motion by others, and now nothing could stop it. He thought of Captain Pryce, saying how he would have liked to be here with them. At the time he had not been so certain, but now he was convinced of Pryce's sincerity. He thought too of the old rear-admiral in Scotland, Ossie Dyer. What would he think when he heard about this last grand gesture by the men and boys he had trained and encouraged when all the odds had seemed stacked against them? Ossie Dyer and his old dog. Walking beside some Scottish loch together, maybe in the company of his Wren.

Home thoughts. They could be fatal at a time like this. And yet, they came. Victoria would be at her desk, or with Pryce while they waited for news . . .

Tucker asked quietly, "All right, sir?"

He looked at him with great warmth. *I am the one who should be grateful.* He said, "I'll let you know later on." They both laughed, and in the control-room Villiers and Murray looked up tensely, and then at one another with disbelief.

It would be another vivid dawn. A time for action.

"I can hear an aircraft, sir."

They all peered into the deep shadows beyond the rounded saddle-tanks. It was difficult to hear anything above the confident growl of diesels. But now they could see the wake creaming astern, the sudden shine of spray across the deck-casing.

Tucker pointed. "Out there somewhere, sir. Port side. I'm sure I heard it!"

Ross had never known him to be wrong in such matters. And there it was. An intermittent buzz, fading away and droning back.

He shouted, "Stand by on deck!" He saw the gunlayer give a thumbs-up sign and lean against the four-inch. He had even thought to wrap his head in a massive bandage, not just as another wounded U-Boat ploy, but to hide his earphones.

Tucker said hoarsely, "Land, sir! Port bow!"

Ross heard the periscope move and knew Murray would be fixing their position again. For the last time.

The aircraft sounded closer, but was probably flying so low that it was still invisible. The light was gaining and spreading and even though there was no real colour, Ross imagined he could smell the land.

Murray's voice bounced up the tube. "I can see the target, sir! Right on the button!" He was obviously using the main periscope at full power.

Ross heard himself say, "*It's there!* The bloody thing is where they said it would be!" He looked around the crowded bridge at their creased and unshaven faces. "So let's go and wake 'em up, eh?"

Two of them laughed. It was a madness; of course it was. Ross lowered his mouth to the voicepipe again. But madness was all they had left.

"Stand by for maximum revs, Number One! Tally-ho!"

He had to wedge his elbows on the side of the bridge to steady his glasses. He had imagined he was shaking, but realized that *Tybalt* was slicing through the fierce cross-current which had made things so difficult for the chariots. It was still blurred, but he could see the target, the *Java Maru,* solid in the water, and probably moored fore and aft to keep her accessible to her charges. Then he caught a glimpse of the low, crouching hulls alongside. At least three, and perhaps others on the landward side. Surely somebody would realize what was happening?

A lookout called, "Aircraft closing from astern, sir. Seaplane." He even found time to clear his throat. "German markings."

Ross straightened his back. "Be ready to acknowledge his signal."

It was strange, but he could feel nothing, as if everything but his mind was frozen in time.

"Here we go!"

The seaplane with the black crosses clearly visible on its wings roared over the water, so low that it tore a deep ridge across the surface.

Ross watched and saw a light blink brightly from the cockpit.

He said, almost to himself, "Wrong signal." He removed his

cap and waved it above as the seaplane began to turn for another sweep. Just for a second he trained his glasses on the depot-ship. Still in shadow, with only her funnel and masts painted in the red-gold of the dawn. He thought he could see the tanker, but it was further up the anchorage, much further than he or the chariot crews had planned for.

He wondered if Major Sinclair's party had reached its objective, the first being to mine and booby-trap the only road which led to this place. He also tried to remember what Villiers had told him about Arado seaplanes. It was a little late now. He felt Tucker's eyes on him, and said, "Surely to God somebody's awake!"

They needed a diversion for the last two hundred yards. At any second . . . He snapped, "What was that?"

Somebody shouted, "Fast launch, sir! Heading this way!" Then he called, "Belay that, sir! It's going about!"

In the strengthening glow Ross could see the launch rocking wildly as her engines were flung to full astern. It seemed to be packed with people, Japanese soldiers, not Germans. It was as if they had all gone mad: some were firing their rifles into the water, and there were muffled bangs, all harmless and unreal at such a distance.

Tucker exclaimed, "Astern of the launch, sir!" His voice was angry, even shocked.

Ross watched in silence as more shots cracked out, then there was yet another bang, and he recognized it as the sound of an exploding grenade which had been lobbed into the water.

It was one of the chariots, either blown to the surface by the explosions or forced into an emergency escape drill. Except that there was nobody left to escape. One figure still clung to the Number Two's position, and through the powerful glasses Ross could see the torn diving-suit, the great bloody gashes shining above the water like part of the dawn.

Whoever it was must have been delayed, perhaps by the tanker changing her anchorage; they had been forced to wait before they could attach their charge. It seemed likely that the chariot had developed a fault, or one of its crew had been overcome by a failure in his breathing gear.

Ross did not even blink as the Arado seaplane roared overhead, the pilot trying to see what was happening.

They had needed a diversion. He wiped his mouth with his hand and called, "Full ahead, Number One!"

Murray repeated the order, his question unasked.

Ross said, "One of the chariots." When he looked again, it and its lone rider had vanished. Maybe they had not even had time to fix their charge to the tanker. They were beyond caring.

He felt the conning tower vibrating fiercely and saw the long bow-wave rolling back from the stem. The water looked muddy in the strengthening light.

There were people on the *Java Maru*'s deck now, and he imagined he heard the sound of a klaxon carried across the water like a challenge.

"Here comes the launch!" The two Brownings dipped suddenly and rattled into life even as the launch slowed down to look at them. At twenty yards they could not miss. Across and up and down, until nothing moved and smoke was beginning to pour from the wheelhouse. And then there were flames. One of the seamen fell to his knees, his head thrown back in a soundless cry as a machine-gun poured a stream of tracer from the depot-ship's bridge wing.

"Fire!" The gunlayer with the head bandage pressed his trigger, and the four-inch deck gun recoiled while the empty shell-case pitched unheeded over the side. The shell exploded inside the depot-ship's forecastle, the hole gleaming momentarily like an evil eye as splinters cracked and ripped through the hull. It was unlikely that many of the German sailors were aboard; they were probably enjoying the rare freedom of quarters ashore. But the effect of the shell would be devastating, especially if word of the chariots' presence had not yet reached the ship and her charges.

A few shots cracked into the submarine's hull and conning tower but a savage burst of fire from the Brownings took care of them, and cut down anyone stupid enough to remain in view.

"Slow ahead!" It was not possible. Ross saw the three U-Boats neatly moored alongside their new mother-ship. There were perhaps two more on the other side. Could it be the whole group?

Fifty yards, thirty, with occasional shots slamming into the hull or glancing off the abandoned deck gun.

Someone shouted wildly, "Another boat comin'!"

Ross stared at the raked bows of the three U-Boats until his eyes watered. The new arrival was too late. He could hear Murray yelling in the control-room, the periscope dipped now to measure the final approach. A scuttle in the depot-ship's straight side opened and a rifle appeared.

Tucker caught one of the Browning gunners as he fell gasping on the rough plating, and took over the gun himself.

"Here, you bastards!" Then he shouted, "Christ, it's the bloody marines!"

The boat which, unbelievably, appeared to be a pilot cutter, crashed alongside, and wild-looking marines and Gurkhas spilled on to the casing even as Murray stopped the engines. Like athletes their arms went up and then over, their grenades bursting almost instantly on the depot-ship's decks.

Major Sinclair was striding through them. "Single shots! Save your ammo! This is not bloody Whale Island!"

Then he clambered up the ladder and said, "Thought the boat would come in handy. It'll get us ashore. After that, it's up to us." He lifted his Sten-gun and fired almost from the hip, and somebody slithered into the sea alongside.

Sinclair snapped, "Get Villiers up here with his bag of tricks. The outboard targets might escape otherwise."

He was watching the seaplane, lifting and circling again like a startled bird.

Ross felt the bows snag into the U-Boats' headropes,

nudging between two of the hulls in a screeching embrace. *Tybalt* felt heavier, and when he peered down at the foredeck he saw that the water was almost up to the open hatch.

"We lost a chariot."

Sinclair barely turned. "I had a spot of bother on the road. Three of mine copped it."

"Dead?" Ross saw the surprise in Sinclair's eyes.

"Well, they are now."

Villiers lurched through the hatch. "What's happening?" He seemed dazed by the silence. Just a few random shots and the dead seaman, and a slow-moving pall of smoke from the riddled launch.

"We're getting out. Go with Major Sinclair and sabotage the moorings on the other side. Where's Number One?"

Villiers looked at his sleeve. It was spattered with blood.

He said quietly, "He was coming up to give you a hand. Stray bullet." He shook his head as if it was all suddenly too much for him to comprehend. "He's alive, but I couldn't move him. He just stared at me and said he'd stay with *Tybalt*."

Sinclair said impatiently, "Well, let's get a bloody move on. Won't be quiet much longer!" He fired two single shots at an open scuttle, and Ross guessed it was probably his last Sten magazine.

Ross ran to the scarred plating and looked at the forward hatch as the first trickle of water overran the coaming.

He said, "Clear the boat. We've got less than half an hour." To Villiers he called, "Don't hang about." He thought of the first lieutenant, down there dying and alone. Aloud he said bitterly, "I know how he feels!"

Mike Tucker tossed the scarlet flag with its cross and swastika over the side. "There. All done." Murray would even have his own flag at the end.

Ross touched his holster and realized that it was still clipped shut.

Another bullet ricocheted from the conning tower and

whimpered away over the smoke. Sinclair's men were retreating to their stolen pilot cutter. Some were being carried, a few just managing to hop over the littered deck. *Tybalt*'s Chief was the last to leave, with barely a glance at the water as it surged through the big forehatch. The bows were beginning to go under.

"Plane's having another go, sir!"

Ross heard the rattle of machine-guns and saw Sinclair's men diving for cover, while one of them fired at the seaplane with a Bren-gun until it was empty.

"Ready when you are, sir!" Youthful and surprisingly fresh-looking, Captain Bobby Pleydell reloaded his revolver without once taking his eyes from the depot-ship's rails and bridge.

"Wait another minute." Should he have sent Villiers when they had already done so much, and paid so dearly?

Pleydell was saying, "It was a bit dicey." He grinned and looked even younger. "But then, it always is in this outfit!"

The pilot boat's engine roared into life, and Ross saw two of the marines holding one of their comrades in a sitting position so that he could see what was happening.

Mike Tucker was also watching. He saw the man die in their arms and be laid at peace in the scuppers. Somehow he knew. The White Ensign he had hoisted for Ross's benefit had been the last thing that dying marine had seen.

Ross said, "It's taking too long." A mooring wire was beginning to fray as *Tybalt* put her full weight against it.

Pleydell said, "I'll send two of my chaps to fetch him. They can get round there over some lighters." He strode away, slim and erect amid so much pain.

The submarine gave a violent lurch and sank swiftly between the two inboard U-Boats. As *Tybalt* hit the bottom the two other boats seemed to crowd together again. Ross turned away. The periscope was still raised: it was as shallow as they had expected. But all he could think of was the periscope. As if Murray was still there, keeping an eye on things.

The air quivered to new explosions: Sinclair's booby-traps offering their challenge. It would slow the enemy down. It would not stop them.

Beyond the depot-ship's protective hull the explosions seemed much closer. Villiers felt his heart beating wildly, his breathing so fierce that he could barely fill his lungs. He could feel Sinclair behind him, see his ramrod-straight shadow as he watched for any threat or movement from the ship's deck.

The tape clung to his fingers and he heard himself sob with anger like some fretting child. He gripped the detonator until his mind cleared again. No time for anything fancy. Ross would be waiting for him.

Sinclair said unhurriedly, "Don't be too long about it. I've got to get your people out of here, in one piece if I can!" He laughed. An odd, menacing sound, but when Villiers lurched round on his knees to look at him, he seemed completely calm, one wrist raised while he studied the compass he carried there.

Villiers turned away, and despite the danger he found that he could attach and set the time-fuse. He had done it so often in training on H.M.S. *Vernon* that he could do it blindfolded, and yet before he had volunteered for Special Service he had had difficulty even re-setting a clock.

It was all so clear and stark. Like the time at the hospital when he and Ross had gone to collect Sinclair, and Caryl had been there too. He stood up. "It's set. Twenty minutes, with a bit of luck."

He watched as Sinclair re-cocked his Sten-gun. "I thought you were in a hurry."

It was as if he had said nothing. Sinclair looked past him towards the shore, the quivering mass of green trees.

"I've known for quite a long time, you see?" He smiled. "It was the envelope I recognized, not the writing." He added sharply, "You were both too bloody clever for that!"

Villiers said, "I think we'd better leave!" He dropped his hands to his sides as the Sten's muzzle moved slightly. "So you found out. What are you going to do, gun me down? You seem to be good at that!"

Sinclair did not rise to the remark. If anything, it seemed to calm him further.

"I shall see her when I go back, of course. Tell her what a hero you were. She'd like that, dear Caryl!"

Villiers stood perfectly still. Sinclair was mad. Somebody should have seen it, have listened. He would shoot, and in a few minutes the charges he himself had just set would explode. And when *Tybalt* went up there would be nothing left. *Nothing.*

If he could reason with him, somebody would come looking for them. Ross would not leave him. But who would know?

He made to move but Sinclair said, "Stand still! Do *something* right!"

Villiers thought of the overgrown garden, the place where he knew he had found his parents and Ross had been with him. He clenched his fists and winced as the sun lanced into his eyes.

"That's the ticket! Nice and easy. Like a gentleman!"

Villiers swayed, unable even to see what was happening. But how could it be? It was like the final nightmare. The sun was in the wrong place. He put his hand to his eyes and saw the glare reflected from a scuttle in the *Java Maru*'s side. Like a mirror, or a heliograph, which his father had often described.

He heard himself scream, *"Look out! For Christ's sake!"*

The amused disbelief on Sinclair's face changed as something in his reeling mind detected the truth in Villiers's frantic warning. He turned lightly on his heels and fired from the hip, an automatic burst this time, the last he had.

Villiers heard the crash of glass and was in time to see a bloodied face fall away from the scuttle. He did not hear the other shot at all. Sinclair lay propped against a mooring bollard, his eyes staring down at his chest, as if he could feel nothing, even as the blood pumped out of him.

Villiers wanted to move but felt unable to grasp what had happened.

He said, "I'll fetch help!"

Sinclair looked at him emptily. "You would, too. You're just the sort."

He must be in agony, Villiers thought. Even so, he was shocked by the intensity of his anger and his contempt. Even his eyes were blazing with hate. A face from hell.

"Spot of bother, old son?" Captain Pleydell climbed over a lighter, his eyes everywhere, a Gurkha and an armed marine close behind him.

Villiers said harshly, "He was shot. From up there. But he got the bastard who did it."

Pleydell nodded. "Quite. Could have been you, y'know." He bent over Sinclair's legs and unbuttoned his denim blouse. "The major's bought it, I'm afraid." He opened Sinclair's wallet and remarked, "Funny thing to carry about, I'd have thought?"

Villiers allowed the young captain to grip his arm and push him around the line of lighters. Once he looked back and saw that Sinclair was still staring after him, but the dead eyes were without menace.

Pleydell waved to the swaying pilot cutter, and Villiers felt himself being dragged bodily over the side.

A muffled explosion boomed around the anchorage, and minutes later they saw the U-Boats' tanker begin to settle down.

Ross lowered his glasses. One of the chariots had made it. They might never know which.

Pleydell said calmly, "If somebody drops a match in that little lot they'll really be in trouble."

Villiers looked up and saw Ross turning the Wren officer's badge in his fingers. From Sinclair's wallet. A souvenir, somebody had called it . . .

Mike Tucker was also watching, sharing what they had all done. Together.

He saw Ross throw the pale blue badge into the sea, and wondered if they would ever get back; and if so, if Ross would ever tell his girl about it.

Right on time, as they stumbled through secondary jungle following their Gurkha scouts, they heard the main charges in *Tybalt* explode. Like an earthquake, so that even here the ground shook. Or trembled, perhaps, at what men could do.

Author Bio

DOUGLAS REEMAN joined the Navy in 1941. He did convoy duty in the Atlantic, the Arctic, and the North Sea, and later served in motor torpedo boats.

As he says, "I am always asked to account for the perennial appeal of the sea story, and its enduring interest for the people of so many nationalities and cultures. It would seem that the eternal and sometimes elusive triangle of man, ship and ocean, particularly under the stress of war, produces the best qualities of courage and compassion, irrespective of the rights and wrongs of conflict . . . The sea has no understanding of righteous or unjust causes. It is the common enemy, respected by all who serve on it, ignored at their peril."

Apart from the many novels he has written under his own name, he has also written more than two dozen historical novels featuring Richard Bolitho, under the pseudonym of Alexander Kent.